KU-222-994

Cathy Kelly is the No. 1 bestselling author of *Woman to Woman* and *She's the One*, both of which spent several months on *The Irish Times* and *The Sunday Times* bestseller lists and were widely praised. Cathy Kelly is a journalist for the *Sunday World* newspaper in Dublin and she lives in Co. Wicklow.

Praise for Cathy Kelly's previous bestsellers:

'Plenty of sparky humour'   *The Times*

'A compulsive read'   *Woman's Weekly*

'All the ingredients of the blockbuster are here . . . a page turner'   *Sunday Independent*

'Sharply observed and readable'   *Woman's Realm*

'Covering topics close to every woman's heart with vivacious good humour'   *Irish Post*

'A *tour-de-force* of the Jilly Cooper genre'   *Lifetimes*

Also by Cathy Kelly

Woman to Woman
She's the One

Never Too Late

Cathy Kelly

HEADLINE

Copyright © 1999 Cathy Kelly

The right of Cathy Kelly to be identified as the Author of
the Work has been asserted by her in accordance with the
Copyright, Designs and Patents Act 1988.

First published in 1999
by HEADLINE BOOK PUBLISHING

First published in paperback in 2000
by HEADLINE BOOK PUBLISHING

3

All rights reserved. No part of this publication may be
reproduced, stored in a retrieval system, or transmitted,
in any form or by any means without the prior written
permission of the publisher, nor be otherwise circulated
in any form of binding or cover other than that in which
it is published and without a similar condition being
imposed on the subsequent purchaser.

All characters in this publication are fictitious
and any resemblance to real persons, living or dead,
is purely coincidental.

ISBN 978-0-7472-6058-5

Typeset by
Letterpart Limited, Reigate, Surrey

Printed and bound in Great Britain by
Clays Ltd, St Ives plc

HEADLINE BOOK PUBLISHING
A division of the Hodder Headline Group
338 Euston Road
LONDON NW1 3BH
www.headline.co.uk
www.hodderheadline.com

For Dad

CHAPTER ONE

The breathless sound of 'Santa Baby' trickled from the sales office's radio next door, a soft child-like voice singing about wanting a yacht, a flat and a string of race horses. At least it was better than 'White Christmas' which Evie had heard about ten times over the past week and which she was now practically singing in her sleep. If Bing Crosby hadn't been dead, she'd have been tempted to kill him.

Evie took a moment to stretch her fingers over the computer keyboard. She was tired; she'd been in the office since eight, typing most of that time, in between explaining *Microsoft Word* to the new junior who'd sworn a hole in a pot she was fluent in it during her interview. From the way she had gazed blankly during most of the morning, Evie wondered if the girl was even fluent in English, never mind computer language.

The fragrant scent of Javan Blue coffee drifted out from the sales office. Evie sniffed the air longingly. She'd have killed for a cup of coffee, the sensation of warm, full-bodied caffeine was just what she needed to give her an energy boost. But she couldn't have any.

She was on fruit tea – preferably lemon – and a litre and a half of water every day. How else was she going to bare her bum and thighs in a bikini on honeymoon if she didn't get rid of some of the cellulite?

1

From behind, her rear looked like a relief map of the moon – not the sort of thing to expose to all and sundry on the romantic isle of Crete. Unless lunar landscaped bums suddenly became the latest holiday 'must-have', on a par with a simply knotted sarong, sun-kissed skin and jelly flip flops.

'Getting rid of cellulite isn't simply a two-week thing, it's a way of life,' the beautician had said bossily the previous week. 'Especially when you're getting older. Over thirty-fives have to be more careful, you know,' she'd added meaningfully.

Evie would have liked to have asked how the hell the beautician – twenty-two at a pinch – could speak so confidently about cellulite and over thirty-fives. But she didn't. It was probably the same as just about every other attribute – after thirty-five, *everything* got shrivelled, wrinkled, droopy and smaller. Except for stomachs and waists, which got miles bigger.

Determined not to look like a whale-sized lump of lard in her bikini, Evie had drawn up an anti-cellulite plan which would give her just over nine months to turn her orange-peeled rear end into a smooth, supple, peach-skinned thing fit for exposure. Over one week into the no-coffee-except-on-special-occasions regime, Evie felt very virtuous. But, God, it was hard.

She tried to ignore the captivating smell of the percolator and stretched her arms and shoulders in preparation for another assault on the word processor.

As she flexed tired fingers, the fluorescent office light caught her solitaire ring and it sparkled richly, the single carat gleaming in the light. She held her hand out, admiring the fat gold band with the simple, large diamond. Simon had wonderful taste, although the ring was bigger than she'd have chosen herself. But when your boyfriend took you out to dinner and presented you with an engagement ring which had probably cost as much as your rackety, second-hand Ford Fiesta, you didn't quibble over whether the ring looked too big on your rather slender fingers.

'My darling, this is wonderful. I've never been to a Michelin-starred restaurant before . . .'

He looked deep into her eyes, his piercing blue ones searching the depths of her hazel eyes, his handsome face alight with adoration. 'I wanted to take you somewhere special because I've got the most important question to ask you.'

A strand of lustrous dark hair had escaped from the elegant knot at the nape of her neck and he gently twisted it behind her ear before his fingers traced the contours of her face.

He loved her face, loved kissing the petite upturned nose and the full, ripe mouth; adored tracing the fine eyebrows that arched over her wide, heavily fringed hazel eyes.

'I should have known you were a supermodel from the moment I met you, my darling Evie,' he always said. 'You are so beautiful, so graceful.'

For once, he didn't say it. Instead, he clicked his fingers autocratically and a trio of musicians appeared from nowhere, playing gypsy violin music that would forever remind her of this magical moment.

He smiled then, the enigmatic smile that had fascinated her all those months ago when they'd met in Venice, both waiting for the power boat to take them to the Hotel Cipriani. Slowly, he produced a Tiffany leather box from his suit pocket, slid to his knees in front of her and opened it.

A cluster of exquisite diamonds shone out at her. Their wonderful shimmer, and the tears of joy clouding her eyes, meant she could barely see his face.

'Will you marry me, my love?' he said . . .

'Have you finished that report yet?' inquired her boss.

Evie gave Davis Wentworth III a quelling glance at the very notion that a report which he needed by twelve wouldn't be ready by that time. Honestly, after seven years as his personal assistant didn't he realise that she'd work her fingers to the bone rather than be late with any piece of work? Even a narcolepsy-inducing document on the latest alarm specifications for one of Wentworth Alarms' most important customers.

'Of course it's ready,' she said evenly. 'It's been on your desk for over an hour.'

'Sorry, Evie,' Davis muttered, his mind obviously elsewhere. 'I should have known better.'

He shuffled off in the direction of his office, open suit jacket flapping around his broad hips. He certainly wasn't sticking to his diet, Evie sighed to herself, watching his bulky figure navigate the small space between the filing cabinets and the new junior's desk.

There really was no point buying Davis low-fat soups and mayonnaise-free sandwiches for lunch instead of his favourite pork pies because when he went home, he obviously sat in front of the fridge all night and just guzzled. Poor thing, she *was* fond of him. But if he didn't go on a diet soon, he'd never make his sixtieth birthday.

Evie glanced at her watch and realised she'd have to go out and buy his lunch soon. She'd better stop daydreaming about handsome men and gypsy music if she wanted to be finished by one.

Stretching her tired fingers one last time, she admired her engagement ring and stared blankly at her keyboard.

Simon's proposal *had* been lovely, in its own way. The Carriage Lamp was a pretty restaurant, although the atmosphere of their romantic evening had been rather spoiled initially because they'd gone there when the Early

Bird menu was still operating. And listening to the three-year-old at the next table screaming lustily for 'More fith and chips, pleeth!' had been a bit off-putting.

'Thank heavens they've gone,' Simon had said with relief when the child and her family departed after twenty minutes of tantrums. 'I couldn't concentrate with that noise.'

'Concentrate on what?' Evie had asked, not really paying that much attention because she was wondering if the waitress was ever going to bring their crab cake starters. She was *starving*.

'On what I have to ask you,' he said nervously.

Evie stopped craning her neck and stared at the man she'd been dating for eighteen months. Simon pushed his horn-rimmed glasses higher on the bridge of his aquiline nose and took a deep breath. His bony face was earnest and his grey eyes were serious. Very serious.

Evie, who hated dramatic moments with a vengeance, caught her breath in momentary fear. What was he going to say? It was all over? Their relationship was kaput? Experience had taught her never to rely on anything or anyone. She'd thought things were going pretty well between them but the hardest lesson she'd ever learned was that you never really knew what another person was thinking. Until it was too late.

'What have you got to ask me?' she snapped, doing her usual trick of sounding sharp to hide her nerves.

Simon said nothing for a long moment. Then he reached into his navy blazer jacket, extracted a small box and opened it smoothly. A ring sat on a fat velvet cushion, a diamond ring that wasn't as big as the Ritz, but was certainly in the same ballpark.

Evie goggled at it. Her first thought was that it wasn't the sort of engagement ring a man like Simon would buy.

5

Good taste was his bible and this large, in-your-face diamond had surpassed the good taste barrier and was rolling down the slippery 'where there's muck, there's brass' slope. Not having much experience in the diamond-ring department, she momentarily wondered how much it had cost, picturing the normally frugal Simon waving his chequebook recklessly in Weir's, saying 'money no object'. Thousands, at least.

Then she gasped. *An engagement ring*. It was an engagement ring.

'Simon!' She blinked at him in astonishment.

'Evie,' he said, searching her face for an answer or at least some encouragement. 'Will you marry me? I know it's a bit sudden,' he went on, before she had a chance to answer. 'But, will you—?'

She went pink with a mixture of pleasure and embarrassment.

How could she not have *known*? She'd always thought those women who claimed they didn't know their boyfriends were about to pop the question were on a par with women who were shocked when they gave birth to babies in the loo, swearing they hadn't a clue they were pregnant and having hysterics when a baby plopped out. I mean, Evie had always thought, how could you *not* know?

But she hadn't. She'd never guessed that Simon wanted to marry her. So much for female intuition.

'Will you?' he asked, his eyes anxious.

Evie clasped his hand warmly and gave him a dazzling smile.

'Of course, you dope. I'd love to!'

He leaned over the table and kissed her swiftly, his lips cool on hers. Sitting down quickly, he grinned at her.

'Do you like the ring?' he asked, his kind face suddenly anxious.

'It's beautiful,' she said truthfully.

Reverently taking the ring from the box, Simon held it in one hand and looked meaningfully into Evie's eyes. He didn't make a move to put it on her finger and she didn't have to glance down at her left hand to know why.

She knew it was there without looking at it: the solid gold band she'd worn for over seventeen years. Tony's ring, her wedding ring. She practically never took it off, except for gardening when dirt always got into the inscription: *Forever*. It was a beautiful inscription, she'd always thought. So romantic.

'Do you want to?' asked Simon softly, eyes on the wedding ring.

Evie nodded. She was used to the gold ring, used to its weight on her finger, its familiar feel. But she slid it off gently. Her fingers were thinner than they had been when she'd first put it on, while pregnant with Rosie, so it came off easily. She put it carefully in her handbag without looking at Simon. He'd never know what that ring meant to her, nobody ever would. When your husband was tragically killed at the age of twenty-one, leaving you with nothing but a tiny baby, your wedding ring was supposed to be the most precious thing in the world to you, a painful symbol of all you'd lost. In those dark days when Evie felt as if she'd lost everything, she'd had no time for mere symbols. But people expected you to take great comfort from things like wedding rings and happy family photos, so she'd never revealed that she wanted to throw out every pain-filled reminder and rage at the futility of life.

Simon was waiting, patient as always. Evie looked up at his kind, hopeful face and smiled, the sort of smile that made her dimples appear.

A huge answering smile on his face, he slid the engagement ring on to her finger.

'I'm so glad,' was all he could say.

He'd been so happy all evening, you'd think he'd won the lottery, Evie thought happily every time she looked at his face which was creased into an idiotic grin.

They'd drunk an entire bottle of white wine – Simon had most of it. She'd never seen him drink that much before: it had been funny. He'd gazed at her from behind thick-lensed glasses, held her hand firmly in his and told her she was lovely.

'I'm very glad you're marrying me,' he'd said, slurring his words a little.

Evie had stroked his sandy hair, smoothing the tufts he'd unconsciously created by running one hand through it.

There had been no gypsy music, no champagne, no electrical charge across the table as their hands met. Simon Todd, a forty-one-year-old loss adjuster with a stylishly decorated town house complete with courtyard garden, and an obsession with squash, was no romantic hero.

He wasn't the sort of fantasy man who'd flirt with a beautiful stranger on an Italian jetty or fall to his knees in front of a packed restaurant and ask her to marry him to the sound of gypsy music.

But then, Evie smiled wryly to herself, she was no supermodel either. Unless they came in thirty-seven-year-old versions with cellulite, stretch marks and a teenage daughter.

Well, there was Iman, who was thirty-something and had a teenage daughter, but she didn't count. She was a Somalian beauty who looked as though she'd been carved out of a piece of precious ebony. Rail thin, she had long, long legs and an enviously full bosom. Evie certainly didn't have the long legs but she did match up when it came to bosoms.

She looked down at her own sensible Marks and Spencer's white blouse. Even if maybe she needed an eye job to get rid of her crow's feet, she certainly didn't need a boob job. 36C was enough for anyone.

Simon loved her boobs. Not that he ever actually *said* anything; it was the way he looked at her, especially when she wore her velvet jersey dress, the one she was wearing to his office Christmas party tonight.

Blast! Evie groaned to herself. She'd almost forgotten her lunchtime hair appointment to get ready for the party. She wouldn't be able to buy Davis's lunch after all. One of the other secretaries would have to get it. And she had so much work to finish before she left the office, not to mention checking whether her latest junior had managed to wipe out the company's entire computer files by mistake when she was supposed to be typing a couple of letters.

Waiting patiently in the hairdresser's an hour later, flicking through *Hello!* and people-watching, Evie wondered if she should go for something different from her usual style. She touched her light brown hair tentatively. She'd worn it the same way since she was twenty. It hung dead straight to her shoulders from a centre parting, and most of the time she tied it back in a neat plait, a style that would have looked severe on anyone else. But it was hard to look severe when you had wide-spaced hazel eyes, an upturned nose and dimples that appeared in plump cheeks when you smiled.

Evie longed to look autocratic: she dreamed of having Slavic cheekbones, a ski-jump nose she could stare down and a steely gaze that reduced people to quivering wrecks.

But with a face that was most commonly described as 'cute', steely looks were out of the question. Being petite with the figure of a pocket Venus didn't help – and the figure of a Venus who was partial to toasted cheese and mayonnaise sandwiches at that. At least Rosie had inherited her father's lean build. Evie wouldn't wish a lifetime of rice cakes and morning weigh-ins on anybody.

She hated being cute, which was one of the reasons she frequently set her face into a frosty glare, her 'cross old cow' face as Rosie laughingly called it.

'I don't know why you do that, Mum,' she objected. 'You give people completely the wrong impression of you.'

Rosie simply didn't *understand*, Evie thought. Cute equalled dumb equalled people walking all over you, and that, she had decided long ago, was never going to happen again.

She sighed and was trying to imagine herself four inches taller, a stone thinner and with a sophisticated short haircut when a tall striking woman with a patrician profile walked past the salon reception desk. Swathed in caramel-coloured cashmere, her hair a gleaming chocolate brown bob, she looked as if being autocratic was second nature to her.

Evie watched the other woman's reflection in the mirror before re-examining herself critically. Maybe a rich brown rinse would suit her, would lift her hair colour. Yes, that was it. She'd have her hair dyed. After all, she needed to get something different for the wedding in September, so what better time to experiment than now?

She pictured herself in a soignée white silk gown, rich, dark hair cut in a bob like the cashmere woman's, a bob that brushed against the triple-stranded pearl choker *he'd* given her for the ceremony.

'*They were my mother's, they're family heirlooms,*' he murmured in his exotic French accent. '*I want you to have them, my darling . . .*'

'Hi, Evie,' said her stylist, Gwen, breezily. 'What am I doing for you today? Cut, blowdry, or complete transformation?' she joked.

Evie hesitated for just one moment at the word 'transformation'.

'A trim and a blowdry,' she said quickly. 'I'm going to a Christmas party tonight and I thought I'd combine getting it cut with having it done for the party.'

'Sensible,' Gwen nodded. 'Let's get your hair washed then.'

Sensible, thought Evie grimly, as the cashmere lady sailed past again in a mist of Chanel No. 5, glamour incarnate. I'm always sensible. It should be my middle name. Evie Sensible Fraser.

As Gwen cut, they chatted.

'What are you doing for Christmas?' she asked, head bent as she wielded the scissors on Evie's wet hair.

'Rosie and I are going home to my dad's as usual. My younger sister Cara's coming too.'

'So which one of you will be slaving over the cooker?' Gwen asked. 'You or your sister?'

'Dad, actually,' Evie said. 'He's always cooked Christmas lunch since my mother passed away. He's a better cook than I am; he's certainly a better cook than Cara. She can barely make tea.'

The stylist laughed. 'I'm a bit like that myself. I live on salads and when it comes to hot food, baked beans are my forte.'

'I doubt if Cara can cook beans,' Evie remarked. 'She lives on takeaways.'

'Can't be good for her,' Gwen said.

Evie thought of her sister: eleven years younger, a good six inches taller so she stood five ten in her socks, and still carrying the puppy fat which had plagued her teenage years. Living off pizzas and chicken chow mein while she'd completed her graphic design degree, hadn't done much for her skin either.

She'd have been so pretty if she'd looked after herself properly and bothered with make-up. But Cara had never

11

been interested in making the best of herself, Evie thought
in exasperation, and never listened to her elder sister's
advice when it came to self-improvement. Look at those
shapeless outfits she wore, baggy combat trousers or hopelessly long skirts that reached her ankles worn with baggy
tunics that covered everything else. She looked like a
Greenham Common woman who'd got lost in time. Evie
had given up trying to beautify Cara, although it broke her
heart to see her sister hiding under all those horribly
masculine clothes.

If she didn't make an effort soon, she'd be stuck on the
shelf watching endless repeats of *Ally McBeal* with a tub of
ice cream for company while other people led fulfilled
lives. And that wasn't much fun, as Evie could testify.

'What's the party tonight? Business or pleasure?' Gwen
asked, wrenching her thoughts away from constant worry
over Cara.

'My fiancé's office do,' she answered. She still felt a
frisson of excitement at the very word 'fiancé'. It was such
an evocative word, representing romance and stability all
at the same time. Someone who loved you so much they
wanted to marry you.

'*Fiancé*! Oooh,' squealed the stylist. 'You got engaged?
Congratulations! But when? Show me the ring!'

Evie blushed and held her hand up for Gwen to admire
her engagement ring.

'I don't know how I missed *that*,' she said, eyes widening
as she admired the large rock on Evie's small hand. 'It's
gorgeous,' she sighed. 'But when did you get engaged?
Recently?'

'Late-September, actually,' Evie explained. 'You weren't
here the last time I came in for a haircut.'

'Tell me everything,' commanded Gwen. 'I need some
romance in my life.'

Evie grinned. 'Don't we all?'

It felt a bit weird to be getting engaged at her age. Evie always associated engagements with besotted twenty-somethings who'd been longing for a wedding pageant complete with seventeen bridesmaids since they were primary schoolgirls playing with Barbie in her wedding dress. Upholding her outwardly conservative image, she'd pointed out that most older brides stuck to sedate cream two-pieces, demure hats and register office affairs.

'I'd hate to look foolish,' she'd told Simon. Looking foolish would have killed her. Evie strove for dignity in everything. It was the only thing she'd had to rely on when she'd found herself a widowed mother while little more than a child herself. People might have taken advantage of a sweet, over-friendly twenty-one year old with twinkling hazel eyes and a smile like a child in a pet shop. But nobody would dream of taking advantage of the solemn, dignified and somewhat wary woman she'd turned into overnight. Which was where her 'cross old cow' look came in useful, even if Rosie hated it.

'Are you having the whole works for the wedding?' asked Gwen.

'Yes.'

Simon had never been married before and he wanted to get married in style. And Evie, who secretly lived for romance, had allowed herself to be persuaded into the whole veil/wedding march/confetti rigmarole.

Her mouth curved up at the corners as she thought of the exquisite medieval cream silk dress in the *Wedding* magazine she'd hidden in her office drawer under her supply of manilla folders. It had parchment silk ribbons criss-crossing the tight bodice and tiny silk roses clustered around the hem. Pure fantasy. All it needed was a knight on a white charger. She'd been cheated out of her ideal wedding dress the first time round: it wouldn't happen this time.

'Rosie, I'm home,' Evie called, slamming the front door shut with her hip and dumping the drenched grocery bags on to the hall carpet. She untied the large headscarf and slid it off, making sure not a drop of rain got on to her carefully styled hair.

It had taken an hour with heated rollers to create the bouncy, wavy style Gwen had recommended and Evie didn't want to ruin the effect with an impromptu shower.

'Rosie,' she called again, more loudly. Nothing. Evie shrugged off her raincoat and dragged the bags into the kitchen.

The debris of her seventeen-year-old daughter's breakfast still lay on the kitchen table: a square of toast with teeth marks in it lying on a crumb-covered plate, a butter-splodged knife slung across the plate and the marmalade jar abandoned without a lid on it.

That morning's half-filled coffee mug would undoubtedly be up in Rosie's room, along with at least six other such cups in varying stages of mould development.

'It's a biology experiment,' she joked blithely, whenever her mother complained about the furry green sludge inside the endless mugs she rescued from the bedside locker and the desk where Rosie did her homework.

'Yeah, well, you never wash your experimental equipment,' fussed Evie, who did not really mind cleaning up after her hopelessly untidy daughter.

'I don't ask you to,' pointed out Rosie, who was well used to her mother's fussing.

'Your room is a health risk,' Evie protested. 'That's why I do it.'

'Mould is penicillin and that can't be bad, now can it?'

14

Rosie would argue happily. There was no winning an argument with her. She didn't care. Careless, that was Rosie all over. Who the hell knew what she'd be like when she'd finished her final year in school and got out into the big bad world officially? Evie shuddered to think.

Rosie looked about twenty already: tall, slender and striking, with an oval face that could adopt a coolly indifferent air with ease. In her black jeans, the three-quarter-length leather coat she never seemed to take off and with her long dark hair offsetting her father's glittering sloe-black eyes, she appeared twice as grown up as the other girls in her school.

She was only three years younger than Evie had been when she got pregnant and was already about ten years more advanced. Teenage years were like dog years, Evie reckoned. For every one normal year of their life, they advanced about seven.

If Rosie made it into the same graphic design course as her adored Aunt Cara, Evie would have no control over her anymore, a terrifying thought. It wasn't in the far-off future either: Rosie had six more months at school. Six months to meltdown.

Watching her beloved daughter grow up so rapidly had presented Evie with a terrible dilemma: should she tell Rosie that she'd got pregnant at twenty; that *that* was why she and Tony had got married? Or would the salutary tale be ruined because Rosie had an image of her late father as some sort of demi-god and would be devastated to learn that the fairy-tale romance she'd been told about as a curious child wasn't so much of a fairy story after all? Evie didn't know. She was simply sorry she'd tried to make up for the lack of Rosie's dad by making him into the sort of hero the little girl could be proud of.

There was no doubt about it, lies always came back to haunt you.

Sighing, Evie stowed the shopping away. She was in a rush but, as usual, she found time to put everything in the right place. Jars and tins stuffed higgledy-piggledy into cupboards was not the way Evie Fraser did things. The antique pine kitchen in her tiny redbrick two-up, two-down may have been what even an estate agent would describe as 'compact', but it was meticulously tidy. Careful use of space meant the large larder had pull-out wire shelves with hooks and saucepan lid holders on the insides of the door so that not an inch was wasted.

When everything was tidied away, Evie quickly made herself a cheese sandwich and a cup of lemon tea and took it upstairs with her. After having a speedy shower so a blast of steam wouldn't make her hair droop, she slathered herself in body lotion and then applied some make-up.

It was just as well that Simon loved the natural look, Evie thought, as she brushed some ochre eyeshadow across her eyelids and gave her thick lashes a delicate brush of brown mascara.

Rosie, who wore eye make-up as if it was tribal war paint, was always urging her mother to wear rich, dark colours to emphasise her hazel eyes.

'Some kohl and a line of gold eyeliner will make the amber flecks stand out,' she'd pointed out the last time she'd sat on her mother's bed watching Evie get ready to go out with Simon.

'Yes, and make me look like mutton dressed as lamb,' Evie argued. 'I couldn't bear it.'

Rosie sighed. 'You're not a hundred, Mum. You're thirty-seven. The style police won't arrest you if you stop looking like a dowager duchess just once in a blue moon.' Rosie picked up the gold eyeliner she'd been proffering and began drawing a delicate line under her bottom lashes. The result was startling, it made her eyes stand out even more exotically than usual. 'Anyway, Sophie's mother is five years older than you and she's thinking of getting her belly pierced.'

'Ugh!' Evie said. 'I can't imagine anything worse. What will she look like? And is that what you want me to look like – a wrinkled mother in belly tops, with peroxide hair and a nose stud?'

'No, Mum.' Rosie unfolded her long, slender, black-clad limbs from the bed. 'But it wouldn't do you any harm to lighten up a little. You're too young to start wearing support tights and floral nylon two-pieces.'

'I don't wear clothes like that,' her mother protested, throwing a bottle of pearly pink nail varnish at Rosie who caught it expertly.

'And they're sheer sexy tights you're wearing now, are they?' Rosie demanded.

Evie looked at the black opaque tights she always wore on the rare occasions she dressed in her one and only on-the-knee black skirt.

'Touché,' she said with a grin.

Evie thought of that now as she looked at herself in the bathroom mirror, pale beige lipstick twisted up and ready to go on. Maybe she was a bit boring. Thirty-seven wasn't a hundred, she knew that. But Evie had been acting as a grown up for so many years, she'd forgotten how to live a little, how to loosen up. Rosie couldn't understand that. *She* had no idea what it was like to be a twenty-one-year-old widow with a six-month-old baby girl. If you weren't mature in those circumstances, you went to pieces and there wasn't much time for worrying about the state of your tights or what sort of eyeliner to use.

Dumping the lipstick back in her make-up bag, Evie

17

poked around in the bathroom cabinet until she found her one bright lipstick: a raisin colour she'd got free with a magazine and had never used.

She boldly coloured her lips with it, layering the rich shade until her mouth was a dark and vibrant slash. It was too much, she decided anxiously. She scrubbed it off with toilet paper and slicked on her original colour.

Ten minutes later, she was ready. Her hair was a mass of rippling curls to her shoulders which offset the long-sleeved black velvet dress with its gentle scoop neck. The dress clung to her waist, flared out over the spreading hips to mid-calf, and Evie wore sheer black tights and her mock croc court shoes. No opaque granny tights tonight. She smiled fondly at the thought of Rosie's delighted expression if she was here.

Evie wished she had some decent jewellery to set the neckline off but since she'd been given the diamond ring, all her other jewellery looked small and insignificant beside it. The tiny opal pendant she'd bought in Spain years ago looked ridiculous on its slender gold chain compared to the magnificent engagement ring. So she left her neck bare.

Her taxi had arrived and she was just leaving the house when the phone rang.

'Mum, hiya. I'm in Sophie's,' Rosie said. 'I won't be too late.'

'What's "not too late"?' demanded Evie, staring in the hall mirror and dusting away a speck of mascara.

Her daughter sighed heavily. 'Eleven . . . twelve at the latest. You'll be out, anyway, won't you? What is it you're going to?'

'Simon's office party.'

'What are you wearing?' asked Rosie. 'Nothing too raunchy, I hope. We wouldn't want Simon's entire firm to get collective heart attacks at the sight of you in your gownless evening strap.'

Evie frowned. She hated the way Rosie mocked Simon's job. OK, loss adjusting wasn't the most dangerously exciting profession on the planet and certainly couldn't match what Tony had done for a living. But then, not everyone could be a policeman decorated for bravery. And finally Tony had been too brave for his own good.

Evie just wished Rosie would stop idolising her father and make a bit of an effort with Simon.

'I don't have any gownless evening straps in my wardrobe,' she said mildly, thinking of the perfectly organised wardrobe in her room, with its small collection of classic clothes. Evie believed in buying little and often, and she loved the conservative elegance of tailored clothes. She was wearing the most daring outfit she owned. 'And if I did, you'd probably have borrowed it long ago, you brat.'

'Mum, if you had a gownless evening strap in your wardrobe, *I'd* have a heart attack with shock!' Rosie joked. 'What *are* you wearing?'

'My black velvet . . . and sheer tights, in case you're wondering!'

They both laughed.

'I got my hair done, it's sort of curly,' she added.

'Great.' Rosie sounded enthusiastic. 'Knock 'em dead, Mum. See you.'

She rang off. Evie sighed. She preferred it when her daughter was home at night, when she knew where she was and what she was doing. But Rosie was nearly eighteen: her mother couldn't lock her away in a plastic bubble.

Maybe that was why she felt so old, Evie thought, grabbing her coat. Having a practically grown-up daughter. Or maybe it was just the sense of loss looming in the future, when her beloved Rosie was so grown up she left home and there'd be no more cosy evenings together, watching telly, laughing over old *Father Ted* episodes and having emergency snack breaks in the kitchen when they'd sat up late talking.

She put one hand on the front door and was about to brave the icy December weather when she stopped. Racing upstairs, she found the raisin lipstick, slicked some on her lips and stuck it in her handbag. Rosie was right, bless her. She had to lighten up a little.

Simon greeted her at the door of the Westbury Hotel function room with an affectionate kiss on the cheek. Dressed in his dark suit, which made his sandy hair appear almost blond, he looked palely handsome and Evie felt that flicker of pleasure that sometimes washed over her when she realised she was going to marry him. He was a good man, a kind man. If only Rosie could see it. She slid a hand inside his jacket, feeling his lean frame through the soft cotton of his white shirt. All that squash kept him very fit.

'I'm so glad you're here,' he said, sounding incredibly relieved.

'Are you?' whispered Evie happily, as he helped her out of her coat. The room looked so pretty, she thought, decorated like the rest of the hotel in subtle festive greens and gold.

'God, yes,' Simon exclaimed. 'Hugh Maguire, the Managing Director, arrived a few minutes ago absolutely plastered and his wife, Hilda, who was supposed to meet him in the hotel bar *an hour ago*, isn't amused. I knew you'd be able to talk to her. Nobody else can. She's so difficult.'

Evie's delight evaporated.

'I don't even know her,' she hissed frantically into Simon's ear. But he was already bundling her across the room to where an icy-faced matron in a black satin tent stood alone beside a stately Christmas tree.

'Hilda,' Simon said in his best client voice, 'this is Evie Fraser, my fianceé. She so wanted to meet you.'

Gritting her teeth, Evie tried to look as if she wanted to meet Hilda Maguire. Hilda didn't look as if she wanted to meet anyone – except perhaps for a Mafia hitman while she arranged a contract on her errant husband.

'Hello, Hilda,' Evie said warmly.

Hilda muttered something unintelligible in reply and kept her eyes on the group of people standing beside the buffet table.

Because Simon was not the chatty sort, Evie didn't know the office gossip. But seeing Hilda's husband nose to nose with a giant tumbler of amber liquid and an attractive girl as he loudly told what could only be ribald jokes, it wasn't hard to figure out that Hugh preferred his partying *sans* Hilda.

As his wife stood beside her, glowering and breathing heavily like a rhino with asthma, Evie wasn't sure she blamed him.

'Isn't this a lovely party?' Evie said, glancing around the room where forty or so well-dressed people were spread out, sipping drinks, nibbling canapés and avoiding her and Hilda like the plague.

'I hate office parties,' she boomed, eyes still fixed on Hugh, a handsome grey-haired man who had drained his tumbler in two seconds flat and was now looking around for a waitress.

'They're a good opportunity for staff to meet each other socially, and of course their other halves,' Evie said, aware that she sounded like a personnel manual on the subject of office relations.

Across the room, Hugh guffawed and put one hairy

hand around his companion's suede-clad waist.

Hilda snorted.

Gamely, Evie pushed on.

'I do love your outfit,' she lied. 'Where did you get it?'

'Had to have it made,' snapped Hilda. 'I've trouble with my thyroid.'

There was no answer to that. 'Er . . . would you like a drink?' Evie asked in desperation. She could certainly do with one. Simon had abandoned her without asking if she wanted anything, she thought crossly. So much for an enjoyable evening swanning around on his arm as she showed off her engagement ring.

Now she was stuck with an enraged Hilda Maguire and everyone was giving the pair of them a very wide berth. From the safety of the other side of the room, Simon gave Evie an encouraging smile. She glared back. When she got her hands on him, she'd *murder* him.

Seeing a uniformed waitress pass by, Evie waved at her and plucked a silver-chased glass cup from the girl's tray.

'It's mulled wine,' the waitress informed her.

'Thanks.' Evie took a deep sip, letting the spicy warm liquid flood into her. It was beautiful, like distilled black-berries with a hint of cinnamon. She decided to take the bull by the horns.

'Hilda,' she said, taking another cup of mulled wine, 'try this. It'll do wonders for you.'

The other woman turned to look at her and Evie saw there were tears in her eyes: fat, unshed tears glistening behind the mascara-free eyelashes. Evie smiled, the first genuine smile she'd given Hilda since they'd met.

'Go on, it's nice. You could do with a bit of anaesthesia,' she urged.

'Thank you,' muttered Hilda. She drained her cup in a couple of gulps and grabbed another one from the departing waitress's tray. 'Everybody else is pretending it isn't happening,' she said bitterly, looking at her husband. 'At least you have the honesty to acknowledge it. Nobody else will say a word because he's the boss and they're toadying desperately to hold on to their jobs. Some boss!'

Evie shrugged helplessly. 'People don't know what to say, Hilda,' she pointed out as gently as she could. 'It's not because they're toadying – it's simply embarrassing for everyone.'

Seeing Hilda's bottom lip quiver, she looked around for somewhere to sit. There was a large unoccupied couch in one corner of the large room and she led the other woman towards it. Hilda sank down and immediately started feeling around in her handbag.

'You're being so kind to me,' she said tearfully as she extracted a tissue from a travel pack.

Evie grinned wryly and thought of all the people who'd come to her with their problems over the years. People gravitated towards her for advice, whether it was about work or their emotional problems.

All the girls at Wentworth Alarms ended up at Evie's desk at some point or another, ostensibly looking for tampons or the petty cash book but really looking for a motherly shoulder to cry on. It amused Evie to think that many of them were only slightly younger than she was, but they still saw her as an older, mumsy figure. Rosie was right: she was old before her time.

Two hours later, after listening to more details of Hugh and Hilda's marriage than she really wanted to know, Evie helped Hilda into a taxi and waved her goodbye.

'You were wonderful, Evie,' said a voice.

She whirled around to see Simon at her side, his tie askew and his hair tousled. He looked as if he'd been overindulging in the mulled wine.

'Well, you were no bloody help at all,' she retorted, still smarting at having been abandoned all evening to cheer up Hilda.

'Sorry, Evie.' Simon tried his best to look forlorn but failed. 'You're so good with people, I told everyone you'd be able to look after Hilda.'

'Hmmph.' Mildly mollified, she let him take her hand and they walked back to the party. It wasn't even ten yet, there was still plenty of time to enjoy themselves.

But once she'd joined Simon's closest colleagues, it was soon apparent that while she'd been listening to stories of what a catch of a husband Hugh Maguire had been twenty years ago, *they'd* all been giggling over mulled wine and endless pints of free beer and were all plastered.

After hearing the same joke repeated twice – and they all laughed as much the second time – Evie decided she wasn't in the mood to be the only sedate one at the party.

Drawing Simon aside, she whispered: 'I think I'll leave you guys to it. I'm tired and after talking to Hilda all evening, I'm not in party mood. I'll go home.'

She half hoped he'd insist she stay, manfully demanding that she had to remain at the party. But ever the peacemaker, Simon nodded and said he'd bring her out to get a taxi.

'I'm sorry, it wasn't much of an evening for you, Evie,' he apologised as they waited outside the hotel door for the second time that evening. 'If you hadn't come along, I don't know what we'd have done. Hugh's definitely developing a bit of a drink problem and we were all sure Hilda would go ballistic when she discovered how drunk he was.'

'And how flirtatious,' Evie said tartly.

'That too,' Simon admitted. 'But you were wonderful,' he said and kissed her – a lingering kiss on the lips.

Evie felt the tension of the evening flood away from her

at the pressure of his mouth. She unconsciously slipped a hand behind his neck, reaching up to kiss him passionately. His body melted against hers, his arms reaching inside her coat to encircle her waist.

'Come home with me, Simon,' she said in a low voice. 'I'm not going to see you for three days over Christmas and I'll miss you. You've done your duty for tonight.'

He pulled away, shocked. 'I can't leave now,' he said. 'Hugh and the other senior partners are still here. I can't go before they do – it'd be incredibly rude.'

Hurt, Evie moved away and clutched her coat around her body, wrapping her arms around her chest. 'Hugh's drunk,' she said, her voice high and angry. 'He'd hardly notice if the bloody hotel disappeared, never mind you. I don't see why you can't leave. But,' she turned away as a taxi drove smoothly in front of her, 'you do what you want.' She could feel herself getting emotional. The last thing she wanted to do was cry.

The doorman, who had been discreetly ignoring both their embrace and their row, opened the car door.

'Oh, Evie,' said Simon wearily.

Without turning around, she hopped into the taxi.

'I'll talk to you tomorrow,' she said in a tight little voice. 'Have a nice party.'

With perfect timing, the doorman slammed the door shut and the taxi driver drove off.

'Where to, love?' he asked.

Evie gave him the address and sank back into the seat miserably. Some party.

As the car cruised through the city, Evie gazed out the window and watched the bright lights go past in a blur. She *was* tired, but not that tired. If Simon had begged her not to leave, she'd still be there. But he didn't. And he was afraid to leave in case he offended anyone. Not too afraid to offend her, she thought, her temper mounting.

What sort of a man would land his fianceé with a babysitting job for the first half of a party, and then let her go home alone after they'd shared a very sexy moment? Evie glowered.

'My darling, I would follow you to the ends of the earth. Of course let us leave this boring party. I have a light supper prepared for you in my penthouse.'

He held her hand to his lips, a little longer than was strictly necessary, his sensual lips brushing against her silken skin.

Evie felt her heart quicken at his touch. She knew what would happen if he took her to his luxury penthouse: he would make love to her. And she, who had resisted his advances in Paris and on the yacht, knew she would not resist this time.

Her handsome, charming prince had been undressing her with his dark melting eyes for weeks, with hot glances across the roulette table and as she danced with the ambassador at the ball. Now he would undress her for real, his hands gently undoing the tiny buttons on her St Laurent gown, letting it slip over her slender figure, marvelling at the swell of her breasts and the length of her elegant long legs.

'Will you do me the honour of coming with me?' he asked again, those eyes boring into her very soul . . .

'That'll be fifteen quid, love,' said the taxi driver. Evie paid him and marched into the house, feeling like Cinderella sent home early from the ball because the pumpkin had got a flat tyre.

Naturally, Rosie wasn't home. It was only half-ten and she'd probably stay out until twelve, sure her mother wouldn't be home before then. Feeling very sorry for herself, Evie heated up a cup of milk in the microwave and took it up. Within ten minutes she was climbing into bed, her clothes put away and her face scrupulously cleaned and moisturised.

It was cold and she snuggled under the duvet, cosy in candy-striped brushed cotton pyjamas. Glamorous they weren't but they were lovely and warm, a major plus when it took ages for the electric blanket to heat up.

After a moment getting warm, she took her mug of milk in one hand, her latest Lucy De Montford in the other and settled down to read.

Monique had just told the duke she couldn't marry him because she was still in love with the dashing Spanish pirate who'd captured her and her maid as they crossed the Atlantic. Evie didn't know how she'd put *Monique's Desires* down the night before. Only the knowledge that she had to get up early to work had forced her to turn off her light just when it looked as if the heroine would have to compromise herself to support her huge, hopeless family. Monique was crying miserably in the turret where the duke had imprisoned her, but Evie knew she wouldn't be there for long. She was wearing a flimsy white gown with a bodice awash with silk ribbons and nobody in Lucy De Montford's novels ever wore anything fastened with ribbons if they intended to stay clothed. Tonight, Evie was determined to stay up until three in the morning if necessary to find out what happened.

Evie could well imagine the duke arriving in the turret to claim Monique for himself, marriage or no marriage. And the Spanish pirate would have to get there in time. There'd be a duel of course . . .

She thought of Simon duelling for her honour, rapier held aloft as he challenged some nasty duke who had evil designs on her body. Well, maybe not. Simon hated the sight of blood and was incredibly squeamish. When Rosie had grazed her shin while rollerblading, Evie had nearly had two patients to deal with. Rosie, who was in pain but trying to hide it, and Simon, who'd practically fainted when Rosie had rolled up her torn jeans to examine the scraped bit.

He was just as bad when it came to female ailments. Brought up as an only child by a mother who treated his conception practically as the virgin birth, Simon had no experience of women's problems. Evie couldn't clutch her abdomen when she had a painful period without Simon averting his eyes as if he'd stumbled on some arcane female secret. God alone knew where she'd have to hide her tampons when they got married. In a separate room in a brown paper bag probably.

So duelling was out. He might shoot someone to save her honour, she thought. Shooting happened such a long way away that he couldn't mind that. Evie took a sip of milk and immersed herself in the racy world of the seventeenth century where men were men and women were glad of the fact.

CHAPTER TWO

Parsnips! She'd forgotten the parsnips, Olivia realised with a start. Stephen would go mad if he didn't get parsnips with his Christmas lunch. He loved them, especially pureéd until they resembled baby food, she thought fondly.

It was just after nine p.m. on December 23rd, the supermarket was about to shut and if she didn't reach a check-out soon, she'd probably be shoved out of the electronic doors into the freezing night – without her shopping. But Olivia who would have died rather than keep the staff in the supermarket waiting for her, knew that she just *had* to get parsnips. Poor Stephen had to face three whole days in her parents' house over the holidays so the least she could do was cook him the sort of food he liked.

Hastily abandoning the jam-packed trolley, she sprinted back to the vegetables, both the fringe of her ankle-length Indian skirt and her long fair hair flying out behind her.

She nearly collided with another late-night shopper as she rounded the bend beside the flowers at high speed and her sudden sprint surprised an elderly lady reaching for the cat food.

'Sorry,' gasped Olivia, without stopping.

There had obviously been a run on parsnips that day: all that remained at the bottom of the display were a few stunted specimens which looked about ten years old and would probably taste like boiled socks.

For about the tenth time that day, Olivia cursed the events which had forced her to leave her shopping so late that she hadn't time to visit her favourite greengrocer and delicatessen to stock up on Christmas goodies. Her father adored those fat Spanish olives drenched in olive oil and she hadn't been able to find them anywhere in the supermarket. The pre-Christmas panic meant the shelves were virtually bare and she was now left with prehistoric parsnips Stephen would hate. Still, she'd manage to revitalise them somehow. What was the point of being a home economics teacher if you couldn't rustle up something wonderful in the kitchen?

Olivia grabbed a handful of the puny vegetables, weighed them and rushed back to her trolley in time to hear a bored voice announce over the Tannoy: 'The supermarket is now shut. Please go to the check-outs. This is the last call.'

It was a bit like being at the airport, hearing your flight was closing, Olivia thought, snatching a big bag of mini Mars bars as she passed the biscuits and flinging them on top of the mountain of groceries. What she wouldn't give to be jumping on a plane right now, heading off somewhere exotic where Christmas wasn't celebrated and the temperature seldom dropped below thirty degrees Centigrade.

For a moment, she dreamed of palm-fringed beaches, white sand and cerulean water so clear you could see the tiny silver fish that swam near the shore. She and Stephen lazing on loungers at the water's edge, listening to the sound of the lapping waves as the heat of the sun warmed their bare limbs. Sasha playing on the sand, toys spread out beside her fat little legs as she sat in her pink swimming costume, her white-blonde hair tied up in adorable pig tails and her cherubic little face lit up with happiness.

Wishful thinking, Olivia realised. The three of them hadn't been on holiday for nearly eighteen months because Stephen had been so busy at work with the merger between Clifden International Incorporated and a giant German bank.

European Information Technology Executive was supposed to be the sort of incredibly high-powered job that came with hot and cold running assistants to do the dirty work, but in reality the combination of Stephen's dedication and perfectionism meant he insisted on being consulted over every crisis – weekends, night-time, whenever.

'I can't let anybody else sort this out,' he'd mutter, handsome olive-skinned face blank, his mind already miles away as he expertly packed his sleek Samsonite case for another trip abroad. 'I don't get paid the sort of salary they give me for nothing, you know. It's tough on you, Olivia, but we've got to make sacrifices to get on.'

Now she was sick of making those type of sacrifices. Their apartment in Blackrock may have looked like the 'after' picture in an interior design magazine thanks to Stephen's ever-increasing salary, but she saw less and less of him as his workload grew heavier. She spent birthdays and anniversaries alone and despaired of ever having a normal family weekend that didn't involve Stephen haring into his city centre office at least once. In the twelve years they'd been married, she'd been alone for six wedding anniversaries, and last-minute business meant Stephen had been away for her birthday on three separate occasions.

They'd had to cancel the longed-for week in Spain in July when there was a crisis in the Amsterdam office and their two weeks in the Dordogne the previous year had been constantly punctuated by the shrill sound of Stephen's mobile phone.

Olivia could have lived without the expensive Swedish wood floors and the high-tech kitchen if only she'd had someone to share her home with more of the time. She absolutely adored Sasha but by the end of a week spent with only her daughter to talk to, Olivia craved adult conversation. Long-distance 'Yes, of course I miss you' from a distant hotel room wasn't quite the same as cuddling up on the sofa with Stephen, having her feet massaged as they talked about their days. But he adored his job and was willing to go to any lengths to advance his career, even if it meant being away from home more often than he was there.

Sometimes Olivia simply couldn't understand him. No job could have made her leave Stephen and Sasha for weeks at a time, not even one with a huge salary, lots of perks, a 5 series BMW and a company American Express card.

Perhaps it was because being a part-time home economics teacher didn't fill her with the same burning drive and ambition to succeed.

Teaching a deeply disinterested 3A how to make a nourishing meal out of a can of kidney beans and a bit of minced beef no longer fired her with boundless enthusiasm. Apart from her enthusiasm for breaktime when she could throw herself into an armchair in the teachers' staffroom, enjoy a cup of tea and discuss what a little horror Cheryl Dennis was, to a universal chorus of: 'When will the principal expel that child?'

Stephen, on the other hand, adored his job and its time-consuming challenges. Running his section like an all-powerful despot suited him down to the ground and Olivia suspected he'd know exactly how to deal with

Cheryl Dennis when she threw mince at her best friend, who promptly threw kidney beans back.

'Next,' yawned the check-out girl.

Forget about sun-kissed beaches, Olivia told herself sternly. She stacked her groceries on the conveyor belt and thought about the sort of holiday season she *would* be having: Christmas lunch with her parents, Stephen and Sasha in the rambling Lodge, a raucous affair where both parents would be roaring drunk before the smoked salmon had hit the table, while Stephen would sit in disapproving silence as bottles of her father's favourite claret moved up and down the table with frightening speed. You'd swear it was *Olivia's* fault her parents drank like fishes.

Her mother would be giggling too much to help with the cooking and Janet, the latest housekeeper-cum-home-help – whom Olivia suspected also made a substantial contribution to the already-stratospheric household drinks bill – had been given the week off.

Stephen was hopeless in the vegetable-peeling depart-ment, and anyway he'd be so tired after his week-long German trip that it'd be down to Olivia and her mother's ancient, grime-encrusted cooker to produce everything.

No wonder the school's selection of prehistoric cookers never fazed her – after learning to cook on the Lodge's rackety appliances, Olivia could have whipped up a four-course meal with a single gas flame and two saucepans.

At least, Mum and Pops would fall asleep over whatever Indiana Jones movie was on that afternoon, so she and Stephen could take Sasha for a walk around the village and call in on the Frasers, her closest friends.

Christmas was always so much fun at the Frasers', Olivia thought longingly, remembering the year she'd sneaked out of a loud Christmas morning party in the Lodge, leaving all her de Vere relatives braying loudly at one another across the fifteenth-century refectory table, swigging back the strongest egg nog imaginable. She'd been a shy, retiring sixteen at the time and slipping into the peaceful atmosphere of the Frasers' small homey kitchen after the enforced jollity of her own home had been bliss.

The scent of a goose roasting in the old black range filled the room, Mrs Fraser and Evie were joking and laughing as they finished setting the table for lunch, Mr Fraser sat in his battered old armchair reading, as usual, and six-year-old Cara was sprawled on the floor, attempting to turn her new doll into Action Man with the help of oven blacking, a ripped khaki T-shirt and a pair of large kitchen scissors she obviously wasn't supposed to be using. The simple table wasn't a quarter as grand as Olivia's parents' table with its Waterford crystal glasses and silverware, but it was a hundred times more inviting.

'Olivia darling, Merry Christmas,' said Mrs Fraser, opening welcoming arms for a hug. *She* didn't reek of early-morning hair-of-dog remedies and mothballs from an ancient twinset she'd dug out of her closet; she smelt of baking and of the Blue Grass perfume she used on special occasions.

Olivia smiled happily at the Frasers, wishing they were *her* parents, and then guiltily suppressed the thought, feeling desperately disloyal.

You were supposed to love *your* parents, not mope around after your best friend's. It was just that Evie's parents were so . . . well, like *parents*, grown-ups. Not like Sybil and Leslie de Vere who still both behaved like the carefree, idle kids they'd been when they'd met at college in the fifties.

Olivia felt more grown-up than they were. Well, *someone* had to be a bit grown-up in the Lodge, otherwise the final reminders would have been shoved in the hall drawer unpaid and nobody would ever have thought of paying the account in the butcher's.

Over twenty years later Olivia still sometimes wished she could go home to the Frasers' for Christmas, although sneaking clandestinely out of the increasingly run-down Lodge for a few hours was no longer possible now that the hordes of hard-drinking distant de Vere relatives were all long gone and the only company her parents had would be herself, Sasha and Stephen.

Olivia stuffed his parsnips into a plastic bag along with the rest of her vegetables and wished he wasn't away in Germany. The apartment always seemed so empty when he was gone and she felt so lonely on her own in their big double bed. Stuffing a pillow on Stephen's side so there'd be *something* beside her didn't work very well.

She loved it when he came home and they could sink into the snowy cotton sheets he preferred and make rapturous love. Stephen's lean, dark-skinned body wrapped around her pale gold one. No matter how much time they spent apart, it only took a few minutes for the passion that had drawn them together in the beginning to be rekindled.

Not that there'd be any time for lovemaking when he flew home the next day, she thought ruefully, unless his parents decided to do the convenient thing for the first time in their lives and left at a reasonable hour. And Cedric and Sheilagh MacKenzie never did anything that was convenient for their daughter-in-law. Take today when they'd turned up at the Blackrock apartment unannounced, just as Olivia and Sasha were leaving for a day's shopping.

'As we're not having you for Christmas Day, we've come to give Sasha her presents,' Cedric told a startled Olivia at ten in the morning, breezing into the apartment lugging a large suitcase, with Sheilagh close behind, beady eyes on the lookout for dust.

'How lovely to see you,' mouthed Olivia weakly. What else could she say? Apart from 'you could have phoned first'.

'Stephen's away in Frankfurt,' she said, as they settled themselves on the cream leather couches in the airy, off-white living room.

Stephen was so proud of those couches. They went perfectly with the blond polished wooden floors, the modern Scandinavian furniture and the single driftwood sculpture on the facing wall. Sasha wasn't allowed to play on the couches or on the butter-coloured wool rug placed just so in front of the fireplace.

'I know he's not here,' Cedric said complacently, 'and I know you're coming to us in the New Year, but we've come to visit you and Sasha now, Olivia, my dear. We thought we could get some last-minute shopping if you'd drive us into the city and, I must admit, I'd love a cup of Lapsang, I'm parched.'

'Sorry,' Olivia apologised. 'I'll put the kettle on.' She was always apologising when Stephen's parents were around.

In the stainless steel kitchen, Sasha was sitting under the bleached maple table playing with her colouring pens: the bright, indelible acid greens and luminous pinks that she loved and that didn't wash off. Olivia was sick with nerves keeping them away from the precious leather couches.

'Are we not going shopping now, Mummy?' she asked in a voice that was surprisingly grave for a four year old.

'No, Sasha,' Olivia said resignedly as she wondered when she'd ever get time to shop now. After a manic two days correcting exam papers so she wouldn't have to do them during the holidays and waste her precious time with Stephen, she had banked on getting everything done today, including buying all the food and picking up a gift for her father, who was impossible to buy for. But how could she go shopping with Cedric and Sheilagh ensconced here demanding to be entertained, fed and kept supplied with copious amounts of Lapsang Souchong at hourly intervals?

Why couldn't they drink normal tea like normal people? And how could she tell them they'd have to leave by six the following evening because she and Stephen had to drive down to Ballymoreen for the Frasers' Christmas Eve drinks party?

Cedric and Sheilagh were already raging that it was Olivia's parents' turn to host Christmas, meaning they'd be eating their Christmas lunch alone. There'd be World War Three if Olivia turfed them out of the apartment before they felt inclined to go.

'Sasha's at that wonderful age when it's a joy to see her opening her presents on Christmas morning,' Sheilagh had said earlier, laying on the guilt with a trowel and ostentatiously wiping away a tear as she placed the presents under Olivia's tree.

Olivia felt like a criminal, denying a little old lady time with her only son's offspring. But as the day progressed with unbelievable slowness, she noticed that neither Sheilagh nor Cedric paid that much attention to their adorable four-year-old grand-daughter even when she was right under their noses: Sasha had spent ages in the kitchen quietly making cards with her pens, gold and silver stars, glitter and the child-safe glue Olivia had bought for her.

Olivia loved watching her: the small face screwed up in concentration, the chubby little fingers remarkably dextrous as she decorated a smiley face with long, golden hair: 'Like yours, Mummy.'

Sheilagh had never ventured in once, except when looking for tea and biscuits. It's as if our home is some sort of posh station waiting room, Olivia thought with a flash of irritation, somewhere to relax after the journey from Navan before being chauffeured off shopping. Seeing Sasha to give her her presents was just an excuse.

Stop it, she commanded. That's uncharitable. They love Sasha, she's their only grandchild and of course they want to spend time with her. They're simply not any good with children. Or with adults, the little devil in her head muttered.

In the end, she'd only managed to escape the apartment late that evening when Sasha was in bed and Sheilagh was settling in for the night with her cocoa and a mountain of shortbread to watch *Emmerdale* and *The Bill*.

'I'll just run to the supermarket,' Olivia said gaily, politely hiding the fact that she was exhausted after a day of cooking and tidying up behind her guests, not to mention the trauma of braving the three-mile traffic jam into Dublin's city centre because Sheilagh had a fancy to pick up some last minute gifts in Arnott's.

'You run along, Olivia,' Cedric said magnanimously. 'I'll wash up here.'

Olivia stifled the retort that the only washing up left were his and Sheilagh's last couple of tea cups, as she had already tidied up after the enormous dinner, scrubbing saucepans until her arms ached while the dishwasher trundled through the dishes. But she'd been so grateful to escape that she'd said nothing and smiled politely as she shut the apartment door as quietly as she could.

'Five pounds and thirty-two pence,' counted the checkout girl as she handed Olivia her change.

'Thanks.' She manhandled the unwilling trolley towards the door.

The security guard pulling down the supermarket shutters gave her a hot, admiring glance as she left, taking in the tall, slim figure and the beautiful face. Men always noticed Olivia, even when she was slumming it in her ancient and very comfortable Indian fringed skirt, too-large black coat with threadbare patches and flat suede boots she'd had for at least ten years.

Flowing layers of fabric couldn't hide the elegant, graceful body or the oval face with slanting silver-grey eyes and pale, full-lipped mouth.

If anything, her eccentric style of dress heightened her unusual looks. Fashionable, tight and sexy clothes were too brash and in-your-face for someone like Olivia, who was more at home in antique chiffon blouses and long Edwardian dresses she picked up in flea markets than in the chic modern clothes Stephen liked her to wear.

Olivia smiled faintly at the security guard, the way she acknowledged everyone, friend or stranger. She couldn't help it: it was a reflex action.

'You're not like most beautiful people, Olivia,' Rosie had said recently, faintly disapproving. 'You're nice to everyone.'

'What's wrong with that?' she had demanded easily. She never minded what Rosie said to her. She adored her bolshie seventeen-year-old god-daughter.

'*Too* nice,' Rosie had pointed out crisply.

Now Olivia stowed the bags in the boot of the Golf, shivering in the icy night air.

She'd love to pop over to Evie's for a few minutes. She had no desire to rush home and she hadn't bought anything instantly perishable. If she had, Olivia thought as she fiddled with the heater, it'd remain frozen no matter how long she spent with Evie and Rosie. It was freezing outside and, since the twelve-year-old Golf's heater only worked sporadically, it was pretty cold *inside* the car too.

That was it, she'd go to Evie's. After the hellish day she'd had, it would be lovely to sit in her pretty sitting room in front of the fire and gossip.

Then she remembered – Evie was at Simon's office party. Shit. Sitting in the car staring blankly at the super-market lit up with fairy lights, tinsel and over-indulgent sprawls of fake snow, Olivia felt like crying. She must be pre-menstrual, she thought, searching blindly in her hand-bag for a tissue.

Everything had gone wrong all week, finishing up with horrible Cheryl Dennis's mince-throwing session on the last day of term. Now she was stuck with bloody Sheilagh and Cedric for the night. They wouldn't go to bed until very late, while she, who had a mountain of quiches to bake the following morning, had to get up at six.

Half an hour chatting with Evie would have cheered her up enough to cope. She blew her nose and thought of what her friend would say about the MacKenzie Seniors. Indeed, what Evie already *had* said about them: 'Those people have no bloody manners – they need the short, sharp shock treatment. They're so thick-skinned, it's the only thing that'll work.' Her advice would be brusque now: 'Tell them you've got a lot to do so you're going to bed early. Explain that they can look after themselves tomorrow and,' Evie would pause for effect, her forehead scrunched up crossly, 'tell them to phone next time they plan to stay with you. I don't know why you can't say it, Olivia. They'll haunt you for the rest of your life if you don't get firm with them sometime.'

Dear Evie was so protective of her but she was right, Olivia was perfectly aware of that. Still, it was one thing *thinking* up all the tough things she'd like to say to her pushy, inconsiderate in-laws. It was another thing entirely actually *saying* any of them. And being so blunt would hurt Stephen dreadfully because he idolised his parents. Olivia wouldn't hurt him for the world.

'I'm home,' she said brightly, dragging the first batch of

shopping into the apartment. That was one of the huge disadvantages of high-rise living – it took several goes to lug the groceries up from the car park because the lift was too unreliable to get it to wait while she dragged six or seven bags to the front door.

More than once, the lift doors had slammed shut on half of Olivia's shopping as she struggled to drag the first instalment across the landing and in the front door.

'It never happens to me,' Stephen had pointed out when she'd complained about it.

Olivia was too loyal to remark that he'd only done the big grocery shop once when she was in bed with bronchitis, so he was hardly an expert on the subject.

Now she dumped the bags in the kitchen and poked her head into the sitting room where Cedric and Sheilagh were watching the news.

Cedric was sitting ramrod straight on one couch, that day's newspaper all over the floor, while Sheilagh lay prone on the other, looking like a giant, plump strawberry in the pink velour tracksuit that did nothing for either her hefty figure or her purple-tinged frosted hairdo.

'I'm home,' Olivia said again. 'I'm just getting the shopping from the car.'

'Oh, hello,' said Sheilagh.

Neither of them moved a muscle.

Olivia turned to collect the second hundredweight of shopping.

She'd just dumped it on to the kitchen floor when Cedric called out: 'Did you remember to get a lemon, dear? You've none in the fridge and I love it in my tea.'

Meaning, Olivia simmered, that you'd like more tea, *with* lemon this time.

She gazed at the shortbread crumbs decorating her previously spotless worktops. For someone who claimed to be a martyr to her wheat and dairy allergies, Sheilagh certainly could put away biscuits like there was no tomorrow.

Count to ten, she thought, as she boiled the kettle again.

Her guests were still animated at half-eleven. Sitting on the couch while Cedric regaled her and Sheilagh with some long-winded story about his optician's shop, Olivia marvelled at how her father-in-law could look so like her beloved husband and yet be so utterly unlike him in every other way.

Both men shared the same lean build, although Stephen was broader thanks to his regular workouts in the gym. And they both had tightly curled dark hair, olive skin and fathomless black eyes that spoke of Italian ancestry somewhere along the way (Cedric's grandmother had been from Naples).

But while Cedric was self-obsessed, strait-laced and very fond of the sound of his own voice, Stephen was outgoing, the life of every party, ambitious and very passionate. That's what had drawn her to him, Olivia thought, wishing he was here right now.

They'd been introduced at a dinner party twelve years previously and had fallen madly, passionately in love with each other. After a whirlwind romance when they'd spent every spare moment in bed, they'd got engaged within three months and married six months later.

At the time, Olivia had been working in the local tech by day teaching home economics, and giving cookery demonstrations at night to make enough money to travel round the world. Stephen had just joined Clifden International.

Once they got married, he told her she didn't need to kill herself with two jobs and then somehow Olivia had found herself with only half a job, working four mornings a week, the way she still did. Her plans to travel around the world had been shelved when she and Stephen got married, which Olivia often thought was ironic: he was now never off a plane and had enough air miles saved to buy tickets to Mars, while she never got farther than her daily triangular loop in the car to the school and the supermarket via Sasha's crèche.

She couldn't complain, she knew. After all, they had darling little Sasha and it had taken her so long to get pregnant that she thanked God for her daughter every day of her life. After seven years where Olivia longed for a baby, even if Stephen had been a bit unconcerned about her inability to conceive, she'd felt gloriously lucky to become pregnant. Sasha had been worth the wait, the little pet.

'Hilarious, wasn't it?' Cedric said, barely able to contain his laughter at his own anecdote.

Olivia blinked. She hadn't been listening – 'wool gathering' was what Stephen called it when she tuned out like that. Sometimes her mind wandered and she always felt so guilty that she hadn't been listening to what he said, especially as she missed him so much when he was away.

'I'm obviously not interesting enough for you, Olivia,' he'd say in mock disapproval, pulling her to him and settling her on his lap.

'But you are,' she'd protest, kissing him to prove her point.

And they'd end making love, a frantic, almost silent encounter with the door of their bedroom ajar as they listened out for sounds of Sasha getting bored with her toys and trundling down the corridor on her solid little legs to see what they were doing. Stephen got very irritated by having to keep quiet.

'Olivia, didn't you think that was funny?' Sheilagh was saying.

'Hysterical,' fibbed Olivia. She couldn't wait for Stephen to arrive home.

★ ★ ★

'There's hardly any need to take more booze to your parents' house and you know I don't like too much drinking in front of Sasha,' Stephen complained the following afternoon as he watched Olivia pack a couple of bottles of wine into the giant hamper they were taking to Ballymoreen.

'We'll have a couple of glasses of wine and I hate to turn up with nothing,' she protested.

They were in the kitchen, with Stephen lounging against the counter, still in his grey suit, white shirt and crimson tie. He'd arrived home from the airport a couple of hours previously, tired and definitely not on top form.

'Bloody thing still isn't sorted out,' he'd said shortly when Olivia inquired. 'I don't want to talk about it.' However at the sight of his parents, he cheered up miraculously.

'It wouldn't be right if I didn't see you until New Year,' he said affectionately as he hugged Sheilagh. 'Has she been looking after you both?' he asked in a teasing voice, giving Olivia's hand a squeeze as he spoke.

'Olivia was wonderful,' cooed Sheilagh.

'Not that we expect her to look after us,' interrupted Cedric. 'She's a busy woman, she doesn't have the time to fetch and carry for us boring old things. We're quite capable of looking after ourselves.'

Olivia stiffened, thinking of exactly how much fetching and carrying she'd done since they'd arrived.

It had taken a considerable amount of effort on Olivia's part not to give Stephen chapter and verse on this when Cedric and Sheilagh finally took themselves off to their room to pack – after yet another enormous meal, naturally.

Instead, she confined herself to saying that she didn't like it being asked if she'd looked after his parents.

'I mean, what do you think I'd do with them, Stephen?' she demanded hotly. 'Leave them watching the TV and go shopping with Sasha? You know I'm always hospitable to your parents. I resent your even mentioning it.'

'Have I ruffled your feathers, Mother Hen?' he asked, tickling her affectionately. 'It was a joke, that's all.'

'It wasn't funny,' she replied.

'Come on.' He tickled even harder. 'Don't be such a grump. It doesn't suit you. Frowning ruins that lovely face and I like to see my girl smiling.'

But Olivia, exhausted after her exertions, didn't feel like smiling any more than she liked being called 'Mother Hen'. She was fed up with that stupid name.

When Stephen was away it suited him to let her run their home and cope with every crisis. When he returned, he wanted her back as fluffly old Mother Hen so he could be master of the house. For once, Olivia wasn't in the mood to be patronised.

Instead of hugging Stephen in return to defuse the situation, she'd gone into the kitchen and started organising things for their drive to her father's house. Now there was a coolness between them, a coolness which meant Stephen was in a bad mood.

Trying to ignore the bad-tempered vibes emanating from her husband, Olivia consulted her list to see if she'd forgotten anything. Quiches. Stephen moved one long arm and stuck the pepper grinder in a cupboard, flicking away a couple of pinpricks of pepper from the worktop.

'We better do a clean out soon,' he said coldly, looking into the cupboard and staring at the slightly untidy arrangement of tins and packets. 'The kitchen really looks better with nothing on view and these cupboards are a mess.'

Olivia rapidly shoved the little silver elephant she'd been given by a pupil into the cutlery drawer. Stephen

45

believed the stark modern look of the room was spoiled by knick-knacks, although she loved little bits and pieces, even if they were hell to dust.

She opened the fridge, wishing she'd kept quiet earlier. Her and her big mouth. She should have said nothing. Now Stephen was in one of his moods and the drive home would be hell. She hated driving with him when he was angry: he overtook other cars dangerously, accelerating like a maniac and flashing his lights aggressively, and didn't seem bothered if Olivia and Sasha went green around the gills with car sickness.

'What sort of quiche did you make?' he inquired idly, still watching Olivia's preparations through narrowed eyes.

'One spinach and cheese, two smoked salmon and a tomato, feta and olive one for Pops.'

Stephen grimaced. 'I hate feta cheese.'

'I know, darling,' Olivia said patiently as she arranged Tupperware in the hamper, 'but you don't have to eat it. I got a big thing of cashews for you,' she added anxiously. He adored them.

'Mmm,' was all he said to that.

Olivia, thinking of the drive ahead of them, tried again. 'I almost couldn't get my hands on parsnips yesterday but,' she gave him a broad smile, 'knowing how much you love them, I managed it. Christmas wouldn't be Christmas without some puréed with a little ground black pepper, the way you like them . . .'

'Jesus, Olivia,' he snapped. 'I've just spent a few tough days trying to sort out a huge crisis in the Frankfurt office and I come home to find you moaning about my parents and bloody parsnips! Can't you think of anything more interesting to say?'

Stung, she turned away rapidly, feeling her eyes brimming with tears. She hadn't said *anything* complaining about his parents, although she could have. And as for the parsnips . . . she was only trying to show him how much she loved him, to make up for being cross earlier.

She could have told him about her hellish week in school, about the horrible kids in 3A or about how Cedric and Sheilagh had sabotaged her entire shopping plans by landing unannounced at the apartment. But she didn't. She'd tried to be the perfect wife to the busy executive by standing smiling at the door to greet him with freshly washed pale gold hair flopping around her shoulders, wearing the elegant silk shift dress he loved and that she hated because it rode up her thighs when she walked. What a pity he didn't appreciate her efforts.

Stephen wanted the gleaming, polished home, the kitchen full of home cooking and a squeaky clean wife and daughter, but he didn't want to know how they got that way. The minutiae of their lives bored him.

She didn't turn round when he marched out of the kitchen but when he walked into the sitting room, she could hear him speaking to his parents in a voice so lighthearted it was as if their argument had never happened.

'Mummy, will I give Daddy his card later?' asked Sasha, appearing beside her suddenly with a sparkly card in one fat little hand.

Sasha's eyes, the same slanting silver-grey as Olivia's, were solemn. Olivia sank to the floor and hugged her tightly, comfort flooding through her as she felt the small solid body snuggle into hers. Her daughter had a better idea how to handle Stephen than she did. Sasha instinctively knew when he was in one of his moods and kept out of his way. Like I did when I was small and Mum and Pops were fighting when they were drunk, Olivia realised with a shock.

Why was she so surprised by how perceptive Sasha was? Small children could be aware of so much. Their finely tuned antennae picked up every nuance of adult arguments. At least Stephen was nothing like her parents, Olivia consoled herself. He never ran through the house like her father had on those few terrifying occasions in her childhood, blind drunk and fuelled by some inner rage. She shuddered to remember it and kissed Sasha's soft shampoo-scented hair. Thank God Stephen was nothing like that.

The drive to Ballymoreen was hell. Stuck in a tailback of Christmas Eve drivers all heading determinedly to family gatherings via the motorway, Stephen got into an even worse mood. Not even the comedy special on the radio could improve his temper. Olivia sat silently beside him, watching the rain stream down the side window as they drove with agonising slowness towards Blessington.

She'd remained calm even during the 'did you remember to bring my . . .' conversation. How Stephen, a man who routinely packed for weeks away without forgetting a single thing, could turn into a man incapable of packing his own luggage when they went away for a family weekend, Olivia had no idea.

By the time they reached Ballymoreen, Sasha was asleep in the back of the car and Olivia was dreading the moment when they arrived at her parents' home. Stephen had never really liked Leslie and Sybil; partly because he knew how tough Olivia's childhood had been, the only child of an eccentric couple who viewed their hectic social existence as their true calling in life; and partly because he resented their wealthy Anglo-Irish background.

Both came from a long line of hunting, shooting and fishing types who thought that jobs were for common people, a view which was like a red rag to a bull for a man who'd won a scholarship to college and had been brought up in a home dedicated to the work ethic. It was immaterial that her parents were stony broke, having had a long line of similarly profligate ancestors who'd squandered the family money. Their rambling, rundown home was four times the size of Stephen's family's home in Navan, a bungalow complete with anti-macassars, spotless lino, regimented gladioli and not a wine rack in sight.

In turn, her parents didn't like Stephen very much because he clearly disapproved of their hedonistic lifestyle and made it plain every time a de Vere family party deteriorated into the customary drunken piss-up.

As usual, Olivia would have to referee.

Stephen drove the BMW past the pretty stone church and Olivia couldn't help but brighten up at the sight of Ballymoreen. Like a picture postcard version of an Irish village, it would have been the perfect location for a movie set in the forties – if only location directors had been able to find it.

Tucked away in a corner of Kildare unhindered by major, un-potholed roads, Ballymoreen was guaranteed privacy by virtue of its inaccessibility.

Nothing seemed to have changed very much in the village since Olivia had been a child, from the small post office – now with a strip of bright green lifting the pale façade – to the pretty stone monument to the Civil War in the centre of the village, where tubs of plump evergreen shrubs sat all around the chiselled grey stone in winter. Village life revolved around the monument and the wooden benches under it. People on their way from the gossip central that was Phil's Convenience Shop stopped at the monument to talk to people who were strolling down the village from the direction of the post office.

On summer evenings the local teenagers sat and chatted

around it, discussing that eternal question Ballymoreen teenagers had been discussing for at least three decades: whether it was worth trying to sneak into Bishop's Lounge Bar for an illicit vodka or whether they'd be thrown out before they got beyond the golden syrup-coloured tongue and groove pine that now decorated the lounge.

On Boxing Day, the monument was where the local hunt started and at ten in the morning the place would be thronged with stamping, snorting horses, aching to go. Tonight it was deserted; the biting December wind and torrential rain had driven away even the hardiest villager.

They drove down the hill past the row of pretty terraced cottages that faced the pub and past the butcher's shop with its familiar red and white awning. Over the stone bridge, past the schoolhouse and up the other side of the hill to where the Lodge stood alongside vast, crumbling stone gate posts with an ancient oak tree standing sentinel beside them.

As houses went, Olivia's old home was beautiful, if totally rundown. A medium-sized Georgian building with an overgrown box hedge in front of it, the Lodge was an almost exact replica of the big house which had stood a mile further up the tree-lined avenue.

The big house was long gone and a fledgling estate of mock-Tudor houses stood in its place now. Olivia's parents hated the estate, grumbling at how the residents ruined the area.

Looking at the huge unswept piles of leaves clogging up the drive outside the Lodge, and at the loose slates ready to slide off the roof, Olivia thought it was definitely a case of the pot calling the kettle black.

'Are we there?' asked Sasha, sitting up and rubbing her eyes sleepily at the sound of Stephen putting the hand-brake on.

'Yes, honey, we're here,' Olivia said fondly. 'It's very wet, so let's get your raincoat and hat on.'

She ignored Stephen, whose face resembled a French aristocrat's about to see the guillotine for the first time. Carefully tucking Sasha's silky hair under her furry brown hat, Olivia spoke gently to her. Sasha was always a little grumpy when she woke up and needed gentle handling.

'We're going to see Granny and Granddad and they've got lots of lovely presents for you for Christmas.' I hope, she thought to herself, knowing how useless her parents were at remembering things. 'And I know that Santa has lots of special presents for you too because you're such a good little girl . . .'

'Ready?' interrupted Stephen brusquely.

'Yes.'

They ran to the front door, Olivia clutching Sasha's hand and trying to hold her own rain hat on at the same time.

Amazingly, her mother was watching out for them and threw open the front door as they reached it.

'My dears,' croaked Sybil de Vere in her forty-cigarettes-a-day voice. A skinny white-haired apparition in a long, tweedy skirt worn with a polo-necked jumper and moth-eaten pink shawl draped around her shoulders, she gestured them into the gloomy hallway with a hand holding a half-smoked cigarette.

'Do come in. Excuse the cold. The heating's off. Blasted thing went yesterday and we can't get anyone to fix it.'

Olivia didn't have to look at her husband to know that his face had darkened to French-aristo-looking-*up*-at-the-guillotine-blade-and-listening-to-the-drum-roll expression.

Still holding Sasha's hand, she went into the hall, feeling a blast of cold air hit her. Cold air mingled with the combined scent of cat pee, mothballs and unaired rooms. Wonderful. If she didn't die of pneumonia first, Stephen would kill her with rage. How she loved Christmas.

CHAPTER THREE

Cara opened one glued-up hazel eye sleepily and stared at the alarm clock. Only five to eight. Good. Stretching an arm out from under her blue-striped duvet, she thumped the snooze button, rolled over and went back to sleep.

Nine minutes later, the clock erupted again, its shrill tone dragging her from a wonderful dream which involved a juggernaut, a giant tennis racket and her boss, Bernard. In the dream, Cara was standing at the edge of the motorway, wielding the tennis racket as she back-handed Bernard into the path of the juggernaut. Satisfying wasn't the word for it. Why did you always wake up at the best bit of dreams? Cara wondered as she rolled over on to her back, raked a strand of tangled black hair from her face and toyed with the idea of getting up.

Only last week she'd been on the verge of an orgasmic five a.m. encounter with George Clooney when the burglar alarm in the flat next door had gone off, destroying any hope of getting George's naked manly arms around her. Talk about coitus interruptus.

'Cara!' yelled a voice. It was Phoebe. 'Are you up yet? You'll be late.'

Since she'd fallen in lust with the bureau de change man who worked at the counter beside her, Phoebe had been sickeningly keen on getting up and going into work in the morning, Cara thought gloomily.

Until he'd arrived on the scene – 'He shouldn't be working in the bank. He should be in films,' Phoebe drooled regularly – her flatmate had been just as bad at getting up as Cara.

They'd spent many companionable mornings cannoning sleepily off each other in the cramped avocado green bathroom, grabbing tights, knickers and bras from the line they'd haphazardly erected over the bath. Well, Phoebe had grabbed tights. As one of the most junior graphic designers in Yoshi Advertising, Cara worked right at the back of the building where no client ever set foot, so she and her two lowly colleagues got away with wearing very un-office-like clothes – in Cara's case, her ancient art school flea market stuff, none of which required barely black ten deniers. Or even ironing, for that matter.

At least when Phoebe had been similarly workshy, they'd had time for breakfast. As she was always the slightly more organised of the two flatmates, Phoebe was in charge of getting the Pop Tarts ready for their hasty departure: two each to be munched on the jog down Leinster Road to the bus.

However, for the past month, Phoebe had been legging it out of the flat by ten past eight so she was on time to get to the counter beside Mr Bureau de Change for a little pre-work chit-chat. And Cara, who needed to be shouted at to get up, tended to doze off again so that when she *did* wake up, she barely had time to wash the previous day's mascara traces off her face, never mind stick the Pop Tarts in the temperamental toaster.

'Cara!' roared Phoebe. 'I'm going. 'Bye.'

She'd better get up, Cara thought dozily. It was the last day of work before Christmas and Bernard Redmond had promised he'd dock the wages of anyone who skived off after the Christmas drinks party in Bellamy's last night. He was such a sadist he meant it too. It had been a good night, though, she thought. Well, the bits she could remember had been good. Those last Tequila Slammers had been a mistake definitely. But her head didn't feel too bad . . .

She stretched languorously. So did the other person in the bed, one hairy limb reaching Cara's long leg and rubbing up against hers lasciviously. Shocked, she shrieked as if she'd been electrocuted and jumped out of bed so fast that the duvet lifted off the bed, creating a breeze that redistributed all the dust in the room.

Who was in bed with her? What the hell had she done the night before? And, Jesus, Cara thought as a wave of numbing pain ripped through her skull like a thousand drums being pummelled in unison, her head hurt.

'Whadidya do that for?' muttered a voice she knew all too well. 'It's freezing.' The figure in the bed huddled the duvet around it again.

The small hairs on the back of Cara's neck reverted to their normal position, although the throbbing in her skull continued unabated. Eric. She'd slept with Eric. Again. She wanted to kill herself.

But there was no need, Cara thought dismally as she slumped down on the side of the bed and stared at the fluff-covered floorboards she hadn't hoovered for at least two months. Everyone in the office would kill her when they found out.

The folks at Yoshi Advertising never missed a chance to poke fun at somebody and sleeping with Eric was a surefire way to get so much fun poked at you that you died in the process. *Eric*!

She hadn't thought there was enough tequila in all of Mexico to get her into bed with him a second time.

CATHY KELLY

Although from the way her head felt, she'd imbibed a fair percentage of Mexico's alcohol output.

Clutching her aching head, she wondered exactly what she'd done and why she'd had to do it with him?

The firm's twenty-three-year-old motorbike courier, Eric was a leather and Brylcreem disciple, believing that the combination of his motorbike leathers and slicked-back dark hair rendered him irresistible to women.

After a disastrous – for her – one-night fling last January following the firm's birthday party, Cara decided that Eric would be much more irresistible if he occasionally hung his tight-fitting leathers out to air and washed his hair instead of slathering it with a fresh coat of Brylcreem every morning. The other reason he wasn't ideal dating material was obvious as soon as he opened his mouth: Eric was a heavy rock fan and always talked as if he'd stepped momentarily out of Aerosmith's tour bus after a serious gig.

He was also, at around five feet six, a full four inches shorter than she was and since Eric's taste appeared to run to petite, sexy blondes, like the office's dainty receptionist, Cara had no idea why he was attracted to her in the first place. Tall, strapping – 'Amazonian' Phoebe always said loyally – and without a petite bone in her body, Cara's unruly ebony curls, hazel eyes, milky white freckled skin and aggressively masculine style of dress meant she was a million miles away from the archetypical platinum-haired rock chick the courier usually went for. But then, she groaned to herself, he was hardly her type either. Necessity wasn't the mother of strange bedfellows – booze-laden Christmas parties were.

'Morning, babe,' Eric growled, sitting up in the bed and leaning over to grab Cara's waist with one hairy hand.

She swiftly slid off the edge of the bed and stared down at him, looking with disgust at the designer stubble, bleary eyes and grease-ridden hair. She'd have to boil wash the pillowcase to get it clean.

It was then Cara realised she was wearing a faded black T-shirt she didn't recognise. On her tall frame, the hem ended about four inches below her crotch, revealing goosepimpled white legs that hadn't seen a razor in months. Angling her head to read it, she saw that *Shake Your Moneymaker* was emblazoned on the front in huge lettering.

'Cool, huh?' Eric said, admiring both his T-shirt and Cara's nipples, which stood out like football studs courtesy of the flat's non-existent central heating. 'The Black Crowes, great band. Hey!' He leaned out of the bed and felt around on the floor. 'You got any smokes? I can't find mine.'

'No,' she said waspishly, wishing she hadn't shaken *her* moneymaker the night before. If only she could remember to what extent she'd shaken it.

But she couldn't bring herself to ask Eric what they'd done. It was quite bad enough that she'd been so plastered that she'd brought him home in the first place, without letting on that she'd been so drunk she didn't even know if they'd consummated things. Cara shivered at the thought. Sex with Eric. Damn Pete for starting that bloody Tequila Slammer chicken game. And damn herself twice as much for participating in it.

There was also the knotty question of contraception. Cara desperately wanted to ask Eric if he'd actually used anything. Her sex life was so non-existent that there was no point being on the pill and she'd never had a cap or IUD. In fact, her last sexual encounter had been nearly a year previously. With Eric. Which meant a spur-of-the-tequila fling with him could result in more than just a sour taste in her mouth. Her head throbbed at the thought. Please let them have used *something*.

'Comin' back to bed, babe?' asked Eric, patting the sheets invitingly.

She glared at him, furious with herself, and therefore furious with him too. 'You've got to go, Eric. I'm late for work. I don't have time for this.'

He gave her a cheesy grin. 'That wasn't what you were saying last night,' he smirked. 'Come on, everybody'll be late this morning. Everyone'll expect *us* to be late too . . .' he added meaningfully '. . . after the way you were all over me last night.'

Cara's stomach lurched. So she'd thrown herself at the motorbike courier in full view of the entire firm? Wonderful. At least she'd started the festive season with a bang.

'Come on,' he added huskily. 'For a big girl, you sure are hot. Let's have another go on the merry go round, babe.' He started to drag the duvet down to waist level, no doubt to display his manly charms.

Cara felt the nausea part of her hangover kick into action and closed her eyes beseechingly. Just let him go, get him out of the flat, and she promised . . . no, she *vowed* . . . never to look crossways at another man again. Please God, Shiva, Allah, whoever.

She opened her eyes. He was still there, grinning lasciviously and running thick fingers through his oil-slick hair.

She tried another tack.

'Eric, I've got a lot of work to finish by tonight, I really need to get into the office as soon as possible. I don't want to be rude, but I'd prefer it if you left so I could get ready.'

'What's the rush?' he said, settling back in the bed to watch her. 'I can get you into the office on the bike in ten minutes.'

'You brought the bike home last night?' she asked faintly, wondering what state he'd been in to drive it.

'Yeah.' He grinned. 'You insisted on it, said you loved

motorbikes. Come on,' he patted the bed again. 'We've got time . . .'

For a brief moment, Cara thought about going back to bed. Eric clearly wasn't going to go without either an argument or another session of rumpy-pumpy. She felt far too tired and fragile for a shouting match. She could always close her eyes and think of the empire.

Then she thought of being stone cold sober and having Eric's unshaven face slobbering all over her. And shuddered.

It was time for desperate measures.

'Eric, leave this instant or I'm going to go into the office and tell everyone you've asked me to marry you. I've even got the ring.' Cara pounced on her jewellery box, found an ornate gold and garnet dress ring of her mother's and waggled it in his face. 'I've wanted to get married for so long, I'm the last unmarried girl in my family and I know we'd suit each other perfectly . . .'

She'd never seen him move so fast, even when he was on his Kawasaki 750 driving out of the car park flamboyantly to show off to any nearby female pedestrians.

'Jeez,' he muttered, dragging on his underpants, 'you're twisted.'

'No,' said Cara, batting her eyelashes insincerely, 'just desperately in love with you. I'm twenty-six, you know, nearly twenty-seven. I don't want to be left on the shelf and you're just the type of man I go for. We could have a June wedding. I've always wanted to be a June bride,' she added dreamily.

Eric struggled so hard with his trouser zip that he nearly broke it.

'I'm never getting married,' he hissed, stumbling out of the room with his boots half-undone and his helmet, keys and jacket in his arms.

'Neither am I,' muttered Cara under her breath in a voice that wasn't meant to be overheard.

He stopped dragging his clothes on and wheeled around to face her.

'You bitch!' he howled. 'You were just taking the piss, you just wanted me out of here!'

There was no point in saying anything, not even that nobody else would be dumb enough to believe her in the first place. Cara opened the front door and stood by it patiently.

'I know your type, Cara Fraser,' Eric said angrily, jabbing a finger towards her. 'I'm fine when you're drunk but I'm not good enough for you otherwise, am I?'

'It's not like that . . .' started Cara, but he didn't wait for her to finish.

'You stuck-up bitches are all the same. You think I'm thick. Well, I'm not.' He looked terribly hurt, his face white. Cara felt suddenly sorry for him.

'I don't think you're thick,' she said, laying a hand on his arm. 'I think you're lovely. But I don't want to get involved, Eric. Please understand that.'

He shrugged off her arm.

'Eric, have you known me date anyone since I've worked in Yoshi?' she asked desperately. 'No, you haven't. Because I'm not into long-term relationships, I can't handle them.' It wasn't a great explanation or even a truthful one, but it seemed to be helping. His expression wasn't as desolate.

'Please understand that. I need my own space, Eric, that's all. I didn't mean to hurt you.'

'Well, why'd you talk to me last night?' he demanded.

Cara hesitated. Saying 'because I was blind drunk and I made a huge mistake I now deeply, deeply regret' didn't seem like a very good idea.

'It's easy to feel close to your colleagues and to mistake

that closeness for romance,' she said delicately, quoting verbatim the recent magazine article she'd seen warning against drunken office flings at Christmas parties.

He seemed to accept this. 'Yeah, I understand.'

'Anyway,' she said, attempting to drag the conversation on to a lighter level, 'why did *you* talk to *me*? I'm not exactly your type.'

He grinned for the first time.

'You're sexy for a big babe. I know you wear all that tough gear and give off "keep away from me" vibes, but you're not as macho as you pretend. See ya around.'

He pulled on his boots and left without turning back. Feeling utterly drained, Cara slammed the door shut and leant against it in relief.

Eric wasn't her type, that was for sure. The irony was that after six virtually man-free years, Cara didn't know what her type was.

In the kitchen, she shuffled over to the fridge and dragged the door open listlessly. Nothing leapt out at her demanding 'eat me'. Which was surprising, as the fridge had so many developing lifeforms inside it, there was a large possibility that one day something *would* jump out. It probably wouldn't say 'eat me', though, Cara thought, rather 'I'm going to eat *you*'. A mutant tube of pâté, perhaps, which had gobbled up all the mouldy low-fat cheese and was on the look out for human flesh.

Cara ignored a lump of Brie that looked as if it was wearing a white angora jumper and, vowing to clean out the fridge that evening, took out the orange juice carton, the butter and Phoebe's Marmite. There was nothing else edible in there.

Then she wrenched a couple of slices of bread off the loaf in the freezer and jammed them in the toaster. She boiled the kettle for tea, buttered and Marmited her toast and drank three glasses of juice to slake her hangover thirst.

Breakfast sorted out, she sat down in front of the telly and switched it on. It was nearly a quarter to nine and she should have been on the bus by now, heading for Mount Street. But she wouldn't have the energy to face the office for another hour at least. Getting rid of Eric had turned out to be exhausting and upsetting. Breakfast telly and maybe a few minutes of a nice black and white film would cheer her up.

It was eleven before Cara finally left the flat, having bundled all the Eric-contaminated bedclothes into the washing machine. While changing the sheets, she'd found a condom wrapper on his side of the bed which was a mixture of good and bad news: they'd *had* sex (bad news) but at least Eric had used contraception (good). She pushed the 'I can't believe you got so pissed you slept with him!' thoughts (very, very bad) out of her mind.

Pulling her ratty ankle-length purple velvet coat on over her favourite black combats and the cotton cricket sweater Phoebe had inadvertently dyed a mottled shade of mandarin, Cara braved the wet morning.

She'd obviously lost her hat in the pub the night before because it wasn't jammed in the pocket of her velvet coat as usual, while her gloves, a necessity in the icy late-December weather, were also missing.

Shivering as she trudged along Leinster Road in the pouring rain, Cara prepared her spiel on how she and Eric had ended up leaving the pub together but had parted company immediately afterwards and had definitely not spent the night together.

Absolutely not.

No matter which way she tried it, the story still sounded lame. By the time she arrived at the office, sodden and even more hungover than ever, she'd almost given up on the 'Eric and I didn't touch each other' saga. It was better not to say anything, she decided. Everyone else was probably paralytic with drink as well, so who'd have noticed what she was up to?

'I knew you were desperate but I didn't know you were *that* desperate,' remarked Zoë, head bent over her desk as Cara pushed open the door to their little office at the top of the building and dumped her bag on the floor.

'What do you mean?' asked Cara innocently as she wriggled out of her coat, now stained blackberry with rain.

Zoë looked up, one red eyebrow raised sardonically.

'I mean,' she drawled, 'to sleep with Eric once sounds like misfortune; to sleep with him *twice* sounds like carelessness!'

'Thank you, Lady Bracknell,' Cara said crossly. 'Does that mean everyone noticed?' she added, wincing.

'Luckily for you, no.' Zoë slid off her seat and began fumbling for something in a giant rucksack. 'After Pete's tequila competition – which you won, incidentally – everyone else went home, apart from you, me, Eric the Greasy and Pete. Pete was almost out cold so I don't think he'd have noticed if you'd stripped there and then and sang a few bars of "Hey Big Spender" on top of the table. Eric was glued to you and my lips are sealed about the whole sordid matter. You are a glutton for punishment, Fraser, I'll give you that.'

'I know,' moaned Cara, sitting down at her drawing board and holding her aching head in her hands. 'I couldn't believe it when I woke up this morning and found him in bed beside me. I nearly cried. I can't believe I did it, I hate myself . . .'

'Stop berating yourself,' commanded Zoë, triumphantly extracting a clingfilmed sandwich from her rucksack. 'It's

Christmas and you were pissed. You haven't murdered anyone so forget it.'

'But Eric . . .' wailed Cara. 'Again!'

'You only go to bed with him because you can manipulate him,' pointed out Zoë, biting into her lunchtime tunafish sandwich, even though it was only half-eleven. They always ate their sandwiches early. 'It may cost £2 to buy them in the shop but it's a saving because at least we wait until lunchtime to eat them,' Cara pointed out, when they were on their frequent economy drives and contemplated bringing in their own lunches. 'When we bring our own in, we *still* have to buy lunch because we've nothing left to eat by one o'clock.'

Cara sat miserably at her drawing board where the unfinished campaign for a brand of laxatives awaited her attention.

'Ewan from copywriting fancies you but you wouldn't dream of touching him,' Zoë was pointing out, 'even if you were plastered, because he might want a relationship or something longer than a fling, so you steer clear of him.'

'I'm not good with relationships,' Cara said. 'There's no law says I have to be.'

Zoë fixed her with a stern look. 'So you'd prefer the odd one-night stunned with dopey Eric, huh?'

Cara gave up. There was no point explaining things to Zoë. It wasn't as if she didn't know what had put Cara off men. They'd been at college together, so of course she knew damn well. But Zoë insisted that her friend should be over it by now. It had been six years after all.

'You wouldn't believe the trouble I had getting him to leave,' Cara confessed. 'I thought he was going to move in. I tried that "I want to marry you" trick you told me about but even Eric didn't fall for that one.'

'Nobody would fall for that,' Zoë interrupted. 'I read

about it in a magazine in the "things I wished I'd done at the time" section. It never really happened . . .'

'Cara, Zoë,' said a booming voice and both women jerked upright on their high stools. Bernard Redmond, Yoshi Advertising boss and bully boy supreme stood at the door, blocking the light from the hallway.

In a dark suit that made him look more like an undertaker than usual, Bernard was a rather frightening figure. Tall, thin to the point of emaciation and with straight dark hair tied back in a weedy little pony-tail, he always reminded Cara of the childcatcher in *Chitty Chitty Bang Bang*. Today, his gimlet eyes took in the fact that Cara had obviously done no work on the laxative campaign. But for some reason, he didn't pounce on her in a temper, screeching about deadlines.

When he walked into the room, Cara discerned the reason: Millicent Ferguson, a matronly fifty year old and his wealthy business partner, was close on his heels bearing two metallic red gift bags. Keen to impress the benevolent Millicent, who'd been left a fortune by her much older besotted husband and was now the firm's sleeping partner, Bernard was a different man when she was around. Cara was convinced he hoped to inveigle his way into Millicent's affections and then marry her. She and Zoë had discussed sending Millicent an anonymous note telling her not to touch him with a barge pole.

'Hello, girls,' carolled Millicent, beaming at them. Her broad heavily made-up face was wreathed in smiles, purple eyeshadow cracking on her eyelids, she'd applied so much. 'Pressies from Santa.' She smiled, handing them each a bag.

They smiled back. They loved Millicent, you had to. It was a pity she wasn't in the office more often because she certainly had a beneficial effect on Bernard.

'Thank you, Millicent,' said Cara, drawing a long crimson wool scarf from her gift bag.

'It's beautiful,' Zoë said, finding a turquoise one in hers.

'I thought we needed something nicer than that bottle of wine you got last year,' Millicent trilled, holding the scarf up to Zoë's cropped red head and admiring the contrast. The wine, not quite a £2.99 screw-topped bottle but close enough, had been Bernard's idea of a Christmas bonus. He was incredibly mean, the sort who'd peel an orange in his pocket, as Cara's dad would say.

'How are you getting on with the campaign?' he asked, leaning menacingly near Cara.

She leaned back, knowing she must reek of last night's booze. Bernard could smell alcohol a mile away because he never drank.

'Fine,' she muttered. 'I hope to have it finished today.' As soon as she'd said it, Cara was sorry. She'd planned to leave work early to do the last of her Christmas shopping as she'd be going home to Ballymoreen on the late bus.

Now she'd have to stay late to finish the campaign because, once you told Bernard you'd do something, he made your life a misery if you didn't.

'Good,' he said, leaning closer as he stared at the unfinished campaign. His hard eyes sought hers.

'Have a nice night last night, then?' he asked, his face so close she could smell the mints he sucked obsessively.

He knew, the bastard. She had no idea *how* he knew, but he did. Cara stuck her chin up defiantly. She was not going to blush because he knew she'd slept with Eric.

'Lovely,' she said.

'Good. ' He smiled at her, a fake rictus of his mouth that didn't get within a mile of his eyes. 'I heard that some of you, a few hardy souls, were there till closing time.'

Gritting her teeth inwardly, Cara kept smiling. 'I love a

good party, Bernard,' she said tightly.

She got up, forcing him to move backwards, and faced him, hands stuck into her pockets in a masculine manner. In her size eight flat boots, she was as tall as he was, a fact which definitely unsettled Bernard. He liked being able to tower over people, especially when they were women and he could peer down their fronts. He never got the chance with Cara, mainly because she never wore any item of clothing that went below the hollow in the base of her neck. Her wardrobe was army surplus in every definition of the word. 'You'll have to excuse me,' she added sweetly, 'there's someone I have to see.'

She marched out of the room, belted down the stairs and barged into the ladies' loo on the next floor.

She did look a little the worse for wear, Cara acknowledged, staring at her faintly bloodshot eyes ringed with thick, heavily mascara-ed lashes. Her normally pale skin was very white and as she hadn't bothered to wash her hair that morning, it hung in limp curls around her face, making her look more like a Central European gypsy than usual.

Phoebe, who had a moon-faced, cheekbone-less face, was always muttering about how lucky Cara was to have high, striking cheekbones, a straight nose and a firm jaw. But Cara hated her looks. She could never understand how she'd been stuck with this strong, gypsyish face when the rest of her family looked so totally different.

Her father was several inches shorter, of lean build, and his hair, before it had turned the distinguished silver it was now, had been pale brown.

Her sister Evie looked like every man's idea of the ultra-feminine woman with her petite hourglass figure, large eyes and adorable little nose; no trace of Cara's exotic looks anywhere.

Even her mother, whom she no longer really remembered except from photographs, had been slender, with light brown hair, and utterly feminine. While Cara was stuck with a frame like an ultra-athletic lumberjack and a face that meant customs officers always narrowed their eyes at her when she walked through the 'EC Nationals' channel in the airport after her holidays.

'He's gone.' Zoë pushed the bathroom door open and peered around. 'He's taking dear Millicent out for lunch.'

They both grimaced at the same time.

'We really owe it to "dear Millicent" to tell her what an out and out bastard he is,' Cara remarked, finding a scrunchie in one pocket of her combats and tying back her unruly hair with it. 'The poor woman will end up married to him and the vows won't be a day old before she's ploughing through the gin like the rest of us in utter misery when she realises he's been conning her with his Mr Nice Guy act.'

'Speak for yourself,' said Zoë virtuously. 'I don't drink.'

'Yeah, you only drink on days beginning with T,' Cara retorted, swatting her friend gently across the behind as they left. 'Today, tomorrow, the next day . . . Fancy a hangover lunch full of carbohydrates?'

'Hell, yes,' said Zoë. 'I'm dying with one. I've drunk eight glasses of water already this morning and none of it was in coffee.'

Munching their way through the Christmas lunch special in O'Dwyer's, Cara sympathised with Zoë over her holiday arrangements. Zoë loathed visiting her Kerry home for Christmas where there was guaranteed to be at least three fights a day between her five brothers and their father.

'You're so lucky having only one sister,' she said, pushing a Brussels sprout around her plate listlessly.

Cara raised an eyebrow. 'Evie and I don't exactly get on like a house on fire, you know. She's so touchy lately, I can't utter a word without saying the wrong thing. For a start she expects me to be practically running the office by now and can't understand why I'm not working on the top accounts with a company car yet.'

'Did you explain that Bernard is a psycho with more complexes than Disneyworld?' asked Zoë.

'There's no point,' sighed Cara. 'She's such a high achiever that she expects everyone to be likewise. Excuses are . . . well . . . no excuse. So far as she's concerned, I've been in Yoshi long enough to have pulled myself up the promotional ladder by my fingernails.'

'But she's hardly running Goldman Sachs herself, now is she?'

'No. But if Evie had ever gone to college, she probably *would* be.'

'It's hardly your fault she got married and pregnant and couldn't go to college,' Zoë said equably.

'I know.' Cara pushed her finished plate away and reached for her glass of mineral water. 'She's just not very pleased with me these days, I think she feels I've let her down in some way. She was like my mother when I was a kid, took over when my real mum died. Except the nine-year age gap has turned into a generation gap. She expects me to do amazing things with my life . . .'

She broke off miserably. Living up to Evie's high expectations had never been easy and had been harder than ever these past few years. Her sister couldn't understand what had changed Cara from a lively outgoing girl into a quiet, distant woman with a combative look in her eyes. It had evaporated the closeness they'd shared since their mother died when, for the devastated six-year-old Cara, Evie had been a life saver, an adoring and over-protective surrogate mother.

'What does she want?' Zoë demanded. 'You to run for president? I'm sorry, Cara, but Evie shouldn't be loading all her own unattained expectations on to your back. Anyway,' Zoë took a quick glance at her watch and then unhooked her coat from the back of her chair, 'she'll have her beloved boyfriend, sorry, *fiancé*, with her this time so she won't have any time to spare for telling you where you're going wrong with your life.'

Cara grimaced before finishing her drink. 'Simon isn't coming for Christmas, so I'll have Evie's undivided attention. Well, *Dad* and I will have her attention between us,' she amended. 'She likes telling him what to do too.'

Which was an understatement, Cara knew, thinking of the way Evie ran through the small Ballymoreen cottage like a whirlwind, tidying cupboards, rearranging furniture and making lists of things she needed to buy for their father when she went back to Dublin.

'Really, Dad, you can't just bung everything into the washing machine at ninety degrees with no fabric softener,' she'd fuss, examining faded towels so rough they could exfoliate an elephant.

He took it very well, under the circumstances, sitting comfortably in his old chair with the paper while she marshalled the place the way *she* liked it. Cara wouldn't have minded so much but Dad was well able to look after himself. He'd been doing it long enough. His wife had been dead nearly twenty years.

The problem with Evie was that she wanted them all to be perfect: she wanted Cara to be a perfectly turned-out working girl with a walk-in wardrobe, Barbie's Ken for a boyfriend and her entire life mapped out with the precision of a flight path. Cara suspected that her sister's almost obsessive desire for everything in the garden to be rosy was because everything had been far from rosy for her. Evie wanted Cara to have all the things *she'd* never had – youth, money, a great career and an equally achieving husband. It was just that Evie didn't seem to understand that Cara didn't want those things. That was the nub of the problem. It was difficult telling someone that their most precious hopes and dreams simply didn't interest you.

Cara pushed open the door of the pub and she and Zoë braved the outside world. A fresh wind whistled around them, insinuating itself under Cara's hair, exploring her neck with icy fingers. She huddled closer into her coat. 'All in all, I'm not sure this holiday is going to be much fun,' she muttered.

They tramped up the street together, heads bent to avoid the wind.

'It'll be more fun than mine,' Zoë said between shivers. 'At least you're having a party tonight. My father wouldn't dream of having a party. It'd be a waste of money buying drink for all the people in the town he didn't like.'

'True,' Cara said. 'Dad gives great parties. He started the Christmas Eve drinks party a few years ago, when he got involved with the painting group. They take it in turns to have other parties but he always gives the Christmas one. The class has been brilliant for him. He paints the most amazing watercolours and he's starting to make quite a bit of money from them.'

'I thought he always painted?' Zoë said. 'He's been painting since I've known you.'

'No. He started the classes eight years ago when he had his heart attack. The doctor recommended some-thing calming,' Cara said thoughtfully. 'There's this woman in his group, she's a widow and she's mad for him – Mrs Mulanny. She's about ten years older than him and she's always phoning, asking him to put a nail in a wall or fix something. We tease him dreadfully about her. She haunts him.'

They arrived at the office and hurried round the side of the building to go in by the back door.

'He's good-looking, though, isn't he? He looks it from photos in your place.'

'He's better in the flesh. He's sort of distinguished, you know. His hair used to be the same colour as my sister's but it's steely grey now. It really suits him.'

Cara thought of Andrew Fraser, his kind, lined face with the warm hazel eyes and the welcoming smile. He *was* handsome, even in his ancient corduroys and the lumpy old jumpers he liked to wear around the house. A smile creased her face. 'Maybe I'll give him a pretend present from Mrs Mulanny: a pair of underpants! He'd love that.'

Zoë shuddered at the thought of giving her own father a joke present. 'Your dad sounds great,' she said. 'Are you sure I can't come home with you for the holidays?'

It was half-six that evening when Cara finally made it back to the flat, wet through and worn out after an afternoon devoted to her laxatives campaign and a speedy half-hour in the Swan Centre on a Christmas version of Supermarket Sweep. The bus for home left from the city centre at half-seven, which meant she had about fifteen minutes to pack her clothes, get out of the flat and get back into town.

'Phoebe!' she called as she slammed the front door.

There was no reply. Either her flatmate had left already for her holiday in Kerry or she was stuck in a pub somewhere, nose to nose with Mr Bureau de Change. Lucky old Phoebs, Cara thought.

She hurried into her bedroom and stared at the mess. It'd been at least a week since she'd done any serious laundry and clumps of dirty clothes lay around the floor like dead bodies. Sighing, Cara rushed around, picking up items, examining them to see how crumpled or dirty they were. When she'd amassed a few possible outfits, she stuffed them into her old rucksack along with a couple of clean things – which meant things she never wore and therefore didn't like – from her wardrobe. Adding the bag of Christmas presents she'd already wrapped, she closed the rucksack and was ready to leave in ten minutes. Just time for a quick shower.

Cara winced at the sight of herself in the bathroom mirror. Her hair clung limply to her face, which was still a hungover shade of grey; her eyes were dead with exhaustion and she was getting a nice big spot on her forehead.

She showered, ducking to avoid Phoebe's tights and a new pink broderie anglaise bra dangling from the washing line. Phoebe must be having a drink with yer man, Cara decided with a grin. Otherwise she'd have packed up all her frillies for her holidays.

Out of the shower, she dragged her combats back on along with a clean white T-shirt, ran a brush through her unruly hair and squirted herself with the remains of Phoebe's deodorant as hers was packed. She was ready. Not exactly party material, but she'd do. Evie would have a fit when she saw her, Cara realised as she hoisted the rucksack on to her back and prepared to leave the flat.

Her sister would no doubt be perfectly turned out in some pristine outfit: hair shining, shoes shining and halo shining.

Well, Dad wouldn't care what she looked like, Cara thought with relief. He was happy to see her, no matter what she wore. Pity Evie couldn't get the message. She'd learn soon enough. Rosie wasn't much of a fan of sedate blazers, long skirts and loafers either.

Bags in hand, Cara pulled open the front door and only then noticed the envelopes on the mat. She picked them up: electricity bill and a Christmas card for herself and Phoebe from Evie and Rosie. Cute Christmas teddies grinned up at her, and Cara smiled. Evie was funny: she always sent a card to Cara's flat. It was one of her idiosyncrasies.

'Looking forward to a lovely Christmas, Cara, and I hope we'll see you, Phoebe, for the New Year. Love, Evie and Rosie.'

Cara stuck the card on the kitchen table along with the note she'd scrawled to Phoebe. Poor Evie, she was trying her best. Cara resolved to sort it all out over the next few days. It was crazy to squabble with your sister, pointless family feuds started that way. They'd have a proper discussion and Cara would explain that while she understood Evie only wanted the best for her, Cara was a grown up now, not a motherless kid.

Feeling better, she slammed the front door, already looking forward to a few peaceful days at home. She could picture the living room: the fire lit, logs crackling and the dogs, Jessie and Gooch, sprawled out on the big red rug in front of it, as close as they could possibly get without getting burned; Dad smiling as he cobbled his special herby scrambled eggs together; Rosie creating havoc with the local young lads, eyeing them up on her constant trips to the shop; Evie fussing over the turkey, the pudding, etc, etc. There was no place like home. It was going to be a good Christmas, she was sure of it.

CHAPTER FOUR

It was late afternoon when Evie parked the car outside the small house in Ballymoreen.

'Thank God we're here,' groaned Rosie, opening her door and stretching long jeans-clad legs out.

Massaging her tired neck with one hand, Evie peered through the fogged-up car window at her father's house. Like most of the houses in the village, it was postcard pretty: a stone façade with two gently curving mullioned windows to either side of a door framed with a tenacious evergreen creeper.

Unusually, there were no lights shining through the tiny diamond panes. The sky was growing darker by the minute but the porch light wasn't on. The place seemed deserted. Evie followed Rosie up the path, feeling a prickle of unease at the strange stillness. There was no frenzied barking from Gooch and Jessie at the sound of their footsteps, even when Evie turned her key in the lock.

'Something must have happened,' she said anxiously, reluctant to push the door open now she'd unlocked it. She clutched her coat around her, shivering from nerves and cold. 'He's had an accident. Otherwise he'd be here . . .' She paused. It was so silent, it was almost spooky. Her father knew they were coming; he was always there to greet them, especially at Christmas.

'Don't be daft, Mum.' Rosie shoved past her and gave the door a resounding push. 'The dogs would massacre any burglars stupid enough to break in, and anyway the neighbours would know in a shot if there was anything wrong with Grandpops and they'd be out giving us chapter and verse. You know what this place is like,' she added sarcastically. 'Breathe too loudly and you're in the papers.'

Evie followed her daughter's tall figure into the dark house, half-expecting to see overturned furniture and the results of a struggle. But when Rosie switched on the light in the small sitting room, everything was in its place, from the faded old brocade sofa with its covering of dog hairs to the nest of tables where her father kept his pipe paraphernalia. The polished copper fire guard sat in the middle of the fireplace with its open brick work and the small card table was in its usual place in the corner, silver photograph frames arranged as they always were with faded pictures of Evie's parents on their wedding day forty years ago.

'See?' Rosie marched past her back to the car and started dragging their luggage from the boot. 'Nothing's wrong, Mum. You're such a worrier.'

Still wondering where her father was, Evie followed Rosie. It was so unlike him not to be there, she thought as she carried in some of the parcels. They were a bit early, she knew, but it wasn't as if Dad had anywhere else to go on Christmas Eve, did he? He was dying to see them, he'd said so on the phone.

They'd just finished emptying the car when the rain started, torrential rain that bounced off the flagstones on the path to the front door and hammered against the windows mercilessly.

'Dad'll be soaked if he's brought the dogs out for a walk,' Evie fretted, peering through the dark green curtains at the downpour.

Rosie looked up from where she was lighting the fire. She'd hoped her mother might disappear off to the kitchen to make tea, so she could sneak a crafty cigarette. She reckoned the smell of the fire would disguise the scent of her fag. If she had to spend four whole days without smoking, she'd go insane.

'Mum,' she said in exasperation. 'He's a grown-up, you know. How does he manage when we're not here to worry about him?'

'You're right,' sighed Evie. Her father *did* manage perfectly well without her. But it was one thing not worrying when she hadn't a clue what he was up to; it was another entirely when he was unaccountably missing. Stop being such a worry wart, she told herself angrily, and rubbed her eyes. She was tired after the drive down; tired, hungry and a little miserable. The thought of all the beautiful food she'd brought was making her ravenous but she'd promised herself she wouldn't overindulge during the holidays.

One lapse could ruin her cellulite-busting plan, although those sausage rolls she'd got looked particularly gorgeous, all flaky pastry and tempting sausage meat. But what was the point of killing herself dieting? Simon wouldn't notice if the night before was anything to go by. He'd hardly be aware if she had her entire body remodelled, she thought despondently.

She'd spent the car journey thinking about the party and how Simon had abandoned her for two solid hours by leaving her talking to poor Hilda Maguire. Evie had been so looking forward to the evening. It wasn't as if she had such a hectic social life that she was going to parties every night of the week. She practically never went out.

That much-looked forward to evening had been the high-light of her week. What a waste going to the hairdresser's.

The more she turned it over in her mind, the more depressed she got. Imagine letting her go home alone because he was afraid to offend his bosses by leaving early. He couldn't love her to do that. Love meant wanting to be together passionately, frantically. Especially at Christmas.

She remembered how Simon had broken the news to her that he wouldn't be going with her to Ballymoreen. They'd been trailing around the shops looking for gifts for each other that cost less than £40 each – Simon's idea because they were saving for the wedding.

'Next year we'll be together, Evie. But I'm not going to be able to go with you this time. I can't let Mother down. We've gone to Uncle Harry's for Christmas every year since I was a child. It's a tradition. Mother would feel so alone among all the relatives without me.'

Seeing how downcast his fianceé looked at this bomb-shell, he had asked her to stay at Uncle Harry's too. A bit of a half-hearted invitation, Evie had felt. Still, she couldn't have left Dad and Cara on their own, so she'd refused.

If last night had been a wonderful party, it would have kept her going over the entire Simon-less holiday. But it had been a complete let down. Which was a bit how Evie felt. Let down. Maybe she'd just have one sausage roll. She felt like it. Yes, and think what your rear end will look like after a few days of eating like a horse, her conscience pointed out.

'I'm going to make some lemon tea,' she announced resolutely. 'Want some?'

Rosie, reed slim with a perfect peaches and cream complexion and not a blemish on her young skin, rolled her eyes to heaven.

'The only thing I fancy with lemon in it is a vodka and Red Bull,' she said wickedly.

Evie stopped in her tracks. 'Rosie! I've told you before: no drinking here. Granddad would have a canary if he saw you drinking spirits. Wine at dinner and that's it. I know you drink beer with your friends, I've smelt it. But not here. This isn't Dublin, you know. If you drink here, the entire village will know about it and, believe me, they'll be talking about you. I don't want that to happen.' She marched into the kitchen.

Her daughter scowled. I suppose a smoke is out of the question? Rosie thought crossly as she blew on the logs in the grate. What's eating her? she wondered. Her mother had been like a bear with a sore head all day. It was that drippy Simon, she knew it. He was such a wet it was unbelievable. Exactly what her mother saw in him Rosie had no idea. At least he wasn't going to be there for Christmas; watching Simon's irritating little mannerisms for three whole days would have driven her to distraction.

Well, she was having a cigarette and if her mother didn't like it, tough. She wasn't a kid anymore. With her head angled towards the kitchen, listening for her mother's approaching footsteps, Rosie fished her pack of ten cigarettes from her pocket and lit one. Then she stealthily opened one of the windows, sat on the ledge and blew the smoke out.

Knowing this place, some old bag would undoubtedly be on the phone in five minutes telling the entire village that Rosie Mitchell was chain smoking Rothman's, she thought crossly. It was like the middle ages. If they saw her drinking Budweiser, they'd probably try and burn her at the stake for being a witch.

Half an hour later, Evie had drunk two cups of lemon tea, neither of which had filled the gap in her stomach like a couple of sausage rolls would. She felt desperately guilty for taking her temper out on Rosie and sternly told herself to stop being such a grumpy pig. It wasn't anybody else's fault that her fiancé preferred to spend the festive season with his mother and a selection of ancient relatives playing Scrabble instead of with her.

She'd also put away the food she'd brought, amazed to find that instead of having none of the drinks party stuff organised, her father had trays of beautifully prepared nibbles ready in the fridge.

Evie, who'd spent some of her meagre Christmas budget buying large quantities of ready-made sausage rolls, mini pizzas and sesame prawn toasts, realised that the things in his fridge were wildly superior to her shop-bought offerings. Delicate little savoury pastries and smoked salmon parcels lined the fridge, elegantly arranged on gold-edged china platters she'd never seen before. Evie hadn't known he could make stuff like that. He must have had help.

When she'd brought her luggage upstairs, she'd been surprised to find a small blue and white china vase of winter flowering jasmine on the bedside locker in the twin room she was sharing with Rosie.

How sweet, she thought fondly, smelling the delicate sprigs. Her father had never been much of a man for flowers. He never painted floral still lifes in his watercolour class: he preferred rugged landscapes. Still, it was a lovely, welcoming gesture. At that moment she heard the sound of dogs barking, the slam of the back door and Rosie's voice raised in greeting. Dad!

She hurried downstairs, taking two steps at a time.

'Dad, I was so worried about you,' she said happily, but the words died on her lips as she rushed into the kitchen to find he wasn't alone.

Rosie was crouched on the floor rubbing Jessie, an ecstatic black spaniel, while Gooch, a golden retriever, was slurping water from his bowl, slobbering all over the stone flags and showering great lumps of white fur into the air as his feathery tail knocked against the table. Her father was taking off his dark green wellingtons. And a strange woman was filling the kettle at the sink, behaving as if she was totally at home.

Evie stared at the stranger in surprise. Sophisticated and elegant even in a heavy Aran sweater and dark trousers wet from the knees down, she was tall with sleek honey-gold hair tied back in a knot. Evie reckoned the woman was in her late-fifties although there were remarkably few lines around the clear grey eyes that stared out from a fine-boned face dusted with the merest hint of a tan.

As she stared at the woman, Evie had the strangest feeling that she too was being appraised, as if the grey eyes were sizing her up. She immediately felt podgy in her jeans: jeans she'd worn because they'd been washed so often they were incredibly comfortable, but which did nothing for her short legs and pear shape.

'Evie! Welcome. Sorry we weren't here to meet you but I had to take the dogs out for a walk or they'd have gone mad.'

Her father grabbed her in a bear hug and the two dogs started barking madly again, jumping up and down and generally making an incredible noise. Evie was about to yell at them to stop when the woman spoke quietly.

'Gooch, Jessie, sit!' she said in a crisp, clear voice. An American voice.

Instantly, the two dogs, who'd never obeyed a command from anyone but Evie's father in their entire lives, stopped barking and sat, both gazing up with such adoration at the woman that Evie gasped aloud.

Rosie laughed delightedly. 'How did you get them to do

that?' she asked, rubbing Gooch's velvety ears.

Andrew Fraser smiled fondly at the woman, one arm still around Evie.

'Vida has them eating out of her hand,' he said proudly. 'They walk beside her without their leads and come when she calls them.'

Vida! Who the bloody hell was Vida? Evie wanted to know. As if answering her question, Andrew reached out and took the woman's hand, clasping it tightly.

'Evie and Rosie, I want you to meet Vida Andersen, a very, very special friend of mine.' His eyes twinkled as he looked at Vida. Not a 'special friend' sort of look, Evie thought suddenly, eyes narrowing. More of a 'lover' look. And that, she realised with shocking clarity, was exactly what Vida was.

'Evie, Rosie, I'm delighted to meet you,' she said, in a low cultured voice. 'I've wanted to meet you both for so long.'

She moved forward and kissed Evie on one cheek, leaving a subtle trail of expensive perfume in her wake. Then she did the same with Rosie, who was gazing with admiration at Vida, taking in the long sweeping lashes, the subtle make-up and the strand of gleaming pearls barely visible under the sweater.

'I'd hoped to be more presentable when I finally met you both,' she laughed, gesturing at the Aran sweater she wore with such panache. 'This old thing of Andrew's isn't the sort of thing one wants to wear to meet future . . .' she hesitated briefly, '. . . friends.'

She was even wearing Dad's jumper, Evie realised with outrage. I bought that for him. In the sales one January. Ten percent off, it was.

'We're delighted to meet you, aren't we, Mum?' said Rosie, appearing beside Evie and giving her mother a surreptitious prod in the ribs.

'Yes,' she said automatically, switching into her gracious mode. 'Will you have a cup of tea?' She busied herself looking for the tea pot, which had always been kept beside the tea caddy but which had now mysteriously been moved. 'Are you staying in the village for a few days or have you just moved in?'

Evie turned around from the worktop in time to see her father and Vida exchange glances.

'I've lived here for nearly a year,' Vida said in that low voice of hers to which Evie had taken an instant dislike.

'In one of the cottages beside the mill,' added Andrew, handing the tea caddy to Vida.

'It's a bit rundown but I love it,' she said. 'I've been having a house renovated here and it'll be ready to move into within a few months.'

She produced the tea pot and quickly made tea with the ease of one who'd performed the same task in the same kitchen many times before. Evie stood to one side with a strained smile on her face and petted Jessie as she watched them move around each other as if they were used to spending time together.

Evie felt like an interloper. The other three, Rosie, her father and Vida, were all relaxed in each other's company. Rosie would fit in anywhere. She had that knack of appearing totally at home, no matter where she was, while Evie had never had the gift and now felt as if she stood out like a sore thumb.

'Where's your new house?' she asked brightly.

Her father and Vida exchanged another meaningful glance.

'On Bracken Road. The Grange at the crossroads.'

'Oh.' Evie knew the house, a large old manor not unlike Olivia's parents' house. 'It's very big for one person,' she said absently. 'Do you have family living with you? Your husband?'

As soon as she said it, Evie realised how bitchy it sounded. *Have you got a husband or are you looking for one? Is that why you're dangling around my father?* She hadn't meant it to sound like that.

If Vida thought the question was barbed, she seemed unconcerned. She poured tea into the china mugs Andrew had laid on the pine kitchen table.

'No, my last husband is dead. He died a long time ago, in America.'

Again, there was a pregnant pause.

'Let's take the tea into the sitting room,' said Andrew briskly.

There they sat around the fire Rosie had managed to light and talked about the drive from Dublin, the weather and what time the guests were coming for the drinks party.

'I said half-six for seven, which leaves us an hour to get ready,' Andrew said, with a quick glance at his watch. 'Early drinks parties are better because then everyone doesn't sit around until the wee small hours getting sozzled.'

'Which would be a huge waste of time,' Vida said to him, a warm smile lighting up her face.

She was beautiful, Evie realised with a pang, feeling like a giant blimp in a room full of sleek specimens. She must have been absolutely stunning when she was younger because she was pretty stunning now.

'We met at a cocktail party,' Vida said in a confiding voice.

Rosie grinned. 'I didn't know you were into cocktail parties, Grandpops?'

Her grandfather grinned back. 'I wasn't, until I met this lady. She's teaching me lots of new things.'

They both laughed.

'Not only about cocktails,' murmured Vida, in a voice she hadn't planned on anyone else hearing, but which Evie, who could hear a whispered comment across four desks in Wentworth Alarms, heard only too clearly.

She couldn't cope with this bizarre conversation any longer. Nobody was telling her anything and she just had to know.

'So, you two are going out?' she asked bluntly.

The beatific look on her father's face told her everything.

'More than going out, darling Evie,' he said slowly, dragging his eyes away from Vida. 'I know I should have told you some of this earlier, but it all happened so suddenly and I wanted to tell you in person: Vida and I are getting married. I wanted to tell the three of you together, you, Rosie and Cara, but since you've asked . . .'

Evie stared at him, feeling as if the bottom had fallen out of her world. Married. He was getting married again? She thought of the photographs on the card table, the faded one of her parents in their wedding clothes, her mother in an oyster satin dress with a bright stain of red lipstick on her mouth. Her wonderful dead mother, whom she'd never stopped missing; the person Dad had mourned for so long. Didn't that mean anything to him at all? How could he even look at another woman, especially one like Vida, with her calculating gaze and silky voice?

'Married?' said Evie blankly.

'Aren't you happy?' said her father in a pleading tone.

'Happy?' said Evie, parrot-like. 'It's such a shock. You should have told me.' She stared at him, so many things left unsaid. Like: 'How could you do this to me?'

'I know.' Her father gave her his mischievous grin, the one he usually used when she was tidying the overflowing

85

magazine rack and found newspapers dating from six months ago wedged in behind his bedraggled crossword book.

She could barely look at him, she felt so betrayed, so left out. 'Why couldn't you have told me before, Dad?' she asked hoarsely, feeling a well of emotion bubble up inside her. 'Why?'

Andrew Fraser rubbed his eyes wearily and leaned back in his chair. He seemed to be about to say something but didn't. Evie looked up from where she was savagely scratching at a piece of loose skin on her thumb so that it was almost ripped off. She stared at him gravely, waiting for him to speak. He wasn't going to. That bloody woman had brainwashed him.

She got up abruptly. 'I'd better change my clothes. The guests will be coming soon.' Without saying anything else, she went upstairs.

Evie sat on the bed in a daze. Her all-purpose black velvet dress was hanging in the wardrobe for its second trip out in as many days and she'd even brought her cordless hot hairbrush in case she felt inclined to recreate the loose curls she'd had done in the hairdresser's. But Evie didn't feel like getting ready for the drinks party. She didn't feel like doing anything. She was stunned, shocked. Her father was getting married: actually *getting married*. After twenty years of mourning her beloved mother, he was going to let another woman into their home, into his bed, and Evie didn't think she could cope with it.

Especially not *that* woman. Who did she think she was – making herself at home in Evie's mother's kitchen and in Evie's mother's bed.

'You nearly ready, Mum?' Rosie stuck her head round the door.

'Er . . . yes,' she stuttered. Mechanically, she unbuttoned her white blouse and pulled off her comfy jeans. She took tights from her drawer, and a black bra to go with the dress, and got dressed. Picking up her sponge bag, she headed for the bathroom. Every visible surface needed a good scrub, she noticed as she shut the door. Her father had never been good at washing away the mildew you got in the old house. And dear Vida obviously wasn't much good at getting those perfect nails dirty, she thought bitchily.

She flipped over her father's old shaving mirror and stared at a face so like her mother's. They both had the same wide open gaze, the same rounded cheeks with dimples, the same warm hazel eyes and upturned noses.

That woman was nothing like her mother. She was thin where Evie's mother had been softly rounded; Vida Andersen was all cool self-sufficiency where Alice Fraser had been warm and welcoming.

Evie sat on the side of the bath miserably, then stiffened as she heard two sets of footsteps pounding up the narrow stairs.

The door to her father's room shut loudly and she could hear Vida's voice through the thin walls.

'You should have told her before this, Andrew. It's not fair to give the poor thing such a shock. If she'd known about me, she could have become acclimatised to the idea, not found it such a surprise.'

Evie couldn't hear what her father replied. Used to the walls in the house, he knew that everything you said in the front bedroom could be easily overheard from the bathroom.

When her mother had died after six months' battling cancer, Evie remembered sitting in the bathroom, listening to the sounds of her father weeping alone in his bedroom.

He never cried in front of her or Cara, seemed to think it was wrong to let them see how devastated he was by his wife's death.

Evie had been seventeen at the time and had listened to him for weeks before she went in and told him to cry *with* them and not on his own. She'd been his rock, Andrew Fraser had always said afterwards. The one who kept the family going.

She remembered how her father had comforted her when Tony was killed by that speeding car. How they'd gone for long walks in the forest with Gooch's grandmother, Sadie, gambolling along in front of them, golden nose in every bush and clump of grass. Her father had been a lifeline in those horrible first few months when she'd been getting used to being a widow so soon after she'd become a wife. Now someone was going to ruin all that: Vida Andersen. Evie didn't know what hurt most – the fact that he hadn't told her or the fact that another person was going to come into their cosy family of four.

Olivia stroked Sasha's cheek gently, pulled the duvet up around her daughter's neck, then tucked in the big woollen rug she'd found in the airing cupboard. It was still cool in the room, even with the giant oil-filled radiator rattling away in one corner. Asleep, Sasha snuggled into her cosy cocoon, happy and warm in her brushed cotton jammies and the Rupert Bear socks Olivia had insisted she leave on.

Exhausted after a busy day, Sasha had fallen asleep quickly. Olivia wished she could join her. Her early rising to get the Christmas baking done had left her worn out. She kissed her daughter and left the room, the door ajar so the light from the landing would shine in. Olivia hated leaving her daughter alone in the small bed in this big double room. Sasha was used to pretty yellow wallpaper with bunnies scampering around and her butterfly night-light on the dresser in case she woke up and was scared. This room had gloomy purple cabbage roses on the walls, an ugly chandelier thing that looked like a dusty octopus and lots of large, shadowy furniture for monsters to hide behind. Your classic childhood nightmare.

'I'll keep an eye on Sasha,' Sybil de Vere had said earlier, waving one hand airily, the other clutching her third gin and tonic. Or at least the third gin and tonic she'd had since Olivia and Stephen had arrived. It was impossible to keep up. At the age of sixteen, Olivia had given up on keeping tabs on the amount of booze being consumed in the Lodge. 'You'd want a degree in quantum physics to know how many bottles they get through,' she'd complained to her best friend, Evie, at the time, not that either of them knew precisely what quantum physics was. All she knew was that she was forever finding three-quarter-empty bottles of brandy stuck in the airing cupboard and empty wine bottles jammed in the bottom of the bin. Why her mother – and it was always her mother who hid them – bothered hiding the bottles amazed her. Olivia knew they both drank like fishes.

'We won't be long at the Frasers',' she said firmly now, not keen on relying on her mother's babysitting techniques. 'We'll only stay an hour.'

'Don't fuss, Livvy,' muttered her father from the depths of his chair where he was fumbling through the TV guide to see what was on next. 'The little mite will be fine here. Although,' he peered at her over his reading glasses, 'I don't know what you want to bother going to Andrew Fraser's party for. The man's a bore and he'll be glued to that horrible American woman as usual.'

Olivia's eyes widened.

'What American woman?' asked Stephen, momentarily surprised out of his bad mood. He'd been poring over his briefcase since he'd got there, muttering that he had work to catch up with and refusing Olivia's offers of tea and sandwiches, and her father's offers of brandy.

'That horrible woman who's bought the old Grange on Bracken Road,' interrupted her mother, voice vicious. 'She thinks she's irresistible. Thinks every man in the village can't take his eyes off her.'

Which meant, Olivia knew instantly, that the horrible American woman was obviously very good-looking. Sybil, who'd been a great beauty before she got stuck into drinking a bottle of spirits a day and developed more spider veins than a spaghetti junction road map, loathed other good-looking women, as Olivia knew to her cost. Her mother hadn't been able to cope the year Olivia had turned thirteen and changed from a scrawny ugly duckling into a slender Nordic swan. Sybil's friends, when she'd had such things, had all shared one particular quality: they were all extremely plain.

'So old Andrew has found himself a woman after all these years?' said Stephen, fascinated. 'Do Evie and Cara know about this?' he asked Olivia.

She shook her head slowly, thinking of what would happen when Evie did find out. Her best friend adored her father and idolised her dead mother. *Nobody*, absolutely nobody, would ever be good enough to fill Alice Fraser's shoes.

But then, Olivia consoled herself, Andrew Fraser probably felt the same way himself or he'd have got a partner years ago. Her parents were making mountains out of molehills as usual, probably because Andrew had stopped asking them to his party when they hadn't turned up three years in a row. There was no way he'd bring a new woman into his life after all these years.

The moment she walked into the Frasers' holly-bedecked hall, Olivia knew she'd been wrong. The small house may have felt like an oven after the icy temperature of the heatless Lodge, but the atmosphere was about a thousand degrees lower.

They were among the last to arrive and through the arch from the hallway Olivia could see Evie standing beside her father, her pretty face uncharacteristically stony. A woman dressed in an elegant rose-coloured cashmere dress stood on the other side of Andrew Fraser. From the smile on his face and the way he kept a hand affectionately stroking her arm, Olivia didn't have any trouble in identifying that 'horrible American woman'.

'Is it my imagination or is there a very unpartyish atmosphere in here?' murmured Stephen as Rosie took their coats, a rictus of a smile on her face.

'Welcome to the house of pain, Aunt Olivia,' she said between gritted teeth. 'The drinks tonight are Hemlock Cocktails, Digitalis Slammers or the Cyanide Seabreeze, which my mother will mix for you.'

'Your granddad's friend, huh?' asked Olivia, looking at the elegant woman in pink.

Rosie raised her eyes heavenwards. 'News certainly travels fast around here. I don't know why they base media networks in London and New York. They should pick Ballymoreen – everyone here knows everything the moment it happens. Yes.' She looked miserably at her godmother. 'The introduction of Grandpops' fiancée has caused an earthquake. Eight point five on the Richter Scale is my estimate.'

'*Fiancée?*' gasped Olivia. 'They're getting married? I didn't even know he was going out with anyone.'

'I'm going to get some food,' Stephen interrupted

rudely, moving in the direction of the kitchen. Olivia suppressed her impatience. He'd refused her offers of a snack at home, now he was going to demolish all the party goodies as if he hadn't been fed in a month. He was still punishing her for earlier.

'Don't talk to me about it,' groaned Rosie, visibly relaxing now they were on their own. She always appeared a little uptight in Stephen's company, although Olivia could never figure out why. He liked Rosie, thought she was clever and destined for great things.

The girl leaned against the hall radiator. 'It's the first we heard of it too. Mum didn't even know he was seeing someone until we got here today. The thing is, Vida's lovely and he's crazy about her. It's quite sweet really,' Rosie added reflectively, 'that old people can fall in love.'

'Excuse me,' said Olivia, gently pulling a lock of her god-daughter's lustrous long hair in pretend outrage, 'he's hardly old, and you don't forget about love as soon as you hit forty.'

Rosie grinned. 'Only joking. You old folks are so sensitive about your age. Anyway, her name is Vida Andersen, she's *très chic*, lived in Manhattan for years and is loaded. She's renovating this big house down the road and she's got a fiercesomely posh Lexus parked outside. Grandpops can't stop smiling at her; the dogs love her and . . .'

'. . . your mother loathes her?' Olivia finished the sentence.

'You said it.' Rosie paused. 'Come on and I'll get you a drink before you enter the gladiatorial arena.'

In the kitchen, Stephen was digging into a plate of tortilla chips with two slavering dogs for an audience.

'You wouldn't like tortilla chips, pooches, they're too hot,' Rosie said, patting both dogs. 'Drink?' she asked Stephen.

'A glass of red wine,' he answered.

'Make that two,' Olivia added.

Rosie got glasses, poured out some wine and, standing in front of the tray of booze so nobody would notice, poured a stiff vodka for herself, filling it up to the top with orange juice.

'Your parents aren't coming, then?' she asked Olivia when everybody had a drink.

Rosie didn't mind Olivia's parents. They always offered her real booze when she visited them, *and* gave her cigarettes. She thought Sybil was particularly hilarious. A real tough old bird.

'No,' Olivia said. 'They're babysitting Sasha.' She hoped so anyway.

'I've got the most wonderful present for Sasha for Christmas,' Rosie said enthusiastically, sloe-black eyes shining. 'It's a doll with a carry cot that can be turned into a back pack.'

They were discussing the merits of a baby doll that didn't scream all night or projectile vomit, when Andrew Fraser and Vida came into the kitchen.

'Olivia,' he said, hugging her warmly. 'I never saw you come in. How are you?'

'Great, Andrew,' she replied fondly. 'You certainly look happy.' He did, she thought. He looked as though somebody had turned a light on inside him. Rosie was obviously right: he was deliriously in love.

'You must be Vida,' she said, turning to the woman beside him. She was even better looking up close. Her skin was remarkably unlined and the soft pastel colour she wore brought out the glow in her skin. Only the faintest crêping around her throat hinted that she was over fifty.

'And you're Olivia,' said Vida with a smile. 'I've heard so much about you, you're like a third daughter to Andrew.'

Olivia coloured with pleasure.

'I'm Stephen, Olivia's husband,' he said, giving Vida the benefit of his most urbane smile.

They shook hands.

'And speaking of daughters, where's Cara?' Stephen added.

'She's coming on the late bus,' Andrew said. 'Poor girl had to work late. She'll be here by nine, I daresay.'

He began checking the pastries heating up in the oven, while Vida took more sliced up vegetables for the dips from the fridge.

Olivia could see quite plainly why her own mother and Evie couldn't stand Vida. She looked like the sort of woman you saw in advertisements for designer mail order clothes for the mature woman, subtly elegant and reeking of style.

That cashmere dress undoubtedly cost more than Evie earned in a week from Wentworth Alarms and the pearls were definitely real. Olivia's mother had had ones just like them until she'd had to sell them.

Olivia knew that her friend could probably have just about coped with her father dating some mumsy, over-weight woman from his painting class, who wore frumpy dresses and wasn't a real threat to the status quo. But Vida Andersen had threat written all over her and Olivia couldn't imagine her getting those manicured fingers covered with paint. Deep down behind her wary façade, Evie was so insecure she couldn't cope with people like Vida at all.

'I believe congratulations are in order?' Olivia said hesitantly, wondering if she was supposed to know or not.

Vida shut the fridge, a radiant smile on her face. 'Yes,' she said. 'We weren't going to tell anyone apart from the family but we're both so happy we want to shout it from the rooftops.'

Putting a baking tray on the hob, Andrew went to his fiancée and put an arm around her waist, momentarily oblivious to their guests. Rosie stifled a giggle and Olivia winked at her.

At that precise moment, Evie hurried into the kitchen, clutching a tray of empty dishes and a stack of glasses. Her face was flushed from rushing around, beads of moisture on her upper lip and tendrils of brown hair hanging damply around her face.

Her expression was that tense, nervous one Olivia hadn't seen for many years. She was not looking her best, but then nobody would beside the cool and poised Vida.

At the sight of her father and his fiancée embracing, Evie went white. Olivia's heart went out to her friend. Poor Evie was taking it very badly. She looked confused and lonely. Quickly dumping her glass on the kitchen table, Olivia relieved Evie of her burden of dishes before kissing her hello.

'Your dress is so pretty,' she said loudly. 'I love black velvet.'

'Do you think it's nice?' asked Evie gratefully, turning big sad eyes to her friend. 'It was the only thing I brought with me . . .' She stopped, suddenly remembering where she was. 'You've met everyone,' she said in a strained voice. 'And you've heard the news?'

'Yes,' said Stephen. 'Wonderful, isn't it? When's the happy day? It's not going to be a shotgun wedding, eh?' He poked Andrew in the ribs and guffawed at his own joke.

Olivia froze with horror at his comment, as did Rosie and Evie. But Vida, who was obviously made of sterner stuff, merely smiled graciously, still holding tightly to Andrew's arm.

'February,' she said. 'We're having a small reception at Kilkea Castle. We hope you and Olivia will be able to come, with your darling Sasha, of course. I've heard so much about her. She sounds a little doll. Maybe she'd be a flower girl? And we'd love to have you as a bridesmaid, Rosie,' she added. Vida's assured expression faltered briefly as she turned to Evie, who was looking bootfaced. 'I did hope you'd be one too . . .' she began.

But before Vida could finish the sentence, Evie snapped at her: 'I doubt if I'll be able to make the wedding. Not that it'll matter to you, Dad, since you didn't consider me important enough to discuss it with in the first place!'

She turned on her heel and ran from the room, rushing upstairs as hot, angry tears flooded down her face.

'I'll go after her,' Olivia said, and hurried past a pale-faced Andrew Fraser.

Upstairs, Evie sat on her single bed and wept.

'Can I come in?' asked Olivia, tapping gently at the door.

'Yes,' sobbed Evie.

'You poor thing,' Olivia said, hugging her. 'I know your dad should have told you ages ago, but he was probably nervous of saying he was going out with Vida . . .'

'That's what I can't understand!' Evie cried. 'He did it all without telling me. I feel so left out . . . how could he? It's like he was never really close to me. All those years I thought we were so close to each other and I was wrong. She changes everything.'

Evie wiped away tears with her hands. 'I was going to tidy out his airing cupboard and sort out the kitchen and . . . I can't now.' She started crying harder than ever.

They didn't talk for a while. Olivia just sat holding one of Evie's hands until her sobs subsided. Finally, she scrubbed her face dry with a tissue.

'Sorry,' she said. 'I shouldn't have run off like that, it's just . . .' She grimaced. 'I really hate that woman! Did you ever meet someone and loathe them on sight? That's what I feel for her. She's so smug and perfect. What'll she be like when she's part of our family?'

'She's hardly a wicked stepmother,' Olivia pointed out.

'I know,' Evie said wretchedly. 'Part of me knows I'm being silly about this – I'm certainly old enough to know better. But it's so upsetting, it's rocked me utterly. I can't explain . . . I loved my mother so much, you see,' she added. 'How could he want anyone else?'

'But *you* were widowed and *you* wanted someone else,' Rosie interrupted, appearing at the door. She sat down on the bed beside her mother and slung one slender arm around Evie's shoulders.

'Mum, you loved Dad but you've moved on, even if it is on to *Simon*,' she added in a disparaging voice.

Evie caught Olivia's eye and the two friends looked at each other for a second.

'That's different,' Olivia said gently.

'Why?' demanded Rosie.

Oh, God, thought Olivia, what have I said? 'Er . . . because you never knew your dad, that's why. It's different when you've lost someone you remember.'

'Mmm.' Rosie didn't look convinced.

'Would you mind one of your parents getting remarried if one of them died?' she asked Olivia bluntly.

Olivia, who wouldn't have been surprised or have cared less if either parent married a Martian tomorrow, pretended to think about it. 'Of course I would,' she lied. 'It's hard to explain. Anyway,' she got off the bed abruptly, 'we should go back down, Evie. There's nothing to be gained by sitting up here. The rest of the guests will wonder what's going on.' She meant that *Stephen* would wonder what was going on.

'They're OK,' Rosie said. 'They're all in raptures about

their new hunky male watercolour teacher, talking their dentures off with excitement. I just landed in a couple of bottles of wine and left them to it.'

'What about Stephen?' asked Olivia anxiously. 'Is he all right?' He hated being left on his own at this sort of party. It was a different kettle of fish when they were at his friends' parties. The talk then would be all about business and Olivia often felt totally out of things, but she never minded really. Stephen had to network to get on. Olivia had to expect a certain amount of the conversations to go over her head, he would always say.

'I prefer beauty to brains any day,' he'd murmur in the car on the way home, when Olivia was subdued and happy to be leaving.

'I'd better go down to Stephen,' she said now, envisioning him stuck in conversation with one of the inebriated painting ladies. He'd hate that.

She gave Evie's arm a squeeze. 'Stick on a bit of make-up and you'll be fine.'

'Don't worry, Mum, nobody downstairs will notice you've been crying, they're all too sozzled,' Rosie added. 'You'd never think those little old ladies could put away that much booze!'

Evie nodded. 'I'll be down in a few minutes,' she said, through a bunged-up nose.

Rosie and Olivia left together, Olivia hurrying down the stairs, distracted by the thought of Stephen being bored. She'd suggest going home, that was it. He hadn't been too keen to go to the party in the first place and offering to go home early would placate him. They'd only been there three-quarters of an hour, but Evie would understand.

She rushed into the kitchen but it was empty. Then she heard Stephen's distinctive laugh coming from the dining room. Peeping round the door, she found him sitting with

Vida, a bottle of red wine on the table between them along with a tray of sausage rolls. Vida's elegant head was thrown back as she too laughed uproariously.

'Oh, Stephen, that's a marvellous story,' she said.

He had an audience, Olivia thought with relief.

'Hello, darling,' she said, going round to sit beside him. 'I wasn't sure if you wanted to go home yet? I know you're tired after your flight. Stephen only flew home from Frankfurt this afternoon,' she told Vida.

'Nonsense,' he said briskly. 'It'd be crazy to go home when we're having such fun. Vida's been telling me about the time she lived in Germany. There's this gorgeous hotel in Krönberg that sounds fabulous and she says I've got to go there next time.'

'It's only ten or eleven miles outside Frankfurt and it's so beautiful if you get a chance to visit it,' Vida added. 'The gardens are exquisite.'

Olivia felt her own twinge of jealousy. Here was this gorgeous and well-travelled woman keeping her husband amused with stories of her jet-set existence when Olivia's own travelling experience was limited to that of a boring working mother. *And* her conversation never kept Stephen amused for longer than it took to remove his clothes and get into bed with her.

'Do you ever travel with Stephen on his business trips?' Vida asked pleasantly.

Stephen put his arm around his wife and answered for her.

'Olivia's a bit of a home body,' he said, squeezing her waist. 'She prefers to stay at home looking after Sasha. You'll have to meet Sasha, she's beautiful,' he added proudly. 'We'd love her to be a flower girl.'

Olivia smiled weakly, instantly thinking that Evie would see this as a betrayal and wondering desperately how she'd explain to her friend that it had been Stephen's idea.

'I hope you'll feel Sasha can be a flower girl,' Vida said, turning to Olivia. 'I know that Evie's your friend and I don't want to create trouble between you. I do so want her to accept me but I can understand how difficult it'll be.'

'Oh, Evie will come round,' Stephen said dismissively. 'She's being immature. She's had Andrew wrapped around her little finger for too long and she needs to grow up.'

Olivia shot him a furious glance. How could he say such a thing about her best friend? It was so disloyal. Vida gave Stephen a long slow look, as if she was thinking the same thing. She missed nothing, Olivia reflected.

Vida filled a fresh glass of wine for Olivia, who'd left her original one in the kitchen. 'Tell me about your job,' she said warmly. 'Andrew says you're a superb cook and that you're wasted teaching youngsters who have no interest in food.'

Laughing at the idea of being wasted doing *anything*, Olivia opened her mouth to speak but Stephen got there before her again.

'She is a wonderful cook,' he said warmly.

Olivia glowed with pleasure.

'Although I hate her teaching those delinquent children. What's the point when they all come from homes where they just eat chips and burgers?' he continued dismissively. 'Olivia's always had this fetish about working but she doesn't need to. It was different when we first got married because we didn't have Sasha. But now,' he shrugged, 'we can manage perfectly well. She just likes being a career girl. Wants "to make her contribution" as she puts it.' He made it sound as if Olivia was earning a paltry ten pounds a week which wouldn't have kept them in loo roll.

She wanted to hit him. How dare he discuss her like this with a total stranger? How dare he insult her students?

There might be a few juvenile delinquents in her classes but every school was like that. Burgers and chips indeed. Stephen was such a snob. And how dare he relegate her work to some whim of a pampered woman who could give up work if she wanted to but amused herself by pretending it was necessary?

Vida laughed infectiously, as if Stephen was teasing Olivia and she had got the joke, an old and affectionate joke between a perfectly-in-tune married couple. 'It's hardly unusual in this day and age for a woman to want a career, is it?' she said softly.

'Exactly,' Olivia said defiantly. She wrenched her chair away from the table until she was out of Stephen's reach, facing him and Vida.

'It's a question of childcare,' Stephen protested in a more conciliatory tone, as if he sensed they were ganging up on him.

'Really?' Vida didn't look at either of them but toyed with the bangle on her wrist. 'I have worked all my life and I feel it's been marvellous for both myself and my son, Max. I firmly believe he benefited from my working because I wanted a job. I would have made a dreadful full-time mother if I'd resented being at home all the time when I wanted to work. A woman needs to be able to choose a career if she wants one and not be made to feel guilty. Women have enough to feel guilty about.'

'Oh,' said Stephen, obviously astonished that a woman like Vida had ever done anything more taxing than lift a bejewelled hand to attract the attention of a passing waiter.

'Just because women can bear children doesn't mean they're unable to harbour the same sort of career ambitions as a man,' she said, this time giving him the benefit of her crystal-sharp grey gaze. 'Surely there are women executives in your company who have children?'

'Well, yes. That's different.'

'How is it different?' asked Olivia, unable to take his attitude any more.

'It's what you're used to,' Stephen argued, still talking to Vida. 'I want my daughter to have what I had.'

His daughter! thought Olivia. What about *our* daughter?

'My mother never worked outside the home,' he explained pompously.

'Goodness!' laughed Vida throatily. 'If we all confined ourselves to doing what our parents did, we'd be in trouble, wouldn't we? My mother was a washerwoman in Hell's Kitchen, married to the most notorious drunkard in New York who beat her every day of their married life when he was around, which wasn't very often, until she hit him over the head with a skillet and he left.'

You could have fitted an entire honeydew melon into the gaping hole that was Stephen's mouth, Olivia thought with amusement.

'That's amazing,' she said, while her husband recovered his composure. 'Your mother sounds like a formidable woman.'

'You betcha.' Vida stood up, a twinkle in her eye. 'You and I must have a cup of coffee some day, Olivia. Maybe you'll be able to persuade Evie to come along too.'

She grimaced. 'I'll do my best.'

'We'd better go,' Stephen announced, finishing his wine rapidly. 'Everyone else seems to have and we don't want to overstay our welcome. Thanks for everything, Vida. We must say goodbye to Andrew.'

He shook her hand quickly and bustled Olivia into the hall to collect their coats.

Olivia grinned to herself. She liked Vida, she decided. Liked the way she'd taken on Stephen, gently but firmly, and yet never appeared to imply that Olivia was somehow a doormat because she let him get away with his chauvinistic attitudes.

Instead, Vida had teased him and showed him that while some women fitted into his vision of life, many didn't.

Olivia would have loved to be able to talk to Stephen like that: standing her ground firmly. Hell, she'd have loved to be able to talk to him at all, to tell him that teaching was driving her mad and that one unruly class had undermined her so much her self-confidence was shot. But if she said she couldn't cope with teaching, something she'd done for years, Stephen would be sure to say she was obviously unfit to work full stop. There'd be no point saying she could teach younger children or maybe at night classes.

She kissed Andrew and Rosie goodbye and they left, trudging through the rain towards the Lodge. Glancing at her husband's set profile as he marched alongside her, she almost regretted getting involved in the conversation with Vida.

But she was entitled to her own opinions, Olivia decided. She'd humour him out of his bad mood. Someone like Vida wouldn't bother humouring him. She'd let him stew for a few hours and get over it. Olivia, however, liked a quiet life. Humouring Stephen was one of her most finely honed skills these days.

'Vida,' said Rosie, standing at the kitchen door with a glass of orange juice heavily diluted with vodka, 'was your mother really a washerwoman and was your father an alcoholic?'

The older woman tidied away the remnants of the party nibbles from the dining-room table.

'Goodness, no, dear,' she said briskly. 'I just needed to take the wind out of that particular gentleman's sails.'

She grinned at Rosie. A conspiratorial grin.

Rosie, who loathed Stephen with a vengeance, grinned back. 'Welcome to the family, Vida!'

The dogs, who were worn out from begging for party food all evening and had retreated to their baskets to sleep off an excess of sausage rolls, started barking manically in the kitchen.

'Olivia or Stephen must have forgotten something,' Vida said.

'Yeah, like his sense of humour,' added Rosie. She ran to the front door and wrenched it open.

Cara stood in the doorway, rain streaming down her face and dripping on to the floor as she fumbled for a door key. Her hair was plastered to her head and her coat looked like she'd been swimming in it.

'Hi, Rosie,' she said, wearily unhooking her rucksack with frozen fingers. 'Sorry I'm late,' she added as her father appeared to greet her. 'Bloody bus broke down and we all had to sit for an hour and a half until they got a new one. Mind you, it's so wet I could have swum here faster.' She grinned. 'What have I missed?'

Dried off, wearing fresh clothes and with her hair frizzing in a halo of curls around her head after a speedy blast of the hairdryer, Cara sat at the kitchen table and wolfed down a plate of reheated party food. The dogs flanked her, drooling every time she raised a succulent bit of sausage roll to her mouth.

Evie, who'd only emerged from her bedroom ten minutes previously when she'd made sure Vida had gone home for the night, sat at the far end of the table and toyed with a cup of lemon tea. They were alone. Rosie had retreated into the sitting room to watch the TV and smoke a forbidden cigarette out the window, while Andrew Fraser had gone next door to return two silver platters he'd borrowed.

'I don't see what's wrong with her,' protested Cara, who'd met her future stepmother briefly. Granted, ten minutes with Vida who'd said, 'I'd better go home and let Evie come downstairs,' wasn't the basis for an in-depth character analysis. But Cara had seen the way her father's eyes lit up when he looked at his fiancée and she was happy for him.

Just because her own lovelife was about as successful as man's attempts to reach Pluto didn't mean she wanted everyone else to suffer romantically. She had a totally different view of her father's future from her older sister. Cara had lived with Andrew for longer as a widower than as a happily married man so she'd seen him enjoy flirting with his neighbours, seen him look a little wistfully at couples. Evie would have snapped at any woman who'd dared to look crossways at her beloved dad.

They also had very different views about mothers. Cara had daydreamed about a real mother when she was younger: for Evie, there'd only ever be one mother and she was dead. Nothing and no one could replace her, Cara knew that. But Vida wasn't a replacement – she was a new partner for their father, someone to love him and care for him when they weren't there.

She attempted to say some of this.

'Vida seems lovely and they're great together. He's been on his own for so long, he deserves some happiness.'

Evie shot her a look that'd curdle milk.

'Jeez, I hope the wind doesn't change and you get stuck like that,' muttered Cara, eyeing her sister's sour face.

'You just don't see, do you?' hissed Evie.

'See what?'

'See that she's after Dad because he's lonely and doesn't understand what sort of woman she is! She'll clean him

105

out in a wet week and what'll he be left with then? Nothing!'

Cara groaned as she speared a bit of mini-brioche. 'Be reasonable, Evie. What's she going to clean him out of? The family fortune? The heirlooms? Last time I looked, the cottage wasn't exactly bulging with the sort of bits and pieces that'd make an antique dealer gibber with excitement, unless the hall table is secretly Louis Quatorze instead of mail-order self-assembly.'

'It's not just that . . .' Evie looked around blindly, still hurting terribly and astonished that Cara couldn't see things the way she did: that Vida Andersen was a money-grabbing professional widow who'd break their father's fragile heart and . . . and . . . *change things*. Change things forever. Cara was so bloody gullible she had no idea what was going to happen. Did she not care?

'Evie,' Cara said gently, knowing exactly how left out her sister was feeling at the thought of being supplanted in their father's affections. Old beyond her years in every other aspect of her life, Evie was still like a six-year-old Daddy's girl when it came to Andrew. 'Dad is entitled to a companion, someone to spend the rest of his life with. I know it's difficult to think of anyone taking Mum's place . . .'

'It's different for me,' cried Evie in anguish.

'What do you mean?' asked Cara, pushing her half-finished food away.

'You don't remember her the way I do.'

'What do you know about what I remember?' demanded Cara. 'You never even talk to me anymore, so what do you know about how I feel?'

'I know you can't remember very much about when she died because you were only six; I was *sixteen*. I remember how much Dad cried when she died, I remember that!'

106

Cara gazed at her sister's flushed face and took a deep breath. She wasn't going to lose her temper. She'd vowed to sort out all the friction between them over the next few days. She couldn't ruin it all with one massive row. 'Mum's dead,' she said gently. 'Dad marrying again doesn't mean he doesn't remember her or miss her. It's a new beginning for him. You're marrying Simon, for God's sake. Can't you be happy for Dad?'

'You're so naive,' Evie said hotly. 'That's always been your problem. You let people walk all over you, Cara. You do it in work or you'd have been promoted by now. I've no control over your life but I won't let Dad get walked all over by that bitch!'

Cara gaped at her, shocked. 'I don't let people walk all over me!' she stuttered.

'Yes, you do,' fired back Evie heatedly, not even thinking what she was saying because she was so hysterical. 'I've told you a hundred times to demand a raise so you can afford more than that ice box of a flat you and Phoebe live in, but you don't pay any attention.'

'It's none of your business what I get paid,' roared Cara, finally getting angry.

'It is because I'm your sister!' roared back Evie.

'Yeah, my sister, not my bloody mother!' shrieked Cara. 'And don't you forget it. You think you can boss us all around, even Dad. Well, you can't. Keep your stuck up little nose out of my affairs!'

'Somebody has to stick their nose into your affairs because you can't handle them very well, can you?'

Evie was scarlet in the face now, her eyes feverish. She barely knew what she was saying. She knew she'd said far too many awful things but shock meant she couldn't stop.

It was all too much for Cara. The misery of the past few days, her awful hangover, and the damned bus breaking down all caught up with her. She finally snapped.

'You don't know anything about me or my life because I don't tell you anything and you don't ask,' she said, her voice icily calm. 'I'm closer to the bus driver on the 16A than I am to my own sister because I can't handle your petty small-mindedness, your conviction that you know everything and your jealousy.'

'*Jealousy?*' screamed Evie, too stunned to care how much noise she made. 'What jealousy? What have I got to be jealous of you for?'

'Because I'm not some uptight cow who's got a pole up her backside and always thinks she's right. And,' Cara said vehemently, 'who's marrying a bloke equally as bloody boring and rigid just because he asked her! I can tell you something – if you're not going to Dad's wedding, I'm not going to put on a brave face of it when you marry po-faced bloody Simon.'

With that, Cara threw her fork on to the table where it hit her plate with a resounding clatter that roused both dogs. She stomped out of the kitchen and pounded noisily up the stairs, the way she had when she was a child and Evie had given out to her for something.

Evie ran a hand faintly over her forehead, feeling the beginnings of a terrible headache. What had she said? Terrible, terrible things. Cara would never forgive her. Whatever had happened to them? They'd been so close once. What had turned them into strangers, people who found it easier to hurt each other than to comfort? What had made Cara so bitter, so angry? Wearily, she sank her feverish head on to the cool of the old wooden table and wished Christmas would disappear in a puff of smoke. She'd meant to sort things out, to tell Cara she loved her and that she wanted the best things in life for her. Now she'd screwed it all up because she'd got the shock of her life. If only her father had told her, if only she'd been prepared. She'd still have been hurt but at least she'd have been able to hide it.

It wasn't his fault, though. Evie knew who'd really messed up Christmas for them all. Vida. Horrible Vida.

CHAPTER FIVE

Evie flicked on the lights in the office reception area with a sigh. Another year. Another January. More snow. Shaking wet flakes off her coat, she walked past the drooping Christmas tree and past the scattering of pine needles that littered the carpet.

Davis Wentworth had this fixation about real Christmas trees and always insisted the company reception area had one. Only because *he* didn't have to placate Marj, the cleaner, who spent hours trying to pick out the pine needles that had knitted themselves into the hard-wearing nylon carpet, Evie thought as she unlocked the door to the stairs. Poor Marj would go mad when she saw the state of the floor. Not to mention how cross she'd get when she saw the amount of fake snow plastered on the plate-glass doors between floors as a result of Kev in Sales getting drunk at lunch on the last day and going berserk drawing rude Santas everywhere. Only Chippendales were supposed to be as rampant as that, Evie laughed to herself as she caught sight of one particularly sexy Santa who was en route to deliver more than just a Christmas stocking.

She hadn't shown she was amused at the time, naturally. She couldn't, not with the impressionable young temps watching. Instead, she'd given Kev one of her fiercest glares, told him he was in an office not the zoo, and warned that if the Santas weren't gone by the time the boss saw them, the only Christmas bonus he'd be getting was his P45.

All of which was untrue, because Davis was so short-sighted he wouldn't have noticed a *real* half-naked Santa standing in the stairwell, and even if he had, he wouldn't have minded. But you had to have standards in an office, Evie felt, otherwise things fell to pieces. If anyone knew *she* had a sense of humour, she'd never keep the place under control.

Reminding herself to help poor Marj clean up the fake snow, Evie flicked on the lights. It was half-eight on the third day of January and the entire administrative part of the office felt as if it had been deserted since the *Titanic* went down, instead of just ten days previously. There were usually plenty of people at work by this time but the combination of the bad weather – heavy snowfall for three days – and the fact that the holidays were finally over, had obviously made the staff of Wentworth Alarms collectively turn over for one final snooze before getting up.

For the first time in her life, Evie wished she could have done the same. She never minded going back after the holidays, not usually. It was guilt. After more than a week of not having to get up for work, she began to get anxious and feel slovenly, as if she should be doing something, *anything*. Which was why her house was always spotless, her airing cupboard more organised than a Benetton shop, and why there were never, ever any clumps of dust and hair under her furniture.

'I don't know how you're going to cope on honeymoon, Mum,' Rosie had remarked the day before, when Evie had routed her from her comfy position on the sofa watching the *Teletubbies*, so that she could hoover under it. Standing there in her socks and dressing gown with a half-finished bowl of Frosties in her hand, Rosie watched while her mother ruthlessly eradicated any stray bit of fluff that had stupidly decided to live under her sofa.

'You'll be bored rigid lying on a beach all day for two weeks,' Rosie remarked.

'I'll take books,' panted Evie, sticking the hoover nozzle into the corners of the sofa to pick up any stray dust or Frosties. 'And we won't be lying on a beach all day. Greece is a fabulous country and we've so much to see. I've always wanted to travel, I've just never had the chance before.'

Actually, she'd never had the money. Bringing up Rosie on her own had been tough and money had been very tight. Apart from holidays in Ballymoreen, she and Rosie had only been abroad three times: twice to a cottage in Cornwall with Andrew and Cara, and once to Majorca with Olivia when Rosie had been eleven. That had been their best holiday ever. Sun, sandy beaches, welcoming local restaurants and a lovely apartment in a quiet, unspoilt part of the island. Sometimes, when she thought about that holiday, Evie wished that Rosie, Olivia and Sasha could accompany her and Simon on their honeymoon. It was a strange idea, she knew that. But the thought of being able to take the other three along seemed so right somehow.

Evie climbed the stairs to the third floor, avoiding the lift because she had to work off the five pounds she'd put on misery eating over Christmas. She hadn't planned on touching the sinful cream confections Vida had left in her father's fridge, but they were impossible to resist. That one forkful of chocolate log turned into two enormous slices every time and before she knew it, Evie was walking around with her jumper worn loosely over the waistband of her jeans to hide the opened top button.

In the large office she shared with two other secretaries,

she dumped her handbag on to her desk and switched on the heating. It was freezing in here, she thought. She made herself a cup of coffee – black, because the milk hadn't arrived yet – and sat down at her desk, cradling the hot mug in her hands and wishing she was elsewhere. On a beach in Greece, maybe. In the sweltering sun where nobody could bother her with queries about missing files, irate customers, lengthy, boring reports or whether she was going to her father's wedding or not. She'd sit back on a lounger, with a wrap carefully disguising her cellulite and her belly . . .

'Is there anyone sitting here, mademoiselle?'

She turned her head, adjusting her Yves St Laurent sunglasses to see who was blocking out the light. At first he was just a shadow with the sun behind him. Then he moved under the umbrella that shaded her striped lounger, and she could see his face.

He was dark, like the handsome Greek waiters who smiled at her each evening at dinner. But his proud, hawk-like face wasn't smiling. The black eyes were inscrutable as he stared down at her from his great height.

She could feel his eyes take in the shape of her beautiful body in its expensive white swimsuit, with the ruched bodice highlighting her full breasts and slender waist. Evie was glad she'd worn her diamond bracelet on a whim that morning, so he could tell she was a woman of substance, not some bored bimbo sitting by the pool in the classy Elounda Mare waiting for a millionaire to walk by.

She wondered if he could tell that her empire of luxury clothes shops in Milan and Paris no longer fulfilled her; that she needed the love of a strong, proud man to do that.

'There's nobody sitting here,' she said softly.

'Good,' he replied. 'I have been watching you from the hotel, I hoped you were alone . . .'

114

'Evie, Happy New Year!' shrieked Lorraine, bustling in through the door wearing what had to be her Christmas present from her boyfriend: an ocelot-print fake fur coat.

'The same to you, Lorraine,' Evie said warmly. She was very fond of the other girl. 'Love the coat. Did Craig give it to you?'

'Yes.' Lorraine, a skinny twenty-four-year-old brunette who was one of the few people Evie knew who could carry off a bulky fake fur coat, did a twirl for her benefit.

'It's beautiful,' she said appreciatively, getting up to run her fingers through the silky synthetic fur.

'You try it on,' urged Lorraine, slipping the coat off.

'No, I've put on five pounds, I'd look like a giant teddy bear in it,' Evie replied gloomily, 'or else something escaped from the zoo.'

Lorraine carefully hung the coat on the coat rack and immediately made her way to the worn tea tray to boil the kettle.

'Tea?' she asked.

'No, thanks, I've got some coffee. And the milkman hasn't been yet.'

'Blast,' said Lorraine who liked her tea very milky. 'So how was your holiday? And what did Simon give you for Christmas?'

Evie brightened up at the second part of the question. Describing her holiday without the use of the words 'complete disaster' would have been difficult and she didn't want to get into a big discussion about her problems in case she got tearful. But talking about Simon's present was different.

Smiling, she hooked back her hair so that one of the tiny seed pearl and gold earrings Simon had bought her were visible. When he'd given them to her after her return from Ballymoreen, she'd been thrilled.

115

'Lovely,' cooed Lorraine. 'Very subtle. It must have been hard not having Christmas together?' she said, poking around in the cupboard under the tea things, looking for the biscuits.

'Well, it's his last Christmas as a bachelor and he and his mother have got into the habit of spending it with their relatives.' Evie paused. 'It was easier this way. Of course I missed him but we'll have next Christmas together.'

Christmas together? She couldn't wait. Lounging around in their dressing gowns, watching soppy movies on the box and snuggling up in front of a roaring fire . . . OK, so neither she nor Simon had a working fireplace in their homes, but they'd see about it.

'You won't miss the time till the wedding,' Lorraine remarked.

Evie grimaced. 'Don't talk to me about that,' she said. 'I've got a list of things to do that's a mile long and I haven't the energy to start phoning people. You have no idea how far in advance you have to book everything. I thought it was just the hotel but you've got to book flowers so early, you'd think they were growing them from seed to your very own specifications.'

'It must be lovely planning your wedding, though,' Lorraine said dreamily. 'The dress, the reception, your bouquet . . .' She went off into wedding fantasy land, obviously imagining herself and Craig sailing down the aisle in a cloud of tulle.

'Yes,' said Evie, brightly. It was funny really, but since hearing about Vida and her father, she hadn't thought that much about her own wedding at all. Maybe it was spending so much time away from Simon over the holidays but she'd barely given September the twelfth a thought.

'Anyway,' said Lorraine suspiciously, staring at Evie's

china mug, 'what are you drinking coffee for? I thought you were on the fruit juice diet?'

Evie smiled ruefully. 'Actually I was on the "sausage roll, Christmas cake and as much stuffing as you can eat" diet so I thought having a cup of coffee to wake me up was harmless in comparison.'

Her phone rang suddenly, its peremptory sound making both women jump. She picked it up wearily.

'Evie,' squeaked the receptionist in a harassed voice. 'This caller is looking for the sales department and she insists she can't wait until they arrive. Will you handle her? I can't calm her down.'

'Of course,' said Evie automatically. The New Year had begun.

'What I don't understand,' she said to Olivia as they queued up for sandwiches in the pub across the road from the barren industrial estate where Wentworth Alarms was situated, 'is why Vida wants me at the wedding in the first place? She obviously can't stand me, and would you want your new husband's disapproving daughter standing at the altar beside you on your wedding day?'

'I don't think she hates you, Evie,' Olivia said, somewhat wearily. They'd been over this subject endlessly since Christmas and she no longer had anything to say about it.

Evie talked about Vida constantly, worrying away like a dog with a bone – wondering why her father loved Vida and did it mean he loved *her* any less. Should she even go to the wedding? It wasn't as if they wanted her at it, she was tearfully convinced of that. And if she did go, what could she wear that would compete with that rich bitch who obviously had a wardrobe full of designer gear thanks to her last bloody husband, whom she'd probably poisoned for his insurance money.

117

Because Olivia loved Evie and knew her so well, she knew her friend's harping on and on wasn't because she actually disliked her stepmother-to-be, but because she was feeling desperately threatened. After years of seeing herself as the most important woman in Andrew Fraser's life, Evie simply couldn't cope with being relegated to second place. It had simply devastated her.

They'd discussed it so often that Olivia had run out of things to say. What she desperately wanted to talk to Evie about was how depressed she'd been feeling since Christmas. Stephen had been monosyllabic all week, as if actually pining for the cut and thrust of the office, and had bitten her head off when she'd suggested going out for a day. Even worse, the end of the school holidays loomed and Olivia felt sick at the thought of facing another year of teaching.

Desperate to be cheered up, she'd left Sasha with her best friend from playgroup and driven out to Evie's office for a spur-of-the-moment lunch because she longed to confide in her friend. But with Evie still incapable of having a conversation without the word 'Vida' in it, Olivia hadn't broached the subject of how utterly dispirited she herself was.

The girl behind the bar ladled out two bowls of mushroom soup, handed them rolls, and they moved along the counter to the sandwiches displayed unappetisingly in clingfilm.

'I'm not going, I've decided,' continued Evie, jaw firm as she deliberated over whether to plump for plastic-looking cheese or dried-up chicken.

Olivia waited until they were sitting down before making her point.

'Evie,' she said gently, 'you're going to hate me for saying this but I'm your friend and I have to.' She paused to take her lunch off the tray. 'I know you feel desperately threatened and hurt because of how quickly they got engaged and everything but, believe me, if you don't go to the wedding you'll regret it for the rest of your life. Don't you understand?' She rushed on before Evie could say a word. 'Think about what you're doing by not going. You're telling your father you don't care and that you disapprove of him in the most public way possible, and you're making Rosie choose between you. She can't possibly go if you don't. She's too loyal to you to do that but she loves her grandfather. Can't you see?'

Hazel eyes huge with tears, Evie stared at her oldest friend. She looked as if she'd been stabbed with her soup spoon. Her lower lip quivered pitifully, making Olivia feel like she'd just clubbed a baby seal. Despite the hard exterior Evie displayed so defiantly, she was as soft as butter on the inside and was incredibly easy to hurt. She'd been hurt so many times before that Olivia hated herself for adding to that. She grabbed her friend's hand in remorse.

'I'm sorry, Evie,' she said desperately. 'I didn't mean to hurt you but I had to say it.'

Her friend bit her lip in misery and for a moment, Olivia was afraid she was going to break down and sob. But instead Evie took a deep breath, hiccuped and whispered: 'You're right.'

Olivia sighed with sheer relief. 'I'm so glad, Evie. I know it'll be difficult but it's the right thing.'

Evie picked up her napkin and wiped her eyes with it. 'You're right about making Rosie choose between me and Dad, and you're right about how awful it would be if I publicly turned against him. I keep thinking about it, worrying about what I should do and hating myself for being childish about this.' She gave a wry little laugh. 'I can't believe it's really practical, common-sense me behaving like a prima donna . . .'

'You're not a prima donna,' interrupted Olivia. 'You're normally very level-headed but this has knocked you for six.'

'Well,' Evie said ruefully, 'the last time I lost my head, I was about seven and somebody broke the leg off my Tiny Tears doll! I'm a bit old for having tantrums now, it's just that I lose control when I think of that woman taking advantage of Dad . . .'

The smile faded and Evie's eyes were as hard as agates as she looked at Olivia. 'You're wrong about Vida. She hates me and I hate her back. I don't trust her and if she hurts Dad, I'll kill her. I will.'

Olivia had never seen such a grim expression on her friend's face, one that frightened her. But she didn't want to start another pious homily.

'Don't be so angry, it'll eat you up inside, Evie,' was all she said. 'Come on, let's have our lunch. I can't send you back to the office looking that angry and red-faced – the rest of the staff will think I slapped you!'

Evie laughed, a high-pitched little sound, and the tension was broken. 'The rest of the staff wouldn't dream of thinking any such thing,' she said, managing a weak grin. 'They think nobody would dare slap me. *They* certainly wouldn't.'

'You don't mean to tell me they're all taken in by your tough-as-old-boots routine?' Olivia asked with her mouth full of tuna sandwich. 'Don't they know what a complete old softie you are?'

Evie shuddered. 'I couldn't bear it if they did. The only way to run an office is with an iron hand in an iron glove,' she said loftily.

'Can you give me hints on how to use that technique with a crowd of delinquent school kids?' Olivia asked. 'Another term of 3A will drive me nuts.'

120

'They can't be that bad, surely?' Evie said, not noticing how dismal Olivia looked. 'You've got to show them who's boss.'

'Easier said than done.' Olivia stared into her soup and felt her heart sink at the thought that in four days' time she'd be facing 3A, all hyperactive after Christmas and ready to make her life hell. Or more hellish than it felt already.

'I never had this problem with the fifth and sixth years,' she said. 'But when the other home economics teacher left last year, the replacement wanted to teach the older girls and, being only part-time, I ended up with the horrible third years. There are a couple of little terrors in that class.' She put down her spoon. Her appetite, which hadn't been good for days, had totally vanished. 'None of the other teachers can bear the troublemakers but I'm the only one who can't control them.'

'They're probably all jealous as sin of you,' Evie declared. An expert at giving orders, she couldn't understand why her friend was having so much trouble with unruly pupils.

Evie had always imagined that one look at the ethereal Olivia would stun any class into silence. She was so lovely looking, with her flowing blonde hair, model's bone structure and long, slim body. If Evie had only looked like that, she was convinced her life would have been different. Like a romantic novel, full of real-life heroes waiting to whisk her off to glorious destinations with sun, yachts, magnificent castles and family jewels. And no overdraft, lonely nights watching TV, months of existing on the cheapest cuts of meat because they were so broke – and definitely no envelope-stuffing at nights to pay for Rosie's school trip to Stratford-upon-Avon.

But Olivia never capitalised on her beauty or even seemed to be aware of it. At school, she'd worn the drabbest clothes and had never hung around with the more advanced girls in St Agatha's who'd been dating since the age of fifteen. Instead, she'd stayed best friends with Evie and together they'd steered clear of boys until they were seventeen. Evie, plump, talkative and a tad bossy to cover her insecurity, hadn't exactly been inundated with offers from the local boys, so this hadn't been too much of a hardship. But the desperately unsure and anxious Olivia could have had her pick of the male populace, if only she'd wanted to.

But then, Evie thought darkly, how could any girl be normal when her teenage years happened to coincide with the worst years of her parents' alcoholism? Having your drunken mother screech abuse at you every second day for no apparent reason wouldn't exactly instill you with confidence, no matter how stunning you looked.

'Are you really dreading going back to teaching?' she asked Olivia.

Her friend nodded glumly.

'Stephen's thrilled to be back at work. I think he's bored hanging around the house with me.' She didn't say that she was sure he was bored by her company. It was as obvious as the nose on his face. Her husband was bored rigid by her, preferred talking to total strangers at parties than spending time with her, and his face became ten times more animated when he was discussing work than it ever was when she was talking to him. Suddenly, Olivia didn't feel as if she could reveal all this to Evie. She felt too raw to discuss it. Too much of a failure.

''Course he's not bored,' Evie interrupted. 'He's probably got the post-Christmas blues like the rest of us.'

Olivia shook her head morosely, thinking that Stephen had post and pre Christmas blues. 'No, it's not that. Yesterday I suggested we spend our last day going for a drive out to Howth and having lunch in one of those lovely little pubs, but he said he wanted to catch up on work and spent the day with his nose stuck in his brief-case,' she said. 'If there hadn't been a decent film on the TV, I'd have gone round the bend. It was *Sommersby*. I love Richard Gere.'

Evie sighed in sympathy and waved at the lounge boy, trying to get his attention so they could get coffee. He ignored her.

'You try,' she said.

Olivia raised her perfect profile, flicked back a strand of fair hair and looked hopefully in the direction of the bar. A barman and the lounge boy arrived at their table like a shot, both looking eagerly at the elegant blonde dressed in sleek pewter wool.

'Two coffees, please?' she said, with a polite smile that didn't reach her silver-grey eyes.

'How do you do that?' asked Evie, shaking her head. 'No, don't bother answering. Anyway, you should have insisted that Stephen go for a drive with you. Heaven knows he spends enough time working, it wouldn't kill him to go back to work unprepared like a normal person.'

'I know. But his job is so important . . .' Olivia said automatically.

'You and Sasha are important too,' Evie pointed out, putting too much sugar in her coffee to give herself energy for the afternoon ahead.

She failed to notice Olivia grow even more morose as she thought of her darling Sasha. Olivia's eyes welled up at the thought of the beautiful little girl with those huge trusting eyes so sad as she watched her mother steeped in misery.

She wasn't even a good mother anymore. She'd cried that morning making Sasha's breakfast, big fat tears raining down on the toast and honey as soon as Stephen had slammed the front door without kissing her goodbye.

That was no way to behave in front of a four year old. She felt so ashamed. Here she was telling her best friend how to sort out her life, how she should go to her father's wedding, while she, Olivia, couldn't sort out anything. She felt useless; boring, stupid and quite, quite useless.

Her head bent so Evie couldn't see her brimming eyes, Olivia took several sips of scalding coffee. She had to get out of the pub before she broke down completely and disgraced herself.

'Gosh, look at the time,' she said with a gasp. 'I said I'd pick Sasha up by two-fifteen and I'll never be back in time. I'd better go.' Feeling dreadful to be racing out on Evie under false pretences, Olivia got up abruptly, grabbed her coat and kissed her friend quickly on the cheek without looking her in the eye.

'I'll drive you back to your car,' Evie offered.

'No, it's only across the road,' Olivia said anxiously. 'I'll walk. Finish your coffee.' And she rushed off.

What she really wanted to do was sit down and sob her heart out to Evie but this wasn't the time or the place. Evie was caught up in her own problems and Olivia couldn't burden her with any more. Olivia had to sort this out on her own.

Back at her desk with a sheaf of messages in front of her, Evie thought about Olivia's rapid departure and felt guilty for rattling on about Vida and her father. Olivia was right, she thought: she *had* been obsessing about the wedding. Endlessly, she realised, shamefaced. And poor Olivia had put up with her for ages and obviously wanted to talk about something but Evie had been so tied up with her own problems, she hadn't noticed.

Feeling ashamed, she picked up the phone and dialled Olivia's home number. The answering machine clicked on, with Stephen's deep, self-important voice announcing that the MacKenzies were not at home and to leave a message after the beep. '*After the beep*,' he emphasised, as if he was talking to some spectacularly dumb caller who'd never heard an answering machine before. God, that man loved the sound of his own voice. He'd make anyone feel stupid with his patronising manner, Evie thought crossly. He did it to Olivia all the time. And he was so self-important, you'd think he was chairman the way he went on and on about his job and how vital he was to the company.

Imagine not wanting to spend the last day of Christmas with his family and refusing point blank to go for a drive in Howth so he could pore over his papers. He really was very selfish. Because he travelled so much, he and Olivia spent very little time together. Yet Stephen never seemed to understand that playing happy families was terribly important to Olivia, mainly because she'd never had one before. Doing normal family things like going for drives or having a cosy day at home stretched out in front of the TV with a tin of biscuits and some tea, instead of a quart of gin and an argument, was Olivia's idea of sheer bliss. The only time she'd ever done normal family stuff as a child had been with Evie's family, which was why they were so close. Stephen just couldn't understand that. And he was so obsessed with his bloody career he didn't appear to care.

'Livvy,' Evie said to the answering machine, using the pet name she'd called her friend by when they were younger, 'sorry I was blathering on and on about Vida at lunch. It must have been a real pain in the neck and I'm sorry. Give me a buzz later, will you? We should have a proper chat – and not a word about my family, I promise. 'Bye.'

125

It was only when she'd hung up that Evie remembered she was going to Simon's for dinner, that she wouldn't be home until late. Damn! She'd ring Olivia later, when she was sure to be home, and have a talk then.

As it happened, she never got a moment to herself all afternoon. When Davis came back from lunch, he called her into his office to get through the mound of paperwork on his desk. He looked tired, as if he'd been burning the midnight oil. His plump face was larger than ever after the inevitable excess of Christmas, the treble chin spilling over on to the collar of his shirt. But there were giant hollows under his eyes, yellowing hollows that gave his rounded face a strangely sickly look. He was ill, Evie realised with a sense of shock.

After an hour spent going through paperwork, he seemed worn out.

'I've some important letters to send to our key customers about the changes in accounting we're introducing,' he said. He sat back in his chair, his face sweating. 'I know what I want to say but . . .' He looked at her pleadingly. 'Could you draft them, Evie?' he asked. 'You know how to do it better than I do.'

She nodded. She'd been in Wentworth Alarms for twelve years and knew as much about the running of the company as he did. She'd been his assistant for seven of those years, from the moment it became apparent she was wasted in reception.

'Of course,' she said. 'I'll handle it. Davis,' she added hesitantly, 'do you want to go home? You look tired.'

'Yes,' he muttered. 'Something I ate the other day, I'm still not over it . . .'

'Food poisoning. That really takes it out of you,' Evie agreed, not believing for one second that her boss was suffering the after-effects of food poisoning. He looked so wretched, so ill, it had to be more than that. But if Davis wanted her to believe he merely had a sick stomach, she'd go along with the subterfuge. 'I'll deal with this and you should go home, via the chemist's maybe to get something for your stomach,' she said idly. 'Or even go to the doctor and get a shot. It never hurts, does it, to get an injection to fight the nausea? Rosie had a very sensitive stomach when she was little and the only answer when she got really ill was to go to the doctor for an injection.'

He didn't answer for a moment. 'Yes, maybe I'll do that,' he said finally.

When he'd left, Evie spent the rest of the afternoon working on the letters. Her mind was half on her work and half on her boss. There was something wrong with Davis, that was for sure. He'd never been the healthiest of individuals but he looked so ill ... As she typed and answered calls, Evie worried about him. Widowed recently, he had nobody else to worry about him. Hopefully the doctor would notice how dreadful he looked and do some tests.

It was five-twenty-five when the sound of Lorraine turning off her word processor with a sigh of relief made Evie look at her watch again. She'd have to race if she wanted to get through the rush-hour traffic to Simon's house by half-six. But she had five minutes to spare to ring Olivia.

Pulling on her coat with one hand, she dialled the familiar number with the other. The phone rang and the machine clicked on again. Strange, she thought. Olivia was always at home at that time, getting dinner ready for Stephen. She was an incredible cook and whenever Evie dropped in on her way home from work, the scent emanating from Olivia's kitchen was always enough to put off the most dedicated dieter. She wasn't the sort of woman to knock together a sausage casserole with the contents of her store cupboard and a tin opener. She went for the whole works, gorgeous and elaborate meals that made your mouth water.

And Evie knew that half the time, they ended up in the freezer because Stephen was working late and couldn't get home in time. If Evie had been married to him they'd have ended up in the bin – or all over his face when he arrived home late for the tenth time in a row.

His voice came on the answering machine again and Evie grimaced. 'Sorry I missed you earlier, Olivia,' she said. 'I'm going to Simon's tonight so I won't be home but please phone me tomorrow so we can have a chat. 'Bye. Chin up.'

She didn't know why she'd added that bit at the end. 'Chin up.' It wasn't as if Olivia had said anything was wrong, but in retrospect Evie was sure there was.

Olivia stood in front of the mirror in her bedroom and let the phone ring. She heard Evie's voice coming from the machine in the hall but didn't move to pick it up. Instead, she stared closely at her reflection. Her mother was right, she was deathly pale. She needed something to warm her up, she decided. Like plastic surgery or an injection of personality.

People often said she was beautiful. Everyone did, in fact. But beauty didn't mean anything. Olivia had no respect for the beauty she was supposed to have, she hadn't earned it or worked for it. It wasn't the same as being vivacious and witty like Rosie or clever and kind like Evie.

It was just there: high cheekbones and perfect lips. Nothing more, nothing deeper. It was shallow. Architecture. A lovely façade when she really needed internal lights and something people were interested in. Evie was pretty, feminine and cute with her little nose and her undulating walk.

But that wasn't what made Simon love her. It was what was inside: her personality and her drive. Beauty was nothing really if you lacked all the other important things and Olivia lacked them all. Even her own husband wasn't interested in her. To him, she was just a lovely cold doll he took down from the mantelpiece when he felt like looking at it.

'Mummy,' said a small voice. Olivia looked down to see Sasha peeping around the bedroom door, her eyes even huger than usual. 'Emily got marker on the couch. Pink marker,' she added. 'I told her she wasn't allowed to bring them out of my room but she did.'

Olivia felt herself go as white as Stephen's precious leather couches. Those bloody markers were almost impossible to erase when they got on something. He would have a fit if he found out, unless she could remove the mark before he got home. She just prayed it wasn't somewhere noticeable and that it was small. Very small.

'Don't worry, Sasha,' she said calmly, bending down to kiss her daughter on the forehead. 'We'll sort it out.'

Sasha didn't look convinced. 'Daddy will be cross,' she said anxiously.

'No, he won't,' Olivia replied, doing her best to inject confidence into her voice. She took Sasha by the hand. 'Show me where the mark is and I'll sort it out.'

Evie sat in her car on the way to Simon's house and day dreamed.

'She was wearing a beautiful evening dress and an ocelot coat, and didn't look like a teddy bear in it. Instead, she looked like a famous movie star en route for a première, more

glamorous than Sharon Stone and utterly untouchable.

'Madame, let me take your coat?'

His voice was like the rest of him: cultured and elegant. But the formal dinner jacket he wore with such panache contrasted with the shock of dark hair that reached his collar and curled gently around the nape of his strong neck. Everything about the stranger's dress was conservative, yet his rippling black curls and the gleam in his dark eyes showed a different side to his nature, a wilder and dangerous side.

Evie moved her head graciously. 'No, thank you, I prefer to wear it. The evening has grown cold.'

Standing on the balcony of the stately house by Lake Geneva, the air had indeed grown cold and she could feel herself shiver in the spaghetti-strapped black silk dress.

She wasn't sure why she was there in the first place, why she'd accepted the invitation from the mysterious Count Romulo to a party in his home when she didn't know the man.

He was a playboy, her friends told her eagerly, as they accepted their own invitations. Whatever that meant, Evie thought. She shivered again, conscious of the handsome man in black watching her.

'Come inside, you are cold.'

'It's too noisy,' she said, thinking of the crowded room of people, all eager to meet their host.

'There's a quieter room upstairs.' He indicated a spiral staircase to one side of the balcony, hidden by a bay tree in a huge planter.

'Should we be making ourselves at home like that?' Evie asked, arching one eyebrow.

'It is my home,' he said simply. 'I am Count Romulo. I threw this party to meet you . . .'

Evie loved Simon's town house. She loved the pastel walls, the neat collection of classical CDs, the pot plants he cared for so carefully and the pale carpet that covered every room, apart from his white-tiled en-suite bathroom which was a bit clinical for her taste. Of course, she couldn't see Rosie ever fitting into Simon's pristine home.

His immaculate bachelor pad wasn't built for a rangy teenager who draped coats over the banisters, left opened magazines on every available surface and leg hairs in the sink, and liked to lounge on the sofa watching TV, eating breakfast cereal and talking to her friends on the phone all at the same time.

Evie and Simon hadn't finalised what they were going to do about living arrangements when they got married. She didn't think his house would be suitable for all three of them, because it was so small. But she somehow couldn't see him living in her home either.

The more she thought about it, the more Evie became convinced that they'd have to sell both houses and buy something else. Which would mean a big mortgage. She hated the thought of being in debt. What would happen if Simon left her or if he died? Where would she be then? Broke and on her own, the way she had been seventeen years ago. She shivered at the memory.

'Evie!' Simon opened the door wearing a butcher's apron over his white shirt. He'd taken off his tie and opened the top two buttons of his shirt, making him look young and vulnerable. With his sandy hair standing up where he'd raked it anxiously, he looked more like thirty-one than forty-one.

She stood on her tiptoes to kiss him lightly on the mouth, smelling rather than tasting onions on his breath.

'What are you cooking?' she asked, as she followed him through into the pale green kitchen.

'Roast chicken, chips and deep fried onion rings,' he replied, glasses steaming up as he peered cautiously into the deep fat fryer.

'Lovely,' Evie murmured, thinking regretfully of the calorific content of a deep fried meal. She had told Simon she was desperate to lose a few pounds, but he'd obviously forgotten in his enthusiasm to use the deep fat fryer his mother had given him for Christmas.

Still, it was glorious to be pampered, to have somebody else cooking dinner for her. Rosie never made dinner if she could possibly help it, and when she did it was beans on toast with yoghurt for dessert.

'Are we having apple fritters for dessert to continue the deep fried theme?' Evie inquired with a chuckle, wrapping her arms around Simon from behind and hugging him.

He laughed. 'I never thought of that or I'd have bought some. I can't help it that I can't cook,' he added apologetically. 'You can't go wrong with this stuff.' He dislodged Evie as he hurried over to the oven to check the chicken, which turned out to be roasting in a pool of grease.

'Simon! That's swimming in fat,' she exclaimed. 'Drain most of it away. It'll taste disgusting.'

'I didn't know how much to put in,' he mumbled, holding the tin uneasily with a pair of hideous pink lobster oven gloves. 'I've never done an entire chicken before, only chicken breasts.'

'Here, let me.' Evie took over, expertly handling the heavy roasting tin. 'You should have made something simple,' she scolded as she rescued their dinner from drowning.

'I wanted to impress you.' Simon stood miserably by the sink, still wearing his lobster gloves. 'I can't dial up the Chinese takeaway every time you come to dinner.'

He looked so forlorn that she relented.

'You don't need to impress me,' she said firmly.

After dinner, they sat and watched TV, Simon's arm around Evie's shoulders. She leaned against his chest comfortably, slipped off her shoes and curled her feet up under her on the couch. He flicked channels until he came to a documentary on the most thrilling car chases of all time. As the world had only had cars for the past century, Evie thought the series title was a bit misleading but she said nothing. Car chases bored her to tears.

After fifteen minutes, she'd seen enough helicopter footage of speeding Corvettes to last her a lifetime. She shifted in her seat, moving closer to Simon. Her fingers curled under the edges of his shirt, gently stroking the bare skin.

Slowly, she unbuttoned his shirt and her fingers slid further up his chest to stroke him tenderly. Then she gently moved her hands down over his torso, lingering tantalisingly close to his nipples. Still Simon said nothing. When she moved her face towards him to nuzzle his neck and he didn't make a single noise of appreciation, Evie gave up. Pulling away, she looked up at his face with vexation. He was gazing at the television raptly and seemed unaware she was even there.

Evie dragged herself upright, snatched a newspaper from the coffee table and sat away from him. Honestly, she didn't know why she bothered. They sat there without talking for another half an hour when Simon decided he wanted another cup of tea.

'Do you want some, darling?' he asked solicitously, seemingly unaware of Evie's temper, despite the glacial expression on her face.

'No,' she said sulkily.

'Yell if you change your mind,' he said, heading for the kitchen, blithely unaware of her mood. 'I'm making a quick cup before that new programme about killers on death row starts. The trailers have been fascinating. There's this guy who's been given a reprieve three times in the past ten years and he's still appealing . . .'

Evie would have choked on her tea if she'd been drinking any. *Killers on death row?* Wonderful. Simon was obsessed with American television. He had all the satellite channels and was glued to any programme about true crime. He'd never bothered with the movie channels or the Gold TV station – which Evie would have adored because of all the re-runs of romantic mini-series. She'd never been able to afford them herself, even though Rosie had begged long enough.

'*Everyone's* got the movie channels,' her daughter had moaned practically every day for a year.

In the end, Evie had nearly given in, because she didn't want her beloved daughter to miss out on anything her friends had, even if it meant she wouldn't be able to afford to buy the new winter coat she needed. And then Rosie had stopped asking for the movie channel.

'We could get it,' Evie had offered. 'I can afford to now.'

Rosie shrugged. 'There's no need, Mum. It's great for kids, you know, but I'll be going out in the evenings more now.'

The ad break was over and Simon's programme was starting.

'Hurry up,' she roared in the direction of the kitchen, 'or you'll miss it.'

It was nine o'clock. She might as well go home. She'd planned to stay until ten but what was the point if he was going to be glued to death row? At least at home she could tidy up and get organised for the next day.

Simon placed a tray with two cups of tea and a packet of her favourite biscuits on the coffee table in front of her. Then he leaned over and kissed her gently on the forehead.

'I know you said you didn't want any, but in case you'd changed your mind, I made you a cup. ' He kissed her again. 'You need pampering and I like doing it.'

134

Speechless, Evie smiled up at him happily, plans to go home immediately forgotten. He was so good to her.

They sat snuggled up on the couch, nibbling biscuits and watching the grim stories of American criminals. When Simon took off her shoes and made Evie put her feet up on the couch, she leaned against him contentedly.

Ten minutes of careful rubbing with leather cleaner hadn't worked: neither had fifteen minutes' scrubbing with cream cleanser. Olivia was pretty sure that cream cleanser wasn't good for leather couches but at this point, she didn't care. She'd have put bleach on the couch if she thought it would remove the bright pink squiggle, anything to avoid the inevitable explosion that would occur when Stephen saw it.

If only four-year-old Emily had managed to leave her mark anywhere other than on the arm of the couch Stephen liked to lounge on when he watched television. As it was, the mark was quite noticeable and unless Olivia draped herself over the arm of the couch all evening, not getting up for anything, he was going to notice it. And then all hell would break loose.

There was bound to be something especially for leather furniture, some proprietary cleaner that would wipe off bright pink marker in a flash. But there was no way Olivia would be able to buy it this evening, which meant she had to hide the offending pink bit until she had a chance to go shopping the next day.

Emily's mother, Carol, arrived mid-scrub, a fresh-faced woman of forty. Her dark hair was in a pony-tail and she wore her usual outfit of jeans and a sweatshirt.

Finding Olivia's cleaning equipment spread all over the sitting-room floor, she immediately realised what had happened and was contrite when she realised Emily's penmanship was responsible for desecrating several thousand pounds' worth of Scandinavian leather.

'Olivia, I do apologise,' she said, hands flying to her mouth. 'I am so sorry. I don't know what to say.'

'Don't worry, Carol,' Olivia replied, as if she wasn't in the slightest bit concerned.

'But your beautiful couch . . .'

'Sasha's daddy will be very cross,' interrupted Emily, beginning to cry noisily with the drama of the whole affair.

Snuffling precariously, Sasha nodded her head. 'He will,' she said, before she too started to cry. 'He'll be very cross with Mummy and me.'

'Don't be silly, girls,' Olivia said gaily, bending down and hugging both children to her.

Carol looked curious. 'Will he?' she asked.

'Gosh, no,' Olivia said, hoping she wasn't going to flush puce with embarrassment. She couldn't bear Carol to think that Stephen was some sort of tyrant. 'He's totally easygoing. *I'm* the one who goes mad about marks on things,' she lied blithely. 'Stephen's such a pussycat he can't get angry with Sasha about anything.'

'Sounds just like my George,' the other woman said. 'I was always trying that "wait until your father gets home" trick until my lot realised it was complete rubbish. He doesn't really care if they ruin the place. Men, huh?'

'Yes, George must be just like Stephen,' Olivia said faintly. 'Men don't care too much about furniture, do they?'

'You'd probably be as well off to leave that stain and get a professional in to clean it,' Carol advised. 'I'll pay whatever it costs as it's Emily's handiwork.' She ruffled her daughter's hair and Emily bawled louder.

'I wouldn't dream of it,' Olivia said. 'I shouldn't have let them out of the kitchen with those markers, it's my fault. Don't worry about it.'

When Carol had gone, Olivia hunkered down beside Sasha. 'Daddy won't be cross,' she said gently. 'I promise.'

Her daughter didn't look too convinced.

'Come on, let's put on a video. How about *The Little Mermaid*?'

Cheering up, Sasha plonked herself down in front of the TV with her favourite soft toy, a much-loved grey rabbit called Muffy. As Sasha became engrossed in Ariel's adventures, Olivia tidied away her cleaning products with a heavy heart. Nothing she had was going to remove the stain, she might as well face facts.

Desperate for a solution, she hit upon the idea of swopping the two couches around so that Stephen would be sitting on the undamaged one and she could leave something, her cardigan perhaps, on the marked one. That was it.

Three hours later, he arrived home, tired and hungry.

He wasn't in the mood for conversation and read the paper throughout dinner.

'Is it all right?' Olivia asked, hovering around with the saucepan containing mashed potato in case he wanted more.

'Fine,' he said, tight-lipped, and went back to the paper.

Olivia, who'd given herself a tiny portion of dinner, pushed her food around the plate. She didn't want Stephen to see her eating nothing because he'd be bound to ask what was wrong.

Yet he appeared too engrossed in the paper to notice anything. After ten more silent minutes, she quietly dumped her untouched dinner in the bin. It was a pity Stephen wouldn't even consider getting the puppy Sasha longed for: no animal would ever go hungry with all the food she threw out.

She cleared Stephen's plate and placed a bowl of his

favourite Apple Charlotte in front of him. It disappeared behind the paper and reappeared five minutes later, empty.

Olivia stacked the dishwasher and was about to ask Stephen if he wanted coffee when she realised he'd left the kitchen. She slammed the dishwasher shut and hurried after him.

The cardigan she'd draped artfully across the marked couch arm was still there. Stephen was draped less artfully across the couch he favoured, the paper in a crumpled heap on the floor, sports on the television.

'Did you want coffee?' Olivia asked.

'No,' he said brusquely. 'I've drunk about ten cups already today. I'm rattling with caffeine. Some bloody fool in the office screwed up the Hong Kong deal and we spent the whole day sorting it out. Not that it's sorted out yet,' he snorted. 'I'll be working till all hours tomorrow.'

And that was it. That was the extent of their marital discussion for the evening. Stephen went back to the television, restlessly changing channels to see what was on the other channels.

Olivia picked up the paper he had discarded and sat down on the other couch, careful not to dislodge the cardigan. He didn't speak again for another half an hour and then it was only to ask her to get a bottle of wine.

'I need it,' he said.

After two glasses, he switched the TV off.

'Bed?' he said.

Olivia checked on Sasha before switching on the bathroom light and going into their bedroom. Stephen had pulled the duvet back and had taken off his shirt. His bare chest was muscular and covered with curling dark hairs that matched the tight curls on his head. His soulful dark eyes were black with desire.

He pulled her to him, kissing her deeply on the mouth before moving down to her neck.

'God, you're so beautiful, Olivia,' he murmured, hands greedily sliding up her jumper to reveal small breasts encased in the expensive cream silk lace bra he'd bought her for Christmas. They sank to the bed. He caressed her urgently, kissing and licking her through the lace before eagerly unfastening the bra. He didn't wait to take it or the jumper off – he pushed them out of his way.

His mouth fastened on her nipple and he sucked hungrily. Olivia always loved it when Stephen did that: she adored the exquisite sensations it sent searing up and down her body. Breasts were such erogenous zones, hers anyhow.

But not tonight, not like this.

She lay on the bed like the doll she felt she resembled, a lifeless marble creature to be displayed and played with. Nothing more.

'You're so beautiful, I could look at you for hours,' he moaned, his voice thick with desire.

He rapidly took off the rest of his clothes and pulled off Olivia's jumper and bra.

She stood up to slide off her skirt and tights.

'Stand there,' he said, holding her waist as she stood, semi-naked in front of him.

'I could watch you all night,' he said, eyes hungry for her. Then he grinned and pulled her down on to the bed under him. 'But maybe not!'

He slept afterwards, worn out after his energetic efforts. Olivia lay beside her sleeping husband in their marital bed and gazed unseeing at the opposite wall. When his breathing became heavy and deep, she slipped out of the bed and peered into Sasha's room. One fat little thumb in her mouth, the child lay asleep, eyelids flickering as she sailed through the world of dreams where daddies never got cross and mummies never got depressed. Olivia wished she could join her daughter in dreamland.

CHAPTER SIX

The doorbell rang loudly. Cara, slumped in front of the telly on the only armchair with springs worth talking about, refused to move.

'It'll be for you, Phoebs,' she roared in the direction of the bathroom where her flatmate was frantically doing things with body lotion and mascara in honour of the gorgeous Bureau De Change man coming on his first visit to Château Chaos.

'Please answer the door, Cara,' hissed Phoebe, opening the door a fraction to let steamy, Eternity-scented air filter out in an overpowering blast. 'I'm still in my knickers.'

'He'd love that,' grumbled Cara, as she levered herself out of the chair. She'd spent all of *Eastenders* adjusting their only cushion into the correct position so that the weird bump on the chair didn't stick painfully into her back. She'd never re-position it properly in time for the big film.

She padded across the floor in her socks and wiped away a droplet of conditioner which had escaped from the do-it-yourself hair conditioning treatment that consisted of plenty of hot oil and a load of clingfilm wrapped around your head for an hour. It made her look like an extra from a very old episode of *Star Trek* but Phoebe swore by it.

Cara opened the door and swore. 'Shit!' she said. The athletic Adonis standing outside clutching a six-pack, a tattered woollen scarf and a plastic bag, blinked long dark eyelashes at her and shook some snow from his silky dark hair.

'I meant . . . er, shit, I didn't hear the doorbell ring,' Cara gasped inanely, hand going instantly to her *Star Trek* hair-do. 'Er . . . did you ring often?'

'Only once,' said Adonis, looking bemused. 'You're Cara, right?'

She nodded, still staring at the chiselled face and the full, sensuous lips chapped endearingly by the cold.

'I'm Ricky.'

He looked like he'd just stepped off the pitch of an international soccer match. He was at the peak of his physical condition, all healthy skin, shining eyes and rippling, freshly washed hair. Faded jeans, so tight they threatened to cut off the blood supply to his legs, were moulded to footballer's thighs. He wore a small gold cross on a chain around his neck and under his dark woollen jacket was a loose white shirt with plenty of buttons undone despite the arctic weather outside.

Cara knew her mouth was open but she couldn't help it. Boy, Phoebe, were you ever right? she said silently. He was gorgeous. Abso-bloody-lutely gorgeous.

She forced her jaw shut. 'Come in.'

He moved into the tiny hall and took off his coat. As Cara lingered to shut the door, she found herself eyeing his bum in the spray-on jeans. It was just as perfect as the rest of him; taut and set off by lean hips. Woof!

'Go on in,' she said, pointing the way through to the sitting room as if it was a palatial drawing room instead of a terminally messy kitchen-cum-sitting room with a moth-eaten fake suede sofa, two shabby green armchairs and a collection of magazines and papers dumped on the glass-topped table in the centre of the room. Cara was too distracted at the thought of being caught with clingfilm on her head to care about the state of the flat.

'I brought beer,' Ricky said, turning round and giving her the sort of heart-stopping smile that made her fervently wish she wasn't in her oldest, grubbiest jeans and the sweatshirt she'd worn on the bus home from Ballymoreen that morning.

'I'll put it in the fridge,' she said, 'although it's so cold in here we don't really need to,' she added, with a little giggle.

Cara, you plonker, she told herself disgustedly as she stuffed the beer into the fridge along with the remains of their Christmas consignment of booze. You actually *giggled*. All it takes is one handsome man to walk into the room and you're giggling like some dozy sun-bedded blonde with zero qualifications apart from a degree in men. Ugh!

'Will I light the fire?' Ricky offered.

And he was useful too. Cara would have swooned if she knew how.

'Sure. That'd be great. It's hard to get those briquettes going. I think they're a dodgy batch.'

'No problem,' he replied, attention turned to the fire-place.

'I'll tell Phoebe you're here.'

Cara tried to exit the room as gracefully as you could with a headful of conditioner encased in clingfilm. She shoved open the bathroom door and was enveloped in a cloud of steam.

'You never told me he was *that* gorgeous,' she hissed at Phoebe as they immediately banged into each other in the six foot by five foot space.

'I did too,' Phoebe said slowly, her attention on getting her tights straight.

143

'Does he have any brothers?' Cara demanded, rubbing a bit of steamed-up mirror to see precisely how hideous she looked.

'No. But he has lots of friends.'

'If they all look like him, I'm coming with you on your next date. Lucky cow,' she added.

Phoebe smiled radiantly. She'd spent ages blowdrying her hair until it was a mass of non-frizzy curls that fell flatteringly around her face disguising her round milk-maid's cheeks. Wearing a short lacy skirt, shiny black tights and a tight little floral top, none of which was suitable for an evening in a flat with no central heating, she looked brilliant.

Cara told her so.

'Do you think so?' Phoebe asked, twiddling with her bra strap to hoist up her boobs, eyes glued critically to the mirror.

'Fabulous. He'll be in paroxysms of lust as soon as he sees you. Maybe I should go out for the evening and give you two the chance to have fun on your own?'

'No,' Phoebe said firmly. 'We're all watching *Gone With The Wind*. I told him we were having an evening in. He's broke too, so we've no money to go out.'

'I'll wash the gunk from my hair,' Cara said, hanging her head over the bath and reaching for the shower attachment.

Scarlett had married poor Charles Hamilton and was living it up in Atlanta purely to spite Ashley Wilkes by the time Cara returned to the sitting room. Her hair was half-dry, she'd changed into a clean sweatshirt and had borrowed some of Phoebe's LouLou perfume. She didn't know why she'd bothered to make herself look more presentable. Ricky was Phoebe's boyfriend after all, and Cara would have rather run around Leinster Square naked in the snow than steal her flatmate's man, but when he'd turned up and found her looking as if she'd just been bathing in turkey fat after spending the day working as a brickie, Cara had felt mortified. She didn't want this handsome bloke to think she was a slovenly slapper who thought washing powder was rationed.

Especially since Phoebe had made such an effort and looked ten times dressier than she usually did when she wasn't stuck behind the bank counter doling out crisp tenners. Phoebe's weekend uniform was jeans and a sweat-shirt, just like Cara's. For slobbing around watching TV, the pair of them generally wore their ragged towelling dressing gowns and looked like they'd stepped off the set of a sit-com about people in hospital.

Cara grabbed a bottle of Beck's from the fridge and slid into her seat again. The furry leopardskin cushion was gone and now supported Ricky's dark head, which was angled very closely beside Phoebe's fair one. One of his long-fingered hands lay snugly on her glossy knee, fingers curved inwards under the hem of her flirty little skirt.

Cara would have bet a week's wages that it wouldn't be long before the fingers and the hand were moving stealth-ily upwards. She felt an unaccustomed stab of envy at the thought.

He turned to look at her as she settled herself into the chair.

'What's happening?' she asked brightly, as if she hadn't seen *Gone With The Wind* at least fifteen times already. It was Evie's favourite film and when Cara had been young, it had been as much a part of Christmas as crackers and a tinsel-encrusted tree that the dogs had knocked into ten times a day.

'Nothing much,' Ricky said in bored tones.

Cara looked at him sharply. What did he mean: nothing

much? He was talking about a wonderful movie, certainly one of her favourites.

She took a swig of beer and tried to concentrate but only a few minutes had gone by before Ricky's hand began its careful ascent up Phoebe's leg and under her skirt. Cara tried not to look.

Phoebe giggled softly and Ricky whispered something in her ear. She giggled again, huskier this time, and moved sideways so he could wrap his other arm around her.

Cara shifted uncomfortably on her chair so she could barely see them and wished she wasn't there. For another ten minutes she tried to block out what was happening in the room and concentrate on Scarlett but it was impossible.

'Another beer, anyone?' she asked, launching herself out of her chair energetically and trying not to look in their direction.

'No,' said Phoebe in a muffled voice.

Cara shuffled off to the fridge, feeling as in the way as a male stripper at a lesbian coffee morning. She was hungry again and the fridge was, predictably enough, empty. About to extract another beer, she suddenly changed her mind. She'd phone Zoë. Perhaps they could go for a drink or even out for something to eat. Anything to get away from the misery of watching young love in action when she was so undeniably a spinster.

It wasn't that she begrudged Phoebe the gorgeous Ricky: not at all. Lord knows, Phoebe deserved a decent bloke after the miserable years it had taken her to get over her childhood sweetheart's dumping her and marrying some-one else. No, Cara wished nothing but the best for her friend.

It was just that the pair of them usually lurched from crisis to crisis together, manless – apart from the selection of losers Phoebe routinely ended up going out with for one drink – and happy. With Phoebs in boyfriend bliss, they were no longer the Two Musketeers. They were One Normal Woman, Now Part Of A Couple, and her Oddball Flatmate who never had lovers, apart from the unmentionable drunken liaisons with office motorbike couriers. Wallowing in self-pity, Cara decided to treat herself to the last Mars Bar ice cream in the ice box. She deserved it. That, and some serious whingeing with Zoë would cheer her up.

Zoë arrived in Slattery's half an hour later looking marginally more depressed than Cara. Her cropped red hair was flattened to her skull with rain that had seeped through her crochet hat, and her nose was like a bulbous crimson lump on her face, thanks to a streaming head cold.

'Heddo,' she said in bunged-up tones. 'I've gob a cold.'

'You poor thing,' said Cara pityingly, putting an arm around her friend's skinny little frame. 'Hot whiskey will cure you.'

Being a statuesque five foot eleven, it was no bother to Cara to push through the crowded pub like a snow plough with Zoë in her wake until they found a couple vacating a table and two stools.

Diving past a slow-moving guy in an anorak who also had his eye on the vacant table, Cara grabbed both stools and sank on to one, giving Anorak Man a hard stare, her gypsyish face haughty. He looked as if he was about to complain until he realised Cara was at least four inches taller than him and fierce-looking, so stalked off, grumbling. There were times when it was useful to be an Amazon, she thought, flicking back her long black hair and giving Zoë a mischievous grin that made her high cheekbones look more Apache princess than ever.

After one hot whiskey, Zoë's nose was de-bunged enough for her to talk intelligibly.

'My brothers and I went into Tralee on Stephen's Night and on the way back, Damien's car broke down. We had to walk the last mile home and it was lashing,' she said, cradling the hot glass in her hands. 'We all got soaked. You know me, I just have to look at rain and I've got the 'flu. This cold just won't go away.'

'I'm so sorry,' Cara said, immediately contrite. 'I shouldn't have asked you out tonight. It's pelting down outside.'

'I'd rather be out than sitting at home watching Christopher and his latest boyfriend drooling all over each other,' grumbled Zoë, who lived in a tiny rented town house with an outrageously camp fashion stylist named Christopher. 'They insisted on watching *Funny Girl* and wouldn't let me watch *EastEnders*. Then they spent the entire film whispering sweet nothings in each other's ears and discussing whether they preferred *Yentl* or *What's Up, Doc?* in between screaming about how "gorgeous" Barbra is. I thought I'd hit Christopher.'

'Join the club,' Cara said. 'Phoebe has finally got Mr Bureau De Change to visit and they're so welded together, you wouldn't fit a ten-pence piece between the two of them. They were probably re-enacting a slushy movie on top of the kitchen counters five seconds after I slammed the front door. True love can be very depressing,' she said in maudlin tones.

'Bugger true love!' exclaimed Zoë. 'It's true lust I'm talking about. I haven't had a man fiddling around with my underwear since I was at the doctor's for that cervical smear last September. I need a man,' she rasped in her best Marlene Dietrich voice.

Several men swivelled around on their bar stools with grins on their faces, eyeing up the tall dark girl and the small redhead huddled in a voluminous cardigan.

'She doesn't mean immediately,' Cara informed the eager onlookers acidly. 'We mean for stud purposes, much later, so we don't have to talk to you.'

'Lezzers,' hissed one discomfited bloke. 'Don't fancy either of ya, anyway!'

They ignored him.

'Ewan at work is very attractive,' Zoë said idly, picking cloves out of her glass, 'and he likes you.'

'But I've practically never even spoken to him,' Cara protested.

'Maybe that's why,' Zoë added wickedly. 'Seriously, he's a decent bloke. He gave me a lift home one night when we were both leaving the office late. He drives an MG.'

'So he's decent boyfriend material because he has a car, is that it?' demanded Cara tetchily. 'It's immaterial whether he's an axe murderer or not because he has wheels?'

'He's nice and just *happens to have* a car. That's not why he's nice, but it helps. You're narky tonight, Cara.'

'Sorry.' She stared into her empty glass glumly. 'I feel a bit depressed, that's all. Seeing Phoebe with Ricky made me feel like some decrepit maiden aunt destined to a life of celibacy and never having anyone to spend time with.'

'I keep coming up with possible men and you keep dismissing them!' Zoë said irritably.

'I know . . . Do you want another hot whiskey?'

'Don't change the subject. You've got to give men a chance,' Zoë argued.

'You know why I don't,' Cara muttered, wishing this conversation would end.

'You should have got over that years ago. I doubt if he's spent the rest of his life brooding over you.'

Cara stared at her friend angrily, eyes blazing.

'That's different!' she said hotly.

'No, it's not. If you never let another man near you again, then he's won and you always vowed you'd never let him win.'

They sat in silence for a moment, Zoë's words hanging in the air like giant icicles.

'I suppose you want another drink?' Cara said finally.

The tension evaporated and Zoë relaxed on her stool.

'I'd love one. But only one. *We don't want to be late for our first day back at work,*' she said, mimicking Bernard Redmond's booming tones. 'I'll hate going back tomorrow,' she added with a grimace. 'Do you think Bernard will have any New Year's resolutions planned that'll turn him into something approaching a human being?'

Cara snorted. 'The only resolutions he'll have are to cut the tea break bill by rationing tea bags and to switch the heating down a few degrees to save money on gas.'

They chatted for another hour before they left for home, Zoë turning up towards Rathgar Road where she lived with Christopher, Cara turning down towards Leinster Road.

When she turned the key in the door, the flat was lit up like a Christmas tree with every light and lamp burning brightly and a comedy show blaring from the TV. Phoebe was nowhere to be seen but the moans coming from her bedroom told Cara where she was. Ricky was apparently staying the night, although sleep obviously wasn't on the agenda.

She went around switching off lights, put the lock on the front door and went into her room. It was just as much of a mess as it had been before she left for Christmas: clothes strewn everywhere, books in leaning Tower of Pisa piles on the floor and boots and shoes scattered around near the dust-ridden dressing table. Ignoring the mess, she went into the bathroom for her night-time ablutions. She still couldn't shake Zoë's words from her head: *'You should have got over that years ago. I doubt if he's spent the rest of his life brooding over you . . . If you never let another man near you, then he's won and you always vowed you'd never let him win.'*

As she brushed her teeth, Cara looked at the tired face in the mirror and remembered what she'd looked like six and a half years ago. Then, her black curly hair had been cut in a shaggy style, soft curls feathered against cheek-bones that weren't as pronounced thanks to the puppy fat that remained even though she was on the verge of making the jump from teenager to twenty year old.

She'd emphasised her hazel eyes with eyeshadow and always wore rich ruby lipstick. It was very different from now when the most make-up she wore was mascara and colourless Body Shop lip balm. Her clothes had been different too: after years of drab convent school greys and the hideous A-line pinafore all St Agatha's girls were forced into, Cara had embraced the world of mufti with delight. Living away from home for the first time, even if she was living in Dublin with Evie and therefore under her watchful, ultra-protective eye, Cara felt grown up, confident and ready for anything. A convert to mini-skirts, she never covered up her long legs and the sight of Cara Fraser striding across the courtyard in black opaque tights and an excuse for a skirt brightened many a dull morning for the male students of Slaney Art College.

And not just the students, Cara thought, her eyes blank. Maybe if she hadn't gone so mad wearing youthfully exuberant clothes, it never would have happened. Those skimpy T-shirts she loved to wear under her regulation black man's cardigan just drew attention to her, and as for the black John Richmond knee-high suede boots with the buckles – fatal. She'd bought them in a second-hand shop in Temple Bar for fun but they looked like the sort of things a serious dominatrix would don for a night of pain. The nineteen-year-old Cara hadn't minded the attention she got when wearing them. She'd loved her new found skill at flirting, loved discovering she was a natural at it.

Having anyone who wanted to flirt with her in the first place was a novelty. Nobody had ever chatted her up before. The boys in Ballymoreen had known her in all her chunky, tomboyish glory and had considered her one of them, an honorary lad. But the guys in Slaney were a ripe crop ready to be picked by the mature reinvented Cara.

Her old friends, used to the tough girl who could play football with as much skill as any of them, wouldn't have recognised her during those first few months in college. The boots were part of her new sexy and independent image. Although you wouldn't think mere boots would drive so many men so wild. She'd thrown them out since, mainly because she'd been wearing them the day it started.

Cara sometimes forgot what she'd done the week before and she could never remember important dates like when she'd had her period or what date the electricity company insisted on being paid by. But the events of that freezing October morning were imprinted in her brain on indelible tissue. She'd never forget it. Never.

She'd missed the first bus from the end of Evie's road and then, when she got on the next one, an accident on the dual carriageway meant the bus was stationary for at least fifteen minutes. By the time Cara flew through the doors of Slaney College, en route for Mr Theal's History of Art class, she was half an hour late.

'I apologise,' she gasped, trying to creep into the lecture hall where the other thirty people in her year sat quietly taking notes. 'I missed my bus. I'm really sorry.'

Mr Theal – sorry, not Mr Theal: 'Call me Owen, class, you're in college now, not school' – had looked at her slowly, a calculating gaze at odds with the avuncular impression he'd tried to create during the previous classes where he'd brought them all to the pub for a drink on him.

With his sleekly brushed back dark hair and deep-set dark eyes, the other girls in her class said he was gorgeous. 'A ride,' according to one admirer. He dressed much better than most of the other lecturers. That day he was wearing a fashionable suit over a collarless shirt. He was sitting comfortably on a low chair, facing the class instead of looking at the slide show on the wall behind him, giving the impression that he knew the painting he was talking about backwards and didn't need so much as to look at it. Then he smiled at her, a warm smile as if they were the only two people in the room; as if they were close, dear friends instead of a teacher and a tardy pupil.

'You'll have to stay back to see what you've missed and how you can catch up,' he said easily.

'Of course,' panted Cara as she made her way to her seat, breathless after her sprint from the bus stop and delighted to be in so little trouble for her lateness. Staying after class was *nothing*. In St Agatha's, being late would result in a ten-minute lecture from the teacher and probably a four-page essay on whatever topic was being discussed as punishment. In the small convent school, punctuality was only one step behind cleanliness in being next to Godliness.

Relieved, and in her naivety never once questioning why a college lecturer would care less about a first-year student missing the initial ten minutes of a lecture, Cara got out her pad and began to take notes.

She loved the History of Art classes. Much more detailed than her secondary school curriculum, the programme in

Slaney College's foundation art course was incredibly varied and all-encompassing. Mr Theal's class on eighteenth-century French painters soon had her enthralled. Told in his rich baritone, Theal's stories about Jacques-Louis David came vividly to life and he imbued the paintings he showed on the slides with more life and vigour than ever Sister Concepta had been able to.

The lecture was over before Cara knew it and as she stuffed her A-4 pad into her bag, thinking of her next lecture, she almost forgot she'd been late and had to stay behind. Owen Theal hadn't forgotten.

'Cara,' he said as she passed, his voice silky. 'We need to talk.'

'Yes, we do,' she said, flustered at how rude she must have seemed. 'I forgot.'

'We've got the Professor in five minutes,' warned one of the male students as he walked out of the room.

'It's all rush, rush, rush,' Owen Theal said, leaning back against his desk and folding his arms across his chest. He was the picture of relaxation, the king in his castle. 'Go to the Professor's lecture, Cara,' he said, his voice amused. '*He* hates people being late.'

She coloured.

'But I do want to have a few minutes with you later today. You're one of the most promising students we've got on the course this year and I don't want to see you drop out for any reason. I'd like to help you and to encourage your talent. Can I do that, Cara?'

He gave her an intense look from those dark eyes. Tortured artist's eyes, she thought irrationally, like a martyr in an El Greco painting.

'Come to my office this evening,' Owen said firmly. 'At half-four.'

Talented, huh? His flattering words buzzing around her

154

head like a swarm of summer midges, she hurried along the corridor with a swing in her step. *One of the most promising students on the course and I don't want to see you drop out for any reason . . .*

She'd always adored art; now this important lecturer was telling her she was talented after all, that she had the skill to make it in the art world! She couldn't wait to tell Evie. It was dizzying, thrilling, especially after that horrible year suffering through the secretarial course she'd loathed. She felt vindicated at last. Her sister had gently nudged her into the small-town secretarial course: 'just so you have something to fall back on'.

In other words: 'in case you make a dreadful artist and can't afford the rent, you can always type'.

Cara had hated it and had longed for the year to pass so she could apply for art college in Dublin. Now she'd barely settled into Slaney when her talent had been recognised. Thank you, thank you, thank you! she sang to herself all morning.

The day passed in a haze. At four, her new friend Zoë suggested a trip to Nassau Street for coffee and a meander about the bookshops.

'Can't,' Cara said apologetically, 'I'm meeting someone.'

She didn't know why she'd covered up her meeting with Owen Theal. After all, it was perfectly legitimate and to do with college work, but she felt it would have been bragging to say she was meeting a lecturer because he thought she was talented and wanted to give her special attention.

It'd be awkward to say it, it'd probably make Zoë feel left out and not-so-talented. So she kept quiet and lived to regret it.

It was a long time later that Cara discovered he tried it on with all of them, all the female students who'd listen,

155

including Zoë. Only Cara had been stupid and naive enough to let him get away with it.

'Naive,' suggested Zoë kindly later on.

'Stupid,' Cara said bitterly.

He'd taken Zoë to the pub and tried to ply her with Scotch, telling her she was talented and very beautiful into the bargain. Streetwise and with a strong head for whiskey thanks to the illegal Irish poteen her father always kept a supply of, she'd downed her first drink in a practised motion and told Owen Theal if he ever laid a hand on her again, he'd live to regret it.

'He's not a lecturer, he's a lecherer,' Zoë said harshly, much later. 'Scum of the earth.'

Blissfully unaware of all this, Cara went to the loo at a quarter past four and fluffed up her hair until it framed her face in a flattering dark cloud. She gave herself a blast of deodorant for fear of smelling sweaty after her early-morning dash through the traffic and put on some lipstick before wiping it off hastily. You're going to be talking about college work, for God's sake, she told herself. Let him see how seriously you take your art – he's probably sick to the teeth of flirty students who bat their eyelashes at him and conveniently forget what they're there for.

At half-four exactly, she knocked on Owen Theal's office door and he opened it immediately, his coat in his hand.

Cara faltered. 'Sorry, did I come at the wrong time? Are you going out?'

Theal smiled, with a glint in his dark eyes. 'No, *we're* going out. It's a bitterly cold day and a drink will warm us up. Besides, it's nice to get out of this place occasionally.'

They walked companionably along the road with Theal explaining that he loved Dublin's Georgian architecture but his favourite city, architecturally speaking, was Paris.

He'd travelled all over the world and by the time they were ensconced in the tiny Dawson Lounge, he'd told Cara about his year in France and the subsequent two years when he explored Europe, journeyed to India, and even spent some time on a New Zealand vineyard.

'You've been everywhere,' she said, eyes shining with admiration. 'I've only been on a plane once!'

'You'll travel, don't worry,' he reassured her. 'What's your poison?'

'Er . . . coffee?' Cara said.

Theal brushed that idea aside. 'Nonsense. You'll have a real drink. Do you like Scotch?' He didn't wait for her to answer but ordered two Scotches with ice.

Not used to drinking anything stronger than wine or beer, Cara found the whisky burned the back of her throat but, not wishing to seem ungrateful or rude, she drank it anyway.

Owen was so easy to talk to. And so interested in her. He really wanted to know all about her: what she liked, what she didn't like. Where she lived, who she lived with, why she'd decided to go to art college . . . Warmed by the alcohol and his interest, Cara found herself talking nineteen to the dozen about how she'd adored paintings when she was younger and how she'd bury herself in library books about the Prado in Madrid until she felt as if she'd really seen all the Goyas and Velasquez.

She didn't notice Owen silently ordering another drink and sliding her empty glass away to replace it with a double. He was drinking very quickly. Ridiculously, she felt she had to keep up, like eating your soup at the same speed as everyone else so you won't keep them waiting for the next course.

'We recognise each other, we artists,' he said solemnly, running one finger around the rim of his now-empty glass.

'I think that's why I brought you here to talk to you – I know you're different, you're like me. You're an artist.'

'D-do you think so?' Cara stammered.

'Of course.' He smiled broadly. 'I can spot it a mile off. It's in your hands.' He picked up her right hand and held it carefully in both of his, his fingers warm and sensitive as they examined hers and caressed her palm.

Cara said nothing. She didn't know what to say. This was all very strange.

'You must let me help you, Cara,' he said earnestly.

'Well, er . . . yes,' she replied.

As abruptly as he'd started, Owen dropped her hand and began talking about college and the syllabus. Cara, who'd been getting nervous what with all the hand holding stuff, relaxed again. He was simply being friendly. He was artistic and didn't operate by normal rules. No other teacher would hold your hand like that: Owen was different, that was all. He got them another drink.

'Please, let me pay,' said Cara, embarrassed, hating him to think she was mean even though her bank account boasted only fifty pounds that had to do her for the next two months.

'Don't be ridiculous. You're an impoverished student, I'll pay,' Owen said fondly.

After their fourth drink, things began to feel a bit hazy. Cara felt her insides lurch from the combination of alcohol and no food. Her face was flushed and she knew she wasn't making too much sense. But Owen Theal didn't seem to mind. He appeared to love listening to her. He sat beside her – not touching her – listening raptly. It was nice, she thought dreamily, nice to be listened to so intently.

She didn't want the fifth, and very large-looking, drink but he insisted.

'We're celebrating,' he said smoothly, pushing the glass

into her hands. 'You'd be insulting me if you said no.'

'I don't want to do that,' Cara said, flustered. She didn't know you could insult someone by not having a drink. She knew nothing, really.

She drank it slowly, wishing she'd said no. As if he sensed her discomfort, Owen became even more entertaining than before. He told her outrageous stories about famous artists, amused her with risqué tales of Slaney College's teaching staff, and generally made her feel like a fascinating and mature woman. With the warm whisky inside her and the warmth of his attention outside, Cara basked in a haze hotter than a sweltering summer's day.

It was around seven when they finally left the tiny crowded pub but instead of turning down towards the college, Owen led her firmly up the street, guiding her with one strong hand on her elbow.

'We've got to eat,' he said in surprised tones when Cara began to protest.

Thinking of Evie waiting patiently at home with dinner in the oven, Cara knew she should phone or something. But he didn't give her a chance. He rushed her towards Merrion Row and she felt almost embarrassed to explain that she went home after college almost every night instead of partying with the wilder students.

In The Sitar, a fragrant Indian restaurant, he ordered red wine and filled her glass up almost before she could say anything.

As he ate his lamb korma, Cara toyed with her Tandoori chicken, aware that the room seemed to be moving in and out of focus. She finally understood that old joke about not being drunk if you could lie on the floor without holding on. At the moment, she felt as if she'd fall off her chair any second. And she was nauseous into the bargain.

She just wanted to go home, to sink into her cosy little bed in Evie's back bedroom and feel the soft sheets wrap themselves around her. She longed for sleep but how could she get out of this?

'I'm tired, Owen,' she slurred suddenly. 'I've got to go home.'

He promised to drive her and they went back to the college. 'Come into my room, I've got to get my keys,' he said.

Like the obedient girl she was, programmed through years of training to do exactly what a person in authority said, she went, her limbs unsteady as she climbed the stairs to his office.

Inside, he turned and grabbed her, pushing her up against the filing cabinet and winching her big coat from her shoulders.

Cara would have gasped but his mouth was fastened on hers, his lips wet and rubbery as they took over hers, slobbering on her face, smelling of wine and whisky.

'I knew you liked me too,' he murmured between driving his tongue into her mouth. 'I know you've been watching me all evening but I had to be sure you wanted it too. You're so sexy, Cara. Mature, grown up and sexy.'

It was the words that did it. He believed she wanted him too, believed she'd been giving him the come on all evening. When she'd laughed at his jokes and taken the drinks he'd bought her, he'd assumed she fancied him too. It was like a mating dance and she'd danced it, too stupid to know the difference, too full of her new-found sexuality to know what she was doing.

Cara felt so out of her depth, but if he believed she knew what she was doing, how could she say she'd never *dreamed* of him touching her like this, that she didn't like it? She'd obviously led him on. It was her fault this had happened. How could she stop it? So she said nothing, just let him kiss her roughly for a few minutes. Then something inside her snapped and she knew she had to stop him, had to get him off her. Now.

'No,' she breathed, her voice faint. 'No,' she said again, more strongly this time.

He kept going, shoving her jumper up around her ribs, big hands wrenching it up over her breasts.

'No!'

'Don't be such a little tease,' he said raggedly. 'You want it, you know you do.'

'I don't,' she sobbed, trying to push him away from her. 'I don't want this. Please.'

He wasn't listening. He'd dragged her skirt up around her waist and was fumbling with her tights. God, he wasn't going to stop! She pushed him away but he didn't budge. Cara was strong but Owen Theal was bigger, much, much stronger, and able to handle alcohol. He wasn't drunk and unsteady. He was utterly in control. His hands were everywhere, touching and groping. Touching her intimately, grabbing parts of her no man had ever touched before. As he grabbed her, she felt sick, truly sick.

Then it came to her. The answer, the way out.

'I'm going to be sick,' she gasped, then made a retching noise, like one of her father's dogs trying to vomit after eating grass.

As if he'd been scalded, Theal sprang back.

'A bag, a bucket, get me something to be sick into,' she said between retches. She clasped her hands to her mouth as if she was ready to vomit and he whirled around frantically looking for something.

'Don't be sick here,' he hissed. 'I'll get something . . .'

He dragged open the door and Cara could see him rush down the hall towards the staff room. This was the chance

161

she needed. There was no time to sob or sink on to the floor crying. Grabbing her coat and bags, she stumbled from the room, pulling down her skirt as she ran. Her coat was trailing on the ground behind her as she ran with one arm in and one arm out, but she didn't care. She simply had to get away.

Her blood was racing in her chest, pumping frantically in terror. She nearly fell on the landing, tripped on the broken tile she blithely walked past twenty times a day.

But she recovered her balance and it didn't stop her headlong flight. She tore past the classrooms, terrified he'd find her gone and run, shouting, after her. But he didn't. She ran past the locker room and pulled open the heavy door and was out in the street in moments. Out in the blessedly safe street.

Cara ran all the way to the bus terminus, her heart still pounding and her breath rattling inside her chest. She ran like someone possessed, as if all the demons of every horror movie she'd ever seen were after her.

Mercifully, a bus sat waiting, lights on, engine idling while the driver waited another five minutes so he could leave at exactly eleven o'clock. Cara climbed the step to the driver and looked at him as if he'd personally saved her from Owen Theal.

'You're in a hurry,' he said, taking in the hot, flushed face and her ragged breathing.

'Yes.' She smiled shakily and showed him her travel card, then went to the back of the bus and sank gratefully into an empty seat. Eyes wide, she stared around at the darkened street outside, expecting to see him come after her any second. He knew where she lived, what bus she got. She'd told him. He'd follow her, she was sure. Please, please don't let him follow me, she prayed fervently, too scared to close her eyes. If she did, he'd appear in front of her like a demon, so she kept watching frantically. Ten endless minutes passed, ten minutes when Cara felt as if she'd have a heart attack from fear.

Her heart didn't stop pounding until the driver closed the doors and the bus pulled away from the kerb. Now she felt totally safe. Owen wouldn't find her now, he couldn't.

She sat back and stared blankly out into the night, too shocked to cry. What had she done? Oh, God, what had she done?

Evie had been in bed when she arrived back, reeking of unfamiliar Scotch and freezing because somewhere along the way, she'd lost the crimson chenille scarf and matching hat her sister had given her as a present. Not somewhere, really. In *his* office. On the floor where he'd thrown them. She'd been too scared to remember them when she raced out of the door with sheer terror in her soul.

'What time do you call this to be coming in?' demanded her sister, face icy with disapproval. 'It's nearly twelve and you're . . .' She paused and sniffed the air disbelievingly. 'Drunk! I've been worried sick about you.'

Standing at the door, gazing into the room that was so Evie – all warm floral fabrics and soft cushions, the pine furniture dotted with lace mats, the tiny china elephants Evie loved to collect and family pictures everywhere – Cara felt suddenly tearful. She longed to throw herself on to the bed, have Evie stroke her hair the way she had years ago, and tell her everything. About Owen and what he'd said, about how he'd made her feel: trapped, scared and totally vulnerable. About how terrifying it had been when he'd started to drag her clothes off and how he hadn't listened to her crying 'no'.

But Cara couldn't say the words. Lost in shock and the terrifying newness of the situation, she was silent.

It was like swimming out of her depth, desperately

treading water and trying to grab a foothold but the bottom was so far away she couldn't reach it. Even talking about what had happened was beyond her.

'I hope you don't think you're going to wander in here every night smelling like a brewery,' said Evie crossly, tired after an evening that had included helping a fractious eleven-year-old Rosie with her sums and trying to fit in some envelope-stuffing overtime in between finishing off the ironing. 'It's not on, you know, Cara. I expect you to behave like an adult not some wild student type. Dad expects me to look after you but I'm not going to if you're going to start drinking heavily.'

Cara stood silently, like a deer startled by a lorry's headlights, every nerve in her body poised to throw herself into Evie's arms and be comforted. She wanted to say that she'd hated the taste of the Scotch, had hated the way it burned her throat, and had hated the way it had tasted on Owen's breath when he'd forced his mouth against hers, stubble grinding into her skin like a cheese grater. But she couldn't think about that now.

'I'm going to bed, Evie,' was all she said. 'Sorry I'm late.'

She'd never told her sister about Owen Theal. She'd wanted to but the guilt had stopped her. It was all her own fault, she knew. Her fault for not knowing better. Zoë had known better, but Cara had stupidly been so convinced she was this clever, mature woman that she'd blundered into a scary part of the grown-up world and there was nobody else to blame for it but herself.

She couldn't bear to have her sister blame her; she wanted Evie to comfort her. She wanted Evie to know instinctively that something had happened. Which was madness. Evie never knew and, irrationally, Cara had not been able to forgive her sister, her surrogate mother, for not knowing. She'd never quite got over it and she never forgot. Owen Theal haunted her as if he slept in her bed every night as she went over it endlessly in her mind.

She wondered what would have happened if she'd handled it differently. If she'd thrown his Scotch all over him and told him he could shove his 'you're so talented' speech where the sun didn't shine. It was a bit like wanting to turn back time after witnessing some awful accident. Standing numbly by the road and thinking if only the van driver had been looking properly, he'd have seen the cyclist coming towards him. And if only the cyclist hadn't swerved to avoid that pothole, he wouldn't be lying on the road in a crumpled heap, limbs at odd angles . . .

If only. She thought that all the time. A mixture of if only and why the bloody hell was she such a moron as to fall for his patter, why hadn't she given in to her instinct and run, why had she let him get away with it? Zoë had faced exactly the same scenario and she'd come through it with flying colours. Caustic as ever, she'd told Theal what she'd do to him if he ever laid a hand on her again.

And she'd even told him he'd better not think about messing around with her grades as punishment. 'I've always got straight As in History of Art before,' she'd hissed. 'I don't want to find myself getting Ds because you want your revenge, understand?'

A week afterwards, Zoë had asked Cara what was wrong.

'You're totally different, you never wear your red lipstick anymore. What's the beef?' she demanded.

Eventually, she'd wangled the story out of her and it was only because Cara had begged her not to that she didn't run to the college head's office immediately.

'That bastard deserves to lose his job and end up in the nick,' she'd howled. 'Please let me tell, Cara? He'll only do it to some other poor kid if you don't.'

Terrified of having to explain what happened, she refused.

The upshot was that they'd become best friends. They'd laughed together, shopped together, got drunk together and gone on holiday together, although they'd never shared a flat because they both knew that Cara's messy style of living would have driven the precise and very tidy Zoë stone mad. She was the only person who knew why Cara was a disaster area when it came to men. Phoebe knew something had happened in her flatmate's dark past but she didn't know exactly what. Which was why she never nagged her to get a date, and why Zoë did.

Her teeth brushed, Cara flicked off the bathroom light and went back into her room. She pulled off her clothes, slipped on a fresh T-shirt and climbed into bed. Zoë was probably right – she ought to stop ending up in bed with people like Eric and concentrate on having a real relationship. It wasn't that easy, though.

To have a relationship, you had to let the other person into your heart and Cara was wary of such closeness. Closeness meant you got hurt; closeness meant letting down your defences and letting people see the tender skin under the carapace. After years of building up the sort of defences that a tank would be proud of, Cara was nervous of letting them down.

CHAPTER SEVEN

'Bugger! I've lost my glasses again. I must have left them in that monstrosity of a shop without the lift. You'll have to find them for me,' said the imperious voice. Then, 'No, wait, maybe they're in here.'

Sybil de Vere hauled her ancient brown leather handbag up by the strap from the floor of Bewley's Oriental Tearooms and started rummaging inside it with nicotine-stained fingers.

Olivia and Evie exchanged weary glances over the coffee pot before Olivia reached over to stop the higgledy-piggledy detritus of her mother's handbag spilling off the table as Sybil lost patience and emptied the whole thing on top of a half-eaten cream bun.

Squashed up cigarette packets with flakes of tobacco clinging to them fell on to the plate, joined by bits of paper, pen tops, lipsticked tissues, what looked suspiciously like cat worming tablets and a baby bottle of Power's.

'In case I needed heating up,' she said, whisking the bottle away from her daughter and pouring it into her coffee. The scent of whiskey rose into the air beguilingly and Evie and Olivia exchanged yet another glance. Without speaking, they both knew what the other was thinking: 'I could do with a drink myself!'

After three hours dragging Olivia's crotchety mother around the streets of Dublin, looking for a suitable outfit for Evie's father's wedding, both women could have done with a quadruple vodka and tonic, if only to ward off the memory of Sybil dropping a very nice crêpe suit to the floor in the changing room of Marks and Spencer's and rudely demanding to know what had happened to Switzer's.

'It's gone, Mother,' hissed Olivia as she tried to smile apologetically at the changing room assistant, a difficult task when your face was set in a rictus of embarrassment.

'It's my favourite shop. Whaddya mean "gone"?' demanded Sybil crossly, attempting to kick the suit out of her way as she reached for a lavender polo-neck jumper that had seen better days.

'Gone, closed down, no more,' snapped Evie, whose own teeth were clenched with temper. 'Let's get out of here, I need a tea break.'

While Olivia, puce with mortification over her mother's behaviour, apologised over and over again to the assistant, Evie swung into action. She gathered up Sybil's belongings and helped her on with her mothball-scented fur coat.

Rosie had grinned that morning when she'd seen Sybil arrive at their house in all her three-quarter-length mink glory.

'You're brave wearing that, Auntie Sybil,' she'd said. 'Some animal liberation rights person might spill red paint all over you.'

'Then I'll spill it right back over them,' declared Sybil.

'She would, too,' Evie muttered.

Luckily, the shoppers on Grafton Street were all too busy wielding brollies and trying to avoid the lashing early-February downpour to bother with a white-haired, gin-mottled sexagenarian in a coat that looked more rat than mink after forty years of hard wear. So the threesome made it safely to Bewley's where they sat with their coffee and Evie wondered yet again why she'd agreed to accompany Olivia and her mother on this shopping expedition.

Well, she knew really. Olivia's begging had done it.

'Please, please, come, Evie! I can't cope with her on my own, you know.'

Realising that Olivia was more than a little depressed, not up to hours of listening to her mother's bitching, and certainly not up to Sybil's imperiously demanding lunch plus copious amounts of wine at five past twelve, Evie had said yes. Which meant she was spending the last Saturday before the wedding looking for something for Sybil de bloody Vere to wear when she still hadn't found anything for herself.

She'd toyed with the idea of going in her best outfit, a red and black suit she'd bought in the sales two years previously. But everyone had seen her wearing it and she didn't want her father to think she hadn't bothered. Now that she was actually going to the wedding, she'd decided to give it her best shot.

Evie didn't approve but nobody was going to call her a spoilt, selfish creature who couldn't bear to see anyone take her place. Well, nobody was ever going to call her that *again*. It had been painful enough the first time Cara had flung the accusation at her. She wasn't going to give her sister the opportunity a second time.

So Evie would dance at her father's wedding, sip champagne and smile for the photos, no matter what her misgivings were. And if she bought something new, it could double for her own going away outfit at her wedding in September.

'I hate that colour on you,' Sybil was saying, glaring at Olivia, immaculate and beautiful in a saffron satin shirt that matched the pale gold strands of her hair and made her look like a mermaid on a day out at the hairdresser's. 'You look washed out.'

Olivia, used to a lifetime of such catty comments, sipped her coffee silently.

And no matter how bad Vida was, Evie told herself, she was nothing like poor Olivia's nightmare of a mother. Imagine growing up with that!

'Stephen doesn't like it either. He told me so, said you looked nicer in grey,' Sybil added triumphantly. 'Yellow is so tarty.'

God, she was such a bitch, Evie thought.

'I think you look lovely,' she told Olivia firmly.

Her friend smiled gratefully.

The conversation died after that and they sat in silence for another few minutes while Evie wondered if they should shop a bit more or just abandon the whole enterprise and send Sybil to the wedding in one of her trademark cat-pee-and-moth-ball-scented rig outs.

Sybil's sense of smell was shot after years of smoking like a trooper and she never appeared to realise she ponged more of Eau de Moggy than Eau de Cologne.

'Don't know why we can't go to a bar for a snifter,' she grumbled once she'd finished her whiskey-laced coffee. 'Shopping's easier with a couple of tots inside you.'

'It'd be easier if we could stop at a *couple* of tots,' Evie said, steel in her voice. 'But then ten or twelve is a *couple* for some people.' She eyeballed Sybil icily until the older woman finally looked away.

Sybil recognised a foe worthy of her steel in Evie.

Olivia gave her friend another grateful grin. Nobody could put her mother in her box like Evie. Nobody else *dared*.

For a few brief seconds, Evie considered their options.

She and Olivia could stuff Sybil in a taxi, give the poor driver a tenner and a couple of aspirin for the headache he'd inevitably have after three minutes, and send her to the train station. Then they could meander along gratefully to The Duke, have a revitalising drink and head back to the shops to buy something for *themselves*.

Idyllic. But, sadly, not realistic. Evie sighed, got up from her chair and marshalled the troops.

'Right, we've got another hour to find you something, Sybil, and I've just thought of the place we should go. It's a little shop that specialises in event clothes and they've got beautiful wedding stuff. I saw an advert for it in *Style* magazine with photos of a couple of very flattering suits.'

'Nothing insipid,' Sibyl said with a bitchy glance towards Olivia.

'Nobody could put you in anything insipid,' Evie said sharply, wishing Olivia would stand up for herself. 'It'd be like putting the Queen in *Sleeping Beauty* in pastel pink instead of black.'

'We *are* in a right mood today,' Sybil said happily. She loved a fight. 'Your betrothed having second thoughts, eh? I hope not. Whatever I'm buying today is what I'm wearing for your bash. When is it anyway? August? I hope you're not sticking on a white dress at your age. Mutton dressed as lamb is what we called it in my day.'

Evie gritted her teeth. Exactly how she got through the next hour she never knew. Enlivened thanks to the shot of whiskey, Sybil was in fine fettle, laughing coquettishly and making smart remarks.

But at least she was in a better mood for shopping and when Evie caught her swigging from a second miniature bottle of whiskey in the changing room, the younger woman said nothing, just passed her an extra strong mint after a moment.

Predictably, a tipsy Sybil liked the post-second-drink outfit the best. The colour of a just-ripened peach, the soft wool braided jacket and skirt actually looked marvellous on her and watching how the subtle hue lit up her worn face, Evie realised what a beauty Sybil de Vere must have been in her day. Her pre-bottle-of-gin-a-day day.

As if she was thinking the same thing, Olivia hugged her mother suddenly, something she rarely did.

'You look great, Mum,' she said, eyes wet with emotion.

'Who's paying for this?' demanded Sybil truculently, oblivious to the Kodak moment. 'You, I hope?'

'What did you get, Mum?' asked Rosie that evening, warming her back against the fire in the sitting room while her mother and Olivia lay like exhausted bookends on armchairs in front of her.

Evie grimaced. 'The sort of thing I was determined not to buy,' she answered. 'A pale blue suit. It's a bit mother-of-the bride,' she added glumly.

Actually, it was very mother-of-the-bride and she was quite sure that as Vida would look stunningly elegant in whatever little designer number she chose to wear, Evie would look like Heap of the Week by comparison. She could just imagine Vida's glamorous guests contrasting the two women and wondering what Vida would do to make over her frumpy step-daughter. A total body transplant and about twenty thousand quids' worth of facial surgery, she reckoned.

'It's not mother-of-the-bride at all,' said Olivia staunchly. 'It's lovely, a pale blue with a duck egg blue stripe running through it, with a knee-length skirt and a high collar.'

Rosie, her head angled to one side as she tried to picture the outfit, thought of how pale blue did absolutely nothing for her mother's colouring and how high collars were on the 'avoid' list for women with big busts. Women like her mother, in fact.

'Sounds fab,' she said enthusiastically. 'Put it on and give us a fashion show.'

Because she half-hoped that the outfit might be miraculously improved by the addition of flesh-coloured tights instead of the black ones she'd been wearing when she tried it on in the shop, Evie ran upstairs to change. The right shoes, she told herself, and those suck-it-all-in knickers would make it look OK, she decided with renewed optimism.

'What did you get, Olivia?' asked Rosie, plopping down on the floor beside the fire and stretching out like a big cat.

'I didn't buy anything new. We spent so much time with my mother, we barely had time to shop. I'm going to wear something from my best wardrobe,' said Olivia, whose 'best' wardrobe resembled the Designer Room in Harrods.

'You could wear that grey knitted dress you got last year in the Design Centre,' Rosie suggested.

Olivia thought of the elegantly clinging gun metal grey knitted sheath with matching cardigan by Lyn Mar. Fashioned from sinuous silk, the dress flowed and clung around her body in all the right places and she was tall enough to carry off its matching ankle-length cardigan. But Stephen didn't really like it.

'Too tight,' he'd said disapprovingly when she came home with it, buoyed up after an adventurous shopping expedition with Evie and Rosie. 'Tight clothes do nothing for you, Olivia, I've told you that time and time again.'

He'd hate it if she wore that to the wedding. The day would be ruined before it would have started.

'I don't think it's the right sort of outfit for your grandfather's wedding,' she said hesitantly.

Rosie shrugged. 'I think it'd be very nice but . . .' She tailed off as Evie walked in, a study in blue.

The right tights and the right shoes hadn't, unfortunately, had a magical effect on the suit. It was still an unforgivingly icy hue which drained the colour from her face, while the skirt, probably a thing of beauty on a willowy creature with legs to her armpits, didn't do a lot to flatter Evie's short ones.

Rosie and Olivia, who both loved her dearly, didn't point any of this out. Loyally, they told her she looked beautiful while Olivia mentally vowed to lend Evie some expensive cream calfskin shoes that would give her some more height, and Rosie quietly vowed to encourage her mum to apply some fake tan the night before to give her pale skin a little colour.

'I'm not sure . . .' Evie twisted around to see herself from behind. 'My legs look horrible in pale tights.'

'They don't,' chorused the other two.

'Maybe I should wear my red suit after all,' she debated.

Olivia's mouth formed a little oval before she snapped it shut. She didn't want to hurt Evie by saying that the red suit would be much, much nicer than the pale outfit she'd chosen. Diplomacy was very difficult.

'No, that's very nice, Evie,' she said instead.

Looking at Evie's pretty face with her large, expressive eyes, upturned little nose and soft, rounded contours, Olivia knew exactly what her friend should do – stop wearing her hair in that severely sleek plait and get it cut differently. Then dump her safe, conservative clothes, all the blacks and the navys, and wear the rich jewel shades that really became her. Amethysts, crimsons, bronzes, Prussian blue.

They'd seen the most stunning outfit when they were shopping: a rich imperial purple trouser suit with a jacket with a nipped-in waist that would show off Evie's hour-glass figure to perfection. But she, as usual, had gone for the restrained safety of the blue, saying she couldn't possibly wear a trouser suit to a wedding.

'Well, it's new and nobody can say I haven't made an effort,' Evie said, gazing at the bit of herself she could see in the mantelpiece mirror. 'I needed a going away outfit for my wedding. Simon will be pleased, he loves blue.'

She went back upstairs to change. Was the red suit better? she wondered glumly. What was she thinking of? Nothing was better. She looked a mess and despite all her plans for a cellulite-free bum in time for her honeymoon, had found it almost impossible to return to her caffeine and sugar-free diet since Christmas. And she still carried those extra five pounds she'd put on comfort eating during the holidays. Evie stripped off her suit and thought miserably of the way she wanted to look: exotic and beautiful. Mysterious, maybe.

Heroines in novels were always mysterious, always able to bewitch the hero with their enigmatic gazes and their captivating beauty. Like Vanessa in *Passionate Fury*. A French TV journalist, she was secretly a Russian princess but had hidden it from everybody for years.

Her background gave her an air of mystery which couldn't be breached – until tough war reporter Dirk came on the scene. Hard-bitten, battle-scarred and wickedly handsome, he'd fallen in love with the intriguing Vanessa.

Evie sat at her dressing table wearing her unbuttoned black cardigan and tried to imagine what it would be like to be a mysterious and enigmatic Russian princess disguised as a French journalist. She wrapped the cardigan around her so that it left her shoulders and neck bare, pulled the band from her plait and shook her head so her hair cascaded around her shoulders and entered her dream world . . .

'Why won't you tell me everything?' Dirk said hoarsely, drinking in Evie's beauty as she stood before him, half-clad in the delicate nightgown that outlined her slim shape against the room's many soft lights. 'You're keeping it a secret from me and I must know. I must know everything.'

She stifled a sob, one hand touching her beautiful face, instinctively hiding the faded scar that ran from one arched eyebrow into her ebony hairline.

'I can't, Dirk. You've got to understand – I buried the past in Russia, I can't drag it up again. I've tried so hard to forget.'

'Dammit, don't block me out,' he growled, losing patience. In one long stride he was beside her, pulling her against his strong, muscular body. He was taut, like a coiled spring ready to unwind in one fierce movement.

His face was beside hers, those fierce blue eyes burning into her hazel ones with a passion she'd never seen before.

His skin was warm and Evie remembered how it had felt to feel his arms roaming over her naked body, bringing her to pleasures she'd never dreamed about. But still she couldn't tell him. He'd kill those men for what they'd done to her if he knew. He'd find them and kill them and she loved him too much to let him even try. It was better that she left his life, crept away silently in the night as if she'd never been there, never loved him.

'Tell me,' he breathed, 'tell me . . .'

She weakened with his arms around her. 'Oh, Dirk, I want to explain but it's not easy,' she faltered, breathing in the male scent of him because she knew that after tonight she'd never see him again.

Then she looked up at him, looked into his eyes, lost herself in their azure depths. 'Make love to me, Dirk,' she said simply.

She let the nightgown slip from her shoulders and felt his mouth fasten on hers, almost brutal in his eagerness to kiss her . . .

'Mum, Olivia's going.' Rosie's clear voice called up the stairs and penetrated Evie's fantasy world.

'I'm coming,' she called back. A pale-faced woman with her hair a straggly mess stared back at her from the mirror. Boring, conservative Evie, not the enigmatic woman who could make tough Dirk throb with passion at her very touch.

The boring Evie buttoned up her cardigan, scraped her hair back into a ponytail with unnecessary viciousness and went downstairs.

Olivia – anxious to get home because after an entire six hours minding Sasha, Stephen would be looking at his watch impatiently – was standing in the hall with her coat on.

Rosie was telling Olivia about the jacket she had her eye on in Miss Selfridge. 'It's fantastic. A fake pony skin long jacket in chocolate brown. My friend Charlotte has these brown PVC trousers I can borrow and I've got a taupe chiffon top for underneath.'

'For the wedding?' asked Evie, not sure if she liked the idea of fake pony skin and fake leather as a wedding ensemble.

'Relax, Mum, it'll be cool,' Rosie said blithely. 'Cara's seen the jacket and she thinks it's delicious.'

'Your aunt's taste leaves a lot to be desired,' Evie said, a bite to her voice. 'Lord knows what she's going to wear.'

She was still angry with her sister over what Cara had said about the wedding. Angry and terribly hurt. Even if Evie had shamefacedly to admit it was true, that didn't mean she wanted to be told she was spoilt and jealous.

After three days of suspended hostilities over Christmas,

Cara had finally lost her temper the afternoon before she was due to return home and had vented her anger on Evie.

'You haven't said two words to Dad today,' she'd snapped, flinging dishes into the washing-up water with blatant disregard for breakages. 'And as for poor Vida . . . If you weren't going to talk to her at lunch, you should have just driven home to Dublin and left us to it. It was so rude to sit like that in silence, like a bloody spectre at the feast!'

'Be quiet!' hissed a startled Evie, nearly dropping the drying up towel. 'They'll hear us.' Her father, Vida and two neighbours who'd been invited in for lunch, had retreated to the cosy living room with Rosie circling and doling out the second pot of coffee.

Cara aimed a wooden spoon at the sink and fired it in, suds going everywhere. 'Who cares if they hear us? They'd want to have been blind and deaf not to have noticed you sitting in icy silence during lunch. *Would you like some gravy, Evie? No. Got all your plans made for your big day, Evie? Yes.* Talk about Ms Chatty! I don't know why you don't get flash cards made so you don't have to actually speak, just hold a card with the words "Yes" or "No" written on it. You'd only need two of them after all.'

Evie reddened. She knew she'd been monosyllabic during lunch but she hadn't thought anyone would notice. They were all having such a nice time, her father and Vida so wrapped up in each other, that she'd felt totally surplus to requirements. Who'd have observed her sitting quietly? Cara, that's who.

'What I don't understand, Evie,' she said finally, abandoning any pretence at washing up, 'is why you spent years teaching me to think about other people, to be a kind, decent, thoughtful person with a sense of responsibility and sensitivity, when all it takes is for one shock to the system and you're behaving like some infantile, immature, witless idiot.'

Evie was speechless but Cara still wasn't finished. 'I know you're finding this wedding hard to take but you're not even trying to accept reality. It's happening so deal with it,' she snapped. 'I'd hate to see what sort of a cow you'd have turned out to be if something really awful had happened to you. You don't know how lucky you are, Evie. You just don't know.'

Cara's voice was bitter now, so bitter that Evie wondered where this was all coming from.

'Get down off your high horse and have a look at the real world. Dad deserves some happiness and if we hadn't both been so tied up in our own little lives, we might have seen he was lonely. I'm grateful to Vida for coming along because I don't want him to spend the rest of his life on his own. And if you could stop thinking about *yourself* for five minutes, you'd agree.'

Cara left the kitchen then and didn't speak to her sister for the rest of the evening. The following day she got the bus back to Dublin. Their phone conversations since then had been brief and all about surface matters, the memory of that heated discussion looming over them like a thunder cloud nobody wanted to talk about.

Evie felt guilty about Cara. Guilty and resentful. Cara was supposed to be on her side, not Vida's. If her own sister couldn't understand her point of view, who could? What niggled her was the feeling that Cara hadn't been speaking in general terms when she'd yelled about having something awful happen to you. She'd been talking about something specific, Evie was sure of it. Something Cara had never told her. That thought nagged at the back of her brain. What had happened to Cara and why had she kept it a secret?

Rosie was still talking about wedding outfits.

'Cara said she'd like to buy a suit but she's a bit broke,' she revealed.

'I hope she does get a suit,' Evie said. 'I mean, you never know what sort of rig out she's going to turn up in. I've been afraid she'll arrive in combat trousers and a T-shirt and show us all up in front of Vida's posh friends.'

At that precise moment, what to wear to her father's wedding was probably the furthest thing from Cara's mind. She was bending over her drawing board putting the finishing touches to a campaign which had been left on her desk when she and Zoë returned from lunch the day before.

'It's an emergency,' Bernard had written on the carelessly scrawled note. 'Get it done by Monday.'

No please, thank you or I'm sorry if I interrupted your Friday, your Saturday or indeed, your whole bloody life, Cara simmered. No. That's because I don't *have* a life, do I? No bloody life and no bloody career either. Just a psychopathic nutcase for a boss who thinks I can work late on Friday and all day Saturday without so much as a bit of common courtesy!

She hated working at the weekends, loathed the way the office was silent after lunchtime on Saturday, couldn't stand the way the building creaked eerily as if there were hordes of unseen burglars shimmying up and down drain pipes and sneaking around the office, concealing themselves behind filing cabinets when she sneaked downstairs to look.

Cara knew the noises were a combination of the heating pipes cooling down and creaky old floorboards, but that didn't make it any less scary.

A final ten minutes of concentrated effort did it. There.

Finished. Wearily, she brought the finished design over to the colour photocopier and made several copies. Then she packed up her stuff, and went downstairs to drop the design on the creative director's desk. She'd just laid it carefully down when she heard footsteps behind her and froze with shock.

'Cara, what are you doing here at half-six on a Saturday night?'

In front of her stood Ewan from copywriting, looking totally different from the way he normally did in a dark suit instead of his usual casual gear.

Like all the copywriters, he dressed down most of the time and she'd never seen him in anything other than jeans or sloppy trousers, dark curly hair flopping over his collar. But the smart grey suit looked good on him.

'You gave me a shock,' was all she could say. Her knees felt weak and she found herself leaning shakily against a desk.

'Sorry.' He touched her shoulder briefly. 'I didn't mean to startle you. I didn't expect there'd be anyone here at this time. Don't tell me,' he said, 'a Bernard special? The "have this for me before the weekend is over" lark?'

'Ten out of ten for observation,' she replied. 'I've been here the whole bloody weekend and I'm shattered and can't for the life of me see what's so vital about a paint shop campaign that we have to have it by nine on Monday. Or will the entire country go into DIY meltdown if I don't?'

Ewan grinned, which showed off a broad flash of very white teeth. He was gorgeous when he smiled, Cara thought, off-handedly. Pretty gorgeous even when he didn't, actually. She'd never gone along with the office gossip that he was a 'fine thing', to use Bernard's secretary's drooling accolade. But now Cara could see

Ewan was actually extremely attractive, with those sleepy greenish eyes, that lop-sided grin and that big mouth of his. She idly wondered if he could kiss. Cara! What are you like?

'I think Bernard likes setting impossible tasks just for the hell of it,' Ewan said, distracting her as he leaned against a desk and stretched out long lean legs. 'He did it to my boss when he started here but my boss – well, you know Ken – he worked one weekend and said never again. Bernard would have to pay him quadruple overtime. Which meant it never happened again.'

'Clever Ken,' muttered Cara. 'But I'd like to see Bernard's face if *I* started demanding quadruple overtime. Lowly graphic designers are on the bottom rung of the Yoshi Advertising ladder.'

'I know what you mean.' Ewan smiled ruefully. 'Have you much more to do tonight?'

'Actually, I'm finished.'

'Great. Fancy a drink?'

Cara didn't need to think about it. Unwinding over a drink and bitching about Bernard seemed like a nice way to end a totally crappy day.

'Sure, I'll just get my stuff from upstairs.'

She sprinted up the back stairs happily, glad that she had something to do that evening. Phoebe was going out to a party and, although she'd been invited, Cara wasn't in the mood to go along and play gooseberry. An enjoyable gin and platonic evening out with Ewan would be a nice alternative to another evening of Blind Date and trying to control her consumption of frozen Mars Bar ice cream. Three boxes a week was just too much for two women to get through effortlessly.

She grabbed her rucksack off the floor by her desk, dismissed the idea of combing her hair and sticking on some lip balm – Ewan was just a guy from work, after all – and bounced downstairs to where he was waiting.

'What are you all dressed up for?' she asked as they walked companionably along the street to the bright lights of O'Dwyer's. He was as tall as she was, which was nice.

'Funeral,' he answered.

'God, I'm sorry!' she replied, shocked. 'Was it anyone close to you?'

'No, a friend of my mother's. I was dragged along for moral support. Or in case anybody started a fight.'

'Wow!' Cara said. 'What sort of funeral was it? A Hell's Angels one?'

'Nothing like that,' he chuckled as they found spare bar stools and ordered two Beck's. 'It's a bit complicated but my mother and the guy who died had been involved for years but then he finally left his wife a couple of years ago and moved in with *another* woman. I can tell you, my mother and his wife weren't pleased! Putting the three of them together at the funeral seemed like a recipe for disaster but they all maintained a dignified silence, amazingly enough. He was a great guy.'

'Was he sort of your stepfather?' asked Cara, intensely curious about this rather unusual family set up.

'No, I never had a real father figure,' Ewan said, not sounding particularly upset about the fact. 'My mother had boyfriends and Stan, the man who died, drifted in and out of our life. But it was really just me and my mother. I never knew my real father. He left when I was a baby. Bit of a free spirit, apparently. He went to Australia and never came back.'

'And I thought *my* family were weird,' Cara said, taking a deep slug from her bottle of beer.

'What's weird about them?'

'Absolutely nothing compared to yours,' she said

jokingly. 'My mother died when I was six and my father never married again until now. He's met this American widow and they're getting hitched on Friday.'

'Good for him.'

'Ah, but the problem is,' Cara interrupted, 'my elder sister has a bit of an Electra complex about my dad and she's foaming at the mouth about the wedding. She's also harbouring conspiracy theories about his fiancée of the Black Widow sort.'

'I get it,' Ewan leaned back in his seat and loosened his tie. 'Your dad is happy as a pig in shit until, two months later, he keels over in his sleep and your new stepmum runs off with the family millions?'

Cara chuckled, amused that he'd put his finger on it so aptly. 'The fatal flaw in this theory is that the family millions don't exist or,' she fingered the frayed hem of her second-hand man's linen jacket. 'I wouldn't be dressed like this.'

'Oh, I don't know,' Ewan said, eyeing her from her tangled curls and flushed, high cheekbones down to the faded, tight jeans she'd only put on that morning because everything else was in the laundry basket. 'You look pretty good to me. That second-hand chic look suits you.'

Cara blinked for a moment, unsure what was coming next.

He continued. 'I can't see you in a twinset and pearls somehow, even if they came from Armani.' He drained his beer. 'Your round, I believe, Ms Rich Bitch.'

She laughed. What seemed to have started out as a compliment had segued neatly into a joke. A flattering joke that she looked good, but a joke nonetheless. And it was her round, as Ewan had pointed out. Cara preferred it when men treated her like one of them, one of the lads.

Standing her own round, being as tough as any of them,

that was the way to be safe. There could be no mixed signals when you swore as proficiently as any male, wore bigger Doc Marten's than they did – she was size eight – and could tower over most of them.

They sat and talked for a couple of hours and Cara enjoyed herself so much, she wondered why she'd never taken the time to talk to Ewan before. Maybe it was the fact that he was attractive and had a certain devil-may-care air about him that had kept her away.

She was wary of men who were gossiped over in the women's loos and always scored high on the 'Who in the office would you like to sleep with most?' games when the female staff were on the piss. Cara never joined in those games.

'Spoilsport,' Zoë would say.

'Trollop,' Cara would answer lightly.

Ewan bought the next round and they chatted, laughed, bitched and generally had a whale of a time.

At half-nine, Ewan said he had to go. 'I'm playing football tomorrow afternoon and the coach will kill me if I turn up hungover.'

'On a Sunday?' she asked, piqued that their cosy little evening out was ending so abruptly.

'It's a charity match for this mentally handicapped school. We do it every year. It's good fun – unless you're dying after a Saturday night bender, that is. Do you want to come?'

For the second time that evening, she was speechless.

'Me, come to your match?' she gulped.

'Yeah, you'd enjoy it.' Ewan grinned at her. 'You'll like the lads on the team, they're good crack. We always go out after this match and have a slap up dinner and some drinks. A bit of a party really. You'll come, won't you?' His face was eager, the green eyes crinkled up attractively at the corners. Cara could see how he scored so high on so many drunken lists from the Yoshi girls.

She considered what she'd be doing on Sunday. Under normal circumstances, she and Phoebe would stagger off to Flames restaurant at about one for a huge brunch of fat chips, nuclear-missile-sized sausages or maybe a Flames special burger, which they'd consume while squabbling good-naturedly over the papers.

But since the advent of Ricky, the Sunday morning ritual now consisted of Cara leaving the flat to get breakfast after listening to much heaving and giggling from Phoebe's room. Going to Flames wasn't so much fun on her own either and finding funny bits in the papers was boring when there was nobody to read them out to.

She looked at Ewan, smiled and said as casually as she could: 'I'd love to.'

'A date? You've got a date with him!' squeaked Phoebe in delight when Cara got home to find her and Ricky ensconced in the kitchen making toasted cheese sandwiches with some Cheddar that looked dangerously gone off.

'It's not a date,' she protested. 'It's an . . . outing. He knows I like football and going for a few drinks, that's all.'

'What, and that's not a date?' said Ricky, his mouth full of toasted sandwich. 'He'll get you plastered at the piss up and try to score!' Laughing happily at his own lame joke, Ricky spewed sandwich all over the counter.

'I thought you were going to a party,' Cara said, ignoring him. Ricky was good-looking but, God, he was dense. Not to mention annoying.

'We did but the music was awful, there was no free booze and they had nothing but about ten packets of salt and vinegar crisps to eat. I only like cheese and onion and

186

we were ravenous. Plus, we're too broke to go out to the pub,' Phoebe revealed with a bite to her voice.

'I don't understand you pair,' Cara said, wriggling past to get a Mars Bar ice cream out of the freezer box. 'You both work in the bank, you deal with money all day, you get well paid – and you never have a bean. My bank account is healthier than yours, Phoebe, and I'm hopeless with money.'

Ricky finished his mouthful and licked his full lips clean with the pink tongue Phoebe claimed left her weak with excitement. 'Yeah, er . . . talking of money, you couldn't lend us a tenner?'

Cara looked at his beautiful vacant face. 'You're right, Ricky, I couldn't. You still owe me a fiver after the night we went to Brady's.'

'Did you borrow money off Cara?' squealed Phoebe, turning to her boyfriend.

'Yeah,' he muttered sheepishly. 'I haven't forgotten it, Cara.'

Not like he'd conveniently forgotten the previous fifteen quid she'd lent him, Cara reflected grimly. She'd learnt her lesson with Ricky. Neither a borrower nor a lender be, etc, etc. Especially to Ricky. It was obvious that he was never going to dazzle the banking world with his business acumen and would always be stony broke unless he figured out how to get into modelling. It was a complete mystery to Cara how he'd managed to get a job in the bank in the first place. After a few months of seeing him every second day, she'd come to the conclusion that Phoebe's joy in going out with such a perfect physical specimen had blunted every other sense in her. Like her common sense, for example.

Ricky was glorious-looking, had a body to die for and had enough sex appeal for four normal people but the space between his two perfectly shaped ears was entirely empty.

Ewan, she reminded herself smugly, was good-looking *and* clever. Not in Ricky's cover-of-GQ league, but still damn good-looking. Ricky was too smooth, anyway. Too perfect. Ewan had that tough edge to him, a sort of don't-mess-with-me edge.

She wondered where he'd got it. She didn't know that much about him, really, or why he had the indefinable air of danger about him. Maybe she'd find out more tomorrow.

The next morning, Ricky had gone by the time Cara arrived back from the shop with the Sunday papers, having abstained from her usual fry up in Flames in favour of a pot of Blue Javan and a croissant in a tiny coffee shop that played mellow jazz music and served every type of coffee imaginable. In the living room Phoebe was aimlessly watching the box and eating corn-flakes at the same time.

When the *Wonder Woman* music blared after the ad break, Cara's immediate reaction was to dump the papers, forget about her plan to tidy up her bedroom and sink into seventies-induced catatonia on the couch. *Wonder Woman* had been her favourite TV programme as a child.

She'd dreamed of having heavy gold bangles that could deflect bullets and a lasso that could knock a villain to his knees with one expert flick of the wrist. But when she threw the papers on to the coffee table and half an inch of dust and fluff shot up into the air like startled dandelion heads, she changed her mind.

'This place is a pit, Phoebe, ' she said in disgust. Piles of old magazines and papers were scattered around the floor so that you could – mercifully – only see bits of the puke-coloured carpet with its putrid green paisley design.

The previous night's glasses and mugs still sat on the coffee table and a few of an even earlier vintage littered the mantelpiece alongside several used up boxes of matches, a candle that had melted down completely and the detritus of several bales of briquettes.

Even the fire burning merrily in the grate couldn't inject a bit of cosiness into the untidy and unloved squalor of the room. It hadn't had a good spring clean for months. Cara leaned against the couch in despair and immediately found her black combats decorated with marmalade fur.

'And how come we have cat hairs on everything when we don't have a cat?'

'Ricky has,' mumbled Phoebe, not taking her eyes off the telly.

Cara gave up. She tied her hair back from her face, rolled up her sleeves and set to work. After half an hour of hauling papers off the floor and removing all the dust, dirt and ash from the fireplace, the room had started to improve. Once she'd started, Cara couldn't stop and she scrubbed, polished and cleaned demonically while Phoebe still sat slumped in front of the box.

When the drone of the Hoover didn't move her, Cara knew something was up.

'What's wrong, Phoebs?' she asked. It wasn't like her flatmate to shirk her half of the cleaning up – once they actually got round to it, that was.

Phoebe snuffled. 'We had a fight.'

'What about?' asked Cara, still not relinquishing her grasp on the handle of the Hoover.

'Money.'

'Oh.' Cara let go of the Hoover and sat down beside her friend.

'He keeps borrowing money from me but I didn't know he'd been borrowing from you too. I said something and he got cross and said I couldn't love him if I felt like that.'

Cara kept her mouth shut. Saying the wrong thing at this stage would be fatal.

'I said I *did* love him but I didn't want him taking your money because he doesn't pay it back,' continued Phoebe miserably. 'He owes me over a hundred pounds now and I've paid the last four times we went out. That's really why we didn't stay at the party. I thought Ricky was bringing a bottle and he didn't. I was so embarrassed when I realised.'

Beside her, Cara winced. In her opinion, there was nothing worse than a relentless borrower, someone who was perpetually broke and perpetually on the scrounge. Even worse was the sort of bloke who never coughed up for an evening out. It wasn't that Cara was one of those women who expected men to pay every time. Far from it. But a fifty:fifty ratio was reasonable when it came to a couple paying the bill. With Ricky, the ratio was obviously twenty:eighty in his favour. And he had to borrow to pay his twenty per cent.

'Why is he always broke?' she asked in a neutral voice.

Phoebe shrugged. 'He buys loads of clothes.'

He does? goggled Cara, thinking of Ricky's selection of ultra-casual togs that looked as if they'd been bought from an outdoor market during a downpour. 'What's he buy – nothing but Gucci underpants?' she joked.

'I don't know,' said Phoebe, her face crumpling miserably. 'He says it's over between us because he needs affection and doesn't think I love him properly.' And she started crying.

Hugging Phoebe, Cara did her best to provide comfort. It took three cups of very sweet tea, a pack of Hob Nobs and a lengthy discussion on why men were such shits to do it. Once they'd gone through the ritual male bashing,

Phoebe's natural exuberance returned. She began to talk about how crazy she was about Ricky, how sweet he was to her and how much she loved the way he scrunched his face up adorably when he didn't understand something.

Which was most of the time, Cara thought with a grimace she managed to turn into a sympathetic smile.

'You're right, Cara,' Phoebe said firmly, wiping away the remains of her tears with a tissue. 'I've got to talk to him about money and say I love him, but I worry about him when he never has a penny.'

It wasn't exactly the advice Cara had given. ('Tell him you can't support him while he squanders his money – it's just not on.')

Cheered up, Phoebe got off the couch and headed for the bathroom, while Cara, worn out by her role as chief cleaner, comforter and tea-maker, lay back and yawned.

She glanced idly at her watch and froze with horror.

In a mere three-quarters of an hour she had to be standing on the sidelines of Ewan's soccer match cheering him on. A soccer match that was at least an hour away by bus. She'd have to order a taxi and that'd take half an hour to get there which left . . . fifteen minutes to get ready. Shit. Double shit.

Despite offhandedly telling Phoebe the night before that she planned to go in her combats and big woolly sheepskin coat 'because it'll be freezing and it's hardly a date', Cara had still toyed with the idea of dressing up a bit. Just to show Ewan that she could look like a girl as distinct from a tough cookie with size eight boots and SAS gear.

Time constraints meant the glamour puss look would have to wait, she realised, leaping to her feet.

'Phoebe,' she roared as she grabbed the phone to ring for a taxi, 'get out of the shower. It's an emergency!'

191

The match had started by the time she belted up to the sidelines, no longer shivering in the cold because she'd ended up getting the taxi to drop her in the wrong place, necessitating a five-minute jog through the grounds to the soccer pitches.

A big crowd of people were gathered watching the match, stamping their feet to get warm and huddled close together as the biting wind whipped down the pitch far faster than the ball. It was a bitterly cold February day, even though a watery winter sun shone low in the sky.

Her eyes stinging in the breeze, Cara stood beside a couple of heavily made-up women and tried to figure out which one of the players was Ewan. She didn't even know which colour his team wore. They all looked the same in their white shorts, twenty-two men in either red or black jerseys, hairy legs purple with the cold.

The men in red appeared to be losing as their opponents had possession of the ball most of the time and kept almost scoring. The goalie for the black-clad team certainly wasn't cold: he was running around like a maniac as the ball rattled around dangerously near his goal.

'Come on, St Helen's!' shrieked one of the women beside her, a tiny blonde huddled up in a giant blue anorak.

'Get your finger out!' yelled her companion, a red head in a black puffa.

St Helen's. That sounded a bit familiar, Cara thought. She peered at the players in red more closely. The St Helen's forward on the far side of the pitch looked a bit like Ewan. His hair was flopping all over the place and he was wirily athletic. Fast, too, she thought approvingly, as he whizzed up the pitch alongside a team mate, waiting for the ball. The crowd perked up as St Helen's took possession of the ball and the shouting grew more frenzied.

Shrieks of 'Come on, St Helen's, score, score!' mingled with enraged 'Get it away, Dems!' as the other team's supporters howled with rage.

Unfortunately, Ewan's team mate's shot at the goal went wide and the Anorak Girlies beside Cara slumped dejectedly.

'Better luck next time, Michael and Ewan,' yelled the red head, glossy crimson lips quivering with cold.

Ewan turned his head at her voice and noticed Cara for the first time.

'Hi,' he yelled, and waved.

The nearby supporters turned to see who he was waving at and the Anorak Girlies gave her an appraising look.

Flushing to be singled out so noticeably, Cara waved back at him.

'You're Ewan's friend Cara,' cooed the red head, cute as a button in a purple velvet hat that set off her ringlets beautifully. 'He told us all about you. Come and cheer with us,' she invited. 'We're his friends. I'm Arlene, going out with Michael,' she said proudly, 'the one who nearly scored. And Barbara's dating Dave, the left back.'

'Coo-ee, Dave,' shrieked Barbara, as if to prove the point.

Dave looked around and a Dems man cannoned into him, knocking them both to the ground.

Barbara giggled nervously. 'I hope he's OK,' she said.

'Probably just concussion or a cracked rib or two,' reassured Cara, a dedicated Arsenal fan who took a dim view of people distracting the players.

Both women giggled skittishly again. 'You are a card,' Arlene said, 'Isn't she, Babs?'

Cara smiled tightly and took a step away. How did she come to get stuck beside them? And whatever did they mean by 'Ewan's told us all about you'?

By half-time, she'd managed to put at least two yards between herself and the Anorak Girls, and St Helen's had managed only to let in two goals.

'Hi, Cara,' said Ewan, emerging from the sea of mud with a broad smile on his face. 'You got here OK, and I see you met Babs and Arlene.'

They were busy waving excitedly at a concussed-looking Dave and a very muddy Michael. But like lap dogs, hearing their names and sensing titbits, they smiled in Ewan's direction.

'They're great, aren't they?' he said fondly, running a sweaty hand through his equally sweaty hair.

'Marvellous,' Cara said brightly, thinking that she hadn't wasted nine-fifty on a taxi to stand beside the sort of women she couldn't bear to talk to under normal circumstances. Over made-up in the extreme, Arlene and Babs looked like they were done up for a disco, not a freezing February football match.

'I told them to watch out for you,' Ewan said sheepishly. 'Didn't want you feeling lost. Are you enjoying yourself?'

Suddenly, it was as if the day had turned tropical. Instead of the icy wind clutching her extremities, Cara felt as if she was being warmed by a benevolent sun.

Ewan had wanted her to feel at home. He'd warned people in advance about her coming. Forget what she'd thought about this not being a date: it *was* one.

'Absolutely,' she replied, eyes shining.

He touched her arm briefly in response. 'Great. I'd better go and discuss tactics,' he said, and then added ruefully: 'Or discuss how not to lose too humiliatingly.'

'You're doing great,' Cara said with an encouraging grin. 'Go get 'em.'

He ran off and she found herself admiring him do it. Those baggy jeans hid a well-muscled form, she realised, as she watched his gluteal muscles ripple under filthy shorts.

'Want a sandwich?' inquired a voice and she looked around to find Arlene opening a Tupperware box containing freshly cut brown bread sandwiches glistening with succulent egg. 'Babs has coffee and we've got a hip flask of brandy.'

'Because it'd freeze your boobs off out here,' said Babs with the inevitable giggle.

'I'm sure you've only got cups for two people,' said Cara, astonished.

'No.' Babs reached into her giant handbag and extracted a mini tower of polystyrene cups. 'I've brought loads. I always do.'

Babs and Arlene went up several notches in her estimation. They weren't as dumb as they looked.

'Thanks,' she said gratefully. 'I'd love a sandwich and I'd kill for a coffee.'

Fortified by coffee, sandwiches and a decent nip of brandy – Babs' flask proved to be of the big variety – Cara watched the rest of the match in comfort and enjoyed herself chatting to the girls.

While St Helen's went on to score two goals, Babs and Arlene gently grilled Cara about herself and she, just as gently, grilled them about Ewan. He'd been at school with Dave and Michael, loved skiing and hadn't brought anyone to a football match since breaking up with his last girl-friend, an advertising executive named Layla who was, according to Babs, 'a complete bitch'.

'She thought she was so clever and looked down her posh nose at us,' sniffed Arlene, who was a beautician, 'because she was a big noise in her company.'

Cara felt a twinge of guilt. She'd been looking down her nose a bit at them too, judging them totally by their girlish giggles and heavy make-up. They could just as easily have judged her on her bolshie, couldn't-give-a-damn clothes, but they hadn't. They'd kindly given her the benefit of the doubt before they judged.

'And her hair . . .' shuddered Babs, a colourist by profession. 'She thought that fat blonde streaks looked nice on jet black hair, God help her. Somebody should have told her it looked awful.'

'If she hadn't been going out with Ewan, whom we love, I'd have certainly told her,' Arlene said menacingly. 'Proper little cow, she was.'

Cara roared with laughter. 'How do I measure up?' she asked gleefully.

Arlene turned away from the match and raised one exquisitely pencilled eyebrow as she surveyed Cara.

'You'll do,' she grinned. 'You're normal, like us. Ewan said you were dead on and he was telling the truth.'

The final whistle blew. Three:two to Dems.

After the usual back slapping and hand shaking, the teams dispersed, running either into the tiny clubhouse or over to the knots of supporters.

Arlene and Babs hurried off to their boyfriends while Ewan loped over to Cara.

'The girls giving you the third degree?' he panted, bending over and stretching his muscles.

'They now know my birth sign, my bank account number and what shampoo I use,' she joked. 'And we shared coffee, sandwiches and brandy which kept me from freezing to death. They're great fun, I like them,' she said truthfully.

'Knew you would.' Ewan stood up straight. 'Well, we got hammered, so myself and the lads feel we should go out and get hammered again, if you get my meaning. You're still on for going out for a meal?'

Even hot and sweaty, his face flushed from exertion, Ewan looked good. That wide, mobile and eminently kissable mouth was waiting for her answer.

'Of course. I wouldn't miss it for the world.'

'Great. I'll give you my keys and you can sit in the car while I shower.'

In the car park, Arlene and Babs were rummaging inside a massive black jeep, the doors open and M People's 'Moving On Up' pumping out of the stereo system.

Cara wandered over to say hello and her jaw dropped. They had come prepared in more than just the catering department, she realised with a shock as they both emerged from the back seat *sans* anoraks, wearing dressy clothes. Babs had replaced her faded denim outfit with a black brocade jacket worn over velvet bootlegs while Arlene was now encased in spray-on black jeans and a long-sleeved purple body that revealed a dizzying amount of cleavage each time the matching cardigan swung open. They'd swopped their pitch-side flat shoes for high heels but, even so, were both at least four inches shorter than Cara. Beside them, she felt more than a bit inadequate, not to mention very tall.

'Girls,' she said equably as she looked at her man's navy overcoat, tattered faded jeans, ancient lace-up brown boots, and Phoebe's crimson chenille jumper – lent for the occasion because Cara had nothing clean – 'you make me sick. How come you pair are done up to the nines after watching a football match in the freezing cold and I look like I've been *playing* in it?'

'Listen, girl,' said Arlene firmly, 'I have to make a big effort to look good because I'm short, put on weight quicker than a pregnant woman, and without blusher I've a face as round as Ronald McDonald. You, on the other hand, don't have to do anything. Look at you,' she said in exasperation, staring at Cara's fine-boned gypsyish face with its plump lips and huge dark eyes. 'You've amazing bone structure, blow job lips . . .'

Babs broke into howls of filthy laughter at this. 'Lucky Ewan,' she shrieked.

'And,' continued Arlene, 'you've got a great body with those bleedin' long legs I'd kill for.'

'Whaddya mean, great body?' muttered an astounded and embarrassed Cara. 'I'm just big, I'm like a man.'

'You're athletic,' Arlene said. 'Not big. If I looked like you do in jeans and that jumper, I wouldn't be bothering with all this slap now. So,' she asked with a smirk, 'does this worrying about what you're wearing mean you're coming out with us? Ewan'd like you to . . .'

Cara swatted Arlene's red ringlets with a gentle hand.

'Does the word "subtle" mean anything to you, Arlene?' she demanded good-humouredly.

Babs roared with laughter again. 'You wouldn't ask that question if you saw the leopardskin bikini she's just bought. It's got so much uplift, her boobs are pushed up around her chin and she could eat her dinner off them.'

By the time the lads arrived back at the cars, wearily carrying sports bags and slugging back cans of isotonic drinks, Cara and the girls were having their own little party in the comfort of the jeep, listening to M People and telling dirty jokes. Babs had produced a bag of diet chocolate bars which they'd wolfed down with the rest of the coffee, spiked with brandy, naturally.

'You were wunnerful,' slurred Babs, flinging herself at Michael when he opened the driver's door.

'You little wagons, you've started without us,' he said, getting a sniff of her boozy breath. 'We'll have to catch up.'

'Not the hip flask again, Babs,' Ewan groaned, appearing at the other door beside Cara, freshly washed dark hair flopping around his eyes. 'I told you pair to look after her, not get her pissed.'

'Nobody got me pissed,' interrupted Cara. 'I'm not pissed.'

'OK,' grinned Ewan, 'get out of the jeep and let's see you walk a straight line.'

Laughing, she tumbled out of the door, caught her boot in the dangling seatbelt and would have fallen flat on to the tarmac if he hadn't grabbed her.

'Shit!' she gasped, head buried against his scratchy woollen sweater, arms clutched around his waist as she tried to right herself.

'Not drunk, huh?' his voice said, surprisingly strong arms holding her safely.

Inside the jeep, the other girls were convulsed with laughter.

'She's pie-eyed!' screeched Babs between snorts of laughter.

Cara wriggled upwards, trying to get her balance back with one hand leaning on the jeep, the other on Ewan's shoulder. But he still held on to her, arms around her waist until they were standing face to face, hip bone to hip bone.

That close, she could smell the just-showered smell of him and feel the warmth of his breath against her cheek. For a brief moment she gazed into his face, letting her eyes roam over the intelligent, sexy eyes and down to the mobile mouth. He was watching her watching him, his gaze intense. The electricity between them was palpable and Cara felt as if time had stood still, as if there was nobody watching them, as if they were alone in the car park and anything could happen.

'Bruno's?' said somebody.

Cara wondered if she'd imagined it, a voice breaking into their own private world.

'Bruno's?' said the voice again. 'What do you think, Ewan? Are you on for Bruno's?'

He moved away from her, just a tiny movement but it broke the tension between them. 'Yeah, that'd be fine.' He looked at Cara. 'Would you like to go to Bruno's to eat?' he asked softly.

She nodded, thinking of what she'd like to do with Ewan and eating dinner in Bruno's wasn't on the list. Not at that moment anyway.

As if he could read her mind, Ewan grinned, kissed her gently on the lips in almost brotherly fashion, and took her hand. 'Let's go. We can go off for a drink on our own later, if you'd like?' he added.

Cara wondered if her eyes could bore into his soul, because she was sure he could see into hers. It was a heady feeling. She gave him a liquid gaze, her eyes dark. 'I'd like that very much,' she said in a voice that sounded huskier than normal.

They piled into two cars – the jeep and Ewan's sports car – and drove to the DART station where they left the cars and took the train into the city. Despite losing the match, everyone was in high spirits and it was a good-humoured group of six which piled into the restaurant, taking a table by the window where they could look through the frosted glass and watch the trendies of Temple Bar walk past.

Sitting beside Ewan, Cara had no idea what she ate. She could barely taste it anyway, although everyone else was in rhapsodies over the food.

'God, this seafood risotto is beautiful,' groaned Michael, shovelling huge forkfuls into his mouth.

'I know,' muttered Arlene, spearing a mussel, 'it's better than sex.'

Michael looked outraged. 'Whaddya mean, *better than*

sex?' he demanded, his mouth full.

Everyone howled.

'Not sex with you, darling,' she amended.

'Sex with who, then?' he said, even more outraged.

Everyone howled even louder.

Ewan leaned closer to Cara and whispered in her ear, his breath tickling the soft skin of her neck, 'Mine isn't better than sex.'

His fingers curled around her jeaned knee, caressing her as if he could feel skin instead of denim. She moaned softly at his touch.

'And you're not even eating the risotto,' Ewan remarked *sotto voce*.

Cara erupted into giggles and Arlene, who'd refused to discuss her risotto/sex comment any more, swivelled around in her chair. 'What's the joke?' she said brightly, wanting to distract Michael's attention from the knotty question of past lovers.

Cara shook her head helplessly.

'Private joke,' grinned Ewan broadly.

After a riotous dinner, the other four elected to go for a drink in The Foggy Dew.

'I think we'll call it a night,' Ewan said.

'Yeah,' added Cara, 'I've got an early start in the morning.'

'Slavedriver bosses are a pain,' said Dave, an arm around Babs as they all walked slowly up the street.

Ewan and Cara nodded earnestly, trying to look as if their desire to get home early was really to do with Bernard Redmond and not their longing to be on their own.

'We're going clubbing next weekend,' Babs said to Cara. 'You'll come, won't you?'

'I won't be around next weekend,' she said regretfully.

'My father's getting married next Saturday.'

'She'll come out with us the following week,' Ewan promised, sliding a warm hand into hers.

Everyone was sad to see her go but adamant she should go out with them again soon. They were so friendly that Cara felt warmed by their goodbye hugs and waves. Used to being always a little on the fringe of groups, it felt nice to be in the middle of one, welcomed and liked.

She and Ewan walked up to Dame Street and, miraculously, managed to hail a taxi without too much difficulty.

'Would you like to come back to my place?' he asked as he opened the taxi door for her.

She nodded.

They sat in the back of the cab, Ewan's hand in hers, and talked about the day. It had been so very long since Cara had been on a date that she knew she should have felt nervous at the thought of one. But today, even though it had been transformed from a casual day out into the pleasurable state of a proper date, hadn't made her in the slightest bit anxious. Now that they were on their own, she still felt relaxed. Sitting close to Ewan felt utterly and completely natural.

The taxi stopped at a crossroads and the glare of a street light shone in, illuminating Cara's profile and dusting her lustrous dark hair with silvery streaks. Ewan silently reached over and stroked the high bones of her left cheek, his fingers softly caressing.

'You're very beautiful, do you know that?' he said quietly.

It would have sounded corny had anyone else said it, if anyone would have dared. And if someone had, her first instinct would have been to punch their lights out.

But when Ewan said she was beautiful, Cara knew it was because he meant it. It wasn't a throwaway line designed to make her fall at his feet. She *was* beautiful to him; what was more, she *felt* beautiful with him, not a giantess with clumsy feet and unusual foreign looks.

'I didn't feel beautiful, not ever before,' she said, softly so the taxi driver wouldn't hear.

'But you do now?' prompted Ewan, his hand still gently touching her face.

She turned to smile at him, letting her face say it for her.

He lived in the basement flat of an old Georgian house in Dun Laoghaire. A young couple with kids lived in the upstairs but they'd cleverly had the floor between the two floors soundproofed, he explained as they walked up a tiny garden path to his front door, which meant that the tenant downstairs could make as much noise as they liked.

'It means I can play my old Abba records at full blast,' he joked.

Letting them into a tiny hall, Ewan touched a switch and the large airy room beyond was filled with light. Huge black and white movie posters dominated cream walls with a Mondrian-inspired rug sprawled out on wooden floorboards. But Ewan didn't give Cara a chance to check out his interior decorating skills. She, in turn, didn't want to.

At exactly the same moment, they turned and moved forward, seamlessly melting into each other. His mouth found hers and this time it was no brotherly kiss like the one in the soccer club car park. This kiss was strong and sensual, their mouths clinging together, probing, tongues twining deeply as they explored.

Cara dropped her rucksack to the ground and pushed off Ewan's coat. He struggled out of it, their lips still locked, before wrenching her out of her overcoat.

Silently, urgently, they clung together, hands touching each other as if they were in a battlefield, afraid a bomb was going to wipe them out instantly. As if every second was precious and none could be wasted with their bodies and mouths separate.

Ewan's lips pressed exquisitely into Cara's skin, moving over her face and neck: kissing, licking, consuming her. Her fingers shoved his jumper over his ribs and they stopped kissing for a moment while he ripped it and his shirt off, buttons pinging off as he dragged the unopened cuffs over his hands. Then they were touching again, his face in her hands as she tried to kiss his face all over, like a blind person's fingers reading Braille.

He moved his head rapidly to suck her fingers, imprisoning them in his mobile mouth and sucking them as if he wanted to eat her whole.

Then her hands were in his hair, pulling him closer to her as he burned a trail down her face and neck with molten kisses.

They half fell on to a couch Cara hadn't even noticed, bodies locked together in a frenzied embrace. She moved so that she was half lying on top of Ewan, her upper body crushed against his. Her eager mouth traced down the smooth skin of his chest to his nipples and he groaned as she nibbled gently.

Unable to wait a moment longer, Ewan sat up so he was propped against the couch back and started to pull her jumper up her body. Straddling him, Cara sat up and ripped Phoebe's chenille jumper up and dragged off her cosy grey T-shirt to reveal her completely plain white cotton bra. Through the soft fabric, her nipples stood out in rosy peaks and she could see his eyes darken as he gazed at her longingly.

'You're beautiful,' he said for the second time that day. Breathing heavily, their lips met passionately and briefly before he pushed her back to the other side of the couch, fingers and mouth exploring her body greedily.

Like dancers in a practised ballet, they seemed to sense exactly what the other wanted, moving in unison. At the same time, they wordlessly moved and stripped off the rest of their clothes, eyes locked on each other as they tore off jeans, socks and underpants. His body was lean and well-muscled, strong shoulders tapering down to narrow hips and long legs.

Naked, Cara stood for a moment, knowing that the harsh overhead lights were on her and not caring. For once she didn't feel too tall or unfeminine. She didn't worry that she hadn't rubbed scented lotion into every part of her body in case she smelt like a woman who'd had her shower over twelve hours previously. And she didn't care that it was at least a million years since she'd shaved her legs.

Ewan thought she was beautiful and when she was with him, she felt beautiful.

His hot eyes roamed over her nakedness, then he wrapped himself around her and she felt that taut, strong body hard against her. She almost shivered at the sensation of his skin against hers, revelling in the sensual experience of making love to this amazing man. She felt wanton, earthy, she wanted him to explore every part of her body, she wanted to lose herself in Ewan and let him lose himself in her. She didn't want it to stop. Ever.

With infinite tenderness, Ewan kissed Cara and led her back to the softness of the couch.

'Are you sure?' he asked as she lay down.

'Absolutely,' she replied. She'd never been so sure of anything in all her life.

He ripped the foil off a condom, not watching what he was doing but looking hungrily at her. Then he was inside her, hard and thrusting, and Cara felt herself open up at that exquisite moment, the feeling of utter closeness, physical and mental. It was glorious: the sensation of his mouth in her hair, breathing her name as they moved together expertly.

Her breath came in short gasps as they came together, their bodies fused in an electric moment, skin on skin, sensual and exhilarating all at the same time.

When she screamed his name as orgasm rippled through her, she felt as if she'd been set free from a prison, like a bird let out of a tiny cage. Her body quivered, high on the vibrating ecstasy of the moment, high on feeling his fevered passion for her before she felt the sweet peace of satiation flood through her.

'Cara,' Ewan moaned raggedly.

She held him to her, clinging to him as if letting go would be a disaster, until he shuddered to a halt, spent and exhausted.

'Just as well you've got an insulated ceiling,' Cara quipped, feeling lost in the silence after her fevered cries a few moments previously.

Ewan laughed and, arms still wrapped around him, Cara felt his flat stomach vibrate at the effort.

'You're right,' he said, 'because that was so good, the neighbours would probably want a cigarette afterwards.'

He turned sideways carefully, not wanting to fall off the couch which seemed far too small for two tall people to lie on it all of a sudden. Propping his head on one arm, he gazed at Cara.

'I gave up smoking four months ago and not having a cigarette now is probably the hardest moment in that entire four months.'

'You mean, you don't bring strange women home every Sunday to do this?' she asked, tongue in cheek.

'No,' he replied, his mouth finding hers again.

She closed her eyes and lost herself in his kiss, loving the sensation of lying tightly beside him, wrapped around each other, limbs tangled up.

Ewan seemed in no rush to move. He ran his fingers lightly over her shoulders, tracing the contours of her body, stroking every hollow and curve. Feeling like a cat lying in the sun, Cara simply lay back and enjoyed the feeling

He had the most incredible eyes, she thought idly. The outer rim of his iris was a deeper green than the rest of his eyes, as if a watercolour painter had carefully ringed the hypnotic cloudy green with a deeper, richer colour, almost the colour of verdigris on old copper. When he looked at her with that sleepy, sexual gaze, she felt as if he had the power to melt her insides.

'What are you thinking?' he asked.

It was Cara's turn to laugh. '*I'm* the one who's supposed to ask that. *You're* supposed to fall asleep and snore while I lie here and wonder where it's all going and should we get married in your parish or mine!'

Ewan didn't stop his gentle stroking, fingers caressing the curve of her waist and gliding down to touch the length of her thigh. 'I'm afraid that if I fall asleep, I'll lose you. That you'll have time to think, get scared, be afraid you've got too close and run out of here without saying goodbye. I don't want that to happen,' he added.

Cara said nothing. She just wondered how he could be so intuitive. Did he know that she'd had practically no relationships over the past six years? Had someone in the office been sneaking? But nobody knew that much about her private life, apart from Zoë.

'You're not going to run out on me?' he asked. 'I have this gut feeling that's your instinct.'

Cara's eyes met his.

'No,' she said. 'What makes you ask that?'

He shrugged. 'I can see it in your eyes. You're like a hedgehog, all prickly on the outside but soft and scared inside. When somebody gets to see the inside, you want to get away from them as quickly as possible.'

'I'm not going to run away,' she repeated. 'I promise.'

His face creased into a smile. 'Brilliant! How about moving into the bedroom, then, before I fall off this thing.'

'You mean, you have a *bedroom* too?' she asked in mock astonishment, looking around the airy living room. 'I thought this was it?'

In retaliation, he burrowed his fingers into her ribs, tickling her mercilessly until she pushed him off the couch.

'Brat,' he said, getting up off the floor. 'For that, I'm going to make you sleep on the wet patch.'

'What wet patch?' demanded Cara, swinging her feet to the floor.

'The wet patch we'll have created in a few minutes,' he replied, bending down and taking her nipple in his mouth.

When Cara opened her eyes, she felt momentarily disorientated. The room was dark but the streetlight that shone through the thin curtains in her bedroom wasn't on. The darkness was suffocating and she panicked, sitting up in the bed in terror. Her breathing got faster, she was panicking.

A hand slid out of the crumpled duvet and took hold of her arm.

'It's all right, Cara. You're with me.'

Ewan. She was in bed with Ewan after a glorious, glorious evening. Relief washed over her and she burrowed under the covers, aware of how cold it was outside the bed. Ewan's naked body was warm and he held her close, still half-asleep but wanting to curl his body around hers.

Spooned together in the warmth, Cara closed her eyes and dozed.

She was tired and she should probably go home soon. After all, they both had work in the morning. She had to be in early. She wondered what time it was and how difficult it would be to get a taxi back to the flat. It had to be after one in the morning anyway.

Then, as her ears adapted to the sounds around her, she became aware that the noises outside Ewan's flat weren't middle of the night noises. They were early-morning noises: the hum of heavy traffic, the sound of people walking up and down the street outside. She sat up again and looked at Ewan's side of the bed where a small Mickey Mouse alarm clock sat. Mickey's big hand was at eleven and his little hand was nearly at eight. Which meant five to eight and very, very late for work.

'Ewan!' she said. 'We've overslept.'

'Don't care,' he replied, stretching luxuriously and pulling her back down into the bed. His lips fastened on hers, his hands slid down her body to see if she was as aroused as he was.

Cara surrendered to his caresses in an instant. Who cared if they were fifteen minutes late in to work? she thought, wrapping herself around Ewan's warm, naked body.

Twenty-five minutes later, she was standing in Ewan's shower, jets of powerful water streaming all over her. What a shower! It even had a massage function. The one in her flat barely had a shower function and you needed to spend ten minutes under its limp drip to rinse the conditioner off your hair.

'Need any help?' inquired Ewan silkily, sticking his head around the curtain and giving her his best lascivious grin. His face was covered with shaving foam and he was brandishing a sponge.

'We'll never get to work if you get in here with me,' Cara said, flicking water at him.

'Spoilsport.'

He retreated and Cara turned her face up to the powerful stream of water and let it wash over her. It was hard not to compare this morning with the last morning she'd woken up with a man in bed beside her.

Although comparing Eric and Ewan was ludicrous. Their names both started with E, she giggled to herself, but that was where the similarity ended. Eric was a huge, alcohol-induced mistake but Ewan . . . he was something different. Something special.

She'd loved snuggling up beside him in bed; loved talking to him softly when they'd finished making love. She adored the way they fitted together so perfectly, the way her frame fitted exactly into the curve of his body, the way his arms held her tightly while he talked nonsense into her ear.

And, more importantly, she loved the way he understood her. He'd been so right about her immediate instinct being to run away after they'd made love. But wrong that it would happen with him. For the first time in years, Cara didn't want to run away from a man.

'You'll wash yourself down the plughole if you don't come out soon,' he yelled from outside the shower. 'I've made coffee for us.'

What to wear was the next problem. For her meeting with Bernard, Cara knew she couldn't turn up wearing her ratty jeans but she didn't have time to go home and change.

'Wear one of my shirts and I have a pair of black denims that are pretty respectable,' Ewan offered, as he pulled on a white T-shirt over grey casual trousers. 'You could try them.'

Dressed in a crisp black cotton shirt that was way too big for her and a pair of beautifully ironed jeans that were very snug, her damp curls tied back, Cara looked smart. Ewan sprayed her with his Eternity for Men, kissed her on the nose, then stood back to admire her.

'Beautiful. And sexy. In fact, we'll have to get out of here quickly or I'll want to jump on you again.'

'Don't be daft,' Cara said. 'Not until we've had breakfast at least,' she amended.

It took them five minutes to swallow two slices of toast each and gulp the remains of their coffee down before hurrying out the door.

With Ewan's car at the train station, they got a bus to pick it up then drove through endless traffic to the office.

'Maybe we should keep our relationship to ourselves,' Cara said delicately as they sat in a line of cars with five hundred yards to go before they reached Yoshi Advertising.

'What do you mean?' asked Ewan, his hand comfortably resting on her thigh, fingers idly sliding up and down the black cotton.

'Well . . .' she paused '. . . just not talk about it until . . . well . . . until we know each other better or . . .' She was really floundering now. 'Until we've been together for longer.'

Ewan didn't look pleased at the idea.

'You mean, hide that we're going out?' he demanded.

'Not hide, just be discreet. Bernard might not like it,' Cara added.

'Fuck Bernard!' Ewan replied venomously. 'He doesn't run our lives.'

'He's certainly trying to ruin mine,' Cara said gloomily. 'He makes my life hell whenever he can.'

'He will if you let him,' Ewan said succinctly.

CATHY KELLY

'Don't be cross,' she begged him. 'I'd just prefer us to keep our relationship to ourselves for a while, not let it become the biggest bit of office gossip since Bernard's secretary was caught in the men's toilet with a client. Can't you understand that?'

She couldn't bear to be the centre of attention, with people giving her knowing glances, the way they had all those years ago. Keeping her private life just that was too much of a habit to be abandoned now.

With shameless disregard for the laws of motoring, Ewan leaned over and kissed her firmly on the lips. 'I understand. I don't want to keep it a secret too long, though, Cara. I want to shout it from the rooftops. I want to be able to take you out to lunch every day and go for walks with you and . . .' he stopped and grinned '. . . drag you into the men's toilets myself!'

'And get us both fired?' she laughed, but felt bizarrely nervous in case anyone from Yoshi saw them together in the car. It would be just her luck for Bernard to be driving along in his Jag and spot them kissing. She could imagine what he'd say: 'No relationships between staff – one of you will have to go,' or something to that effect, and Cara would be out on her ear, jobless and referenceless. She couldn't risk that. 'I'll hop out here in case anybody sees us. I'll phone you later, OK?'

'And pretend to be my aunt in case anybody else answers,' he said drily.

'I won't be your aunt tonight,' Cara said huskily, a promising look in her dark eyes.

She clambered out into the heavy traffic, eyes darting around looking for Bernard's distinctive maroon Jag. He hadn't been able to get the vanity plates he wanted: BR 1.

Zoë reckoned he should have got DCKHD – abbreviation

212

for dickhead. But the car was nowhere in sight.

Cara marched along the road and swung into the lane by the office, hoping nobody would notice her new clothes or the gleam in her eyes. She couldn't wait to tell Zoë.

CHAPTER EIGHT

Cara and Evie weren't speaking to each other. Sybil and Leslie de Vere weren't speaking except in hushed voices because they were nursing horrible hangovers. And Olivia and Stephen were barely speaking at all.

Rosie was sick of the lot of them. She fidgeted in her pew at the front of the church, hands jammed in the pockets of her pony skin jacket. She could feel the new packet of Marlboros in her right pocket, still encased in their shiny paper. For her grandfather's wedding, she'd splashed out and bought twenty instead of ten and now they were just screeching to be smoked.

Well, she reasoned, after driving down in the car with her aunt and mother, both of whom were simmering on about Gas Mark 7, she reckoned it was going to be a long, long day and she'd be glad of the comfort of a fag. She wanted one now, in fact. But you couldn't leave the church while you were waiting for the bride, could you? Only if you were sitting down the back and could sneak back in unnoticed after she'd arrived. Rosie wished heartily she was sitting down the back and not beside her silent and bad-tempered extended family.

Even the great-aunts, Al and Elizabeth, who were usually game for a good chat whether they were in church or not, were quiet. Probably asleep, Rosie grinned to herself, looking at the two elderly ladies sitting beside her, both dressed in their Sunday best.

Grandpops looked great, she thought, pleased for him. In a smart grey suit with a cream rose in his buttonhole, he looked elegant and distinguished. Definitely not like a man in his late-sixties. Standing talking to his best man at the altar, he kept turning around and giving her encouraging winks, his kind eyes twinkling at her. She winked back.

Rosie sneaked a look at her watch under the guise of stretching out and flexing her wrists. Her mother would kill her if she saw Rosie openly looking at the time.

Ten past two. Vida was ten minutes late. Still, you were allowed to be late to your own wedding. Rosie decided she'd be at least half an hour late if it was *her* wedding. Not that she had any plans to get married. But if she did, she'd rather enjoy making them all wait for her so she could sweep up the aisle fashionably late, blowing kisses to ex-boyfriends and making them wish they were the lucky bloke at the altar.

Bored, she admired her chrome-coloured nail varnish for about the hundredth time. It was seriously Space Age and she loved it. Cara had given it to her before they'd started out that morning.

Rosie couldn't see why her mother had got in such a tizz over Rosie keeping them waiting an extra five minutes while she painted her nails with it. They were leaving way too early anyway.

Mind you, any time would have been too early to travel with her mother and Cara. The atmosphere in the car had been awful, so Rosie had plugged herself into her personal stereo and ignored them pointedly ignoring each other.

Her mother had addressed one sentence to her aunt.

Namely: 'I hope Vida isn't wearing white.' To which Cara had replied: 'Well, you're wearing it to your wedding, aren't you?'

After that, Rosie had given up all hope of reconciliation and had buried herself in an old Ella Fitzgerald tape that had belonged to her father.

She was keeping out of it.

Why couldn't her mother see that Cara didn't want a fight but wanted to make friends? And why couldn't Cara see that her mother hated being in the wrong, hated being criticised and had no idea how to apologise without feeling she'd let herself down in some way? God, Rosie just wished the pair of them would grow up.

Evie couldn't help admiring the flowers. In a wicked thought she'd immediately regretted, she'd half-hoped the Ballymoreen church would be done up like a bordello with a riot of mismatching bright blooms vying with each other for supremacy, maybe with some garish ribbons thrown in for good measure. It would have been proof that Vida Andersen wasn't the queen of taste she pretended to be, a Martha Stewart clone.

But there wasn't a clashing crimson, lilac, delphinium blue and daffodil arrangement in sight. Instead, the mellow stone of the old church was decorated with velvety roses in the palest ivory, tied up with fragile grey ribbons. Very elegant. Evie had to admit it looked lovely.

She caught her father winking at Rosie. Her daughter, who hadn't stopped fidgeting since they'd sat down, winked broadly back. Evie leaned forward and shot a glare along the pew in her direction but Rosie was pretending to stretch her arms in an attempt to see what time it was.

Evie wished she could sneak a glance at her own watch

217

or even ask Rosie the time but, sandwiched between Great Aunt Al and her mother's second cousin, Fidelma, who'd turned up out of the blue for the wedding, she couldn't move. And she wouldn't ask Cara, who was sitting the other side of Fidelma. Evie could feel the waves of hostility coming from her sister. It had been that way all morning.

Cara was just so irritating. Couldn't she see that Evie didn't want to continue their row?

But once she got in a mood, that was it. Evie had even tried to talk to her that morning but had got her head bitten off in the process. She'd only made a simple comment about hoping Vida wasn't going to turn up in a ludicrous white fluffy dress and Cara had been so bitchy in return. I mean, how dared she make that smart remark about Evie's wedding dress? Evie felt herself flush again with remembered indignation.

If she wasn't the elder of the two and with an example to set, she'd have loved to have slapped Cara's face.

At a signal from the priest, the organist sprang into action and the low throaty warble of the elderly organ vibrated around the church. Everyone sat up straighter in their seats and craned their necks for the first glimpse of the bride. Evie, with a suddenly developed lump in her throat, looked at her father instead. His lined face, as dear and familiar to her as her own, was illuminated with joy. The furrows in his forehead magically disappeared as he watched Vida walk slowly up the aisle. He looked happier than Evie had seen him for a long time.

The tears pooled in her eyes, brimming over the fringe of bottom lashes. Evie held her breath, desperately, trying to stop them from starting to fall.

She hated herself at that moment, hated all those jealous thoughts she'd done her best to quell but hadn't quite been able to. How could she not want her beloved father to be happy? He deserved happiness. Cara was right, she was a cast-iron bitch. She was sorry she'd been so adamant about not letting Rosie be a bridesmaid either.

Too late, she realised the tears were falling. She snuffled frantically, hoping nobody else could see. Thankfully she was hidden behind Aunt Al's vast puce wool bulk and hopefully if anybody *did* notice her crying, they'd think she was overcome with the usual wedding weeping fit. She couldn't help it, though.

Watching her father stand at the altar and replace her wonderful mother was still so very painful. But, Evie decided with a resolute snuffle, she'd mourn during the ceremony and afterwards she'd start again. She'd show her father she was happy for him, she'd dance at his wedding – tight skirt suit and Olivia's toe-crunching shoes permitting – and she'd smile at his new bride.

If only she could warm to Vida. If he'd been marrying anyone else, Evie could have been totally, one hundred per cent happy for both of them. Yahoo, where are the balloons, let's all celebrate! Yet she wasn't happy. There was something about the cool-eyed American woman she didn't like. Evie couldn't admit to herself that the problem might be her own jealousy.

As the organ wheezed asthmatically, the bride finally came into her line of vision, looking just as wonderful as Evie had secretly suspected she would.

Radiant in a discreet grey suit, Vida smiled at her husband to be. Her hair was held up in its usual classic chignon, with a jewelled clip the only adornment. In her own conservative blue, with her hair done up in rock hard curls and wearing an overbright lipstick in an attempt to look cheerful, Evie felt like a 'fifties Avon lady by comparison.

Vida handed her ivory bouquet to her one attendant, her very unmatronly-looking best friend from New York who was just as chic in a darker grey suit with a helmet of perfectly coiffed Ladies-Who-Lunch hair. Evie sighed. How could you compete with that? Vida and her matron of honour could have stepped out of a *Vanity Fair* editorial on Manhattan style. *She* felt like she wouldn't make the grade in the style section of *Lumberjack Weekly*.

Don't get maudlin, she told herself firmly. Try and enjoy the wedding.

Four-year-old Sasha, adorable in white raw silk with a big silvery grey sash, looked trustingly up at Vida, who held out her hand to the little girl.

She was a poppet, Evie thought, eyes filling up again as she remembered Rosie at the same age. At least Olivia and Stephen had each other, even if they weren't getting on brilliantly. When Rosie had been the same age, Evie had been on her own, a lonely widowed mother.

She still felt as if she was on her own. Simon hadn't been able to make the ceremony and was coming later, so Evie had to endure yet another wedding feeling like the only single woman in a sea of married ones. She felt another tear wobble on her eyelashes. Weddings were so difficult.

While the priest welcomed the congregation, Cara hoped Vida understood that being a bridesmaid wasn't her thing. She'd been terrified she'd have to wear the requisite horrible pink/peach/baby blue satin dress that'd make her look like something that had just come back from the upholsterer's.

Vida's best friend, Katherine, didn't look like the sort of woman who'd take kindly to being jammed in a pink frilly thing, so maybe that was why she was wearing a very unbridesmaidy suit. Cara was pretty sure that if *she'd* said yes to her stepmother-to-be's request, she'd have been looking ugly in pink.

Or maybe not. Ewan thought she always looked beautiful so perhaps she *could* have worn a bridesmaid's dress without looking too hideous.

Ewan . . . Just thinking about him sent a pleasurable shiver down Cara's spine. What an incredible week it had been. They'd spent every evening together: going out to dinner in a tiny Italian restaurant, going to the cinema to watch the latest Spielberg movie, and sitting in a quaint little pub laughing and talking nineteen to the dozen over far too many bottles of Beck's afterwards.

And then there'd been the lovemaking. They'd gone to Ewan's place the first couple of evenings and once inside the door had fallen on each other hungrily, barely waiting to take their clothes off before making love, frantically and passionately. Afterwards they'd sit half-dressed and watch TV and sip coffee before turning to each other again, limbs entwined, as they made love at a more leisurely pace.

Cara would have loved to have stayed with Ewan each night and he asked her to, but she didn't want to stagger into work in borrowed clothes again so he dropped her home every time, sitting in the steamed up car outside her flat for at least half an hour as they said their goodbyes.

She'd taken him to her place on Thursday, after a mammoth cleaning up session that morning when she'd hoovered and tidied her room in an attempt to get rid of at least three months' worth of dust and unwashed socks lurking under the bed.

Phoebe had been out so Ewan and Cara had had the place to themselves. They'd cuddled up on the old sofa and had a couple of Cara's beloved Mars Bar ice creams before retreating to the dust-free bedroom and losing themselves in hours of blissful pleasure.

On Friday night, Ewan had to visit his mother who was still devastated over the death of her one-time lover, so Cara had to go home on her own for the first time in a week.

She'd felt empty and lonely as she sat in the silent flat, flicking channels listlessly and wishing she'd gone out for that drink with Zoë. She missed Ewan, she realised, missed his arms around her and missed his good-humoured teasing.

When he'd phoned late that night, missing her just as much as she was missing him, it made up for being on her own.

'I wish you were coming to the wedding,' she said, cradling the phone as if it was a part of him she was caressing. 'I should have asked Vida if I could bring you. She wouldn't mind.'

'It's a bit short notice,' Ewan said easily. 'They probably have the numbers worked out and another guest would screw things up for them.'

'Another guest would make it perfect for me,' breathed Cara, 'if the guest was you.'

But Ewan was playing football on Saturday, she hadn't mentioned him to Vida and she was going to have to endure an entire twenty-four hours without him.

Sighing, she wondered if anyone could see the glow on her face, what Phoebe called her 'Sugar, I got me a man!' glow? Evie hadn't, that was for sure. Cara had been dying to tell her sister that she'd just found the most incredible man in the world but after ten seconds in Evie's company that morning, it had been clear that her sister was still in the throes of her anti-Vida syndrome.

There was no point talking to her when she was like that, Cara decided, irritated. She'd never seen Evie behave so badly in all her life. Usually, Evie was a rock of good

sense, too damn' sensible in fact. But their father's marriage had rocked her like an earthquake and now Evie was
behaving like a spoilt child denied that extra chocolate.

Cara knew she ought to make things up with her sister
but she was fed up with Evie's childishness – and too
engrossed in thinking about her beloved Ewan to bother.
Evie was a grown up after all, let her deal with it.

Olivia watched her daughter standing at the altar, her mind
far away on this morning's row. Everything had started out
so well. She'd brought Stephen breakfast in bed: coffee,
orange juice, scrambled eggs, toast and the newspaper.
Sasha had been scampering in and out of the room in her
Winnie the Pooh pyjamas, trying on the artificial floral
head-dress Olivia had bought to get her used to the real
thing, a delicate wreath of real rosebuds.

Bright sunlight filtered in through the window, casting
pools of glorious light on the crisp white bedclothes and
shining on the carefully polished dark dressing table where
no clutter was allowed. As Stephen sat in state, eating his
breakfast, Olivia perched on the side of the bed, sipping
coffee and kissing Sasha each time her daughter rushed in.

'Aren't you eating?' Stephen asked finally, mouth full of
scrambled egg.

Olivia shook her head, smiling at him. She didn't want
to tell him her appetite had disappeared so that forcing a
piece of toast down her throat felt like Chinese water
torture.

'You must have something.' Stephen looked mulish.

'I had some fruit,' lied Olivia.

Her husband harumphed, letting her know that in his
august opinion fruit was no substitute for a proper breakfast. 'I suppose you're dieting? I don't know why, you're
too thin already.'

Olivia bit her lip and said nothing.

Half an hour later, she stood in the shower stall and let the steaming water flood over her face and hair, revelling in the solitude and the blissful warmth of the water. She loved the shower, loved the aquamarine mosaic tiles on the walls and floor that made it feel like showering in a Mediterranean villa.

'Olivia!' yelled Stephen, impatiently opening the bathroom door and standing right beside the steaming shower. 'I can't find my blue shirt. Where is it?'

Knowing exactly where the shirt was – in the washing machine half-way through the cotton cycle – Olivia felt that familiar wrenching feeling in her gut. 'Give me a minute, darling,' she stammered, thinking that if she finished the wash cycle early and stuck the shirt in the dryer, it'd be ready in thirty minutes.

This didn't suit Stephen.

'Christ! Didn't you know I wanted to wear that shirt with my good suit?'

No, I didn't, Olivia wanted to say. I'm not psychic. I wash and iron all your stuff on the off-chance you might feel like wearing some of it. I never know exactly which suit you feel like wearing on a particular day. Instead, she grimaced meekly and apologised again.

Stephen had been irate after that and Olivia knew there wasn't a snowball's chance in hell he'd be civil during the wedding. She mentally tried to work out which guest she could beg Vida to put him beside so he wouldn't be bored. Vida would understand, she thought blindly. Vida wouldn't mind upsetting her carefully worked out seating plan if it came to making sure Stephen didn't throw a tantrum during the day.

She and Sasha got ready silently, the joy of dressing her daughter in the fairy-tale flower-girl dress diminished by the icy mood in the apartment. The sunlight streaming in at the windows felt wintry now and Olivia shivered in her thin dressing gown, goosebumps all over her too-slender body. Stephen certainly knew how to create an atmosphere, she reflected as she tried to smile gamely at Sasha. She knelt on the floor and did up the tiny covered buttons.

'We're going to have a lovely day,' she chanted, 'lovely, lovely day.' The little girl knew better.

'It'll be all right, Mummy,' she whispered. 'I asked Santa to make it better.'

It was all Olivia could do to stop herself breaking into hysterical sobs. Poor little Sasha. In her innocence, she'd asked the most powerful person she could think of to fix things, not realising that it'd take more than a cuddly old man in a red suit to make things better between her parents.

'Sasha,' she said quietly, so Stephen wouldn't overhear, 'there's nothing to make better. Mummies and daddies have fights sometimes, that's all.'

The little girl regarded Olivia for a moment from serious silver-grey eyes.

'Scary fights?' she asked.

Her mother hesitated. How could she say, 'Yes, scary fights,' when she knew that lots of people didn't have arguments the way she and Stephen did: vicious and bitter comments from him, cowardly silences from her. Fights that must be utterly terrifying to a child. She didn't want to lie to Sasha but how could she tell her the truth? Four year olds shouldn't hear stuff like that.

'Yes, scary fights because daddies get tired from working and having lots of things to worry about . . .' Sasha was still gazing at her with those big eyes but Olivia ploughed on. 'And they're not really scary because we know that Daddy loves us and doesn't mean it, don't we?'

Sasha didn't look convinced. I'll have to learn how to be a better liar, Olivia thought anxiously. And then an idea sparked in her head, like lightning hitting a church spire, frightening and fierce. Why should she learn how to lie? Why lie at all? Surely, if she and Stephen didn't have the sort of relationship where Sasha could live without fear, then they shouldn't be together. It was that simple.

Like the church spire after the lightning strike, Olivia's mind remained white hot with her own astonishing idea. Her thoughts raced, frantic and turbulent, as the notion stuck in her head. Why stay with somebody who made you so miserable and who was clearly so miserable with you? And why stay when the daughter you adored was driven to asking a mythical Christmas figure for help when her father lost his temper and vented his all-too-frequent rage? The solution was clear. It was simplicity itself.

'Olivia!' roared Stephen and, as if scared that he could see into her mind and discover the forbidden thoughts lurking there, she got up nervously and ran to the door.

'Yes?'

'You're not wearing that to the wedding, surely?'

That was the simple navy trouser suit she'd decided to wear with a cream silk knit top underneath. It was very plain but that was partly why she'd chosen it: she didn't want to upstage Vida, and anyway, the way Olivia felt, she *wanted* to blend into the furniture.

'You'll look like a little mouse. It's too boring, far too dull,' sniped Stephen, holding the suit at arm's length and looking at it as if it was infectious. 'Wear your white wool dress with the black jacket. You've never worn it and it cost me a fortune in London.'

Starkly geometric and quite startling, the outfit would make her stand out in the crowd as plainly as if she had a halo of flashing lights over her head screeching 'Bought At

Great Expense in Harvey Nichols'. The dress was short and showed off far too much of her legs, and it was white, for Godsake! You couldn't wear white to a wedding, it was unfair to the bride.

'Stephen,' she started. 'I don't really want to wear that . . .'

But he didn't let her finish. Utterly used to getting his own way, it never occurred to Stephen MacKenzie that his wife might not want to wear his choice in clothes.

'Olivia, wear it. You haven't a clue, have you?'

He turned on his heel, convinced that the matter was now over. Olivia would do what he'd asked – she always did. It was that dismissive action that decided her. The simple 'the conversation is over' gesture that sent Olivia hurtling over the edge.

Under normal circumstances – normal, placate-Stephen-at-all-costs circumstances – she would have smiled sweetly at him, done what he wanted and said nothing. Like she'd done on myriad occasions before when Stephen screamed at her because the tea tasted funny or she'd bought the orange juice he didn't like or, worst of all, when she'd got his car repaired at the wrong garage while he'd been away.

But on the morning of Andrew Fraser's wedding, when she was doing her best to keep her husband in a good mood so he wouldn't get too bored during the day, something snapped inside Olivia MacKenzie. Maybe it was thinking about Cheryl Dennis's latest exploit which had involved joking loudly and throwing paper aeroplanes throughout a whole double period, blatantly ignoring Olivia's attempts to quieten her down. Maybe it was because she was worn out with misery and her blood sugar level was non-existent because she couldn't eat. Or maybe she'd simply had enough of her domineering husband.

227

She slammed the door shut so that Sasha wouldn't hear and faced him, eyes blazing.

'Are you ever going to stop telling me what to do, Stephen, or are we going to live like this for the rest of our lives – you shouting at me at the very end because I died in the wrong place, at the wrong time, and it didn't fit in with your plans?'

He almost gasped with shock. For one brief triumphant moment Olivia saw astonishment mixed with bewilderment on his face. His dark eyes were wide open, the same as his mouth.

She was breathing heavily, stunned that she'd said anything but unable to stop, the momentum pushing her on.

'I'm sick of it, Stephen! Sick of you treating me like some cretinous child who can't make up its mind about anything! You think I'm an idiot. Well, I'm not!'

He recovered with dizzying aplomb, taking her victory and shattering it.

'My God, Olivia, you're turning into your mother,' he said, lips curled in disgust. 'Hysterical and ranting, like some crazed banshee. I never thought I'd see the day. You're not fit to be a mother to Sasha. Do you want to destroy her the way your mother destroyed you with these ridiculous tantrums?'

Olivia stared at him, devastated. She wasn't anything like her mother, was she? And she wasn't hurting Sasha. She loved her daughter, adored her. She'd never do anything to hurt Sasha.

Stephen wasn't finished.

'I don't know what you're hoping to achieve with this behaviour, Olivia,' he said, his voice vicious. 'I only want the best for you but you're determined to twist everything I say into something negative. Maybe it runs in your family. Your mother can't open her mouth without savaging someone and you've gone the same way.'

She crumpled. Unused to voicing any opinion these days, she was utterly unaccustomed to being angry with Stephen. She'd wanted to say something for so long but because the mirror never answered back when she practised her rage on it, she'd totally forgotten that he could respond, that she wouldn't be speaking in a vacuum.

And Stephen *was* responding. When he was angry, his ice-cold rage had the power to cut through anyone. It ripped through Olivia's soft centre like a rapier slashing through feather pillows.

'I didn't mean . . .' she said hoarsely, wanting to say that she was merely standing her ground about what to wear to the damn' wedding.

He didn't want to hear. 'I know exactly what you meant, Olivia,' he said coldly. 'Wear what you want. You de Veres always do what you want anyway.'

He slammed the door behind him and she sank on to the bed, too stunned to cry. Was she turning into her mother? It was her greatest fear, to become like the vicious and cruel woman she'd had to fight hard to love.

You were supposed to love your mother, but it was just so hard sometimes. She tried to be different, tried to be soft and gentle instead of unyielding and selfish like Sybil.

Perhaps she was kidding herself that she was soft. Perhaps she was really a bitch, a stupid bitch who'd end up lonely and unloved, having turned her only daughter and her husband away from her.

Shaken to the core, Olivia sat white-faced, one hand nervously scratching at the unmade bed, bringing up little bobbles on the sheet.

After ten minutes, she knew she had to move. She could hear Stephen pottering about inside, could almost feel the white hot rage he'd been in. What had she done? Why had she said anything? Her outburst hadn't solved anything; it had only made matters worse. Now Stephen would be in a total fury all day.

Olivia's head throbbed at the thought of an entire day like this. How would she cope?

The solution came to her – the tablets Stephen had been given for his back. Valium. The doctor recommended both a muscle relaxant and a painkiller when Stephen's back went into its rare but agonising spasm. He'd never taken any of the valium, of course, preferring to suffer, and not in silence, either.

The little container was still in his part of the bathroom cabinet, full to the brim. She took one and peered at it. Five mg. Washing the tiny tablet down with a splash of water from the cold tap, she was about to put the container back but thought better of it. She took another two tablets for later. Better safe than sorry.

Now, vaguely anaesthetised, Olivia sat beside the surly figure of her husband and listened to the priest going on about the holy state of marriage.

She closed her eyes and tried to tune his voice out. She'd rather not think about the state of her own marriage and, she thought caustically, he was hardly speaking from experience, was he? What the hell did he know about family rows and bitter arguments between man and wife? If he'd ever been married or in a relationship with someone as difficult as Stephen, perhaps he wouldn't be quite so keen to discuss love in that general, rose-coloured-glasses way.

Ahead of her sat Evie, a small upright figure in blue, unmoving as a marble statue while her father got married.

Olivia wondered idly what it would be like to give a fiddler's toss about your parents marrying again. Although at least if her parents stayed married to each other, they wouldn't have the chance to make two other people deeply unhappy as well.

Evie had taken Andrew's remarriage badly at first although she was coming round.

'We're going to have a wonderful day,' she had said firmly on the phone the night before when Olivia had rung to see how her friend was bearing up. 'I won't let you down, Livvy. I promise not to scream and roar,' she'd joked. 'Honest! If I can dance in those perilous shoes you've lent me, I'll dance away like a mad thing and show Dad I'm delighted for him.'

'I'm so glad,' Olivia said with relief. 'You'd hate yourself afterwards if you didn't. It's going to be a lovely wedding and Sasha is terribly excited about being a flower girl. She's in bed now, quivering with excitement at the thought of wearing a princess dress and having flowers in her hair!'

Nothing had worked out quite as planned, though. Sasha was subdued after the row between her parents, while Cara and Evie were sitting as far apart on the church pew as was possible, a sure sign of trouble. Olivia could never quite figure out what had ruined their once incredibly close relationship. They'd been best friends for so long, more like mother and daughter than two sisters. It was sad that they were feuding. Olivia would have done anything to have a sister of her own, someone who could share her horrible childhood. Someone who could have diluted the alcoholic misery of the Lodge when she was growing up.

In her mind, once you actually *had* a sister, you had to appreciate her. Under the benevolent haze of the valium she'd taken an hour and a half previously, Olivia decided to sort out Evie and Cara. She'd do something wonderful for other people, even though her own life was a disaster.

★ ★ ★

'Daddy, Daddy, are we nearly there?' asked Sasha plaintively, looking out of the window and ignoring the glorious countryside Olivia was admiring.

'Ask your mother,' he snapped. 'She knows everything.'

Olivia didn't even flinch.

'Yes, darling,' she said calmly. 'Another few minutes and the photographer will be taking lots of lovely photos of you in your princess dress.'

'With Auntie Vida and Uncle Andrew?' asked Sasha, brightening up.

'Yes.'

They pulled up outside Kilkea Castle and Stephen was out of the car and rummaging around in the boot before Olivia had time to take off her seat belt. Charming, she thought. He can't bear to spend two minutes more than necessary with me. She wondered whether his icy demeanour would last till bedtime. In her experience, his desire nearly always overcame whatever sulk he was in.

Stephen actually believed that an energetic sex session could make it up to Olivia when he'd been rude or sharp with her. He'd never quite grasped the concept that sex in itself wasn't an apology.

As far as Olivia was concerned, you might have decent lovemaking *after* the apology, but you never had anything but one partner tearfully on the verge of breaking down if you had sex *without* the 'I'm sorry, darling, I *do* love you, honest.'

Because of that, she'd gone through far too many staring-up-at-the-ceiling-trying-not-to-cry nights. No, she decided tranquilly, Stephen would never last the night in a glamorous four-star hotel without wanting to make full use of the facilities. Tonight, she thought with a small smile, she didn't think she'd be in the mood.

★   ★   ★

Cousin Fidelma was wedged into the passenger seat of Evie's car and no amount of pulling could get her out. The combination of Fidelma's unsupple seventeen-stone-plus body and a wonky right leg that couldn't bend meant she was imprisoned by the dashboard of the small car.

'I should have put you in the taxi with Al and Elizabeth,' Evie said anxiously, wondering how she was ever going to lever Fidelma out. It had been difficult enough getting her *in*. That in itself should have set alarm bells ringing but Fidelma had been adamant about travelling with Evie 'so we can catch up on all the gossip'.

They hadn't caught up on very much because Fidelma, who was on tablets for the pain in her leg, had dropped off immediately they drove out of the church car park, leaving Evie to fume in indignant silence about how Cara and Rosie had both conveniently jumped ship and gone off in a rackety old Volvo with the great-aunts, cigarette smoke and laughter bellowing out the windows as it shuddered off.

As soon as I get there, Evie thought crossly, I'm having the biggest glass of champagne I can get my hands on. Stuck at the back of a convoy of big, expensive cars en route to the hotel, she got crosser still.

'Vulgar gas-guzzlers,' she muttered as a great big tank of a German car swerved dangerously in front of her to avoid hitting a poor cyclist. 'That thing is a threat to the environment!'

'I'm sorry, Evie,' said Fidelma piteously from the depths of the front seat, bringing her firmly back to reality.

'No, don't be,' said Evie, immediately contrite. 'We'll get you out of there in a trice. Just wait.'

Fidelma's sweet rounded face relaxed a fraction. Around seven years older than Andrew Fraser, she somehow looked years younger thanks to her moon face which didn't have a wrinkle in sight.

Only the floral print two-piece and matching turban squashed on her grey curls gave a hint that Fidelma wouldn't see seventy again. But when she spoke, her sweet little-girl voice made her appear like a child in a grown-up's body.

'I'm terribly sorry,' she said again meekly.

Evie sensed that if it took much longer, Fidelma would begin to panic. It was time for speedy action. She looked around the hotel car park blindly. As most people had arrived before she did, abandoning cars at frantic, haphazard angles in order to get at the free champagne before it was all gone, the car park was now empty of any member of the wedding party. Evie didn't want to leave Fidelma on her own but she needed to get some help.

A smooth clicking noise from the car parked nearest to her caught Evie's attention.

Sleek, black and very expensive-looking, the car reminded her briefly of the one Richard Gere had driven in *Pretty Woman*, one of Evie's favourite films. In her dreams, she'd been the beautiful young Julia Roberts many times, desperately in love and hoping for the fairy tale.

A low-slung door opened and a man stepped out. He wasn't Richard Gere, Evie thought, startled, he was better. Tall, darker than your average Irishman, and with his shock of jet black hair sleeked loosely back from a tanned, strong-boned face, he was devastatingly attractive.

Then he smiled at her, a broad, amused smile that opened up his bronzed face and displayed a flash of very white teeth.

For a moment, she could only stare. With those big solid shoulders and long, long legs, he looked like every romantic, bodice-ripping hero she'd ever read about, except that he wasn't quite as lantern-jawed as the he-men oil painted beautifully on the covers of *Davina's Desires* or *The Jade Princess*.

He was real flesh and blood instead of one-dimensional paint. He wore what was obviously a very continental suit, something grey with a sheen to it. A buttoned-up shirt but no tie. *And he was coming over to her and Fidelma.*

Evie gulped and moved closer to her car, instinctively smoothing down her skirt which had got wrinkled during the drive. Had her lipstick all gone? Was her hair all right? Would he notice if she bent down to check how she looked in the mirror . . .

'I think you may need some assistance?' he said. He loomed over her, dwarfing her with his size and sheer presence.

Up close, Evie could see that his eyes were the deepest blue imaginable with long dark lashes, almost like a girl's. They were the only feminine thing about him. Otherwise, he was all male. All six foot something of handsome, healthy masculinity.

The heroine of *Davina's Desires* would have known what to say to such a creature, Evie thought blindly, something provocative or intriguing. She just gawped at him.

'Do you need help?' he asked again.

His voice was rich and dark, like finely aged whiskey rippling over gravel. Not Irish but she couldn't put her finger on the accent. She refocused, aware he was watching her with the faintest glimmer of a smile. God, he was waiting for her to answer!

'Er . . . well, yes,' she said blankly. 'We do have a bit of a problem.' With an expressive flick of her eyes, she tried to let him see what the problem was without actually saying anything in order to save poor Fidelma's blushes.

He took in the situation instantly.

'You know, modern cars don't have much room in them,' added Evie, for Fidelma's benefit.

'I agree,' he said, amusement glinting in his eyes. As if a man with a state-of-the-art sports car wasn't quite aware that Evie's battered Ford Fiesta was at least ten years old.

'People were always getting stuck in this model, I believe,' he lied gently, as he leaned into the car and took Fidelma's arm. 'I heard they recalled quite a few of them to the factory.'

'Did they?' she asked with relief.

How kind of him, thought Evie. What a lovely man.

'If I support you like this,' he was saying to Fidelma, 'then we can get you out.'

For thirty seconds, Evie looked on worriedly as the big man carefully helped Fidelma to freedom, lifting her not insubstantial upper body with ease. He chatted comfortingly to her all the time, nonsense about car companies and how they forget that modern ladies like a bit of leg room. Finally, they managed it and Evie's elderly relative got to her feet and grabbed her rescuer's hands in gratitude.

'Thank you so much,' she tittered. 'I don't know what I'd have done if you hadn't come along, my dear.'

Evie looked at Fidelma in amazement. She was actually red in the face, blushing like a shy seventeen year old under the stranger's gaze. How astonishing.

'I'm glad I could help,' he said, turning to Evie and taking her hand in his.

To her own shame and amazement, she could feel herself flush up like a ripe peach. It was the *way* he was looking at her, she thought, an undress-you-with-his-eyes look.

She snatched her hand back.

'Thank you,' she said crisply, determined to reassert her

dignity. Yes, he'd come to their rescue but now she was finished with him, he needn't hang around like the conquering hero whose next question was going to be: 'Would you have a drink with me, ladies?'

No way, Jose.

The dark eyebrows rose a fraction at her abruptness and Evie could imagine them sitting low over his eyes in anger or rising in amusement at will.

'I don't suppose I could buy you ladies a drink to get you both over your ordeal?' he asked, directing the question at Evie.

'Ooh, yes, we'd love that! Wouldn't we, Evie?' squealed Fidelma girlishly.

Evie shot her relative a quelling glance but it had no effect. Fidelma was gazing at the man in rapt delight.

'It might do you good to have a brandy to settle your nerves after your ordeal,' he said to her, 'before you go into the wedding.'

Fidelma blossomed like a Georgette Heyer heroine asked to a ball by a previously girl-hating marquis.

'How do you know we're going to a wedding?' demanded Evie suspiciously, for once feeling much more hard-eyed female private eye than frilly Regency heroine.

'I'm going to it and I'm sure you ladies are, too, because you're both so beautifully dressed,' he replied in that cultured, deep voice.

Evie hadn't known that Fidelma could giggle but she did.

'Oh, go away out of that, young man,' she cooed girlishly, hitting him a whack on the arm with her handbag.

He grinned, the combination of white teeth and tanned skin making him appear positively wolfish. He was dangerous-looking, Evie decided with an exquisite little shiver, sophistication and elegance wrapped around a rogue in Italian wool. She wasn't sure if her rapidly increasing pulse was because she liked him or not.

'Forgive my rudeness,' he apologised. 'How can you go for a drink with someone you don't know? I'm Max Stewart.'

'Fidelma Burke,' said Fidelma quickly, 'and this is Evie Fraser.'

'Nice to meet you both. May I call you Fidelma or is it Mrs Burke?' he inquired.

'Fidelma will do for me and Evie doesn't stand on ceremony either,' replied Fidelma coquettishly.

Evie looked around to see if a *Mrs* Stewart was going to emerge from the black sports car, all gazelle-like limbs, sleek South of France blonde hair, gold jewellery like cow chains and wearing something with Dior on the label. That was the sort of woman a man like Max would be married to, surely.

'I came on my own,' he said gravely, as if he'd noticed her surreptitiously wife-spotting. 'So I'd love two elegant ladies on my arm.'

No sooner were the words out of his mouth than Fidelma was glued to him like a limpet. Evie wondered what had come over her. It must be those tablets.

'Evie?'

She'd been about to smile and walk in by herself but there was something about the way he said her name that stopped her.

His blue eyes were serious now, as if he really wanted her to have a drink with him. It was flattering to have this debonair man looking at her in that warm, frankly admiring manner. It certainly made a welcome change from Rosie and Cara's earlier defection. Here at least was one person who obviously didn't think she was boring, grumpy and best left to entertain elderly, drugged-up-to-the-eyeballs relatives.

'Please?'

Sensible, circumspect and outwardly proper, Evie Fraser found that she couldn't resist, even though she felt she should. There was something quite dangerous about Max Stewart. Dangerous, unpredictable and yet vastly exciting. Nothing like Simon, she thought, immediately hating herself for being disloyal.

But he was miles away, detained by some boring meeting he'd refused to miss because it was: 'With the directors, Evie, and I couldn't let them down, you know that.' He'd prefer to let her down by arriving at the wedding after the ceremony and the meal.

Well, what Simon didn't know about couldn't hurt him, could it? It was only a drink after all. What harm could there be in that?

'Yes, I'd like that,' she found herself saying.

Max took her arm and Evie felt a thrill of excitement shoot up from her elbow as all the tiny hairs on her arm stood up straight.

He was so big, he made her feel like a little sprite of a thing, a tiny, fragile creature instead of a woman constantly warding off a garage full of spare tyres. God, she wished somebody could see her now, Evie Fraser being escorted by this incredible guy.

Inside the hotel, she barely noticed the elegantly vaulted ceiling, the suits of armour or the rich medieval pennants hanging from stone walls. All she was aware of was Max Stewart standing close to her. He was talking to Fidelma, making her giggle. But Evie still felt utterly conscious of his every movement. She wanted to watch him, to see his head thrown back laughing at something silly Fidelma had said, to see the lines around his glittering eyes when he

CATHY KELLY

smiled. It was exhilarating just being close to him but she was too excited to work out why or worry about it. Enjoying the moment was the most important thing; Evie couldn't think of anything else. It was dizzying and scary all at the same time.

'I think we need a drink in the bar so you can relax before facing the wedding party and put on your lipstick in privacy,' he was saying to Fidelma.

'Wonderful,' breathed Fidelma, who, to the best of Evie's knowledge, rarely drank and never wore any cosmetics apart from a dusting of the baby pink Max Factor powder she'd had for decades.

Max steered them into the bar which was a wedding-free zone because the champagne frenzy was in another part of the hotel.

Settling Fidelma comfortably in a deep chair in front of a massive stone fireplace you could roast a boar in, Max sat down beside her and pulled his chair marginally closer to the one Evie had chosen. After the chill of the day, the fire warmed their bones beautifully.

Evie instinctively stretched out her legs in their unaccustomed gossamer-thin seven deniers to warm them, before she suddenly realised she was actually displaying her horrible calves instead of keeping them hidden as per usual. Whipping them back under her chair, she peered up at Max to see if he'd noticed.

He didn't seem to have done. He was asking Fidelma what she wanted to drink.

'A Harvey Wallbanger,' she said with enthusiasm.

Evie's eyebrows shot up in alarm.

'No,' Fidelma added thoughtfully, changing her mind. 'A Long Island Iced Tea. Or maybe a Singapore Sling . . .'

'Fidelma,' interrupted Evie, hoping to intervene before the other woman ran out of decent cocktails and got to the

Sex on the Beach variety, 'don't forget you're on . . . er . . . *painkillers*,' she emphasised.

'A Banana Daiquiri!' announced Fidelma happily. 'I had one of those the night I nearly got engaged.'

Max caught Evie's eye and they both grinned.

'Perhaps a restorative brandy or a glass of white wine,' he suggested. 'Because,' he murmured for Evie's ears alone, 'I'm not asking the barman for a Vestal Virgin or a Long Sloe Comfortable Screw . . .'

She had to stuff a sleeve into her mouth to stop herself collapsing into laughter and then felt her heart thud at the way Max looked so very pleased with himself for making her laugh.

They sipped chilled white wine and Evie watched in astonishment as Max gently drew Fidelma out of herself, getting her to talk about the risqué cocktails she and her pals had drunk as dizzy teenage girls.

'Movie stars drank cocktails and champagne then,' Fidelma said, misty-eyed as her mind travelled back nearly fifty years. 'We wanted to be just like them. I wanted to be Katharine Hepburn and my best friend wanted to be Jane Russell. Not that she had the . . . you know, embonpoint,' she added discreetly with a glance at her own considerable bosom.

After Fidelma's reminiscences of watching *The African Queen* in a tiny fleapit in Limerick with a young man who was too scared of her father's prowess with a shotgun to hold her hand, she playfully asked Max who his heroes were.

'I wanted to be Sean Connery,' he said ruefully, sitting back in his chair. 'My father took me to see *Thunderball* when I was ten or eleven and I had never seen anything like it in my life. I wanted to be a spy, to be supercool, when in reality I was this skinny beanpole of a kid who

241

couldn't walk two steps without tripping over my feet!'

Evie laughed, not able to imagine this suave man ever being a grubby ten year old.

'What about you, Evie?'

She remembered being in love with Harrison Ford in *Star Wars* and longing to be Carrie Fisher as Princess Leia, even if it did mean having to wear her hair in those ridiculous ear-muff plaits. And she'd never forget herself and Olivia admiring Goldie Hawn's picture in one of her mother's glossy magazines. At least Olivia had had rippling blonde hair and *some* hope of looking kookily sexy like Goldie, when with her mousy rat's tails, Evie hadn't a hope in hell.

'Go on, tell us. Or are you embarrassed to admit to being a sweet eleven year old dreaming about wearing Olivia Newton-John's gear and snogging John Travolta.'

It was Evie's turn to laugh. She'd been seventeen when *Grease* came out, not eleven.

'You are a rogue, Max,' she admonished, waggling a finger at him. 'As if I look thirty! What's your game?'

He pretended to look shocked. 'You mean you're younger than thirty? Forgive me.'

This time she slapped his knee, an instinctively familiar gesture.

'I'm *older* than thirty, you lunatic. As if you didn't know.'

In reply, he gave her a heavy-lidded look that was meant for her alone. A dark look that sent a bolt of excited lightning through her belly. Terrified in case she went pink again, Evie took a giant slug of her wine.

'I do believe he's flirting with you, Evie,' twittered Fidelma, who had drained her glass and was now looking happily tipsy.

'I'm flirting with both of you,' Max replied, giving Evie another intense look.

Arch looks were not Evie's thing. She'd long realised that a snub nose and rosy cheeks meant her chances of looking wryly amused and sophisticated at the same time were nil. But today, she thought, she'd managed it.

'You look very fierce when you do that,' Max remarked.

'Do I?' she asked, astonished. 'I didn't mean to. I was trying to look . . .' She paused. She couldn't very well say she was trying to look like a soignée heroine who was trying to slap down an eager suitor. '. . . tougher, I was trying to look a bit tougher, more autocratic,' she said, suddenly overwhelmed with the desire to be brutally honest. 'Not a pushover.'

Max laid one big hand softly on her arm. 'You're no pushover, Evie Fraser,' he said, his voice truthful. 'But you're not a hard-edged, autocratic woman either. Believe me, I've had more experience of women like that than I care to remember. You're warmhearted, funny and gentle. That's why I'm sitting here with you.'

Evie almost couldn't breathe, her heart swelled so with his compliments.

'Oh, I almost forgot,' Max added, wolf's teeth showing. 'You're one hell of an attractive woman too.'

The Jade Princess, Davina or any one of Evie's other paper heroines would have said something clever or sexy in return, something guaranteed to knock Max for six and prompt him to produce red roses, champagne and an item of jewellery that came with its own security guard.

Evie simply beamed at him. For the first time that day, she felt really, truly happy.

'Was it Olivia Whatsit-John you liked?' demanded Fidelma, who was trying to attract the barman's attention by waggling her empty glass meaningfully in his direction.

Max took pity on her and ordered another round of

white wine. 'But we'd better go up to the party soon,' he warned, 'or the bride and groom will murder us.'

Evie momentarily wondered whether he was a guest of her father's or Vida's but didn't want to break the mood by asking. She was sick of those 'I'm his auntie's second-cousin-twice-removed' conversations you regularly had at weddings where everyone got headaches trying to place everyone else in the complicated family tree. Her father had a wide circle of friends and Max could be anyone. She'd find out later. This spell was too magical to be broken with formalities.

'I was never mad about Olivia Newton-John,' she answered. 'Although I'd have killed for a figure like hers. I still would,' she added as an afterthought, one hand patting her waist.

'What do you mean?' Max said, brow furrowed as he looked at her.

The heat of the fire had given her pale face a rosy flush and had made the previously stiff curls drop into more natural waves around her face. With her huge hazel eyes animated as she talked, Evie's little face was as pretty as it had ever been.

'Well,' she said, searching for the right way to explain it. 'Olivia's a real model girl, isn't she? Gorgeous.'

'And you're not, is that it?' he asked, still perplexed.

His expression said he genuinely couldn't imagine Evie's not being happy with the way she looked. As if it was ludicrous that she had a problem with herself. After a lifetime of feeling not-quite-right, Evie felt her world shift on its axis. What if she didn't have anything to feel anxious about, what if she was really gorgeous and she'd just been locked in a cycle of hating herself all her life? What if it was OK to be Evie Fraser, petite, curvy Twix bar fanatic instead of a lanky celery fiend?

'Women fascinate me,' Max remarked, 'but I'd hate to be one. There's so much to live up to. Men might want to *be* the top Grand Prix driver, yet they don't want to *look* like him.'

'I don't want to *look* like someone else,' protested Evie. Well, she did actually. But she couldn't reveal *that*, no matter how bizarrely open she was being with this complete stranger. 'It's wanting to be looking you know . . .'

'Thinner?' supplied Max with a wry look.

'What's wrong with that?' said Evie hotly, hating to feel that her entire personality had been reduced down to her desire to be thin.

'Nothing,' he replied softly. 'Except that you don't need to be thinner. You're wonderful the way you are. I saw you hiding your legs earlier. You don't need to bother, believe me.'

His eyes swept admiringly over her body, his practised gaze making Evie feel as if he could expertly predict her bra size and judge her waist span to within a centimetre.

'We'd better go up,' interrupted Fidelma mournfully. 'Andrew wouldn't like it if we spend the whole afternoon here, even though I'm having such a ripping time.'

'You're right.' Evie gathered her reeling senses. It was half-three in the afternoon and she was feeling as headily drunk as if it was half-three *a.m.* 'They must have finished taking the wedding photos by now,' she added, 'and we don't want to be late for the meal.'

'I'm ravenous,' Fidelma said. 'I could kill for some soup.'

'We'll have to get something tasty for you to eat, my dear,' Max said, helping her to her feet. 'Otherwise all those wonderful cocktails I'm going to buy you later will go straight to your head!'

Fidelma's delighted shriek of laughter could be heard echoing all round the room.

Evie began to think about food too. It was a long time since breakfast and since she was already thin and gorgeous, she could eat what she wanted.

The three of them walked towards the ballroom slowly.

'You're very kind to Fidelma,' Evie whispered. 'I really appreciate it. You must have a raft of female relatives who adore you. I bet you're the apple of your mother's eye,' she added jokingly, thinking that she'd never met a man less like a mummy's boy.

'Well, my mother isn't the sort of woman who requires looking after,' he remarked fondly. 'She's very independent. After losing two husbands, you've got to be.'

Evie felt a flicker of suspicion in her gut. A premonition. Her father had told her something about Vida's son, a television producer. He'd been asked to the wedding but had plans to be in Australia at that time and hadn't been able to promise his disappointed mother anything.

Max couldn't be . . . No, he wasn't . . .

They had reached the ballroom and he pushed the double doors open effortlessly.

'Max, you made it! I'm so glad.' Vida's serene face was wreathed in smiles as she ran gracefully across the room and threw her arms out to embrace Max. He enveloped her in a bear hug, careful not to mess up the sleek honey-blonde hair, before holding her at arm's length and admiring the elegant wedding outfit.

'Mother, you look beautiful,' he said affectionately. 'As always.'

Evie felt her heart sink to the bottom of her stomach like a concrete block. Max was *Vida's son*. Who knew what he was really doing when he was chatting Evie up. Probably trying to figure out how much trouble she'd be to his beloved mummy who'd undoubtedly primed him on what to do.

Why else would someone like him be interested in her? Why else indeed. He was a sickeningly attractive man, almost movie star material. Why would someone like him bother even talking to her without an ulterior motive? And as for all the bullshit about her being gorgeous and thin enough without needing to worry . . . With a mother who was so slender she looked like an ex-*Vogue* model!

Rage flooded through Evie's body with the same ferocity as excitement had earlier. That bastard! He'd been using her, teasing her! She'd kill him.

Shooting Max's back a fierce scowl, she took Fidelma by the arm and bustled her down the ballroom to a table where Cara and Olivia sat, Sasha between them, slowly dismantling a rosebud from her floral headdress.

'Can you believe it?' Evie squeaked, her face aflame. 'That bloody man was chatting us up and look who he is! Just look!'

'What man? Who are you talking about?' asked Olivia, wondering why Evie looked so distressed.

'He's lovely,' crooned Fidelma, sinking heavily into a chair and immediately grabbing a spare glass of champagne. 'There he is.' She pointed. 'Max. If I was twenty years younger,' she added with a sigh.

Cara and Olivia followed her gesture and stared.

'Oooh, baby, he's a fine thing,' said Cara, taking in the tall, striking figure at the far end of the room. Even at this distance, she could see he was pretty damn' gorgeous. Too old for her but still fine. Great body, great face. 'What a hunk! He was chatting *you* up, Evie?' she asked incredulously.

'Yes,' wailed Evie. 'And you needn't sound so astonished,' she added indignantly. 'I'm not quite at the paper bag over my head stage, you know. You just wouldn't believe who he *is*.'

'A movie star visiting "Oirland" to research a role?' suggested Olivia.

'He could certainly be a movie star,' Cara said enthusiastically. 'He'd give George Clooney a run for his money.'

'No,' Evie said in exasperation. 'He was chatting me up and never told me he was Vida's bloody son, that's who. *Vida's son!* I bet she put him up to it for some reason,' she added dramatically.

Both Cara and Olivia turned to look at her.

'Evie,' Olivia started, wanting to be gentle, 'Vida would hardly get her son to chat you up on the off chance it'd benefit her.'

Cara, who wasn't as sensitive as Olivia, put it differently. 'Evie, will you stop with the conspiracy theories. You're worse than Oliver Stone. Exactly how would it help Vida to make her son flirt with you?'

'To . . . to . . . embarrass me by forcing me to flirt back!' said Evie fiercely, thinking of how she'd responded to Max's dalliance. She'd fluttered her eyelashes, simpered like a bloody schoolgirl. She'd even *touched his knee*! How awful. What must he think of her? Well, she knew what she thought of *him*. He was just a dirty double crosser to make her fancy him. And she did fancy him, she realised, feeling as deflated as a party balloon.

'Have a glass of champagne,' suggested Olivia kindly, seeing Evie's sad little face.

Defiantly, she took the proffered glass and downed half of it in one go, gasping and hiccuping as the bubbles exploded on to the back of her throat.

'Evie,' said an awestruck Cara who'd never seen her normally sedate sister whack back a drink like that before. 'What did he do to you?'

Eyes narrowed, Evie snarled: 'It's not what he did to me,

it's what I'm going to do to him when I'm talking to him! I'll rip off his . . .'

Her discussion on which part of Max Stewart's anatomy she wanted to divest him of first was cut short by the best man calling for order.

Boiling with rage, Evie had to watch Max sitting at the table close to the bridal party reserved for Vida's guests.

To her embarrassment, he caught her looking at him. His tanned face lit up with a big 'Where did you get to?' smile.

Evie flashed him a killer stare, perfected after years of enduring builders' wolf whistles, and whipped her head around as if her tablemates had just said something thrilling, which was unlikely given who she was sitting beside.

She was stuck between Olivia's father, Leslie, who was already reeking of booze, and Aunt Al, because there weren't enough men at their table for the traditional ratio.

Bloody Max, she raged inwardly. How dare he? She hoped he wasn't looking at her. She was sure he was, convinced of it. Well, he could look all he wanted. She wasn't even going to *glance* in his direction again, never mind actually talk to him. He could forget it.

Throughout a beautiful meal, Aunt Al whipped out her cigarettes every time she'd finished a course, oblivious to a stony-faced Evie who hated smoke blowing in her face. To make matters worse, Al loved jokes, the dirtier the better, and could relate filthy ones from her collection of joke books for hours on end. Stephen MacKenzie, sitting boot-faced across the table, wasn't impressed as Al stage-whispered rude limericks to her neighbour, Rosie. On the plus side, at least Leslie de Vere was sitting quietly beside Evie, mainly because he was pickled from all the brandy and ports he'd consumed to cope with his hangover.

Everyone, apart from Stephen, appeared to be having a great time, Evie realised gloomily. Everyone except her. Cara was chatting animatedly with Fidelma and Aunt Elizabeth. Sybil de Vere was listening in to Aunt Al's jokes in between picking at her food.

Even Olivia looked happier than she usually did when Stephen was in one of his moods. Her beautiful face was serene, as if she wasn't aware that her husband was glowering across the table at her volcanically. Evie wondered why her friend looked so unconcerned. Normally the very thought of Stephen in a temper gave Olivia palpitations but today, even though he looked as if he was about to go into orbit with temper, she was chatting happily to Fidelma in between cuddling Sasha, who'd left her place beside Vida to talk to her mother.

Olivia must have got high on the champagne, Evie decided. Those bubbles really gave you a buzz. What a pity she had been wasting her time with horrible Max drinking wine when she should have been guzzling Moët.

Evie took a cautious glance in Max's direction. He wasn't even looking at her, she realised crossly. His body was angled towards his neighbour, a very attractive forty-something woman with a striking Cleopatra haircut and sloe eyes to match. She was obviously his latest conquest. Evie hated him at that moment. How could he have flirted with her like that? How could she have let herself down by responding?

Cleopatra said something funny and Max laughed, a rich happy sound that made Evie narrow her eyes with jealousy. Not that long ago, *she'd* been making him laugh. He'd seemed enthralled by everything she'd said, gazing at her as though she were the most fascinating creature on earth. And now he was giving Ms Ancient Egypt the same treatment. Cow. Evie'd bet a tenner she dyed her hair. And that heavy eyeliner was very aging. Up close, she probably looked like she'd spent a month in a kiln.

Vaguely satisfied at the thought that her rival was nothing more than a dried-up prune with a good wig, Evie sat back in her seat and pretended to enjoy herself. It was no use. She wasn't interested in Al's jokes and Leslie had nothing to say for himself, apart from 'Red, please, fill my glass up' every time a waiter cruised by with wine bottles.

The speeches began and, turning in her seat to face the top table, Evie found she was in a perfect position to spy on Max and his current squeeze. She didn't hear a word of the speeches, even when her father's best man slipped up and said, 'I'd really like to spank the matron of honour . . . sorry! *Thank* the maid of honour.'

The room erupted into salacious laughter.

'What?' asked Evie, bewildered. 'What happened?'

'Fellow wants to spank the matron of honour,' Leslie de Vere informed her with glee. 'Wouldn't mind meself. Bloody fine-looking woman, that.'

By the time her father started to make his speech, Evie had decided that the only way to get back at Max was to flirt outrageously with some of the other guests. Some devastatingly handsome single man who'd make Max pea green with envy.

The only question was, with whom? Devastatingly handsome single men were thin on the ground under normal circumstances and after a quick recce of the room, Evie couldn't immediately spot anyone who'd fit the bill. Apart from Max, her father was the best-looking man around. Stephen was certainly good-looking but even if he hadn't been married to Olivia, he'd have been out of the question too on the basis that he was a grumpy sod currently looking as if he was undergoing painful colonic irrigation under the tablecloth.

Evie's gaze landed on the Higgins family, owners of the Ballymoreen butcher's shop. They had an unfamiliar man at their table; presentable, tall and wearing a decent suit. He didn't appear to have anyone with him. He'd do.

Andrew Fraser's speech was winding down. 'Now we have the perfect opportunity for our families to get to know each other,' he said with a fond look in Evie's direction.

He's got some chance of that, she thought grimly. She wouldn't spit on Max Stewart if he was on fire, so she was hardly likely to welcome him into the bosom of her family. And as for Vida! She'd obviously put her son up to it. What sort of woman would do that? A manipulative one, that was for sure.

The speeches over, people drooped in their chairs waiting for the next stage of the party. While musicians began setting up in one corner of the room, Evie excused herself.

In the loo, she stared at her tired, flushed face. How could she have thought she looked pretty earlier? She looked like a raddled old bag with stupid curls, worn-off lipstick and a smudge of mascara like a Rorschach blot on one cheek.

Leaning towards the mirror, she rubbed at it with a finger.

'Isn't he a complete sweetie?' said a voice.

Evie straightened up when she saw who'd just pushed into the room: Cleopatra accompanied by another woman.

'The way he looks at you . . . God!' she was saying suggestively. 'You wouldn't kick him out of bed for getting toast crumbs on the sheets, would you?'

The two of them screamed with licentious laughter, oblivious to Evie.

Quietly, she rummaged in her handbag for her lipstick,

trying to watch Cleopatra but not wanting to be caught doing it.

Far from the oven-baked, wig-wearing harpy Evie had hoped she'd be, Cleopatra was exotically attractive with remarkably unlined skin for someone that particular shade of mahogany. Evie had never seen anyone that tanned who wasn't actually Indian but the *café au lait* colour looked good on her.

Evie revised her original guess and put the other woman in her late-thirties instead of early-forties.

'Since the divorce, I *have* been on the lookout,' Cleopatra was saying. 'Max would fit the bill perfectly.'

'Judith, you're a howl,' said the friend. 'He seems interested . . .'

Judith, huh? Evie swept out of the room into the corridor and slap bang into Max.

'Why didn't you say who you were?' she blurted out accusingly.

'Why should I have?' he asked in bemused tones.

'You knew who *I* was,' she stressed, 'but I had no idea who you were.'

'What difference would that have made?' Max inquired.

She glared at him.

'The thing is, Evie,' he said, taking her arm to accompany her back into the ballroom, 'when I realised you were Andrew's daughter, I wanted you to like me for myself, not because I was about to be your . . .' he paused '. . . stepbrother.'

'Stepbrother! You're not my stepbrother!' she said, aghast.

'Actually, I'm afraid I am,' he pointed out mildly. 'And my mother is now your stepmother, although I gather you're not too wild about that idea either.'

Evie knew she was going pink. She was sick of her

traitorous skin giving her away like this.

'You don't approve of her so you don't approve of me, is that it?' Max asked.

'That's *not* it,' she said hotly. 'I just don't like being made a fool of.'

They were at the ballroom door now. His face was serious as he looked down at her. 'I'd hardly consider having a drink with you and chatting you up making a fool of you, Evie,' he said slowly. 'I thought we were getting on very well. I was having a lovely time.'

She could feel the beginnings of a smile on her face when Judith's strident tones could be heard from the direction of the loos.

'Max darling, have they started dancing yet?' she called. 'I'm aching for a whirl around the floor.'

Even Max could hear Evie's sharp intake of breath.

'You're getting on even better with dear Judith, *darling*,' she said sweetly. 'She's husband-hunting after her divorce apparently so I'll leave you to it.'

With that she was gone, determinedly tip-tapping into the ballroom in Olivia's high shoes.

'Great legs,' said Max behind her.

Damn him, Evie fumed. Nothing fazed him.

Her father and Vida were dancing their first dance while the band played 'Come Rain or Come Shine', a gloriously melancholy saxophone riff rippling around the ballroom. People were smiling at the newly weds, everyone happy for them. Evie stood to one side and watched. They both looked so happy, so serene. She'd go and talk to them after a while, tell Vida she looked beautiful and remind her to make sure her father got his vitamin tablet every morning.

When the song finished, he left Vida and walked towards Evie.

'May I have this dance?' he asked, the small upturn at the corners of his mouth belying his formality.

'Of course.'

A singer with a throaty cigarettes-and-whiskey voice was belting out 'It Had To Be You' as Andrew and Evie took to the floor. Other couples joined in, and at the far end of the room she could see Max and Vida dancing together. Tall and elegant, they moved gracefully. Evie watched them wistfully.

She didn't know what had come over her, she'd been so rude to Max. And just because he was Vida's son. It was ridiculous really, childish. This behaviour had to stop. Apologising to her father came first.

'I'm happy for you, Dad,' she said truthfully. 'I'm sorry I took it so badly at first. I've been horrible to you and Vida. I apologise.'

'You don't have to say anything,' Andrew replied. 'I understand that it was hard for you. I knew it would be. That's why I took the easy route out and didn't tell you I was involved with her at first,' he revealed guiltily. 'I was afraid you'd want me to end it before it began.'

Evie was mute for a moment. 'I'm so sorry, Dad,' she gasped. 'I didn't know I was such a bitch you'd even dream I'd do that. And then, when I heard, I saw red, couldn't handle it. I never meant to hurt you.'

They were barely dancing now, just shuffling slowly around the floor, oblivious to the music as they talked.

'You're not a bitch, Evie,' he said earnestly. 'You're good and kind and I'm proud of all you've done in your life. But I know how much you loved your mother, how you idolised her. That's why I never got involved with anyone else when you lived at home after Tony died. You'd gone through so much and I knew you'd never cope, seeing me with another woman.'

'Dad, that was so unfair of me, I'm sorry,' Evie said. She was practically crying now. 'I never meant to . . .'

'Shhh,' he comforted her. 'I know you didn't.' He put his hand under her chin and turned her face up towards his. 'But you're happy for me now, aren't you?'

'Yes, Dad.' The words came out in a big sob. 'So happy. Just forgive me for earlier, please?'

Andrew hugged her and, seeing that her face was blotched with tears, escorted her off the dance floor to their table. Vida immediately hurried over.

'Is everything all right?' she asked worriedly.

'Fine,' Andrew said.

With a reassuring smile, Vida was about to move away, anxious not to intrude, but Evie caught her arm quickly.

'Don't go, Vida. I wanted to apologise for being so cold to you, it wasn't fair. I want to wish you every happiness.'

The other woman's face was momentarily frozen, as if she didn't quite believe what she was hearing. Then her mouth curved, the smile reaching her eyes. She leaned down and kissed her new stepdaughter on the cheek.

'Thank you, Evie. I appreciate that and I do know how hard it has been for you.' She straightened up. 'I'd better reclaim my son before he goes off.'

'You've got to meet Max, Vida's son,' Andrew said eagerly.

'Yes, you must,' Vida echoed. 'You'll love him. He's so funny.'

Bloody hilarious, she thought to herself. At least the pig hadn't told his mother he'd already met Evie.

'And you've got to dance with him,' Vida added.

'Love to,' she said brightly. Just not yet. Not until she had shown him how popular she was. Then she could be magnanimous and frostily polite. But only then.

The Higginses were delighted to see her, promising her

some lovely chops and a nice rib roast if she made it into the shop during the weekend.

'Thank you,' Evie said coquettishly, perching on a chair and looking inquiringly at the man she'd earmarked earlier as suitable make-Max-jealous material.

'Our son, Paul,' beamed Mrs Higgins. 'Home from London. You must have met when we first bought the shop.'

'Of course, I remember,' Evie lied. Then, seeing Max bearing down on her from the top table, no doubt under instructions from his mother to make friends, she said recklessly: 'I don't suppose you dance, Paul?'

'Er . . . yes.' Startled, he blinked at her. He wasn't as handsome as she'd thought from across the room, but he'd do nicely.

Evie stood up, grabbed his hand and they whirled away from the table, just in time to see Max giving her a bemused look. She smiled sweetly back.

Conscious that he was watching her, Evie put on a bravura performance. Paul had two left feet and no conversation, but from the way Evie smiled up at him adoringly, any onlooker would have thought he was the most fascinating man in the room.

She was aware that she was behaving with abandon and that if Cara, Olivia or Rosie had any clue what she was up to, they'd be open-mouthed in shock, but she didn't care. She was at her father's wedding for God's sake, a wedding she'd sworn never to go to so normal rules didn't apply.

She stuck it out for three dances, refusing to let Paul sit down. 'It's so much fun,' she said gaily, ignoring the pain in her toes from several altercations with the tug boats he had on his feet.

Max whirled by, Judith attached to him like a barnacle.

Evie's smile grew brighter. He was a wonderful dancer, she realised crossly, that big body of his remarkably graceful. Judith was enjoying herself immensely, laughing like a drain and pouting up at Max at every opportunity.

The music finished and the band announced that they were taking a break.

'I could do with a drink,' Paul said, wiping the perspiration from his forehead. 'Would you like one?'

'Yes,' Evie answered absently, still staring at Max and Judith. 'Oh, no,' she said, spotting Simon at the ballroom door. 'Sorry, Paul,' she added. 'Somebody I must greet.'

Simon had come straight from work and looked worn out. His tie was imperceptibly crooked, his eyes were tired and his sandy hair was standing up straight the way it always did when he'd been on a long drive, unthinkingly running his fingers through it at traffic lights.

Evie nearly knocked him over with the strength of her embrace. 'Darling Simon,' she breathed, snuggling into his neck like a vampire scenting lunch after a month in its coffin.

'Evie, hello,' he answered. 'Missed much, have I?'

'You missed a wonderful ceremony and much more,' said a deep voice. 'I'm Max Stewart, Vida's son.' Max, large as life and twice as handsome, held out one hand to Simon.

'Simon,' said her father's voice. 'I'm so sorry you couldn't make the wedding.'

'But we're glad you're here now,' added Vida, arriving with a glass of champagne. 'Andrew has told me all about you.'

It was like being ambushed, Evie thought. She recovered gracefully. 'Yes, Vida, I want you to meet Simon, my *fiancé*,' she emphasised, managing to give Max a steely look and to wrap an arm around Simon at the same time.

Everyone shook hands.

'Evie, you haven't met my son Max yet,' Vida exclaimed.

'How nice to meet you,' she said between gritted teeth.

'Isn't she a joker!' he chuckled, waggling a finger at her playfully. 'We met earlier and she promised me a dance, didn't you, Evie?'

With her father and Vida looking on happily, thrilled to see this further sign of Evie's being reconciled to their marriage, she couldn't say no.

'But there's no music,' she said suddenly, giving him an angelic look. As if by magic, the band came back to life with a twang of a double bass, Max held out his hand and Evie took it, unable to prevent the sudden tremor she felt as his skin touched hers.

She was going to get lockjaw from smiling so inanely, she realised, as her assembled relatives beamed back at her happily.

'You didn't look as if you were missing your fiancé too much earlier,' Max whispered into her ear as they walked to the dance floor.

'I cherish the ground he walks on,' hissed Evie.

'Lucky man,' answered Max, eyebrows raised quizzically.

She'd planned to stand on his feet and make him sorry he'd ever asked her to dance, but the strains of Glenn Miller meant she just couldn't. On the dance floor, Evie came to life. Born with natural rhythm and a fluid grace, her body flowed and moved to the music as if she'd trained for years with the corps de ballet while moonlighting at a jazz club.

Max, one arm holding her more closely than strictly appropriate, appeared to have a similar gift. His large frame moved expertly, flowing with hers to the point where she felt like Ginger Rogers dancing with Fred Astaire.

Other dancers moved out of the way for them, admiring their expert moves. Evie loved it. Her heart thumped with exhilaration.

'Are we Fred and Ginger or what?' Max murmured, as she rippled back into his arms after a spectacular twirl.

Evie laughed in spite of herself.

'Don't forget, Ginger did it backwards and in high heels,' she gasped.

The music soared and she let herself go, enjoying the moment as if she'd never danced before. Her hair flowed out behind her and her body obeyed her every command, moving in perfect time with Max's.

Time passed in a blur of dancing feet and the sensation of his body next to hers. His eyes danced as well as his feet and Evie couldn't stop herself from smiling up at his face, knowing that his laughing mouth mirrored her own.

That close, she admired his sleek black hair, raked back from his forehead, and the eyebrows that could speak volumes, arching in amusement or furrowing in concentration.

It seemed like only a few minutes until the musicians took another breather.

Without letting go of Evie, Max glanced at his watch. 'Half an hour of dancing. I think we'd better stop or they'll think *we're* the ones getting hitched.'

'Half an hour!' she exclaimed. 'It doesn't feel like five . . .'

'Minutes?' he supplied.

'Exactly! I was having such fun.'

He regarded her solemnly, glittering blue eyes sober. 'Me too.'

Aware that the dance floor was clearing and that they were still standing in the middle, like statues, Evie tried to let go of Max's hands. He held firm.

'I'd like to see you again,' he said softly, so softly that at first, she thought she'd imagined it.

'What?' she asked in astonishment.

He repeated himself. 'I'd like to see you again.'

A welter of emotions surged in Evie's breast: shock, delight, excitement at the thought that Max Stewart wanted to see her again. And then the sudden guilt of knowing she couldn't.

'Simon,' she breathed. 'I'm seeing him . . . we're engaged . . . I can't.'

The cobalt eyes roamed over her, searching for some sign of hope in her distressed little face. 'It's a pity I'm too late,' he murmured. 'We'll just have to be brother and sister to each other then, won't we?' he added softly.

He walked her back to her table in silence.

'Thank you for lending me your fiancée, Simon,' he said loudly, his good humour apparently restored. 'She's a wonderful dancer.'

'Isn't she!' said Simon, who himself did everything possible to avoid setting one foot on a dance floor.

'I'll talk to you later,' Max said, the picture of joviality.

''Bye,' said Evie in a small voice.

Max's gaze lingered on her a moment and she couldn't draw her eyes away from his. She hoped nobody else noticed but she couldn't help herself.

Then he was gone.

Simon moved in his chair and in the process his elbow caught a wine glass and sent it flying, ruby liquid staining the white linen tablecloth.

Irritated, Evie was about to berate him for being clumsy but stopped herself.

It wasn't his fault he wasn't Max.

Olivia was enjoying herself. Happy to let the music drift over her, she sat with Sasha comfortably on her lap and

261

watched Evie dancing with Vida's son. Her friend looked wonderfully animated, she thought.

A tap on her arm woke her from her reverie.

'Olivia, it's getting late. Sasha should be in bed.'

Stephen's mood had mellowed slightly although he was still frosty-faced.

'Did you check if they have a baby sitting service or not?'

'God, no, I didn't.' Olivia felt instantly guilty for being a bad mother. 'I sort of thought we'd take it in turns to sit with her. The party won't last more than another couple of hours or so.'

It was just before half-eight and Vida had explained that she hated long drawn-out weddings. 'The die-hards can sit in the bar all evening but Andrew and I will be retiring early,' she'd told Olivia earlier. 'It's been a long day and we're getting up early to drive to the airport.'

They were going on a cruise for their honeymoon and Olivia could feel her eyes take on an emerald green hue when Vida spoke about cocktails on deck, day trips to Santorini and the glamour of the captain's table.

'I'm not tired, Mummy,' piped up Sasha, still bright-eyed after her exciting day.

'Darling, you have to do as you're told,' Stephen said gravely.

Like your mother, Olivia surprised herself by thinking.

Automatically, she got up and swung Sasha into her arms. 'OK, Munchkin,' she said, nuzzling her daughter's face, 'let's say goodnight to everyone.'

Stephen arrived in their hotel room when she was tucking Sasha into bed.

'Will I read you a story?' he asked.

Sasha nodded and squirmed delightedly in her small bed. Olivia put Sasha's flower-girl dress away and listened fondly as Stephen read the story of Flopsy, Mopsy and Cottontail for the zillionth time.

She put her navy jacket back on, reapplied some lipstick and waited for him to finish. If she went downstairs to the party for another half an hour, she could speak to everyone and then retire to bed while Stephen went back for an hour. That suited her fine. She was tired anyhow.

Slipping the lipstick back in her handbag, she adjusted her waistband and stood quietly by the door.

'Where are you going?' asked Stephen, total amazement in his voice. 'You're sitting with Sasha, surely?'

Olivia blinked. He obviously expected her to stay. It wasn't even open for discussion. Stephen had already worked out that Olivia would forfeit the rest of her evening to mind their daughter. It wasn't that Olivia didn't want to sit with Sasha; she simply couldn't bear the fact that Stephen hadn't given her a choice or offered to take his turn.

She was the woman therefore she looked after the children – that was it. QED. End of story. He was the hunter-gatherer and couldn't be bothered with menial tasks like caring for their daughter.

Like lava boiling dangerously under the earth's tectonic plates, her anger suddenly came volcanically to the surface. Face suffused with rage, Olivia motioned shakily for Stephen to join her in the corridor.

'You never think about me for more than one second, do you?' she whispered fiercely. 'You blindly expect me to do as you want, without even asking me what I think. It never even occurred to you that I might want to go back to the party for a while and that *you* could look after Sasha.'

Flustered, Stephen searched for words to give his side of the story. Thanks to several glasses of decent Fleurie, he couldn't think of any. This was not usual, Olivia flaring up twice in one day. It wasn't even unusual; it was unheard of.

She wasn't finished. Her eyes strangely bright, she poked him in the chest with one finger.

'*You* can stay up here. *I'm* going to enjoy myself with my friends. You didn't even want to come to this wedding, Stephen, so *you* can have an early night. I'll be downstairs if Sasha needs me urgently.' She swept him with a disgusted look. 'You don't spend enough time with her to know what to do if she gets sick.' She swivelled regally and swept off towards the stairs.

She made straight for the bar, anger making her determined to have a huge drink that would irritate Stephen. She rarely drank but when she did, he hated it. A modest white wine spritzer fitted in with his version of cosy Mother Hen, she thought venomously.

Vida's son was standing at the bar and Olivia detected a slight sag to his shoulders.

He'd been so charming when she'd met him earlier, very debonair and polite, although he'd had eyes for no one but Evie. Now he greeted her warmly and asked her if she wanted a drink.

'Something very strong,' she answered flintily. 'Something that'll knock me out so I don't murder my husband in his bed tonight!'

Max's eyes gleamed with amusement.

'Far be it for me to interfere,' he said gravely, 'but I believe alcohol is more likely to make you murder your husband.'

Olivia's eyes met his and they both laughed.

'I was getting a Brandy Alexander for my mother because she adores them but only allows herself one as a special treat. Can I get you one?'

The party was indeed winding down, with people sitting in little groups and the musicians playing softly in the background. Max and Olivia sat in a quiet corner and watched the last few dancers swaying merrily on the floor.

Olivia didn't know if it was the Brandy Alexander, the soft lighting or the fact that Max proved to be such a good listener, but she found herself telling him about her row with Stephen. And about her crisis of confidence.

'I love cooking and teaching people how to cook but . . .' She broke off in frustration. 'It's so difficult to teach when you've got a few brats in your class and I'm not strong enough to control them. I feel so useless when they misbehave and I can't stop them, as if every other teacher in the school is standing outside the door listening in shock.'

''Course they're not,' Max said reassuringly. 'I doubt if you'll find many teachers today who don't have problems with their classes. It's a tough job, teaching, I wouldn't like to do it. Kids are so clever, they instantly pick up on it if you're nervous.'

'You can say that again,' Olivia sighed. 'I wish my husband understood this,' she added. 'He'd only see it as proof that I shouldn't be teaching in the first place. He thinks I should be at home glued to the oven, cooking him dinner and polishing the silver, instead of teaching what he describes as "juvenile delinquents",' she said bitterly.

'Your husband doesn't understand you,' Max said gently, a twinkle in his eye.

Olivia laughed, a throaty sound that surprised her. She hadn't laughed in so long, not a real laugh, anyway. 'He doesn't,' she replied candidly. 'I think he understood me once, about a million years ago, and he thinks he still does. He has me neatly in a little box, labelled "Olivia". That's me. I'm not allowed to change in any way, inside or out.

He can, but I can't.' She paused, and looked at Max, taking in the glittering eyes that were so kind as he returned her gaze unwaveringly. He'd looked like a wolf in Armani earlier, a real lady killer, dangerous with a capital D. Now he looked like the most compassionate, sympathetic man she'd ever met. 'I don't know why I'm telling you all this. I never talk to strangers, certainly not to strange men.' She gave a little false chuckle. 'My husband doesn't like it. He thinks I'm throwing myself at them.'

'Today seems to be a day for doing things your husband doesn't approve of, ' Max remarked.

Her face lit up. 'Order me another Brandy Alexander,' she declared. 'I fancy another one and as I'm not driving, I'll have it.'

Halfway through the second drink, Max said something that startled her into almost spilling champagne on her jacket.

'I told you I'm involved in TV production,' he said. 'Mainly those two-hour mini series but I did a lot of straight TV work years ago. The thing is, a friend of mine is working on this morning TV show and they've run into difficulties with their cookery presenter. It's a slot three times a week and this woman has just been offered a job in Paris so she's pulling out. They're going mad because they need someone to take her place immediately. I think you'd be perfect for it.'

Olivia just stared at him. Was he on drugs? 'Me?'

'Yes, you. You're beautiful, you're an expert cook, and I think you'd look marvellous on television.'

'Me?' she repeated, practically gasping this time. 'I'd panic, I'd be hopeless, I'd look terrible, I'd . . .'

Max shrugged. 'I've been on one side of the camera for twenty years now and if there's one thing I've got a feel for, it's how somebody translates on to the screen. I don't know for sure and it's not an exact science, but I'm convinced you'd be wonderful.'

Olivia was still staring at him disbelievingly but he pushed on.

'It's just in front of a small TV crew, smaller than an average class, and at least they'll be hanging on your every word. The slot is fifteen minutes long and you'd have researchers to help you.'

'I've never done anything like that before,' Olivia said, feeling stupid. 'I was never in the drama club in school, I just wasn't a performer.'

'This is different.' Max's face was earnest now. 'All you have to do is cook something on television. You can plan and test it all beforehand and make several different versions at different stages, otherwise it's just doing what you do now. Except you'd get paid more. But,' he paused, 'I can understand if you're nervous about Stephen not wanting you to do it.'

Olivia's grey eyes flashed like quicksilver. 'That's not it. Don't try and manipulate me, Max.'

He put up his hands in surrender. 'Forgive me, you're right. I wanted to prod you into doing this, just a screen test, that's all. I was wrong to try that . . .'

'Just a screen test?' she interrupted.

'Two hours of your life,' he said, 'between make-up and shooting. Then you'll know for definite.'

She breathed heavily, wondering if she was going to regret this. 'I'll do it. But don't tell anyone,' she added hurriedly. 'Nobody is to know.'

Max crossed his heart. 'Scout's honour.'

Olivia gave him a wry grin. 'I can't see you as a scout, somehow.'

Max chuckled, eyes flashing mischievously. 'I can make a fire by rubbing two girl guides together. Seriously, Olivia, I bet you anything you'll be great.'

Olivia banished the notion that she didn't know what exactly she was getting herself into and gave him a gutsy smile. 'We'll see,' she said, crossing her fingers. 'And you're right – Stephen will hate it.'

Evie waved the Butlers goodbye at the hotel's front entrance. She was tired and ready for bed.

'Long day, huh?' said Cara, leaning against the wall and not bothering to stifle a yawn.

'Yes, I'm ready for bed,' Evie replied.

'Ms Evie Fraser?' said a voice.

The receptionist held a white envelope in her hand.

'Yes?'

'A letter for you, Ms Fraser.'

Too weary to think who would be sending her letters at this hour of the night, Evie unthinkingly ripped the envelope open. Inside was one sheet of paper.

The message was simple, written in a bold hand: '*If you change your mind, phone me. Max*'. And a phone number.

She ran her fingers over the message, as if touching him.

'What's that?' inquired Cara, peering over her sister's shoulder.

Evie hastily stuffed the paper into her handbag. 'Nothing. A fax for Simon, the hotel addressed it to me by mistake because we're sharing,' she lied.

They walked to their rooms, Evie's mind seething. She couldn't deny she'd felt something intense when she'd met Max Stewart but she couldn't do anything about it. He was just a fantasy, not real, not for her. She was in love with Simon. How dare Max try and rock her boat? She'd clearly told him she couldn't see him again.

'It was a lovely day,' Cara was saying. 'Vida looked

marvellous. Her son was very nice too, wasn't he? Dishy really,' she added dreamily. 'I told Dad I'd take him out, get to know him better. He's sort of related to us now, like a brother.'

'He's a rogue,' Evie said shortly, thinking of the note and of her engagement ring. 'Personally, I'd be happy if I never saw him again.'

CHAPTER NINE

Olivia closed her eyes and let the make-up artist do her best. She felt a sponge smooth foundation on to her face, pressing into every crevice relentlessly. With one eye open a smidgen, she realised it was a dark honeyed shade she'd never have worn.

'Don't worry,' reassured the make-up artist, seeing Olivia's long lashes flutter in horror. 'You'll look as if you're anaemic on TV without a dark base. This Screen-face stuff is perfect for you, I promise.'

Seeing as Olivia knew absolutely zero about the world of television, she said nothing. Perhaps it was good to look tangerine on camera? What did she know?

Since she'd arrived at the studio half an hour ago and been whisked up to make-up without a by-your-leave from the producer she was supposed to meet, Olivia had felt like a kid on the first day at a new school. People sped past her at every moment, bearing clipboards and important expressions.

The denim-clad teenager who'd brought Olivia up to the make-up department had nearly had a seizure en route when the mobile phone hooked on to her jeans went off with a jarring trumpet call.

'*What? I said I wasn't to be disturbed!*' she screeched into the phone, seemingly oblivious to the fact that Olivia was with her.

Wow! Olivia thought. If even the gophers had mobiles and attitudes, what the hell would the programme's movers and shakers be like? Bloody nightmares, she reckoned.

'You've lovely bones,' sighed the make-up lady, getting to work on Olivia's eyes. 'It's a joy to work with you. You weren't a model, were you?' she asked suspiciously.

Olivia grinned, knowing she was crinkling up her eyes and therefore, ruining the other woman's chance of applying eye shadow. 'No,' she said with an ironic laugh.

'You could have been,' sighed the make-up lady. 'It's a shame really. When I think of some of the cows I've got to make up in here. They come in looking like unmade beds and throw tantrums if they don't go out looking like Claudia-bleedin'-Schiffer.'

Olivia and the rest of the make-up department erupted into laughter. A spot of bitching ensued, with a discussion of which TV star had the biggest head and the least chance of ending up looking like a supermodel.

After fifteen minutes, Olivia was able to admire herself in a mirror which really did have lightbulbs around it.

Her silvery eyes stood out even more dramatically than usual and her full lips were glisteningly plump in a lilac colour that picked up the amethyst trouser suit she wore. With her blonde hair shimmering around her face in silky strands, she looked beautiful.

'Thank you,' she told the make-up lady. 'You made me relax and I was so nervous.'

The woman smiled. 'It's a pleasure working on someone like you. Someone lovely who appreciates it.'

Downstairs, Olivia followed another production assistant, a much nicer, less volatile personality, towards the studio. His name was Kevin and he was young, attractive and chatty, a huge change from Ms Bitch From Hell earlier. His platinum crew cut suited him, making his dark skin look exotic by contrast.

Outside the double doors to Studio One, a red light was shining brightly.

'Do *not* enter when the red light is on,' proclaimed a huge notice on the wall.

'Should we go in?' asked Olivia anxiously, seeing the light glowing crimson in the television building gloom.

'No prob,' replied Kevin breezily. 'They're getting ready to record a segment for tomorrow morning but they'll never hear us here. It's a band, The Wild Men. You could let off a nuke in reception and nobody would hear it in Studio 1.'

'Oh.' Wondering if she was ever going to know anything about the TV world, Olivia followed Kevin's denim-encased bum into the studio.

It was an enormous room with black-clad walls full of cables hidden behind the terracotta screens of the *Wake Up Breakfast Show* studio set. In the shadowy behind-the-scenes area, men and women in sweatshirts and denims stood around with radio mikes and bored expressions, while to the left of the cuddly morning sofa set (two bright raspberry velvet sofas awash with primary-coloured cushions), a very wrinkly rock band all wearing orange sunglasses belted out their latest hit.

The noise was phenomenal, even though Olivia would have sworn blind that the band weren't playing live.

'Do it to me, baybee!' went the lyrics over and over again as the lead singer practically stuck the mike in his huge mouth as he mimed to the words theatrically.

Two camera operators performed an elaborate dance on the studio floor, weaving in and out of the cables as their cameras whizzed up and down, taking in every twitch and pelvic thrust of the band.

'I'll just tell the producer you're here. Her name's Linda Byrne, she's expecting you.'

Ignoring the action on the floor, Kevin sashayed over to a forty-something woman in black leather jeans and a grey T-shirt who was talking into a radio mike. Olivia, feeling totally in the way, tried to blend into the background. There seemed to be an inordinate amount of people in there, some watching the band through narrowed eyes, some talking to each other.

Linda was eyeing her up and Olivia turned nervously away. What the hell was she doing here? She must be mad. She'd kill Max when she saw him again. I mean, if she couldn't control a classroom of kids, how the hell did she think she could appear calm and poised in front of this load of TV veterans? They were all so blasé that nobody was even *listening* to The Wild Men. I mean, they'd been a huge band once and the people in the studio were looking as bored as if somebody was racing earthworms across the floor. How did she even imagine that anyone would be bothered to look at *her*?

Just then, a vision in aquamarine swept into her line of vision and abruptly ended Olivia's anguished soul-searching.

The vision was a blonde woman with a frosted, upswept hairdo and a tight blue taffeta jacket vainly trying to stay buttoned over her considerable bosom. She stalked through the back of the studio with a make-up artist trailing in her wake. Olivia instantly recognised the woman as Nancy Roberts, one half of the morning show's presenting team. Voluptuous, with flashing blue eyes, a cute snub nose and a permanently working mouth, she was the picture of vibrant animation. The public loved Nancy, both for her unashamedly down-to-earth manner and the fact that she flaunted her size 16 figure, defiantly refusing to lose weight for the unforgiving television cameras, which had made her an icon for 16+ women all over the country.

You couldn't pick up a newspaper without reading about Nancy, a woman who proudly eschewed the champagne lifestyle of the TV personality for quality time spent with her family and her beloved vegetable garden.

In the week since Max had convinced her to audition for the breakfast show, the only thing that had kept Olivia from cancelling through sheer nerves was the thought that no matter how bad she was, at least she'd meet the famous Nancy.

Then, Olivia had been informed that her screen test would take place in the afternoon, which meant she probably wouldn't meet the star after all.

So it was a real bonus to see Nancy Roberts on set. But from the way she was storming in from the back of the studio with a mobile phone jammed against her ear, she didn't look at all like the lovably down-to-earth woman of the newspaper features. In fact, she looked positively outraged.

The make-up artist hurried alongside her, a velour powder puff held aloft in one hand.

'Nancy, I need to get rid of the shine on your nose . . .'

'Shut the fuck up!' screeched Nancy, before resuming her conversation on the phone. 'Who the bloody hell do you think I am? Nancy-fucking-Roberts, that's who! I'm not doing some pissing little shop opening in the back of beyond for a measly grand. You'd better cop on quick, you little shit, or I'll be looking for a new agent!'

She snapped the phone shut with such force that Olivia reckoned it'd break. Then Nancy stopped dead, turned her face to the make-up artist and calmly waited to be powder-puffed. A thin woman dressed in grey appeared beside her and received both a withering look and Nancy's mobile phone to hold.

Finally, the TV star closed her eyes, took a deep breath that reminded Olivia of a yoga video she'd once bought, and waited for the band to finish.

As if by magic, her face composed itself into a beatific smile and she bounced on to the set, clapping as if the mimed song was the most wonderful thing she'd ever heard instead of a woeful comeback record from a band who'd spent all their past royalties on serious cocaine habits and were now in financial straits.

On the monitors, Olivia watched in amazement as Nancy's snub nose wrinkled up in that idiosyncratic, lovable way.

'Boys, that was fan-tas-tic!' she cooed. 'You make me feel nineteen again, which wasn't that long ago, you know,' she added archly, giving the lead singer an affectionate tickle.

Taking his cue after a lifetime of TV performances where flirting with the hostess was a prerequisite, no matter how much of a dog she was, the lead singer grabbed Nancy in a bear hug. Clutching her to his sharkskin-suited body, he gave his trademark sexy roar. 'Baybee! How about you and me gettin' out of here and havin' some fun?'

Nancy squealed with delighted laughter. 'Don't tempt me, Barry,' she sighed with a pout, wriggling out of his grasp in a way that guaranteed maximum exposure of her cleavage. 'I'm a happily married woman.'

'No!' Barry groaned, running a hand through a leonine mass of dyed hair. 'You're breakin' my heart, Nancy baybee. You've been promisin' me for years. I'm all alone now and I need the love of a good woman.'

She shook her head resolutely, as if she'd just been offered a double cream and strawberry shortcake dessert but had to say no. 'Dickie would never forgive either of us. But you'll come back for another session on the show when the album is out, won't you Barry?' she added.

'You betcha, baybee,' drawled Barry, before going seamlessly into plug-the-record mode. 'The album is out in three months and we're off touring the States next week with fifty dates.'

'Oooh,' breathed Nancy, 'I bet you've a woman in every state?'

'None like you, Nancy.' he said, a touch of longing in his voice. With that, he walked off set over to where his model girlfriend, rail-thin and with a face like a Greek goddess, stood waiting patiently. Having seen Barry in action before, she hadn't even raised an eyebrow when he'd sucked up to Nancy.

'Great!' yelled the floor manager. 'Thanks, everybody.'

Nancy, who despite her frantic onscreen flirting hadn't looked once in Barry's direction since he'd ambled off the set, sat down on one of the raspberry couches. Her face rearranged itself back into bad-tempered mode.

'Gimme some water, Nita,' she yelled at her grey-clad assistant. 'You know I need two litres a day or I dehydrate.'

Kevin sidled up to Olivia and, seeing the ultra-astonished look on her face, whispered into her ear: 'She's a nightmare, isn't she? But she's such a professional on screen, nobody talks about what she's really like.

'You'd understand if you worked around here. Nancy knows instantly and instinctively where to stand, what to say . . . you name it. She's a complete pro. But what a bitch!'

'What about all this stuff about her being a lovely, sweet woman who's mad on gardening and hates champagne and all that?' Olivia whispered, aghast.

Kevin quivered with suppressed laughter. 'Gardening!' he hissed. 'The only trowel La Roberts ever lifts is when she puts her make-up on. Somebody in her agent's office dreamed that one up and she went ballistic.'

He led Olivia over to the woman in leather he'd spoken to earlier, whispering in Olivia's ear all the time: 'Still, the Great Unwashed love the idea of their favourite telly star up to her eyeballs in tulip bulbs and potting compost, so she keeps it up. You'll notice she never actually mentions any flower by name. One journalist asked her which fuchsia she liked best. What a howl!' He giggled at the memory. 'All she knows about flowers is how to judge exactly how much money the bouquets she's been sent actually cost. And, believe me, she's an expert at that.'

His voice returned to normal levels. 'Linda, this is Olivia MacKenzie. Olivia, this is Linda Byrne, the show's producer.'

The two women shook hands. 'MacKenzie?' said Linda thoughtfully.

'Max Stewart and Paul Reddin arranged for me to come for the cooking slot,' Olivia said, thinking the producer didn't recognise her name.

'Oh, no, it's not that.' Linda waved a hand airily. 'It's just that our astrologer is a MacKenzie too, believe it or not. We can't have two on the show. People will think you're related. What's your maiden name?'

'De Vere,' Olivia replied.

'De Vere!' said Kevin and Linda approvingly in unison.

'That's much better,' Linda added. 'Olivia de Vere . . . Olivia de Vere,' she repeated. 'Marvellous. Now, let's see if you can do it. Have the researchers gone over what we've organised with you?' The way Linda asked the question made it plain to Olivia that it was practically rhetorical. Linda was quite sure the researchers *had* sorted everything out and she'd only asked automatically.

So Olivia hated having to say 'no'. But she had to. She hadn't seen any researcher and had no idea what she was supposed to do.

'I'm afraid not,' she said candidly.

'Shit!' Linda said. 'I'm sorry, Olivia, they were supposed to bring you up to speed on what we've organised . . . I'll fucking kill that stupid Carol. I told her to talk to you. You'll have to wing it – we've only got another half an hour before the camera men's shift ends.'

Thinking that things couldn't really get any worse, Olivia idly wondered if everyone in television swore like troopers and how did they stop when the cameras were rolling? Nancy's tongue could rival any docker's, yet she never lapsed into 'shit' on air.

'You don't mind winging it?' Linda asked.

Olivia, feeling remarkably calm for a woman who'd needed valium to get her through a wedding the previous week, grinned at her. 'As long as you give me a brief explanation of what I'm supposed to do.'

'You're a star.' Linda patted Olivia's arm and led her over to the cookery set. Stuck in the farthest corner of the studio, the cookery set was actually a high-tech stainless steel kitchen with everything you could possibly need, from a giant American fridge to a sleek double oven and state of the art microwave. Windows complete with flower-filled window boxes looked out on to a fake city scene of shimmering skyscrapers. The kitchen was so perfect that it was hard to imagine it didn't belong to some sprawling loft apartment in Manhattan.

The only difference between it and a normal kitchen was the long TV-style freestanding unit with another sink and two hobs where the cook stood and faced the cameras. On the unit lay a bizarre assortment of foods: one shrivelled, schizophrenic pepper that wasn't sure whether it was yellow or green, a bunch of bananas, some creamed coconut, two small onions and some crusty bread.

Olivia laughed out loud. No researcher needed to tell her what she had to do – it was like those TV cookery programmes where a celebrity spent a fiver buying the most ludicrous combination of food and then a harassed chef had to turn it into a reasonable meal.

'Carol hasn't worked on the cookery slot before,' Linda said with a sigh as she looked at the groceries. 'She hasn't a clue. What we want is for you to talk us through making a dish with this stuff. You can just start the dish, you don't actually have to cook it.' She looked at her watch. 'We don't have time, really. But if you start and we film you, we'll get a good idea how you perform, right?'

'Right,' Olivia replied evenly. It was funny feeling this calm, she thought. Ironic really. The thing was, because she hadn't been prepared properly by the TV people, she could hardly do a very good job, could she? So if she failed miserably, they'd think it was because of that, not because she was a useless coward who quaked in her boots at the thought of teaching 3A.

When it was all over, she'd just slip out quietly and never set foot in a TV studio ever again. She'd promised Max and she wouldn't break a promise. But never again. She'd be terrible, she knew it, but all she had to do was get through this next half an hour calmly and leave. That was all.

Linda spoke into her radio mike: 'Can we get a sound person over here to mike Olivia up?'

In two minutes she was wearing a microphone, the bulky unit attached to the waistband of her trousers at the back.

'You'll be great,' Kevin said encouragingly, as he opened cupboard doors to show her where everything was.

'I hope so,' she replied fervently.

'Afterwards, I'll steal some of Nancy's champagne so we can celebrate,' he whispered wickedly.

'Nancy's champagne?' asked Olivia. 'I thought she . . .'

'Didn't drink champagne?' Kevin grinned. 'She doesn't drink it – she slurps it up like a dehydrated camel. If she gave up Cristal alone for a month, she'd lose a stone!'

Olivia was still laughing when Kevin left her alone on the kitchen set. She found a couple of knives, a chopping board and some Chinese-style dishes. The cupboards yielded some interesting spices and store cupboard staples. The last cookery person had known her stuff, Olivia thought, discovering treasures that would make her banana-and-onions combo edible. She knew exactly what to do.

'Ready to go whenever you are,' said a strange voice. Olivia whirled around to find two cameras on her and the crew of radio-miked, clipboard-wielding people staring at her with interest.

For a moment, her mind went blank. She stared at the camera directly in front of her and there was nothing in her head. Nothing. Her mind felt the way it was supposed to when you couldn't sleep and tried to imagine nothing at all so you'd drop off instantly.

During sleepless nights, Olivia found she just couldn't imagine nothing and ended up worrying about all the things she had to do the next morning.

But today, in front of an entire television studio, her mind was like the blackboard before a lesson – utterly blank. Why was she here? She'd been mad to think she could do this. Absolutely mad! Those Brandy Alexanders Max had bought her, the row with Stephen and a false sense of bravado had got her into this hideously embarrassing mess and now she was going to screw up publicly and desperately.

Feeling herself start to sweat with fear, she looked around the studio in a panic, looking for Linda so she could beg to go home and apologise for wasting all their time.

And then she saw Nancy. The presenter was still sitting on her raspberry couch and staring at Olivia with interest. The sort of emotionless interest assassins display in films before they pull the trigger on their quarry. Or perhaps not that emotionless, Olivia realised, as Nancy smiled spitefully at her predicament.

The famous, pink-lipsticked mouth curved up in a contemptuous smirk, one that clearly said: 'Amateurs.'

God, she was a bitch but she could turn on her TV persona like turning on a kettle, Olivia realised. A viper in real life, Nancy could switch on her television charm instantly because she had to. She couldn't possibly display her real self on TV so she acted. Well, if acting was all that was required, Olivia could do that too. She was acting all the time at home these days – acting happy families and acting as if she wasn't going slowly mad. Acting was a doddle. She eyeballed Nancy, took a deep breath and faced the camera again.

'This,' said Olivia, smiling as she held it up in one hand, 'is a pepper.' Her voice was nervous and slightly quavering. She had to make it firmer, slower. Concentrate, Olivia! Imagine you're in the classroom with a schools' examiner down your back, scrutinising your every move.

'Peppers are wonderfully nourishing and incredibly sweet and rich if cooked properly. They're the basis of lots of simple sauces. But what do you do if you're rushing in and out of the supermarket and end up at home with a sad specimen like ours?'

She was getting into her stride now. 'Bin it and send out for a pizza? Or get inventive with your store cupboard contents and make a delicious meal?'

From the corner of her eye, Olivia could see people watching her. They were interested, actually interested in what you could do with a mean little pepper that probably had less flavour than a used teabag. They weren't like 3A, bored rigid by the very notion of making things with peppers.

Olivia smiled at her audience, feeling a surge of confidence. If she treated the studio people like an interested class, she could do it. She might even enjoy it.

'The answer,' she said, her face animated, 'are these things.' Whisking out a jar of chilli flakes, a container of sun-dried tomatoes and some dried porcini mushrooms.

'Wait till you see what we can do with these,' she added enthusiastically.

Kevin's face, lit up with a huge, congratulatory grin, leapt out at her from the crowd. It was working, Olivia realised.

'Now who knows what to do with chilli flakes?' she asked.

She could see Linda looking suddenly nervous, as if Olivia had made the fatal inexperienced-TV-person mistake of expecting the technicians to join in. But Olivia, accustomed to asking questions in class and answering them herself because bored students doodling pop song lyrics on their textbooks couldn't be bothered, hadn't actually expected anyone to answer. Seamlessly, she explained exactly what you could do with chilli flakes. She chopped, she puréed, she sautéed . . . and she had her audience in the palm of her hand.

Afterwards, when she wondered how she'd actually stood in front of around thirty people and two cameras and talked to them for ages, she realised the secret was that she'd forgotten about the cameras. She'd tried to concentrate on the people watching and on the actual cooking, which she loved. And it had worked. These people looked at her with fascination as she spoke passionately about creating a beautiful meal with fresh ingredients.

Fourteen year olds couldn't care less about healthy eating and how a little garlic was one of the best medicines around. They wanted three-minutes-in-the-microwave food so they could go out afterwards and flirt with seventeen-year-old boys.

But the grown ups in front of her loved the idea of making their own tomato sauces and relished the thought that a couple of little jars from the delicatessen could rescue them from a daily diet of heat-and-serve dinners. Even if they didn't actually *make* tomato sauce, they liked knowing how to do it.

They let her run on for fifteen minutes, five longer than originally planned.

'Fantastic,' enthused Linda when the cameras went off. 'You're a natural!'

Olivia slumped against the unit, suddenly exhausted by her efforts. 'Really?' she asked, suddenly doubting herself. She'd *thought* it was OK, but how could she tell? She hadn't been *hopeless* but she was hardly up to broadcasting standard, surely?

'Brilliant,' said the floor manager.

'Absolutely brilliant,' echoed Kevin. 'You are a complete star, Ms de Vere. I can't believe you've never done that before.'

'I just kept imagining the worst class I teach and thinking you lot were nicer, so it was easy,' she said.

They all laughed. 'It certainly worked,' Linda confirmed. 'I was hungry just listening to you talk. I'm going to the canteen for something as soon as we're finished. Come on and watch yourself in the control room.'

Olivia blanched. 'I couldn't.'

'You will and you'll be amazed. You were great. In fact, I reckon you're hired, although I can't say officially until Paul sees the tape.' Watching herself on video in the control room, Olivia felt she was in a dream. The glamorous blonde woman who behaved as if being in front of the cameras was the most natural thing in the world couldn't be her, could it? Her onscreen self smiled at the camera tranquilly and shook her curtain of shimmering golden hair out of the way occasionally, a habit she'd noticed in Sasha but which Olivia had no idea she shared herself.

And her eyes . . . they looked huge in her face, like two silvery orbs shining with enthusiasm. She looked, Olivia thought with utter surprise, beautiful. Not doll-like or expressionless, the way she felt when Stephen told her she was beautiful, but lively, vivacious, animated.

'You look great on television,' Linda repeated, peering carefully at the screen. 'Very natural. I thought you weren't going to be all right in the beginning, you hesitated and I thought, "Oh-oh, rabbit on road in front of oncoming car time." But you gathered it all together and gave us quite a performance.'

Olivia, feeling a little shell-shocked by everything, grinned to herself. She couldn't very well tell Linda that the sight of Nancy Roberts smiling like a venomous Cheshire cat had spurred her on to perform in a way she'd never thought possible.

As if she was reading Olivia's thoughts, Linda said: 'You must meet Nancy before you go.'

Olivia wasn't sure that she wanted to but she could hardly say that.

'If you're going to be working with us, you'll be working specifically with Nancy. She hosts the cookery slots and you two should . . . er . . .' Linda hesitated '. . . get on.'

Obviously, the producer wasn't going to say that getting on with Nancy was vital to remaining on the show but Olivia could read between the lines. She briefly wondered if the previous cookery person had got on with Nancy.

They walked along a corridor to the dressing rooms, with Linda explaining how often they'd need Olivia if she was to be hired. Two mornings a week for a fifteen-minute slot at ten-thirty, which would involve discussing the menu with the researchers and coming in at half-eight to get the preparation done.

As they walked past several open doors, Olivia could see that the dressing rooms were compact little boxes each containing a tiny sink, a clothes hanging space, a few chairs and wall-to-wall mirrors.

Then, they reached Nancy's dressing room.

Nita, the star's beleaguered assistant, opened the door gingerly when Linda knocked and let them into a large airy room that looked like at least three ordinary dressing rooms knocked into one. Painted in Nancy's signature pink, the room contained a zebra-print armchair, a cherry pink and gilt chaise-longue and a coffee table groaning under the weight of fan letters and a glossy magazines opened on purpose at fawning profiles of the star herself. There was even a pink-tiled bathroom.

One light-bulb-edged mirror was a shrine to Nancy with scores of pictures of her stuck haphazardly on to the glass: Nancy with Frank Sinatra, Neil Diamond, the President and Barney. A vase of fresh pink roses sat beside the shrine, with another cellophaned bouquet of baby pink ones on the floor, waiting to be arranged.

The star herself was arranged on the chaise-longue, feet up and a glass of champagne in her hand.

In her pink boudoir, on the pink and gilt chaise, Nancy looked like everybody's vision of a brothel's madam. She was tough enough for the job, too, Olivia reckoned, imagining Nancy personally throwing punters on to the street for not paying up.

'Olivia, how lovely to meet you,' Nancy said in her

television voice. Thrilled that Nancy had decided to be nice to her, Olivia held out a hand. Nancy, however, wasn't into hand shaking. 'So formal,' she tittered, giving Olivia an air kiss on both sides of her face. The waft of overpowering Hypnotic Poison left Olivia reeling. Nancy must have used half the bottle in one go.

'Do sit.' Nancy patted the end of the chaise and Olivia sat down, waiting to see how the encounter would progress. It was a bit like entering the lioness's den and finding her no longer hungry for fresh meat but in the mood to toy with you. One false move and you were dead.

'Where did you find Olivia?' Nancy asked Linda, still in sweet mode. Nancy was obviously wary of Linda, Olivia decided, which was why she was being so nice to the producer.

'She's a friend of Max Stewart's.'

Nancy's eyes turned into slits at the word 'friend'.

'Really?' She gave Olivia the once over. 'You're his type, I'll say that for you.'

'I'm happily married and Max isn't my type,' she replied tartly.

Nancy giggled girlishly. 'Poor pet, you'll have to get used to our bitchy ways in television,' she said in a patronising voice. 'You won't last long if you can't develop skin a little thicker than that, Olivia. This business is very incestuous, you know, that's why I asked. We all live in each other's pockets. Everyone sleeps with everyone else eventually. How do you know Max, anyway?'

'He's a friend of my husband's,' Olivia lied, innocently thinking that was one way to scotch rumours of anything between herself and Max.

'What does he do?'

'He's in banking.'

'What's his name?'

'Stephen MacKenzie.'

'Never heard of him.' Nancy continued the interrogation. 'What did you do before this?'

'I teach Home Economics.'

'Ooh.' Satisfied at last, Nancy sat back against her plump cushions and drank more champagne. She'd not offered any to Olivia or Linda. 'Cookery classes.'

'It's more than cookery,' Olivia said hotly.

'I'm sure it is. Do you do sewing as well?' Nancy asked facetiously. 'Linda,' she turned to the producer, who'd been silently watching the exchange, 'maybe we should get Olivia to sew as well? I seem to remember making a lovely little gingham apron when I was in home economics classes. Useless, of course, but so pretty. Wouldn't that be a nice slot – Olivia teaching people how to make aprons and clothes for Barbie dolls?'

'Well, I don't know, Nancy,' said Linda in a thoughtful tone, getting to her feet. 'That's not a bad idea. We'll think about it. Come on, Olivia, we've people to meet.'

Olivia, outraged by Nancy's comments and just as outraged by the producer's obsequious response, felt herself go white with rage.

'So nice to meet you,' Nancy said disarmingly. 'You were good on camera.'

Taken aback, Olivia stared at the other woman, her longing to lacerate Nancy with a smart comment subsiding. She was never good with smart remarks. Evie would have thought up something devastating.

'Er . . . thank you,' she stuttered.

Linda held the door open and Olivia was nearly in the corridor when Nancy hit her with a parting shot.

'Of course, it's easy to be competent with no audience and the knowledge the show isn't live,' Nancy said, her voice so treacly it was hard to reconcile it with her bitchy words. 'Try it for real, sweetie, and you'll get a big shock. Live television sorts out the amateurs from the professionals.' She gave Olivia a withering look that left her in no doubt as to which category Nancy had placed her in.

Linda slammed the door before Olivia could say anything in response. 'She's quite a character, isn't she?' the producer said weakly.

Character, Olivia thought, wasn't the word.

Evie laughed delightedly and hugged Olivia.

'I'm so pleased for you,' she said. 'Olivia de Vere, TV star! How wonderful! We'll have to have a girls' night out to celebrate.'

Thinking of Stephen's feelings about girls' nights out, Olivia smiled weakly, the buzz she'd felt after leaving the television centre abating somewhat. Driving through the traffic to Evie's house, she'd felt high on adrenaline and thrilled with herself. Now, sitting at Evie's kitchen table with a mug of weak tea in her hand and some ginger nut biscuits on a plate in front of her, she began to wonder if she'd hallucinated the whole thing.

She was Olivia MacKenzie, mum-of-one, wife to the disgruntled Stephen, hardly a TV star. Evie was the lively one, the animated one.

'I don't know, Evie,' she sighed, 'am I mad even to think of doing this? What if I do go to pieces when it's live . . .'

But Evie wouldn't hear a word of it: 'Don't listen to that bitch,' she said, fierce in her loyalty. 'I may not know anything about the world of television, Olivia, but I know jealousy when I see it. She's jealous as sin, that's all. Jealous because you're better looking, thinner *and* naturally blonde.' Evie didn't care about verbally mangling a woman she'd hitherto admired for being one of the few voluptuous-and-proud-of-it women on TV. Nancy

Roberts had been vicious to her beloved Olivia and for that she deserved to die! Or be slagged off as a talentless bleached blonde.

'It's a compliment really,' she added. 'She feels threatened by you and that's why she lashed out. If she'd been as sweet as pie, then you'd have reason to worry because it'd mean you were terrible.'

Delighted with her logic, Evie carried on. 'I was worried about you doing the audition in the first place,' she admitted. 'Not because I thought you wouldn't be able for it,' she added hastily. 'But because Max Stewart,' she almost spat his name out, 'organised it. I was sure he was simply bullshitting you.'

'I don't know what you've got against Max,' Olivia said mildly. 'He's a lovely man, very kind and friendly.'

Evie snorted.

'You don't still think he was trying to set you up when he chatted with you at the wedding, Evie, do you?' Olivia said. 'He's not that sort of person.'

You don't know what sort of person he is, Evie thought grimly. She hadn't told Olivia about Max wanting to see her again, even though he knew she was engaged to Simon. It was despicable, dreadful. She hadn't been able to stop thinking about it and him.

He filled her thoughts and she'd had endless screaming matches in her head when she'd told him exactly what she thought of him. The words 'rogue', 'chancer' and 'bastard' came up a lot in those imaginary conversations. Who did he think he was, asking her out when she'd already said no? And what sort of woman did he think *she* was?

'Is this the latest wedding dress brochure?' asked Olivia, to change the subject. She picked up the glossy brochure that was lying under a newspaper and flicked through the pages. Brides in elegant shift dresses and medieval princess gowns vied for attention on every page. 'These are beautiful. Which are the three you like best, the ones you were telling me about?'

Evie glanced at the brochure dispiritedly. She'd lost interest in wedding dresses for some reason. The medieval fantasy dress she'd dreamed of for so long no longer gave her little shivers of delight when she looked at it, imagining herself at the altar beside Simon in front of awe-struck guests. Until recently, she'd loved day-dreaming about the wedding. When she was tired and couldn't sleep, imagining every detail of the day had been her favourite way of dozing off. But that didn't work anymore. Thinking about the long-anticipated day just made her strangely edgy and unable to sleep.

In fact, the only time she'd dreamed about the wedding at all, recently had been a veritable nightmare where she'd found herself at the altar wearing a long diaphanous white nightie, with flowers in her hair, bare feet and – worst of all – no underwear! Even stranger, when the groom had turned round to greet her, he wasn't Simon at all. It was Max bloody Stewart looking like a pirate in the sort of buccaneer's linen shirt men wore in her favourite novels. Then he grinned at her, baring those wolf's fangs as if he was going to sink them into her. After that dream, Evie had woken up abruptly, sweat beaded to her forehead and her brushed cotton nightie glued to her body.

'This is so you, Evie.' Olivia showed her a picture of a Regency-inspired dress that had Jane Austen written all over it. Demure and sexy, it was just the sort of thing Evie would look beautiful in.

'Mmmm,' she said listlessly, 'I don't know. I still haven't sorted out the menus. I don't know why the hotel are so keen on knowing what we're going to eat now when the wedding isn't for six months. I can't figure out if we want poached salmon and Wicklow lamb or trout with almonds and Beef Wellington. It's so far away to be planning specifics.'

Olivia looked up from the brochure, jolted by the depressed tone of her friend's voice.

'I thought you were enjoying organising the wedding?' she said quietly, scanning Evie's face carefully.

Aware that she'd almost revealed something she was barely able to admit to herself, Evie backtracked. 'Oh, it's just wedding jitters,' she said hurriedly. That was it, she told herself. Wedding jitters. Every bride got them.

Olivia was still studying her.

Evie rattled on. 'Poor Simon won't know what to do with me when we're married,' she said brightly. 'I'm getting as moody as hell. We still can't decide where to buy a house when we're married. He wants a larger town house, something near the city, and I'd prefer to move out, maybe to Dun Laoghaire.' She beamed at Olivia, as if whether to live within a stone's throw of the city or miles outside it was the biggest issue in her life at that moment.

She couldn't say, *daren't even think*, that there was any other issue throbbing in her head like an abscess. An abscess named Max Stewart.

'So, what does Stephen think of all this television stardom?' she asked cheerily, getting up to make more tea.

It was Olivia's turn to look guarded. 'That's the other big problem,' she said slowly. 'He doesn't know.'

'Stephen doesn't know?' Evie asked in shock. 'Do you think that's wise?'

Olivia put her head in her hands and groaned. 'I know, I know. I should have told him. I knew he'd hate me doing it and put me off, or at least convince me I'd be so hopelessly bad that I'd be bound to make a mess of it. Destroying my self-confidence is what he does best nowadays.'

Evie stopped messing around with the kettle and sat down quietly at the table. 'I didn't know things were so bad,' she said finally.

Olivia fiddled with a cuticle, not meeting her best friend's eyes. 'It's not the sort of thing you talk about, is it?'

'It is to *me*,' Evie said earnestly.

Olivia shrugged. 'I couldn't tell you, I couldn't tell anyone. I don't know where it all started to go wrong, but it did and it has.' Her eyes filled with tears. 'I love him, Evie, but he doesn't love me, not really.' The words came out in a rush. 'He loves having a wife who looks like me and knows how to say the right things but he doesn't care anymore about me as a person. It's as if I don't exist, I'm just another thing in his life. Like the car or the apartment or his state-of-the-art laptop. I hate it all.' She broke off, tears running down her face now. 'I don't say anything to him now,' she continued. 'I let him go on believing that it's all OK when inside I hate him sometimes. That's why I did this, the television audition. Because I thought it'd show him I could do something, that I wasn't stupid.'

'You're *not* stupid!' Evie said, putting her arms around Olivia.

'I feel stupid,' she howled. 'Stupid and useless. I can't even teach my classes without screwing up, I can't do *anything*. Why do I think I can do this?'

While she cried on to her friend's shoulder, Evie held her tightly, wishing there was more she could do or say. But there was nothing, apart from 'I told you so', which wouldn't have been true, anyhow.

Evie had never really liked Stephen, wary of his brusque self-assurance and suspicious of the way he'd treated Olivia. He was domineering and almost obsessive about her from the very start. The way he watched her across a

293

room made some people smile fondly but it had made Evie wrinkle up her nose in distrust. A man who trusted and loved a woman didn't stare at her like a gaoler guarding a prisoner on day release, which was the way Stephen looked at Olivia.

But Evie had never said any of this. She'd never said, 'Have you really thought about this?' The type of plain speaking she was renowned for. Olivia had been so very in love with him. Anyway, still reeling from Tony's death, Evie hadn't exactly considered herself an expert in male/female relations at the time, so she'd kept her misgivings to herself. And watched her closest friend carefully for signs that the fairy-tale wedding hadn't worked out.

As the years went by, Evie convinced herself that Stephen and Olivia were happy together, which just went to show that you never knew what really went on behind closed doors.

'Do you want to talk about it?' she asked now. 'Stay for dinner and we'll talk, you can't go home now. You need to get this off your chest.'

Olivia sat up, wiping her tear-streaked face. 'No, I can't, Evie. Thank you for the offer, but I've got to get home.' She was visibly pulling herself together, dragging on the 'happy' face she presented to the world.

'Olivia,' said Evie sharply, 'stop it. That's what you've been doing for years and you never told me. Now stop and talk,' she commanded. 'You've got to or you'll go mad!'

Olivia dropped her façade and her lovely face looked instantly ravaged, the mask gone and hollows of misery left in its place. Haunted eyes stared out at her friend.

'Oh, Livvy,' Evie cried softly. 'You can't go on like this.'

'What else *can* I do?' she asked. 'Leave him? Be realistic, Evie. I can barely cope with the world *with* him – what would I be like without him?'

'You could be your old self again, the person you were before Stephen.'

With a tissue, Olivia dabbed away the tears from her eyes. 'I don't know who that person was,' she said dully. 'I don't know what sort of person I am now. At the wedding I told Max that Stephen didn't see me as a person anymore.' She gave a little laugh. 'That's not exactly true. *I* don't know who I am any more, so I can hardly blame my husband for not knowing, can I?'

'I want to help,' Evie said anxiously.

Olivia shrugged. 'You can't help me, not really. I have to do it myself . . .'

'Please, Livvy, don't shut me out. Let me help,' interrupted Evie.

'I won't shut you out, I promise. Who knows? You may have to put me up on your sofa for a few nights.' Olivia got up from the table, letting her words sink in. 'I really have to go now. I know I have to tell Stephen about all this sometime.' She gestured to the heavy television make-up. 'But not tonight. He's got some people over from Germany and they're coming to dinner, so I'm going home to play the good hostess with something exotic for dinner and a perennial smile on my Stepford Wife face.'

Her voice was bitter. There was nothing Evie could say.

They hugged goodbye and Olivia got into her car. With sunglasses hiding her eyes and her perfect profile outlined in the low March sun, she looked the picture of an elegant working woman as she drove away from Evie's front gate.

Looking into her pocket handkerchief-sized front garden, Evie watched a fat pigeon waddling around digging for worms in the soft clay. Unease sat in her belly like a rich meal, curdling ominously. She thought about Olivia and Stephen, on the surface the perfect couple. Underneath it was all a sham.

Was she mad to want to get married? Evie wondered. She'd been happy enough with her life so far.

Being half of a couple had seemed so important for such a long time. Or maybe it was just that *not* being half of a couple made it seem to matter. Was that why she and Simon had clicked – because they'd both desperately wanted someone else and didn't really care who? In any case Simon was practically married to his mother, which was why he'd taken so bloody long to decide actually to do the desperate deed and ask someone to marry him.

He'd been burned once before, he'd told her. A long relationship that hadn't worked out. Perhaps whoever she was hadn't been able to compete with his maternal devotion. Evie watched the pigeon mournfully. Perhaps they were both making a huge mistake.

She shook her head as if driving the thought from her mind. Daft, that's what she was. Plain daft. She was marrying Simon in September and that was that.

CHAPTER TEN

It was five to three. Still. Evie wondered if she was in the
Twilight Zone because no matter how often she looked at
the alarm clock, the time seemed to change with brain-
numbing slowness. Not looking at it was obviously the
answer. She sat up in bed, shook her pillow around a bit
and sank back down on to the cool side of the bed,
determined not to look at the time. Four minutes to three
winked the luminous numbers on the clock.

Evie felt like crying. She was exhausted and yet she
couldn't sleep. The memory of Olivia's weary face earlier
that day kept running through her mind; Olivia and
Stephen, Evie and Simon, an ill-fated foursome and their
problems. And Max. No matter how she tried to wrench
him from her mind, he was still there. Smiling wolfishly at
her, eyes caressing her in a way Simon's never did.

Shit! She sat up again, feverish and furious. She had to
stop thinking about bloody Max Stewart. It was positively
sickening. His presence loomed over her even when she
was in bed, never mind what it did to her when she was
up. Since she'd met him a week ago, he was everywhere:
grinning at her, taunting her, eyebrows raised in amusement as if he could see the effect he was having upon her.
It was no use trying to sleep. She might as well get some
hot milk and read.

Trying not to think of how shattered she'd be after a sleepless night, Evie warmed some milk and brought it up to bed. Propped up with pillows, she picked her book up and tried to read. Even that didn't work.

The dashing South American polo player in *Venetia's Victory* reminded her of Max; he had the same glinting eyes, the same devil-may-care attitude. Every time the polo player crushed Venetia to his chest with his powerful mallet-wielding arm, Evie could see herself being crushed against Max. She threw the book down in disgust and rummaged through her bedside locker for a replacement. Jammed at the back was one of Cara's forensic pathologist thrillers. Cara adored blood, gore and serial killers and had been trying to get her sister to read one for years. Evie had resisted until now because she hated the thought of reading about murderers preying on vulnerable women before she went to sleep. Strangely enough, the idea seemed very appealing now. Surely an axe murderer would be able to get Max out of the picture?

By five-thirty, she was a serial thriller convert – and very, very tired. How come you can only sleep when morning is lurking around the corner? she thought exhaustedly, sinking her head on to the pillow as the birds began to sing energetically outside the window.

They appeared to be singing the same song when the alarm clock erupted with the breakfast show and Tom Jones purring 'Kiss' at seven-fifteen. Evie dragged herself out of bed, yelled at Rosie to get up, and yawned her way down the stairs, only just avoiding tripping over her dressing-gown belt. Strong coffee and some breakfast didn't help her as much as she'd hoped.

'You look wrecked, Mum,' Rosie remarked, the picture of health as she bounced into the kitchen in her school uniform.

'Couldn't sleep,' Evie mumbled, head bent over her plate, 'and I've a terrible day ahead. The auditors are in. God, I could sleep for a week.'

'Caffeine tablets,' pronounced Rosie, 'that's what you need, Mum. They're ace at waking you up. All the girls use them for exams.'

Normally, Evie would have said something about how she hoped Rosie would never use any sort of chemical stimulant. This morning, however, she only just managed to stop herself from asking where she could get her hands on some caffeine tablets and how many could you take for maximum effect.

Rosie switched on the radio, which immediately foretold horrible delays on Evie's route to the office.

'I don't believe it,' she mumbled miserably, ignoring her usual rule about only having one cup of coffee in the morning and pouring herself another. Her cellulite would just have to like it or lump it.

'Poor Mum.' Rosie gave her an affectionate hug. 'Now if you'd teach me how to drive your car, I could drop you into work and you wouldn't have to face the traffic,' she added with a mischievous grin.

Her mother groaned. 'Have you ever thought of going into the legal profession, Rosie? You're an expert at arguing at the right time and the right place.'

Grinning, she shoved a couple of slices of bread into the toaster. 'Is that a yes?'

'I'd be the wrong person to teach you to drive,' Evie pointed out. 'Maybe Simon could teach you.'

Rosie grimaced. 'Not Simon. Maybe Grandpops would. Or perhaps Vida!' She brightened up at the thought of driving Vida's stately Lexus and impressing all the young fellas in Ballymoreen who hung around the monument. She could picture them with their mouths open in astonishment and admiration, particularly that guy who lived above the post office. It was a pleasing picture.

'What's wrong with Simon teaching you?' her mother asked irritably.

'Oh, Mum, come on,' said Rosie. 'You know . . .' She broke off without finishing the sentence.

'No, I don't know.' Evie was cross and very tired.

Rosie sighed. 'Let's not have a fight.'

'This isn't a fight,' Evie said grumpily. 'I simply wish you didn't have such an attitude about Simon.'

'I don't have an *attitude* about Simon,' her daughter retorted.

'You do,' Evie snapped back.

'It's not an attitude,' Rosie said, taking her coffee cup off the table. 'I just don't like him, that's all.' She slammed the kitchen door and a millisecond later her toast sprang up from the toaster with a twang.

What have you done? Evie groaned to herself. Just because you're in a bad mood, you don't have to take it out on poor Rosie.

She quickly buttered and marmaladed Rosie's toast and took it up to her daughter's room. The door, usually open in the morning because the two of them chattered nineteen to the dozen as they showered and dressed, was ominously shut.

'Rosie love, I'm sorry. I'm grumpy this morning because I couldn't sleep,' Evie said from the landing.

The door opened. Slightly mollified, Rosie took the toast from her mother.

'I *am* sorry,' Evie said again.

'It's OK,' Rosie said. 'I'm sorry about what I said too. About Simon. I don't dislike him,' she lied. 'I just don't want him to teach me how to drive. I'd love you to do it.'

Evie smiled for the first time that morning. 'I don't know

why, love, when I'm such a bad-tempered old cow of a mother. But I'll teach you, I promise. When you've finished your exams, I'll put your name on the insurance. It'll be my post-exam present to you.'

'Ace!' said Rosie joyfully.

'Ace' was the word of the moment, Evie thought, shuffling back into the bathroom for her shower. She felt anything but ace at that precise moment.

Sitting at her desk at nine on the dot, she still felt spectacularly aceless. She felt terrible, in fact, and she was damn' sure that she looked it too, particularly as she'd been too tired to wash her hair. Greasy hair, a 'safe' black suit and a pale, exhausted face meant she looked as if she'd just arrived from a funeral, a fact Lorraine remarked upon.

'Lord, Evie, what were you up to last night?' she demanded, resplendent in an eye-catching red mini in honour of the auditors' visit. The last time they had been at Wentworth Alarms, she'd spent three thrilling days flirting with the junior member of the team, a Diet-Coke guy lookalike.

'Nothing exciting,' sighed Evie, who wasn't looking forward to a day of the auditors' demands combined with Davis in the inevitable bad temper. Since he'd been diagnosed with ME, he was only in the office on rare occasions and then he was like a hungover JCB driver: cross and determined to take it out on everyone.

'You can tell me what you were doing,' Lorraine said saucily. 'Your Simon doesn't look like he's a goer but he must be. The silent ones are always the worst, that's what my mam says.'

The thought of placid Simon being described as a goer brought a wry grin to Evie's face.

'I couldn't sleep, that's all.'

Lorraine winked. 'I bet.'

The morning passed with interminable slowness. Davis failed to arrive at work and when Evie rang him at home the answer machine switched on every time. The financial director, Davis's nephew and proof positive that nepotism was generally a mistake, did his best to help but only succeeded in looking bewildered most of the time, and asking Evie where everything was.

'I wish I'd studied bloody accountancy,' she hissed at Lorraine finally.

'I wish I'd stayed at home today,' the girl answered wretchedly. The Diet Coke guy from the previous year hadn't turned up. His replacement had the sort of bad breath that could knock you out at fifty yards.

Neither of them had got anywhere near either the kettle or the ladies' loo all morning and when lunchtime arrived, they were both shattered. At one o'clock, Evie leaned back in her chair and decided for once to ignore her phone as it rang incessantly.

'I'm too tired to put on my lipstick,' Lorraine said, lolling in her swivel chair, her feet on the desk. 'Will I order us a pizza so we don't have to go out?'

Evie was about to say 'yes' when the sales department's secretary stuck her head around the door.

'Evie,' she said, round-eyed, 'your lunch date is in reception. And he's *gorgeous*. Who is he? We're all dying to know.'

Evie's heart skipped a beat. She didn't have a lunch date. But she could think of only one person who'd have the female staff of Wentworth Alarms in such a tizzy: Max Stewart.

'I can't imagine,' she said, trying to look nonchalant, and picked up her still-buzzing phone.

It was the receptionist.

'There's someone waiting for me?' Evie asked coolly.

'Max Stewart,' breathed the receptionist, with the same reverence she reserved for speaking about Mel Gibson.

'Tell him I'll be down in ten minutes.'

'Who is it?' squeaked Lorraine, knowing something was up from the way Evie's eyes shone.

'My stepbrother,' she said as calmly as possible.

'*Stepbrother?*' Lorraine repeated incredulously. 'You never mentioned him.'

'Didn't I?' Evie scooped up her handbag and wondered if it would be a complete giveaway if she asked Lorraine for a squirt of her perfume and a lend of some concealer to hide the suitcases under her eyes. It probably would, but who cared?

Trying to calm the excitement that bubbled up inside her, Evie did her best to hide the ravages of a sleepless night. At least she didn't need blusher, she thought wryly; her cheeks were already rosy from a mixture of pleasure and embarrassment. Then she began to worry. What if Simon rang and was told she was seeing Max Stewart for lunch? What if he drove past unexpectedly and discovered them in the pub?

Well, Evie decided firmly, she wouldn't go out to lunch with Max, it was that simple. He hadn't made an appointment, so she wouldn't go with him. She'd make an excuse.

Squinting as she zigzagged her dark brown mascara wand up her lashes, she realised that it wasn't so simple. She wanted to go. It would all be perfectly innocent, she told herself. He was her *stepbrother* after all. What could possibly be wrong with meeting him for lunch?

But as she hurried to the stairs, eyes shining and a bounce in her step for the first time that day, Evie knew in her heart of hearts there was nothing innocent about Max's visit – or about her reaction to it.

At the bottom of the stairs, she peered into reception

through the glass fire doors. Her heart swelled instinctively at the sight of him. Max was sitting in one of the squashy chairs, a giant thing she could never sit in comfortably because she was too short.

He dwarfed it, long denim-clad legs sticking out across the room. He looked casual today, wearing a tan suede jacket with suede workmen's boots. She could see that much from behind the paper he was reading, his face set in concentration.

Like a child gazing at a spaniel puppy in a pet shop window, Evie stared at Max. The rock-breaker jaw was set firm as he read, dark brows hid his eyes. He looked different out of his elegant suit: less formidable, younger.

Then he saw her.

He unfurled himself and got to his feet. Evie shoved the fire door open and hoped he didn't realise she'd been watching him for a few moments.

The receptionist and her lunch-time replacement were staring at Max with unabashed curiosity.

'Evie, your . . . guest,' the receptionist said, her lip-glossed smile on full beam, obviously dying to be introduced.

'Thanks,' Evie said politely, equally determined not to introduce her. She stood in front of Max but didn't make a move to hold out her hand.

'Evie, how nice to see you.' He smiled at her, a warm, glinting smile that lit up his cobalt eyes as if somebody had flicked on a button inside him.

Evie blinked. She hadn't imagined how attractive he was. He was devastating in the flesh, better than she'd remembered, better than in her bizarre wedding dream.

'I was in the area on business and thought I'd see if you were free for lunch,' he said.

'Well, I wasn't going to . . .' began Evie, suddenly remembering how she'd meant to tell Max where to go if ever she saw him again. 'I have a lot of work to do this afternoon.'

'Please, I'd like to talk to you.'

The way he said 'please' did it. A low, soft caressing sound that slithered up her spine as if he'd just asked her to take all her clothes off and get into a jacuzzi with him to play doctors and nurses.

She couldn't resist. 'OK.'

Max pushed the front door open and they went outside. Evie could feel fascinated eyes burning into her back as they walked towards Max's car. She half-turned to look at the office and saw Lorraine, the receptionist and the sales secretary all peering out past the reception blinds like spectators at a tennis match eagerly waiting for the umpire to call a shot.

'Do they always do that?' Max asked innocently, looking back too.

'They're waiting for the sandwich delivery man,' Evie fibbed. 'He's late and they're ravenous.'

'They're probably wondering who I am,' he remarked.

Evie laughed at his perceptive reading of the situation. 'You have no idea,' she said, shaking her head ruefully. 'I'll probably be on the six o'clock news for going off with a strange man at lunch. *Nearly-married woman seen getting into flash car with stranger – police alert!*'

'But I'm your stepbrother,' he pointed out in a mock-innocent voice, opening the passenger door of the sports car for Evie.

'So you are,' she replied sweetly, shutting her door with a resounding bang.

'Where's a good spot for lunch round here?' he asked, driving out the gate.

'I assumed you knew this area since you said you were around on business?' Evie asked suspiciously.

The laughing eyes crinkled up with amusement. 'You've caught me out, I'm afraid. I've never been in this neck of the woods before. I came to see you. And not because you're my dear stepsister, either,' he added in a tone that made Evie feel very hot suddenly.

'The pub at the roundabout is nice,' she said, her voice sounding an octave higher with nerves. 'Turn left here and take the next two rights.'

She sank back into her seat, eyes fixed straight ahead. She didn't even want to look at Max. What had she got herself into? She should have sent him away, refused to meet him, bluntly told him he had a nerve turning up after she'd told him she was engaged. She'd never handle him, he wasn't like Simon: easily dealt with. Max was a whole different kettle of fish. Piranhas, in fact.

'Difficult day?' he asked companionably, manoeuvring the car into a parking space.

Evie, who'd been expecting a different sort of conversation, shot him a sideways look.

'Yes,' she said reluctantly. She was too edgy to be comfortable.

'The receptionist said you had the auditors in,' he said, still not looking at her as he parked.

'Just as well she isn't working for MI5,' Evie said, raising her eyes to heaven.

'She was only making conversation,' he said mildly.

'I suppose.'

They joined the soup and sandwiches queue in the pub. To cover up what she felt was an uneasy silence, Evie found herself rattling on about the dreaded auditors and how difficult it was dealing with them when her boss was out of the office.

At first, her chatter was stilted but as they sat down with their food, she began to enjoy telling him about her manic day. Max was surprisingly easy to talk to, or maybe it was that he really listened. He asked the right sort of questions and was interested in her answers.

When she'd finished telling him about Tom, Davis's dopey nephew, he told her about a television production company he'd once worked in where the boss appointed his four sons as middle managers: 'Each one more stupid than the last,' Max said, grinning. 'None of them could make a decision about making programmes and when you got the four of them together, they just fought. They were like crabs in a bucket – none would let the others do anything independently. They'd drag him back in so they could argue some more about where to get the paper cups for the water dispenser or what colour to paint the conference room. Their father had this happy idea of letting them take over the company when he retired but after six months he fired them all.'

'What happened then?' asked Evie.

'My partner and I bought the company and within a year we'd turned it around so profits were up fifty percent. Then, the four of them tried to sue us, saying we'd taken away their birthright and that if their father had given them time, they'd have turned a profit.' He laughed at the memory.

Evie swallowed a bite of her sandwich. 'Is that the company you have now?' she asked, eager to know more about him but not wanting to appear too interested.

He shook his head. 'I still own shares in it but somebody else runs it. My new company is called DWS Productions. We make mini-series. The old company makes technical videos, there's a lot of money in that. But producing mini-series is more fun.'

'I'd no idea that's what you did!' Evie exclaimed. 'Your mother never really explained what sort of producing you did. I had visions of tacky game shows.'

He allowed himself to smile at the comment.

'Mini-series, huh?' Evie added. 'What are you working on now? What have you done?'

'We've just finished a production about the famine and now we're in pre-production for a *Gone With The Wind*-type series, set in Ireland and Louisiana.'

'You must travel all the time?' Evie said, sandwich forgotten. This was so exciting, far more thrilling than stories about auditors and alarm companies.

'I spent six months in Australia for the famine one, *The Wilderness*,' Max explained. 'We made it primarily for the American and Australian markets. The new one is more European. My partner is going to handle most of the American side of things which means I'll have more time to myself. I've travelled nine months of every year for the past ten years. I need a break. I'm thinking of buying a house in Ireland and putting down some roots.' He pushed his plate away and smiled at Evie.

'Sorry to change the subject, but I know you've got to get back to work. Do you know why I've asked you out?' he asked abruptly, eyes boring into hers.

Evie could feel her pulse rushing along like a freight train. She could imagine what he was going to say. *Because I can't stop thinking about you, Evie. Because I'm crazy about you. That's why I want to spend more time in Ireland, to be close to you. I know you're engaged but . . .*

'. . . I don't know what you'd think about that,' he was saying.

'Sorry, what?' Evie reined in her imagination, which was now on a windswept beach with herself and Max in a clinch beside frothing waves and a sandy cove that was a dead ringer for the one in *From Here To Eternity*.

One of Max's eyebrows veered upwards. 'I was telling you about this idea I have for a summer holiday to bring both families together. I know you usually spend some time with your father during the summer and I thought we could combine that with my gift to the newly weds.'

'What gift . . . combine what?' asked Evie stupidly. What was he talking about?

'A villa in Spain. I've booked a villa in the south of Spain for two weeks at the end of July. It's my wedding present to Andrew and my mother but your dad is understandably worried because you normally spend time with him for the summer. Mother doesn't want to upset things, she knows their marriage was difficult for you to accept, so I thought that if you, Rosie and Cara came with us, it'd solve lots of problems.'

'With *us*?' Evie asked again.

'Naturally I was going to go too. If you don't object?'

There was that grin again, a wry grin, as if he *knew* what she'd been thinking. Wrongly thinking.

'I don't know,' Evie said coolly, recovering her composure somewhat. 'Where in the south of Spain?' she asked, as if she were intimately acquainted with every centimetre of the Costa del Sol instead of only knowing it from holiday programmes on TV.

'Puerto Banus.'

'Oh,' she said in a blasé tone, making a mental note to look it up on the atlas when she went home. 'I'll have to think about it.' She drained her coffee cup in one go.

'It's a beautiful part of the coast,' he said, as if reading her mind, 'and it'd be a wonderful chance for us all to get to know each other.'

Evie eyed him suspiciously.

The amused expression disappeared from his eyes. 'I mean that,' he said softly. 'I'd love to get to know you better.'

The way he looked at her was like nothing she'd ever experienced before. Those incredibly blue eyes roamed over her face, drinking her in. The moment was unbearably charged, incredibly seductive. Evie felt the rest of the world melt away, as if there was no other sound or movement around – just her and Max, his gaze fastened on hers.

'Rosie, Cara and me?' she asked, deliberately misunderstanding him.

'Just you.'

'Oh.'

He was speaking in a very low voice now, the words electric. 'I know what you said last week at the wedding but I wanted to see you again.'

She looked away, as if he could see inside her and know she'd been longing to see him too. To talk to him, laugh with him, touch him.

'You never answered my note.'

'How could I?' she demanded fiercely. 'You know about Simon, how could I possibly meet you?'

They were so close now, both leaning across the table towards the other, almost touching. Intimate, like lovers. Evie didn't know what she was going to do next. It was heady, this feeling of being carried away with emotion. That's what Max did to her – changed her, made her like someone different, someone who followed her instincts and not a prepared script.

'I know you're engaged, Evie, but I can't help the way I felt about you the moment I met you. I thought you felt the same way too?'

His hand reached across the table to hers. She watched it, fascinated. His skin was a golden tanned colour, the strong wrist covered with surprisingly pale hairs for a man with such a shock of Italianate dark hair.

'Evie!' shrieked someone. 'Fancy meeting you here!'

Startled, she jerked back in her seat and looked up to see

310

one of Simon's colleagues bearing down on them, a tray jammed with a plate of chips and sausages in his hands. Younger than Simon but a partner in the firm, Phillip Knight was always promising Simon he'd play squash in the evenings. But judging from the man's vast stomach, it seemed unlikely. Of all the people to meet now.

'Phillip, how nice to see you,' Evie said dishonestly. 'Phillip works with Simon, my fiancé,' she added with heavy emphasis for Max's benefit.

She felt a tell-tale flush of guilt rise from her throat to her face like a crimson tide. Phillip, though not the brightest man she'd ever met, would be sure to mention to Simon that he'd met Evie with Max and then where would she be? Nobody with even a quarter of a brain cell could misconstrue the body language between them. She grinned inanely at Phillip, shock making her incapable of saying anything else. OmiGod, omiGod, went a little voice in her head over and over again.

Phillip stood there with his tray clutched to his vast, pin-stripe stomach, obviously waiting to be invited to sit down at their table. Beautifully brought up and endlessly polite, he wouldn't have dreamed of plonking himself down without being asked. Which was why Evie found dinner in Phillip's house such a nightmare. She was always afraid she'd make a terrible faux-pas by using the wrong family-crested knife for her bread.

In one swift movement, Max got to his feet.

'Max Stewart,' he introduced himself genially, 'Evie's new . . .' he hesitated, as if he had only just come up with the notion '. . . stepbrother. Imagine that! Her father and my mother have just got married and we're hatching a plan for the newly weds.' He slapped Phillip on the arm, as if letting him in on some wonderful secret.

The tray wobbled.

'Phillip Knight,' he said formally, still holding his tray.

'Yes,' Evie said brightly. 'A wedding gift! Gosh, it won't be too long until it's Simon and me getting hitched!' She got up and slapped Phillip's other arm heartily. The tray wobbled some more.

'I'd love to stay, Phillip,' she gushed, 'but I've got to get back to work and Max has got to . . .' she faltered '. . . pick up his wife from the . . .'

Both men were looking at her expectantly.

'The hospital!' she said triumphantly, it being the first thing that had come into her head. And a wife. That was a master stroke, she thought. Phillip couldn't get the wrong idea now.

She ignored Max's face, which was a picture of barely suppressed mirth.

'Is she working in the hospital?' Phillip said politely.

Evie blinked a couple of times. 'No, she's . . . er . . . having a baby!' Even better. What man would be flirting with his stepsister when his wife was expecting?

'Lovely. Congratulations,' Phillip said.

Max took the tray from him and put it on the table.

'Thanks,' he said. 'I'd better go. Mia hates to be kept waiting. Especially,' he glanced at Evie mischievously, 'as she's the size of a house.'

'*Huge*,' supplied Evie, rounding both arms to make a pregnant belly gesture that would surely signify a hippo baby instead of a human one.

She pecked Phillip's cheek, smiled as brightly as she could and sailed away, Max in her wake.

He managed to stay silent until they reached the car park. 'Thanks for the pregnant wife,' he said conversationally. 'That was a neat touch.'

'I thought so myself,' Evie said lightly.

'Did she have to be quite so enormously pregnant or,

indeed, did we have to be married?' he inquired. 'I'm only asking because Simon will hear about it and will probably wonder what I've done with the said pregnant wife, especially when I don't bring her to Spain. I don't want to get a reputation as a complete bastard.'

'I was desperate,' hissed Evie.

'I could see that. But why lie quite so outrageously?'

'Phillip may be stupid but he's not blind,' she retorted. 'And he'd have to be blind not to notice the way we were sitting so close to one another, staring into each other's eyes!' Evie shivered and didn't know whether it was from the shock of seeing Phillip so unexpectedly or the thought of the conversation she and Max had been having when he'd showed up.

'Since you now have the perfect alibi for meeting me, and since I'm officially "safe" because of my pregnant missus, can we meet again?' Max asked. 'Before the quadruplets are born, I mean.'

'How can you ask that?' Evie demanded furiously. 'You can see I can't meet you.'

Max drove into Wentworth's car park. The onlookers weren't at their posts, Evie noticed idly.

'No, I don't see that you can't meet me,' he said softly, and turned the ignition off and faced her for the first time, making her aware of how small the car was inside and how disturbingly close they were. 'If you don't want to see me again, that's one thing.' His face was in shadow, the hard planes shaded in, making him look saturnine, devilish. 'But if you're afraid to take the chance, that's different. You do want to see me, don't you?' he asked, sounding strangely vulnerable for a moment.

He reached out and touched Evie's full bottom lip, letting his thumb caress it gently. She closed her eyes briefly, letting the sensation ripple through her. It was the most erotic sensation she'd ever felt. Unexpected, unusual. She could smell his skin, smell the warm, musky maleness of him, could taste the saltiness of his skin. She almost kissed his thumb as it rolled lazily over the plumpness of her mouth. Then she pulled back abruptly. What was she doing? What was *he* doing?

'Who the hell do you think you are, touching me like that, coming into my life and trying to screw it up?' she screeched at him.

A muscle moved in his jaw, just a tiny flicker.

'I don't want to see you again,' Evie said, her voice growing hoarse.

He said nothing but just stared at her, his face dark.

'It's impossible for me,' she said in anguish. 'Don't you understand?' She fumbled with the door and finally opened it, dragging herself out of the car frantically.

Aware that she could be seen from the office, she tried to set her face into some sort of normal expression. It was almost impossible. Her pulse was pounding in her veins and she wanted to cry, longed to cry. Smile, Evie, she told herself. Don't cry. Don't look back. She knew he hadn't driven off yet, could feel him sitting quietly in the car watching her walk into the office.

The muscles in her neck were corded with the effort of smiling as she pushed the office door open and marched straight for the stairs. Please don't let anyone speak to me, she prayed. Nobody did. She walked up the stairs to her office slowly, her senses reeling. Had she done the right thing by sending him away? She had, hadn't she? You couldn't be engaged and about to be married *and* have clandestine meetings with another man, especially a sexy, single and utterly handsome man. She *had* done the right thing, definitely. She was sure of it. But why did it hurt so much, then? Why did she have a lump in her throat that made her want to sit on the floor and wail? Why did she want to run back down to the car park, throw herself into Max's arms and beg him to hold her tightly?

Lorraine's eyes lit up when Evie walked into their office.

'Wow, your stepbrother is something else,' she said. 'He's a stud. Can you have sex with your stepbrother? No, sorry. Can *I* have sex with *your* stepbrother?' She crowed with laughter at the idea. 'Craig need never find out, I won't tell him!'

Evie dug her nails into the palm of her hand and tried to join in. Even to her own ears, her laughter was very forced.

She'd turned Max down for the second time. He'd never come back, never bother her again, that was for sure. So why did she feel so utterly depressed at the thought?

Simon positioned the jack under Evie's rusty Fiesta and expertly began to elevate the car off the driveway. He'd taken his sweatshirt off and she could see the muscles in his back ripple through the thin fabric of his T-shirt. All that squash made him very lean. Probably too lean, she thought. He was getting positively scrawny.

He'd never had a big appetite and he wasn't using his deep fat fryer as much since she'd remarked that she didn't want to be eating chips morning, noon and night when they were married.

'It's lucky I noticed this nail in the tyre, Evie,' he said, only slightly out of breath after the job of unscrewing the ancient nuts. 'If I hadn't, you'd have ended up with a flat one day with nobody to change it for you.'

'Yes, thanks, dear,' Evie said, not bothering to point out that changing a tyre wasn't beyond her capabilities. She was glad he'd noticed the nail when the car was parked safely on her driveway but didn't want to spend the entire evening discussing it. She stood behind Simon and stared absently over the roof of her car. It was a warm March evening and Countess Street was waking up after a long winter where the residents had been forced to stay indoors. A spurt of Mediterranean heat and a balmy evening meant the place was positively buzzing.

Evie's next-door neighbours were cutting the grass; a man two doors down was labouring over his overgrown borders: a couple pushed a pram leisurely on the opposite footpath and three young boys played soccer on the road, the ball whacking into the trees regularly. It was time she cut the grass, Evie realised, looking at the tiny lawn she rarely had time to do anything with. The heathers she'd planted two years ago looked terribly straggly, as if they wouldn't last a wet week on a genuine Highland bank. She ought to replace them. Especially if she was going to sell up to buy a place with Simon. Evie felt a heaviness in her chest at the idea.

'When did you last have it serviced?' he asked. 'You're probably due one, you know. Well, actually, you should think of getting a new car, Evie. Or a newer one. Of course, when we're married, you'll be able to drive mine.' He stood up and beamed at her.

She smiled back, a fleeting smile, and then busied herself pulling a weed from the rock-hard flower bed beside the gate. 'Look at this,' she muttered, 'I've really got to do some weeding.'

Simon bent back down to roll one tyre off and replace it with Evie's spare. 'Don't forget to get this fixed,' he said gravely.

She controlled the impulse to hit him with the tyre iron.

By the time she'd pulled up most of the weeds in that bed, Simon had gone inside to wash his hands and had made a cafetière of coffee. Irritated that he'd made coffee at eight in the evening, despite the fact that she hadn't slept at all the night before and could do without an injection of caffeine, Evie took a cup and a biscuit.

Simon sat at the kitchen table, lost in the sports supplement.

'Do you ever wonder why people fall in love?' Evie asked idly. 'There are millions of people in the world and then we find one and that's it. It's so . . . random.'

Simon ruffled her hair affectionately without looking up from his paper. 'You're always dreaming, Evie,' he said fondly.

'I don't mean it like that,' she pressed on. 'You know – how do we find the right person? Lorraine and I were talking about it today. Does true love really exist?' She gave a little laugh, as if talking off the top of her head.

Simon stopped reading about Inter Milan's most recent million-pound transfer for a moment. 'You're such a romantic, Evie. I've got a more cynical view of life. I've always believed you meet someone and then fall in love with them, whatever that is,' he added. 'You know, gradually. It's about trust and familiarity. Like my parents,' he said thoughtfully. 'I don't think they were madly "in love", as you'd say, but they grew to love each other. She still misses him, you know.'

'Yes, I see what you mean,' Evie said faintly. But Simon had gone back to European football.

Trust and familiarity, he'd said. Nothing about passion, the spark of electricity that threatened to overwhelm you or a fire that burned deep in your soul.

Evie sipped her coffee and gazed blankly into the middle distance, for once not seeing bits of the kitchen that needed a good going over with cream cleanser and a J-cloth. She wanted fierce passion and Simon wanted a kind companion, someone to sit in front of the telly with or play bridge with in the distant future. That was the amazing thing – she really did want fierce, intense passion; that flooding feeling of desire and longing rushing over her like a tidal wave.

For years, she'd read about it, immersing herself in the fantasy world of beautiful women and sensual, cruel men, and daydreaming about being one of the heroines in her stories. But that's all it had been: a daydream, a fantasy.

Then, for some reason, she'd begun to want that in real life, passion and hunger and excitement. Well, not for some reason. She knew the reason. It was six foot something of laughing, almost mocking eyes and a dark face that lit up when Max saw her.

'It's time for the news,' Simon announced, looking at his watch. 'Shall we put it on?'

They watched the news at nine in the sitting room, Evie's feet on the coffee table and her mind elsewhere. The weatherman was forecasting another sunny day when Simon nuzzled Evie's neck hopefully.

'What time is Rosie due back?' he asked in muffled tones, his mouth buried in his fiancée's neck, inhaling the faint scent of Anais Anais. Ordinarily, Evie loved him kissing her neck: it was one of her most erogenous zones. Tonight, it felt stiff, very unerogenous, not sensitive to kissing.

'Very soon,' she said. 'Jenny's mother is dropping her home before ten. They've been studying together. Anyway, Simon, I can't right now . . .' She paused delicately. 'It's that time of the month,' she said, knowing very well he wouldn't know she was lying.

Enough said. Simon sat up as if he'd been bitten by a wasp. He really was so incredibly inexperienced when it came to women, she thought with a rush of irritation. And so gullible.

How many periods did he think women had every month – two? She'd only just got over one and had had the most terrible cramps, but Simon wouldn't know that. Just mention 'women's problems' and sheer embarrassment meant his brain ceased to function.

She remembered Rosie giggling while she'd told her about a male maths teacher in school who went puce at the very thought of any female gynaecological difficulty. Rosie claimed that all you had to do to get out of maths was stand in front of the teacher, press one hand to your abdomen and moan about 'not feeling very well, sir'.

'You're out the door in a shot to the nurse,' Rosie cackled.

'That's terrible, Rosie,' Evie had exclaimed. 'Women fought long enough not to be considered the weaker sex and you'll put the cause of feminism back hundreds of years by that sort of "I'm a poor little girl" carry on.'

'Aw, Mum, we've got to suffer periods, we might as well get some benefit out of them,' joked Rosie. 'Anyway, that's the new feminism – using *everything* to get what you want, the way men always have.'

Evie took a quick sideways glance at Simon now. She couldn't imagine him being ruthless to get what he wanted. Not like Max.

'Sorry, darling,' she said, putting a hand on his.

'It's all right,' he said awkwardly. 'Shall we watch the film or,' his narrow face became animated, 'there's a programme on about the Cold War.'

'Cold War, definitely,' Evie replied quickly, hoping Simon wouldn't begin to make comparisons between the Berlin Wall and the one which had suddenly grown up between them. She snuggled against him and tucked her feet up under her on the couch. 'This is lovely, isn't it?' she said and wondered for whose benefit she'd said that. Hers, to convince herself it *was* lovely? Or Simon's?

Rosie drifted in at ten, looking far too relaxed and happy to have been studying English poetry in Jenny's house. Her

319

sloe-black eyes gleamed with some secret Evie vowed to winkle out of her when Simon left.

But Rosie took one look at what was on the TV and announced she was going to bed. 'I'm tired, Mum,' she said, giving Evie a kiss and pointedly avoiding saying goodnight to Simon. Evie was too distracted to glare at her angrily.

By the time Simon left, Rosie's light was off and Evie had to go to bed without discovering what mysteries were tumbling around in her daughter's beautiful head. It had to be a boy. Who else would put that sort of dreamy look on Rosie's face? Had she really been studying with Jenny and had Jenny's mother dropped her home? If not, where exactly had she been hanging out? Questions without comforting answers rushed through Evie's head. She had to trust Rosie. After all she was seventeen, not a child.

Mothers who couldn't let their children grow up lived in the worst kind of dream world, Evie had always thought. But theory and reality were very different.

Rosie had never had a serious boyfriend before, apart from dates with a selection of guys who never quite measured up to her exacting standards and didn't last beyond one trip to the cinema.

The positive side of this was that Evie had always been convinced none of these rejected suitors would ever make her strong-willed daughter do anything she didn't want to. Rosie was obstinate, almost bullheaded. No mere callow youth could lead a girl like that into trouble. But a guy who lit her face up, that was another matter entirely. Evie twisted and turned in her bed for the second night in a row. When she'd fretted for at least an hour about Rosie, she moved on to Max and her encounter with him.

This wasn't a game anymore. Not a fantasy from one of her romantic novels. This was real. Undeniably, absolutely real. Max wasn't a fictional hero, one who could be put away when she closed the book at night. He was flesh and blood, and he was coming between her and Simon. Poor Simon.

Whatever was she going to do? Forget Max, that was what she had to do, must do. And as for going to Spain in two months, forget that altogether. Anyway, she'd only be able to get a week off work what with the time she was taking for her honeymoon, so she could hardly go, could she?

Olivia practised. 'Stephen, you know the way you don't like me teaching those "juvenile delinquents" as you put it . . .'

No, that sounded dreadful. She shook back her hair, stared at herself in the bathroom mirror and tried again.

'Darling.' That was better. 'Darling, I know you'll be cross with me because I kept this a secret, but I've got a new job. Max Stewart . . .'

No, leave Max out of this, she told herself. Stephen would hate the fact that Max was involved. 'I heard about this cookery slot going on that morning television show . . .'

'Mummy,' called Sasha from her bedroom. 'Daddy's home.'

Olivia abandoned her how-the-hell-do-I-tell-Stephen masterclass and ran into the hall.

Stephen stood there with three strange men in suits, all sniffing the lamb ragout-scented air appreciatively, all slightly glassy-eyed.

'Darling.' He swept her up in a hug, holding her closely to the new grey silk suit he'd worn in honour of having the German businessmen over from head office. He kissed her on the lips and she could smell red wine on his breath.

Letting her go, but with one unseen hand cupping her buttock in an uncharacteristic move, he introduced her to his guests. 'Olivia, my beautiful wife. See,' he added with a wink to the oldest and obviously most important guest, 'I told you she was beautiful.'

They all giggled like noisy schoolboys caught reading *Playboy* behind the bike shed.

'You must forgive us for being late, Mrs MacKenzie,' said the senior man once the introductions had been completed. 'We took your husband for a celebratory drink once our business had been concluded.'

'It must have been very successful business for you to get my husband to the pub,' Olivia teased gently. 'He's not much of a man for pubs.'

Unseen by the others, Stephen's hand fondled her buttocks some more through her silky skirt until, embarrassed the others would notice, Olivia slipped out of his reach.

'If you'd like to come into the dining room, gentlemen, dinner is ready.'

As she orchestrated the complicated starters in her immaculate kitchen, Olivia decided that tonight would be the perfect time to break the news of her impending TV debut to Stephen.

Slightly drunk, pleased about his business meeting and obviously as randy as hell, he'd be in the ideal mood to hear that his wife was starting on a new career. As long as she could keep the news of her television name from him for as long as possible, so he was accustomed to the *idea* of her working on TV before he realised she was using de Vere instead of MacKenzie. But that shouldn't be too hard. Stephen wasn't a heavy drinker and with a bit of help from her, he'd be merrily pie-eyed by the time she got him into bed.

She resolved to find the recipe book with the vodka

crème sauce in it. Just the thing to add extra flavour to her between-courses sorbet. She'd eaten it in Switzerland once and so could claim that the meal was international in honour of the international guests. Another dollop of the seriously alcoholic Irish Mist in the pudding should help too.

An entire bottle of vintage port was gone, along with two bottles of white wine and three of red by the time the deeply appreciative guests had been decanted into their taxi by a swaying Stephen. Olivia stared at the devastation of her dining-room table and decided that she'd leave the tidying up for the morning.

'That was wonderful,' said Stephen loudly, when he arrived back in the apartment and slammed the door. Olivia winced at the thought that he'd wake Sasha but reasoned that if the little girl had slept through Stephen's slurred rendition of 'Seven Drunken Nights', then she'd sleep through anything.

'I'm going to bed,' he muttered, nearly cannoning into Olivia's prized peace lily in its Spanish pottery container.

'Me too,' she said.

He looked surprised. Olivia normally didn't go to bed while the place was a mess, no matter how late the party. She always stayed up to fill the dishwasher, wash the saucepans and restore order to the dinner party mess.

In their bedroom, Olivia pulled off her slingbacks and took her hair down from the knot she'd tied it into for the dinner party. She'd only removed one earring when Stephen came out of the bathroom, clad in shirt and socks that showed off strong, hairy legs, and took her in his arms. His dark face was relaxed, his mouth, sometimes harsh, was smiling.

'I like having people over when you cook but I didn't like the way Gerhard was looking at you,' he murmured, clumsily unbuttoning her blouse.

'Don't be silly,' Olivia answered, aware that Gerhard had been eyeing her up in a less than surreptitious manner. He'd been so charming, too, offering to help her in the kitchen, something Stephen would never dream of.

'He was.' Stephen's voice was hard. 'When you weren't watching, his eyes were all over you. I'd kill anyone if they ever touched you,' he said. His fingers slid greedily inside her blouse. 'You're mine, Olivia, all mine. I couldn't share you with anyone.'

A tremor ran through her body at his words. Not sharing her with anyone presumably included the viewers of a morning television show.

As his mouth closed fiercely on her nipple, she closed her eyes in resignation and chickened out of telling him. Maybe in the morning, she thought hopefully.

Morning brought a raging hangover for Stephen and an argument about clothes for the two-week trip he was taking that afternoon.

'I didn't know you were going away today,' said a startled Olivia.

'It came up yesterday,' he said curtly from the depths of his wardrobe where he was searching for his black Ralph Lauren polo shirt. 'I rang you twice but you weren't home. Where the hell were you?' he said in annoyance.

'Out,' she said. 'You know, out and about. Buying food for the dinner party.'

'Got it,' he said triumphantly, extracting the missing Lauren shirt. 'Now where's that blue one . . .'

Tempers were very frayed by the time Stephen's case was packed to his satisfaction, having mentioned twice that he'd have liked to have taken the blue polo shirt with him.

'If you'd remembered to tell me last night, I could have washed everything you needed,' Olivia said, feeling she couldn't take all the blame for a last-minute trip she'd known nothing about. 'And I'm going to miss you,' she added placatingly, which wasn't entirely true.

'I know. My poor baby will have to be Mother Hen while I'm away,' he said, pulling her to him. 'Last night was very sexy,' he added.

Mother Hen! thought Olivia. Is that all I am to him? *Mother bloody Hen!* That was it. She was telling him about her new job. He could do with a shock of the short, sharp variety. If she wasn't Mother Hen she was the damned Irish washerwoman. There had to be more to life than that.

'There's something I've been meaning to say to you, Stephen,' she said coldly.

'What?' He gave her a sharp look.

Under his suddenly belligerent gaze, Olivia felt herself quake. 'I might go down to my parents' house for a few days if you're going to be away,' she said quickly.

He looked puzzled. 'You normally can't get away from them quickly enough,' he said, before shrugging in a 'Women, who understands them?' way. 'Do what you want, dear.'

When he was gone, she tugged at a strand of her hair with impotent self-disgust. Stupid, stupid bitch! Couldn't you have had the courage to be honest, just for once!

She'd only returned from leaving Sasha at playgroup when Paul Reddin – Max's producer friend whom she hadn't met – phoned to say he was delighted with her audition tape and could she please come in the next day to sign a contract?

'Of course,' Olivia said, delighted. Then, because she didn't want to appear too unprofessionally excited about the whole thing, she inquired about fees and expenses.

Putting the phone down, she danced around the kitchen with glee. Her fee was twice what she earned for a morning's teaching. She should have gone into the TV business years ago.

When the phone rang a second time, Olivia answered with a lift in her voice that hadn't been there for months.

'Olivia, it's Max. I wanted to find out how you got on with the audition?'

'Max!' she said, pleased he'd rung her. 'Wonderful! I got the job, can you believe it?'

'Of course I can,' he responded warmly. 'I spotted your potential as soon as I set eyes on you. What did you think of Paul?'

'I never got to meet him,' Olivia confessed. 'But I met Nancy Roberts and I got such a shock. She's nothing like I imagined . . .'

Max's rich laugh interrupted her. 'I could tell you stories about that lady that'd make your hair curl. I'll tell you what, how about I take you out to lunch to celebrate. Are you free this week? Today?'

Faced with the prospect of having nobody else to celebrate her good news with, Olivia jumped at the chance.

This was the beginning of a new life for her, she decided, singing to the radio as she raced around the apartment tidying up before she left. With Stephen and his glowering bad mood gone, the place felt lighter, a happier home altogether. Olivia felt capable of anything.

The dishwasher was humming with dirty dishes, the crumbs had been hoovered up from the dining room and the kitchen gleamed like a showroom specimen by the time she hurried out of the front door, wearing a business-like striped suit in honour of the occasion. Well, Olivia reasoned as she jettisoned her original choice – a rose pink slub silk dress – in favour of the suit, she had to start looking like a professional woman now.

Max drove up just as she was jamming coins in the pay and display machine on Merrion Square.

'You look lovely. Very "woman in the media",' he said, kissing her hello on the cheek.

'I normally get dressed in five minutes,' Olivia replied. 'This look took ages to get right.'

'Suits you.'

The number of people who greeted Max when they entered Patrick Guilbaud's made Olivia aware of his status as a mover and shaker.

He greeted everyone by name, chatting urbanely and charmingly to all comers as he moved easily to their table in the restaurant ante-room. He was graceful for such a big man, she thought. She'd always thought that Stephen had the most fluid gait of all the tall men she knew, but Max, though of a more powerful build than her athletic husband, was positively feline.

When he introduced her to a media tycoon whose name she'd only ever seen in the world's richest people list, and the tycoon slapped Max on the back and demanded to know when they were going marlin fishing again, Olivia realised that he really was a man of influence. And that he'd gone out of his way to use that influence to help her.

His friend Paul was a big name in the world of television yet a word from Max had secured her, a complete novice, a much sought after audition. The question was: why had he done it?

'Why did you fix me up with an audition?' she asked bluntly as they sat with the menus and glasses of mineral water.

'Do you think I did it with an ulterior motive in mind?' he responded.

Olivia grinned. 'That's like that joke that goes, "Do you

know that an Irishman always responds to a question with another question?" And the Irish guy replies, "Who told you that?" '

Max chuckled. 'Fair point, Mrs MacKenzie,' he conceded. 'Or should that be Ms de Vere?'

'You've spoken to Paul,' she said accusingly. 'I wanted to fill you in on the details.'

'Sorry.' He looked unabashed. 'I only rang to ask him how you got on after you'd told me you'd got the job. I wouldn't have gone behind your back to ask otherwise, but I do think it's a marvellous idea to use your maiden name. It's much more interesting but . . .' he paused delicately '. . . problematic.'

She exhaled heavily. 'Yes. I haven't told my husband about either the interview or the name yet. He'll go mad. I'd hoped to tell him this morning but he went off on another business trip and there never was a moment to talk. Well, there *was* but I fudged it.' She looked up at Max, startled. 'What is it about you that makes me divulge my innermost secrets to you within three minutes of meeting you? Are you a wizard or something?'

She was only half-joking. It was utterly bizarre the way she felt she could speak to him on the sort of subjects she'd normally only discuss with Evie. Here she was telling him *everything*. She'd never had that sort of relationship with a man before.

Platonic and yet truthful. Because it was totally platonic between her and Max. There wasn't the faintest spark of attraction there, they were comfortable with each other but that was it.

'I mixed up eye of newt, wing of bat and a few hairs I stole from your brush,' he said solemnly. 'That's the secret.'

If they hadn't been in such a classy restaurant, Olivia would have flicked her menu at him. As it was, she restricted herself to a stern look that vanished as soon as she caught the gleam in his eyes.

'Really,' she said reprovingly, 'what is it with you?'

He shrugged. 'In the nicest possible way, I'm not interested in you, Olivia. I'm sure that's very rare in that you are a very beautiful woman and most men probably drool openly in your presence or else are rendered speechless.'

She would have gone red if any other man had said this but with Max speaking, she merely grinned in mild embarrassment.

'I appreciate your beauty,' he emphasised, 'but I don't want to possess it or you. And you instinctively know that. *That's* the difference. You're not threatened by me.'

'It's like having a marvellous gay friend,' she said wickedly.

'Well, you've found all my secrets out,' he said dead pan, 'so we're equal.'

When the waiter had taken their orders, she returned to the subject.

'Right, so you don't want to get me into bed,' she quipped, as if ticking off an imaginary list, 'and I don't think you're doing it to get my *husband* into bed, so why did you fix me up with the interview?'

Max steepled his fingers in front of his face and regarded her through suddenly veiled eyes. 'I wanted to do something for my new family,' he said.

'I'm not a member of your new family,' she pointed out.

'No,' he said slowly, 'but you're a close friend of . . .' he was about to say something else but stopped himself just in time '. . . the family.'

Olivia knew he was hedging but she left him alone. Because she instinctively knew which member of his new family he really wanted to help, which name he'd nearly blurted out: Evie. Olivia had seen the way Max's

329

gaze had lingered on Evie at the wedding, the way he'd stared at her and Simon with fierce concentration, only breaking away when either of them turned his way. Poor Max was crazy about Evie, she was sure of it. But would any good come of it? Had he tried to make his interest plain already and was that why Evie was so vehemently anti him?

'That's all, that's my motive,' he said firmly, making it clear the subject was closed. Olivia would have liked to discuss it more but Max obviously didn't want to.

During a marvellous lunch, he regaled her with stories of the television world and the dreaded Nancy, who was as sexually voracious – if Max's terrible stories about innocent young camera men seduced in hospitality were to believed – as she was malicious.

Olivia hadn't enjoyed herself so much in ages. Max was a wonderful raconteur and by the time he'd finished his potted biographies of the people she had either met or soon would, she had a stitch in her side from holding in roars of laughter.

He told her that Nancy Roberts would be out for her blood and had in fact already made an attempt to have Olivia fired.

'Even before I was given the job?' she said, amazed.

'Paul won't take any of her crap,' Max remarked. 'Lots of producers let the stars boss them around wholesale, and sometimes,' he grinned ruefully, 'if the star is big enough, you have to kowtow or they won't work. I have a leading lady a bit like that. However, Nancy needs Paul Reddin just as much as he needs her so she can't out-manoeuvre him. He won't let her, which is why you're perfectly safe. Well, your job is safe. What nasty little tricks Nancy has up her sleeve to dissuade you from a TV career is another matter entirely. But you'll manage.'

The way he said it, so confident of Olivia's ability, gave her self-confidence an enormous boost. She would handle Nancy Roberts. During the coffee, he finally came back to the subject of the Frasers, like a dog returning to the place where he'd buried a particularly tasty bone. 'Have you known Simon for very long?' he asked, trying to be subtle but failing miserably. His long fingers played with the fine handle of his coffee cup.

'Only since Evie's been going out with him,' she replied. 'Nearly two years, I think.'

'When are they getting married?'

'September.'

His fingers tightened around the handle and Olivia feared for the delicate china.

She hadn't imagined it: he *was* crazy about Evie. Olivia decided gently to explain a little bit about her friend.

'Evie was on her own for a long time, although I'm sure your mother knows that. She didn't have it easy, bringing Rosie up without a father, and I rather think she'd given up on men and love when Simon came along.'

'He seems like a nice guy,' Max remarked.

'He is. He's very . . .' Olivia searched for the right words. 'Sweet and kind. Not the sort of man I'd have thought Evie would go for, in fact.'

Max sat forward, face alive with interest. 'What sort of man would you think she'd like?'

'More macho, stronger, more streetwise perhaps.' Olivia felt marginally guilty about Simon, of whom she was fond, but she was being honest.

The sensitive, rather unworldly Simon had always struck her as an odd choice for her friend, a woman who would probably name Rhett Butler as her ideal man, if she wasn't trying to hide her love of romantic fiction behind her hard-boiled façade.

331

'Evie's husband was totally different from Simon.'

'What was he like?'

It was difficult remembering anything about Tony Mitchell, although Olivia had been a bridesmaid at their wedding in his icy little Kerry hometown. There'd been no heating in the tiny stone church and, shivering in the off-white plain wedding dress the two of them had bought hastily a week before, Evie had looked blue with cold. Her new mother-in-law had looked blue in the face from pressing her lips together disapprovingly. The only person who'd appeared to be enjoying themselves was Andrew Fraser – stoic in the face of disaster as usual, Olivia thought fondly.

In the context of that wedding, she could just about picture Tony, impenetrable sloe-black eyes so like Rosie's giving nothing away. He was what they called 'black Irish', descended from the Spanish Armada that had sunk off the Irish coast in the Elizabethan era, leaving Spanish sailors to father a whole race of dark-eyed, dark-skinned children who looked very different from the pale, blue-eyed Celts.

That's what had drawn Evie to him, Olivia remembered. The fact that he was very different from all the callow boys she'd gone out with before. Wearing his dark blue police uniform, gypsyish face curved into a taunting grin, he was positively dashing. Very Rhett Butler. What a pity he hadn't turned out to have the same kind, strong heart as Rhett.

Maybe that's why Evie had given up any hope of finding a real hero and made do with a palely decent man like Simon, who'd never light any fires within her – and who'd never light any for other women either. Olivia jerked herself out of her daydream. Max was still waiting for a description of Tony but she felt that she

332

couldn't give away all her dearest friend's secrets, no matter that it was to a man who seemed to embody all Evie's hidden needs.

'He was very brave, a member of the Gardai,' she said, giving Max the official line. 'He'd been decorated for his police work but was tragically killed in an accident.'

'Certainly sounds tragic,' Max said. 'Poor Evie. I guess she was really in love with him?' he added wistfully.

'Yes,' Olivia replied briskly, draining the last of her coffee. 'Now, much as I'm enjoying this wonderful restaurant, I have to go and pick up Sasha and her friend. We're going swimming.'

After an afternoon spent in the shallow end and then ages getting two wriggling children dry to shrieks of: 'I'm cold, Mummy!' Olivia felt in need of more adult company. As Stephen was away, she was free to do whatever she wanted and the thought of an hour chatting to Evie felt good.

Evie was cooking something that both Rosie and Simon would eat when Olivia arrived, a tired Sasha in tow.

Installing her daughter in the sitting room with Barbie and *101 Dalmatians*, Olivia retreated to the kitchen and, seeing Evie wearily browning bits of chicken, boiled the kettle.

'I'm dying for a cup of tea,' Evie said, brushing hair from her forehead with the back of her hand. 'And I'm ravenous. I'm back on the Ryvitas again,' she added gloomily. 'I don't know why but I just can't lose those five pounds I put on over Christmas.'

'Poor thing,' Olivia said comfortingly. 'I just had the most wonderful lunch with Max,' she added gaily.

Evie couldn't believe how jealous she felt. *Olivia had had lunch with Max*. Jealousy pierced her like a metal skewer stabbing the soft flesh of a roast chicken to see if it was cooked. Only the metaphorical juices flowing down the sides weren't clear like that of a perfectly cooked fowl – they were green with envy.

'Lunch?' she asked, feigning indifference. 'That sounds nice. Where did you go?'

'Guilbaud's,' answered Olivia, too thrilled with her wonderful day to notice the hurt tone in Evie's voice.

'Guilbaud's?' asked Evie, not even bothering to feign indifference now. The most exclusive, most glamorous and most talked-about restaurant in Dublin. She longed to go there, dressed to kill with a handsome man by her side, with fleets of attentive French waiters ministering to her every need. Simon, eminently prudent, wouldn't have dreamed of taking her there. But Max would. It was just his sort of place – elegant and luxurious. And he'd brought Olivia there. Evie was amazed at how much it hurt.

What an indiscriminating rake he was! If he couldn't have one woman, he went after another like a drunken, womanising sailor, not caring which port he was in so long as there was something warm and female waiting for him there.

Olivia was talking about the food. 'Seared scallops, soft as butter,' she moaned. 'I am telling you, Evie, I have never tasted anything like them in my life. That chef is a genius. I wonder if I could cook scallops on the show . . .'

Olivia had her priorities all wrong, Evie thought crossly, pushing the browned chicken around the pan aggressively. If *she'd* been eating in Guilbaud's with Max Stewart the food would have been the last thing on her mind.

'He was very good to me,' Olivia continued. 'He told me all about Nancy Roberts, said he wouldn't have dared to tell me *before* the audition in case I bottled out. Max says he's known her for years and that she's the biggest prima donna in the business. Apparently, she was on the phone to the executive producer, his friend Paul, immediately after my audition, demanding to know why they were auditioning amateurs. Which means,' Olivia grinned, 'that you were right all along, Evie. She's dead jealous, or so Max says.'

Evie quelled her desire to point out sharply that Olivia's conversation was littered with 'Max says this' and 'Max says that'. Or that the Olivia of the previous day had been so nervous about the idea of a vengeful Nancy Roberts that she'd toyed with the idea of never going near the television studio again. Now, Olivia was speaking as if Nancy was nothing more than an irritating nuisance, certainly nothing to stand in the way of her television career.

'The problem is that Nancy has been trying to get a prime-time evening show for years, only when she tried it the programme flopped disastrously. The Nielsen ratings were horrendous,' Olivia said, sounding at ease with the TV speak. 'So now she uses all her muscle to make everyone's life a misery. What's wrong, darling?' she asked in concern as Sasha came into the kitchen, a tremulous expression on her face. 'Is the film over?'

Sasha shook her head mutely, stuck her thumb in her mouth and put out her arms for her mother to hug her.

Olivia put the little girl on her lap and enveloped her in a hug, kissing the soft baby fine hair gently. She smelled clean and fresh, of peach shampoo and baby soap, and Olivia felt overwhelmed by love for her. After a moment, Sasha wriggled down and trotted into the sitting room.

'She's very clingy these days,' Olivia said worriedly. 'She can sense the tension at home and she's back to sucking her thumb, which she hasn't done for months. I don't know what to do. No matter how badly Stephen behaves, I can put up with it, but not if it affects Sasha.'

Seeing Olivia's anxious expression, Evie felt a stab of remorse at even thinking her friend had been deliberately flirting with Max. Poor Olivia had enough on her plate as it was and wouldn't dream of having an affair with anyone. Despite all his flaws, she was still in love with Stephen, still committed to her marriage.

It was Max who'd done all the running and Evie grimly awarded him another black mark.

They chatted for another few minutes before Simon arrived straight from work, tie askew as usual. Not noticing that Evie was cooking, he said he'd booked dinner for two in the hotel in the city centre where they were having their wedding reception.

'I want to see what their rack of lamb is like,' he said eagerly, pushing his glasses on to his narrow nose, as he did at least fifty times a day.

Usually, Evie vowed to get him new glasses. Tonight, it merely irritated the hell out of her. She banged the pan on the cooker top to draw his attention to it.

Unperturbed, Simon patted her arm. 'Rosie can eat that, can't she?'

'We'd better go,' Olivia said, sensing a row was imminent and collecting up Sasha's coat and toys. 'This honey bunny has to go to bed,' she added, tickling a squirming Sasha.

Olivia was halfway down Evie's road before she remembered that she'd meant to mention how often Max had talked about her. Olivia was convinced that he'd asked her out purely as an opportunity to find out more about Evie. It was charming the way he'd deftly drag the conversation around to her again and again, then forget to be subtle when he asked about Simon and how long they'd been going out. He was crazy about Evie: it was as plain as the nose on his handsome face.

She'd tell Evie another time. It was only fair that her friend knew how Max felt about her.

★　★　★

'Lovely, isn't it?'

Simon gave Evie's hand a surreptitious squeeze under the tablecloth. He wasn't the sort of man who'd hold her hand on *top* of the table. Public physical displays weren't his sort of thing. That was too touchy-feely. Not Simon at all. His idea of being demonstrative in public was the Heimlich Manoeuvre.

Aware that her hand felt about as responsive as a dead halibut, Evie tried to smile back at her fiancé. But she couldn't. It was like trying to beam merrily at the dentist when he said, 'Now that didn't hurt, did it?' while your mouth ached as if it had been hit by a dump truck.

'Is something wrong, Evie?' Simon asked with a flash of intuition.

Yes, she wanted to scream. Yes, it is. We shouldn't be sitting here discussing the wedding meal. We shouldn't be getting married in the first place. It's wrong.

But she said nothing. Instead, she summoned all her energy and tried to look as if she was merely lost in the misty joy of imagining herself as a bride stuffing her face with lamb and creamed courgettes, trying not to spill any on her fairy-tale gown.

'The wedding . . . you know,' she said, just in case Simon hadn't got the message. 'I hope there isn't another one being held here on the same day,' she added cleverly, knowing that nothing got his mind working faster than the notion that he was somehow being cheated by the powers that be. The idea of *two* bridal parties should do it.

'Lord, I hope not!' he said in alarm. 'I never asked in the first place. We should do.'

Evie nodded encouragingly. 'Yes, you'd better.'

While Simon hotfooted it in search of a wedding co-ordinator, who was probably at home glued to *EastEnders* by that hour of the evening, Evie enjoyed the bliss of being alone with her thoughts.

A young waitress brought their aperitifs and Evie gratefully sipped her Campari and soda. She glanced at the other couples out for a meal in the quiet restaurant, people who seemed for the most part happy in each other's company. Nobody else looked like they'd spent years wishing for a husband and, now that they were on the verge of marrying one, wished he'd vanish into thin air.

No, no, she didn't mean that. Evie didn't want Simon to disappear. She loved him, cared deeply for him. But she didn't know if she was in love with him anymore. How did you know? she wondered.

Up until ten days ago, she hadn't known there was a difference. Loving and being in love were pretty much the same things. But it had all changed in the blink of an eye.

Simon sank down into the chair opposite her.

'Sweet Mother of God, I thought we were in trouble there,' he said, wiping imaginary beads of sweat from his forehead.

'Really?' Evie said, desperately trying to sound interested.

'Only kidding,' he said jokily. 'The deputy manager explained that they only have one wedding party at a time. Bit of luck, that.'

'Yes,' she replied faintly. 'Bit of luck.'

An hour and a half later, replete after a meal she had no real memory of tasting, Evie sat woodenly beside Simon as he drove her home. They reached the junction on the Stillorgan dual carriageway where they'd turn left if they were going to Simon's house and right for Evie's. Suddenly, it was important that they went to bed together, that they made love. It might exorcise the thoughts in her head, Evie thought a little frantically.

She touched his arm. 'Let's go to your place for a while,' she said abruptly. 'Just an hour.'

She couldn't see his eyes because he was concentrating on the road, but Evie knew he was pleased at the idea from the way he cleared his throat and patted her knee as he daringly swung the car into the left-hand lane.

In his house, she went into the immaculate kitchen while Simon was pulling the sitting-room curtains and switching on the lights.

'Could we have a drink, love?' she said, going straight to the cabinet where Simon kept the booze. She wanted a drink for some reason. Something to blank out the things short circuiting all the sensible thoughts in her mind.

If he was bewildered by this sudden and unusual desire for a nightcap, he didn't say anything.

Evie poured herself a generous vodka and topped it up with orange juice. She'd seen Cara have one of those once. Not really used to drinking spirits, she liked the fact that the sweet juice masked the harsh bite of the vodka. She gulped back half of it and turned to Simon, kissing him while still holding her glass in one hand. He kissed her back, then pressed his body against hers, proof that they hadn't made love for at least ten days evident in his sudden erection. He groaned and moved even closer to her, pelvic bones grinding.

Evie pulled away. 'Let's go upstairs.'

'Yes,' he said thickly.

He ran ahead of her, probably to make sure the impossibly tidy master bedroom was still as clutter-free as it had been that morning, Evie thought. She finished her drink on the way up the stairs, wincing as the last, least diluted bit of the vodka hit the back of her throat with a kick.

Simon was eagerly unbuttoning his shirt when she entered the room. Evie unsteadily put down her empty glass and began to take off her cotton jumper, feeling about as unsexy as was humanly possible. Amazingly, Simon didn't seem to notice her lack of interest, even though she'd been the one to suggest bed.

He ripped off his trousers, pulled his socks off and then carefully put his clothes on the back of a chair, making sure to get the trouser creases just so.

Max wouldn't have done that, she thought irrationally. He would have been so mad to touch her that he'd have taken her as soon as they'd got inside the front door. He couldn't have waited. He'd certainly never have let her take her own clothes off. He'd want to slowly strip every item from her body, gazing at her with those hungry eyes as he did so.

Mindful of the lights, Simon left his underpants on while he pulled down the striped navy duvet and slid under it, patting the side of the bed invitingly. Evie overcame the desire to back out of her side of the bargain. It'd been her idea, after all.

Still clad in her bra and pants, she automatically switched off the overhead bedroom light, plunging the room into darkness only relieved by the street light shining in through the thin pale blue curtains. Simon was a hump in the bed.

She climbed slowly in beside him and his bare arms wound themselves around her, his mouth reaching for her shoulder, sliding down to her breasts immediately.

As his lips fastened voraciously on her nipple, Evie lay back against the pillows. For the first time in their relationship, she found herself merely enduring his caresses instead of enjoying them. His body, the one she'd been getting used to after years of celibacy, felt alien to her. His familiar caresses felt awry, almost improper. As if she shouldn't be doing this at all.

Furious even to be thinking such a thing, Evie pulled Simon closer to her and found his mouth with hers. She kissed him with fierce abandon, desperately trying to obliterate traitorous thoughts. She wouldn't think about Max Stewart, couldn't.

Encouraged by Evie's renewed passion, Simon couldn't control himself any longer. Fumbling briefly under the covers, he removed his underwear and hers, struggling as usual with the clasp of her new Dunne's lace bra. He pushed himself inside her, groaning heavily into the pillows as he did so. Evie's hands roamed up and down his back on auto pilot, stroking him as he moved because it was what she'd always done.

Every few moments, he planted kisses on her shoulders and neck before resuming his fevered thrusting. She could hear his breathing become rapid and suddenly her eyes filled with burning tears. Why couldn't she be happy? Why was she lying here, enduring this, when she should have been in raptures with her adoring lover?

'Evie, are you ready yet?' he asked, panting. 'I'm sorry but I'm so ready for you. We'll stop for a minute if you want.'

She knew what he meant: he'd lie beside her and fumble earnestly between her legs until she was ready to come, then he'd plunge back in and they'd come together. Well, that was the theory.

Evie was ashamed to admit that she'd faked it more often than not. Faked a shuddering orgasm because it would take about three times as long as they usually spent on foreplay to give her any satisfaction at all. Simon was considerate enough to want her to have an orgasm whenever he did, but sadly not experienced enough to tell the difference between when she did and when she pretended to.

'Will we stop until you're ready, darling?' he asked now.

Faced with the prospect of even longer in bed wishing she was with someone else, Evie chose the easy way out.

'No,' she said, injecting a bit of passionate panting into her voice. She moaned softly. 'I'm nearly there. Oooh,' she groaned.

'Darling,' he said thickly, increasing his tempo.

Evie moaned some more and raked his back with one hand to show enthusiasm. She matched his moving body, wriggling as passionately as she could.

Simon was beyond noticing.

With a hoarse cry, his body spasmed and Evie, wishing momentarily that the Academy Awards people could see her performance now, did the same. It wasn't quite Meryl Streep in *Out of Africa*, but it wasn't bad. She moaned convincingly, injected a little sigh and let her body relax in time to feel Simon slump on top of her.

'Oh, Evie,' he sighed, burying his face in the pillow.

'Darling,' she muttered mechanically.

He shifted slightly so that his entire weight wasn't on her, and Evie moved until she was linked to Simon only by one leg and the arm he'd draped over her rib cage. She could tell by his even breathing that he was on the verge of going to sleep, but she lay there open-eyed and let the tears that lay halfway down her cheeks dry.

What have you done to me, Max? she asked silently as if he was in front of her in the darkened room, standing on Simon's rather old-fashioned shag pile and staring down at the figures in the queen-sized bed. What have you done to me?

CHAPTER ELEVEN

Zoë's red head was bent studiously over her desk but she knew exactly what Cara was up to.

'I never thought I'd see the day when you were wearing lip liner, Fraser,' she remarked without turning round.

Cara jumped guiltily, one hand still holding the tiny compact mirror she'd bought the previous weekend, the other wielding the small pencil as if it was a Class A drug instead of Boots 17 lip liner in Morticia.

'I'm just looking for my lip balm . . .' She started, jamming the lip liner and compact back into her rucksack hastily.

'You're just looking for lurve with Lurve Doctor Ewan Walshe,' Zoë chuckled, finally turning round. 'You don't have to apologise to me, Cara, I'm only teasing you.'

She relaxed with a rueful grin. 'Arlene gave it to me when we were all in Ryan's the other night, insisted I took it. Said it would "define my mouth". I haven't worn anything like this for years.'

'It suits you,' Zoë said, birdlike head angled sideways as she admired the effect of the lipliner and mauve lipstick on her friend's voluptuous mouth. 'Does Ewan like kissing it off?'

They both laughed.

'Yes.'

'Where are you going for lunch today, 007?' Zoë asked, resuming her work at the drawing board.

She was referring to Cara's insistence on meeting Ewan in out-of-the-way places so that nobody at work would know they were going out with each other.

Both Ewan and Zoë thought this obsession with secrecy insane, but at least he was prepared to put up with it on the basis that he was a very private individual and preferred it when people didn't know too much about him. Zoë, who'd blithely discuss her most personal details with someone she'd met in the supermarket queue, simply couldn't understand her friend's reluctance to date Ewan openly.

Cara had tried to explain that she preferred to keep her private life just that because she'd never really got over being the butt of jokes once Owen Theal told a couple of students how she'd thrown herself at him. But Zoë, who'd pointed out that all that had happened a long time ago, refused to entertain the notion.

Cara was actually sloping off to meet Ewan on the canal, guaranteed to be free from all Yoshi Advertising staff because it was Thursday, or pay day, and they were all blueing their wages on big, beery lunches of steak marinated in Guinness.

'We're meeting on the canal,' she admitted grudgingly, 'in five minutes.'

'If I was going out with Ewan, I'd have a site on the Internet telling everyone about it,' Zoë said, abandoning any pretence of working.

Cara snorted. 'So speaks the woman who discusses her sex life with the woman at the launderette.'

'Lack of a sex life, you mean,' Zoë retorted. 'I'm gagging for it and you're getting it every day and won't tell anyone. I don't know why.'

'Well, you know, dating someone you work with,' Cara said defensively. 'It's bound to be frowned upon. You know how difficult Bernard is. He'd fire one of us and it'd be me, I know it.'

'Fuck Bernard,' said Zoë, echoing Ewan's sentiments. 'Anyway, haven't you heard about employment law? This isn't a dictatorship. There are laws about hiring and firing people, you know.'

'It bloody well *is* a dictatorship,' Cara retorted. 'I was here till half-ten last night purely because Bernard wants to throw his weight around, and you were here until nine the night before.'

'Yeah, well, I might not be here for much longer,' Zoë said enigmatically.

'What do you mean?'

'I'm thinking of looking for another job,' she announced. 'Actually, I've applied for several and I've got an interview tomorrow.'

Cara stopped fiddling around in her rucksack and looked at her friend in horror. 'You can't be serious?' she said, astounded. 'When did you decide that? Where are you going?'

She didn't voice her final question: What will I do without you? They'd been together since college, worked side by side in Yoshi Advertising for four years and endured Bernard Redmond's temper tantrums together. Cara couldn't imagine working in Yoshi without Zoë grumbling good-naturedly by her side, slagging off Bernard whenever she got the opportunity. There was nobody around she could team up with to compose filthy limericks about their colleagues, nobody to laugh with till they were sick at lunch, nobody to discuss life, the universe and everything with.

'I don't know for definite,' Zoë answered. 'The interview

tomorrow is with *Solve* and I don't think I'd like to work there. But I've got to get out of this place. Bernard's so mean he'll never increase our wages beyond the national wage agreement and the only way we're going to get promoted is if somebody dies, although I can think of a few people around here I'd personally pay to have wiped out purely for the good of humanity.' She stopped joking and gave Cara an apologetic look. 'I'm never going to get on unless I leave here. I was reading an article in *Cosmopolitan* about your career and in cases like this, when you've got the boss from hell, it makes sense to cut your losses and find another job.'

'Oh.' Cara couldn't think of much else to say. 'You're right but . . .' she blinked back a tear at the thought of a Zoë-free office '. . . I'll miss you so much.'

Zoë threw a pink highlighter pen at her teasingly. 'Jaysus, missus, I'm only leaving the company, not the planet. You won't be banished from my organiser because we're not in the trenches together anymore.'

'I know.' Cara still looked gloomy.

'Go on,' Zoë said with a quick glance at her watch, 'you'll miss lover boy if you stay here any longer talking to me.'

Ewan thought it was a great idea. 'Zoë's right.' He sat on one of the canal benches and extracted his chicken sandwich from its little plastic triangle. It was a warm March day and the clusters of daffodils planted along the edge of the water were brilliantly yellow in the lunch-time sun. A family of ducks swam serenely in front of them, muttering quietly among themselves in duck language.

'But she's going to leave the company,' Cara said miserably, sitting down beside him and ignoring her own cheese salad sandwich.

'I'll probably bugger off myself in a year or so,' Ewan remarked, mouth full of chicken.

'Jesus, what do you mean?' Cara was utterly astounded now. 'It's like the bloody diaspora around here. Where are *you* going?'

'Relax,' he said.

Cara loathed it when people said that.

'I *am* relaxed,' she hissed in a most unrelaxed tone. 'I simply want to know why all my friends are leaving the company where we work. Is that too much to ask?'

'Well,' Ewan said equably, 'if I was working somewhere else, you'd feel able to admit that you were going out with me and you wouldn't be afraid that Bernard would fire you.'

'It's not so much that he'd fire me,' she prevaricated, not having explained the real reason to Ewan because she couldn't bear to get into a discussion of the trauma she could never quite forget. 'It's . . . Anyway, don't change the subject. Why would you want to leave Yoshi?'

'It's great experience working under my boss, but if it wasn't for Ken, I don't think I'd be here at all. Bernard is a complete space cadet and I'd have better opportunities somewhere else. I'd quite like to work in *Déjà Vu*. They've a great creative team. Zoë should try applying there if tomorrow's interview doesn't work out.'

'What about me?' Cara asked mulishly. Ewan was thinking of jobs for her best friend but not for her. It wasn't fair.

He leaned over and gave her a chicken-scented kiss. 'You should consider up-dating your CV too, my little apple blossom, because without Zoë, you'll be doing her work as well as your own until Bernard bothers to rehire.'

Cara poked him roughly in the ribs. '*Little apple blossom*, my backside!'

347

He grabbed her with the non-sandwich-eating hand and planted another wet kiss full on her mouth. 'That's not what you were saying last night,' he joked. 'I could have called you my little cuddly-wuddly bunnikins and you wouldn't have minded.'

She kissed him back, feeling a flare of excitement in her belly at the thought of the night before. A bottle of Body Shop massage oil and the dog-eared copy of the *Kama Sutra* they'd found in a second-hand book shop in Rathmines had combined to produce their most erotic evening yet.

'Point taken, my little chicky-wicky teddy bear-ums,' she laughed.

'Now eat your sandwich so we can go for a romantic stroll in the sun and breathe in some lovely Dublin pollution,' Ewan said as a truck belching exhaust fumes beetled past, sending a black cloud over at least a mile of the canal.

Cara listlessly splashed water over her breasts, watching the bubbles in the bath redistribute themselves into vanilla-scented mounds with every movement. The water was at the just-hot-enough to be comfortable stage and the bottle of Beck's she held in the other hand was just cool enough to be refreshing.

'I think she's off her rocker.' Phoebe plucked out another eyebrow hair and stood back to consider the effect. It wasn't good. She'd taken too many out of one eyebrow so unless she evened them out, she'd look permanently surprised on one side of her face and normal on the other. 'I mean, how does Zoë know she'll get a better job if she leaves?'

'Being in graphic design isn't anywhere near as secure as working in the bank,' Cara said, splashing a few more bubbles out of the way and thinking that she couldn't stay there forever. 'Agencies go under and people move companies within the advertising industry all the time.'

'You haven't,' Phoebe pointed out. 'Although Ricky said he was thinking of chucking his job in soon.'

Cara closed her eyes in disgust. Only Ricky would be dumb enough to give up a pensionable, decent job, which he'd only got in the first place by a complete miracle, to do something else. 'What does he have in mind?' she asked, waiting for Phoebe to say her boyfriend was joining a boy band or taking up a new career as a stripper. You could never tell with Ricky.

'He's thinking of going back to college.'

Cara sat up in the bath. It was a mystery to her how he'd ever got through college in the first place; she couldn't imagine what course he'd take up to further his studies. Scrounging 101, perhaps. 'But the bank would pay for him to do a degree,' Cara said.

'Ricky doesn't want to feel tied down.' Phoebe plucked some more. 'And he'd have to go back to the bank afterwards if they paid for his course. He'd like to do physiotherapy or something like that. He's very good with his hands,' she added with a little smirk.

'Well, Phoebs,' Cara said, getting out of the bath and not mentioning that the brain-dead Ricky hadn't a hope in hell of getting into any physiotherapy degree course no matter how good he was at bringing his girlfriend to the heights of ecstasy with his thumbs, 'if he gives up his job and becomes a full-time student, he'll never have a bean and you'll end up practically supporting him.'

'Don't say that,' she pleaded. 'I'm trying not to think about it. And don't mention any of this to him, will you? Promise?'

'I promise,' Cara said. 'I've got enough on my plate at the moment what with Zoë going. I'll miss her so much.

She's a complete wagon for not telling me until now.'

Ricky was buried in the fridge when Cara mooched into the sitting room. A plate surrounded by a sea of crumbs was evidence that he'd made himself a sandwich and was now looking for something else to eat. Cara hated the way he treated the fridge as an extension of Phoebe's body – available for his sole use at any time. She wouldn't have minded so much if he'd occasionally bought any food by way of a contribution. But no, Ricky's idea of contributing to the household was cleaning out the cupboards when he was hungry.

'Hi, Cara,' he said breezily, emerging from the fridge with the last rhubarb crumble yoghurt.

'That's mine,' she said indignantly.

Ricky gave her his puppy dog look, the one he used when he was trying to borrow money. That was probably how he'd got by in college, Cara thought grimly. One beseeching look and no female lecturer could resist him.

'Sorry,' he said dolefully and pulled back the tin foil lid anyway.

He was so incredibly good-looking, with a face like a Calvin Klein model and the body of one too. Yet once you knew Ricky for any length of time, Cara maintained, you stopped noticing how wonderful he looked because he was such a gigantic pain in the neck. Beauty was only skin deep, whereas being dense cut to the bone.

Knowing she was being a softy for not screaming at him about snaffling up her food, but unable to say anything because he *was* Phoebe's boyfriend after all, Cara sat down in the good armchair and turned on the TV. As she flicked through the channels, she hit upon some rally cross on RTE 1 and quickly flicked to the next channel. Even Ricky wouldn't have the nerve to demand to see rally cross when it was time for *Friends*.

'Oi,' he said in outraged tones, 'that's the programme I wanted to watch!'

Cara spun around in her chair and fixed him with her steely gaze. Rhubarb crumble was one thing, *Friends* was another. 'Tough.'

They were watching *Friends* in grim, very unfriendly silence when Phoebe walked in, scented and made-up in another of the hot little numbers she'd bought 'specially for Ricky. This one was a body-moulding floral see-through top worn with tight metallic sheen trousers. It was wasted on him tonight. Like a petulant child who wanted a squabble refereed, he flicked back his silky hair and said: 'It's a repeat, Phoebe, and the rally cross is on!'

'Ricky . . .' said Phoebe, looking torn.

'It's our television, Ricky,' snapped Cara angrily. 'If you want to watch rally cross, go home!'

'It's a repeat!' he cried back.

They both looked at Phoebe expectantly.

'It *is* a repeat,' she said reluctantly, looking meaningfully at the television where Rachel was wearing her Princess Leia outfit for Ross.

'Fine,' Cara said, getting to her feet, furious that Phoebe had taken sides in this delicate matter. It was her flat too. 'You two watch whatever you feel like, but when you want the rent paid, Phoebe, don't forget to ask Ricky for his cut, seeing as the big gobshite lives here now!'

With that, she stormed out of the room, only stopping long enough to grab her coat and purse, before marching out of the flat.

The sunshine of earlier had given way to a consistent drizzle and she ploughed into the rain, not really knowing where she was going but determined to go somewhere. She couldn't visit Zoë because there'd been a faint sense of restraint between them since her friend had announced her intention to move jobs. Ewan was at soccer practice. To cap it all, she realised guiltily, she'd managed to antagonise Phoebe, sweet, good-humoured Phoebe who wouldn't hurt a fly. It wasn't her fault she had a thoughtless, feckless boyfriend who thought work was a four-letter word and believed that *mi casa*, *su casa* only worked in the *su casa* variation. It was bloody Ricky's fault, Cara thought miserably, pulling the collar of her jacket up to protect her neck against the rain. What a wonderful day. Everyone she could have talked to was either not really talking to her or doing something else. Premenstrual, depressed and feeling as if the entire world was against her, Cara decided she had only one real option – she'd go and get terribly, terribly drunk.

'Zoë's at the dentist,' Cara heard herself say in a sprightly voice when Bernard's secretary rang their bolt hole office at half-nine the next morning. 'Didn't she mention it? No? Root canal, I think.'

She slammed down the phone and sank her head on to her arms, anything to relieve her thumping headache.

It had been a mistake to go to McSorley's in Ranelagh where she'd bumped into a crowd of Phoebe's bank pals and ended up spending a riotous evening with them, slurping back beers as if the girl from accounts in the Dame Street branch was going to Mars on a space shuttle for the rest of her life instead of to Sydney for a year. Nobody could party like the bank people, Cara thought ruefully. It must have been looking at all that money every day and not being able to touch it that made them aware of how fleeting life was and how they had to enjoy it now. Or something like that. She had a vague memory of discussing this theory with somebody in the men's toilet when she and all the bank girls had barged in past a couple of frightened blokes, claiming there was an endless queue for the women's and they were desperate.

Cara hoped that was the worst thing they'd done. She couldn't keep up with those women. They must have constitutions of iron because when she'd finally decided she had to go home at half-eleven, they were all warming up for a night in Club M where the guest of honour was promised a ducking in the jacuzzi, clothes or no clothes.

It was small compensation to think that somewhere in the city of Dublin, there had to be a few people who were feeling more hungover than she.

Unfortunately, that tiny glimmer of pleasure was dimmed by the fact that she hadn't been up in time to see Phoebe that morning, so her plan to apologise for storming out of the flat hadn't come to fruition. She hated not being friends with someone, hated uncomfortable silences. It was bad enough engaging in a Cold War with Evie, without starting battles with anyone else. Before long, she'd have no friends, she decided mournfully.

'Cara,' said a voice and she whirled around to see Bernard Redmond staring at her in an unnerving way, as if she were a rare species of bug and he was a collector with a net who'd been searching for something new to pin in a glass frame. 'I was hoping I'd find you here.'

Instantly on her guard, she looked at her boss warily. Bernard never looked pleased to see anyone except his bank manager and his sweet sleeping partner, Millicent. If he *did* look pleased to see you, experience had shown the staff that it was only because he was looking forward to screeching abuse at you for something.

Bernard didn't drink, smoke or hang around bars so he only had two hobbies: sneaking around the building, surprising people who'd taken a crafty early fag break in the ante-room off the canteen, and screaming blue murder at people for no reason whatever. Cara didn't smoke, she was at her desk working – in theory, anyway – so it had to be a bollocking. She prepared herself for it.

'Hello, Bernard,' she responded carefully.

'We are alone?' he asked, as if someone very small was lurking behind the filing cabinet in the corner.

'Yes.'

'Good, good. I need to talk to you. Privately.'

Cara gulped. This didn't look good. Ewan. He knew about Ewan, that had to be it. Fraternising with colleagues was bad for business and meant nobody got their job done properly, she guessed.

'I believe Zoë is looking for another job,' he said conversationally, sitting down on her chair and fixing Cara with his best television evangelist's stare.

If Cara had been expecting anything, it wasn't this. She'd been waiting for Bernard to launch into a speech about employees dating each other and how this wasn't allowed by the company. But Zoë! How the hell did he know she was contemplating leaving? The place must be bugged. She wouldn't put it past him. Transmitting toilet rolls in the ladies' and concealed microphones in the light sockets, that'd be Bernard's idea of keeping up with what the staff were up to.

He was frowning less than usual, which meant he was attempting to look quizzical, expecting an answer.

He could stuff it, Cara thought with a momentary surge of rebellion.

'Really?' she said in astonishment. 'Gosh,' she added, blinking and trying to look like the sort of person who said 'gosh' instead of the 'for fuck's sake!' she'd have normally used. 'She's never mentioned it to me.'

The quizzical expression disappeared and his gimlet eyes got even smaller, if that was possible. 'Yes, she's leaving,' he said. 'I thought you'd have known.'

'I'm sure I would.' She paused. 'If Zoë were actually leaving.'

Bernard swiftly recovered from his shock at Cara actually being impertinent.

'Well, she is,' he said smoothly. 'And I have another applicant for her job. I expect you to make the transfer of accounts run smoothly. This is an important department within the company.'

He never said that at wage review time, she reflected. But Ewan was right. Zoë's going meant she'd have to do twice the work until her replacement was up to speed.

'She's the daughter of a dear friend of mine,' Bernard emphasised,' so be nice to her.'

Correction, Cara thought grimly, make that twice the work forever. Any daughter of a pal of Bernard's was bound to be some intellectually challenged bimbo who didn't know one end of a pen from the other and would require babysitting for at least six months before she was capable of drawing a straight line or finding the coffee machine unaided.

'Of course,' she said automatically. 'But,' she added hastily, 'if Zoë isn't going . . .'

Bernard didn't let her finish the sentence. 'She is.'

Zoë took the news remarkably well for someone who'd only been toying with the idea of leaving and was now as good as fired. The last person who'd decided to leave was given half an hour to clear their desk and Bernard had made the deeply embarrassed security guard stand over the recalcitrant employee as he packed a bin liner with his possessions.

'I still have a month to work out my notice,' she said.

'He'll probably tell you not to bother coming back as soon as you hand your resignation in,' Cara fretted.

'Remember Dino. You'd have thought he was going to steal half the computers in the place the way Bernard had him watched.'

Zoë shrugged. 'If that happens, it happens, Cara. Besides, the interview went very well this morning. I'm sure they're going to offer me the job and I'd like to work there. Better than here, apart from working with you,' she added, seeing Cara's downcast face. 'Come on, think of the leaving party we'll have.'

'I'm too hungover even to think of having an alcoholic drink ever again,' Cara said gloomily.

'Spoilsport,' Zoë said. 'A couple of Screwdrivers and you'll be right as rain, I promise.'

'Why is it that whenever anyone says "I promise", it's always detrimental to my health,' Cara muttered.

Retail therapy, thought Olivia, swinging the shopping bags into the passenger seat, was definitely one of the most enjoyable pastimes in the world. Better than sex. *Far* better than sex, she corrected herself. Her current sex life was hardly very therapeutic since it consisted of no sex when Stephen was away (endurable because it meant he wasn't bossing her around either) or the sort of soulless encounter she found herself tolerating (because actually to discuss what was wrong with their relationship would be to start them on a rocky road from which there'd be no turning). Under the circumstances, spending a huge chunk of a month's wages she hadn't even been paid yet on clothes for her TV appearances was fifty times more therapeutic than any lovemaking.

She patted the selection of orange Karen Millen and cream Kilkenny bags fondly. If scientists could bottle the euphoria you experienced after buying new, change-your-life clothes, then no woman would need Prozac, she decided.

In the teacher's loo in St Joseph's, she changed into one of her new outfits: a pinstripe grey trouser suit which was cut with the sort of sharp modern tailoring she'd never worn before. Stephen liked her in classic clothes, double-breasted blazers and elegant twin sets you could wear with pearls and scarves with horses on them. The sort of thing her mother had by the drawerful but which she loathed.

She was sure he'd disapprove of this Karen Millen suit with its fashionable edge and outrageous red lining. Yet it gave her a surge of confidence to wear it.

Of course, it wasn't precisely the sort of outfit you'd wear to teach 3A but Olivia needed to try it out, to get comfortable in the suit before she wore it to the television studios the next day. A trial run with the worst-behaved class ever to tramp down the once-silent halls of St Joseph's would be perfect.

It was a different Mrs MacKenzie who walked calmly into the big Home Economics room ten minutes later. Her face didn't have the hunted look teachers' faces usually had when about to face the bane of their lives. Instead, she looked quietly confident, a look her pupils were not familiar with. They took very little notice when she shut the door to the classroom. Mrs MacKenzie, along with the young Geography teacher with the stammer, wasn't the sort of person to strike fear into their souls. Seriously in need of painting, the room stank of a bizarre mixture of cookery smells, most of which were overpowered by the stench of burnt onion from some previous culinary experiment.

3A were already at their desks, some waiting quietly, the remainder shouting at the top of their voices in the happy expectation of an undemanding class where they could chat, tell jokes and discuss which member of Westlife they wanted to marry without any fear of Mrs MacKenzie stopping them.

'Good morning, class,' she said. Apart from a few mumbled hellos from the good kids, who were too afraid of the troublemakers to be seen to be paying much attention to the teacher, nobody responded. The noise level continued unabated.

'I said, good morning, class. Now sit down and be quiet.' Her voice was harder, louder and brooked no opposition.

She gave them a cool, clear stare, a look that had worked well when she'd tried it in front of the camera.

The class sat up straighter and most of the noise stopped, which was a first, Olivia realised smugly. Only the few troublemakers kept talking, the secondary school version of giving someone a two-fingered salute.

Cheryl Dennis, Olivia's particular *bête noire*, chatted the loudest. You can't touch me, she seemed to be saying, running a hand through her short dark hair unconcernedly.

Olivia gazed at the pupil who'd tortured her for so long, the girl who was single-handedly responsible for making her reconsider her career as a teacher. Before Cheryl, she'd been a decent teacher and had never lost control of a class. But from that first day Cheryl had stared at her shrewdly, sensing like a temperamental horse with an inexperienced rider that here was a person who could lose command in an instant, Olivia's confidence as a teacher had plummeted like a stone.

Her fear of losing control in class had spread to every lesson she took, until the point where she'd entered even the first years' class with trepidation. She'd endured it for the seven months since Cheryl had moved – meaning expelled, they reckoned knowledgeably in the staffroom – from another school. Not anymore.

Olivia eyed up her opponent, trying to remember how

she'd stared Nancy Roberts down. Cheryl was short, tomboyish and made her school uniform look as un-uniform as possible with the addition of blocky fashionable shoes, a seriously turned up skirt and an over-large school jumper. Her eyes were rock hard and bristled with attitude.

Action was required, Olivia decided. If she could quell a television studio with her performance, she could certainly shut up a little cow like Ms Dennis.

'I said, be quiet,' she said, staring straight at the troublemaker with menace in her voice.

The class, sensing something was very different today, fell silent. Even Cheryl.

Olivia walked to the back of the classroom, as slowly and casually as if she was going for an afternoon stroll. She did look different today, very cool, admitted a couple of the girls to themselves grudgingly.

'Nice suit,' whispered one fashion-conscious soul longingly to her best friend, recognising superior tailoring, the sort of thing they admired in their mothers' magazines.

They both yearned to look like Mrs MacKenzie, all slim, blonde and elegant. It was just that she was such a pushover. They didn't want to *be* like her. They wanted to be strong, powerful women. But it occurred to at least some of them that Mrs MacKenzie wasn't acting her usual pushover self today.

Mrs MacKenzie stood beside Cheryl, staring down at her with an amused expression on her face.

The girl stared back at her insolently.

Olivia, knowing that this had to be done and silently praying she could act tough for long enough to do it, stared her down. With a superior look, she raked her eyes over the schoolgirl. Not for nothing was she descended from a long line of aristocrats. The supercilious gaze she'd inherited from her mother and never before used meant that the fine bones of her face fixed themselves into an elegant sneer of sheer disdain. Centuries of de Veres had used this look to put lesser mortals in their place. Her mother used it all the time, especially when she thought the butcher was short changing her with lamb chops. As looks went, it was devastating.

Cheryl Dennis reddened under Olivia's gaze.

'Get up and go to the front of the class,' she drawled, deliberately adopting the clipped tones of Sybil de Vere instead of her own soft voice.

The girl moved clumsily and Olivia allowed herself a smile, knowing that it wasn't a very teacherly thing to do but deciding that the end justified the means. The class members who were sick of Cheryl's bullying giggled.

Olivia sank gracefully into the vacant seat.

'Now, Cheryl,' she said coolly, 'as you're so keen to keep talking while I'm here, *you* teach the class. Today's lesson starts on page 124.'

For once, the class troublemaker was at a loss. 'Me, teach?' she said, laughing nervously, hoping someone would laugh with her, back her up and make a fool out of the teacher. That was the way things usually went for Cheryl: a few smart comments, some sniggering behind her hands and the ritual humiliation of whichever pathetic teacher was attempting to tell them what to do. Because *nobody* told a Dennis what to do. Nobody.

She glared at her comrades, willing them to laugh with her. But the class, with the new-style Mrs MacKenzie sitting among them, watching them like a hawk from behind her icy facade, stayed quiet as mice.

'Yes, you teach,' Mrs MacKenzie repeated ominously. And waited.

Cheryl looked around her in shock, suddenly aware that

she'd lost her acolytes and was alone. It was very lonely at the front of the class.

'We're waiting,' Mrs MacKenzie said caustically.

Unsure what to do next, the girl turned to page 124 of the book and found herself facing a page full of long, complicated words.

'. . . Transoleic fat . . .' Jesus, she couldn't read that.

'Is it too difficult for you?' the teacher asked.

Cheryl glared at her mutinously.

'Perhaps if you ever paid the slightest bit of attention in class, you might be able to understand,' Olivia said succinctly. 'But you prefer to play act and ensure that the pupils who do want to pay attention, can't hear.'

Cheryl tried to interrupt. 'But . . .'

'*Don't interrupt me!*' snarled Olivia.

Cheryl shrank back before the venom in Mrs MacKenzie's voice. 'If you want to spend the rest of your adult life shuffling to the dole office or flogging lighters on Henry Street, then leave my class and don't come back. And I'll explain to your parents exactly why I won't teach you. I'm sure they're tired of kitting you out in a new uniform every time you have to leave another school.'

Cheryl flushed at the jibe.

'But if you want to learn, if you want some chance of a future, then you'd better behave when you're in my class. Understand?'

'Yes,' mumbled Cheryl, defeated.

'Yes, *what?*' demanded Olivia.

'Yes, Mrs MacKenzie.'

Olivia rose. 'Sit down at your desk, Cheryl,' she ordered. She took her own place at the top of the class and looked at all the nervous, silent faces staring back at her. It was a pity she'd had to be so mean to the girl in order to regain the respect of the class, but it had had to be done.

Cheryl gave her an angry, vengeful stare.

'I meant every word I said, Cheryl,' Olivia said, ice in every syllable. 'Don't forget it.'

Gazing at her round-eyed pupils, she felt that adrenaline rush she'd felt when she'd completed her television audition. Thanks, Max, she breathed silently.

Cheryl Dennis had been a walk in the park compared to this, Olivia thought as she entered the brightly lit make-up department the following morning to see Nancy Roberts sitting like the mother alien from *Aliens* in a make-up chair, a cover draped over her protectively. Nancy's eyes were closed so Olivia slipped into the chair farthest away from her and prayed that nobody said 'Hello, Olivia' and gave her presence away.

Her striped suit may have been the battledress which had defeated 3A the previous day, but today, unless it was armour-plated to deal with Nancy's daggers, it wasn't going to be as effective.

Three more people arrived to be made up and created a safety buffer between her and Nancy, obliterating any chance the star would notice her.

Olivia sank into the soft, dentist-style chair, closed her eyes and prayed she'd be left alone until they were on set at least. Paul Reddin would be there and, according to Max, he'd prevent Nancy from being openly vicious.

The gods were smiling on her. Ten minutes later, from the corner of her eye, she saw Nancy rip off her gown, peer querulously at her image in the mirror and bark: 'It'll do!' before teetering off on baby peach sandals that would be out of place anywhere but at a Cannes cocktail party. Olivia relaxed and tried to breathe deeply, letting the make-up artist work her magic.

She slipped downstairs and made it to the studio

without encountering Nancy. The production team were hovering by the kitchen bar, waiting for her.

'Olivia,' said Linda Byrne. 'You're still wearing your suit?' she asked in surprise.

'Yes,' she replied. Was that wrong? They'd all appeared to approve of her business-like outfit at the production meeting an hour earlier.

'Well . . .' the producer said hesitantly '. . . it's not what I had in mind for the show's cookery expert. We'd prefer you to wear something more casual. That's too . . .'

'Harsh,' said a plummy voice. 'Office girl trying too hard, perhaps.'

Nancy, beatific smile on her face, stood behind them. Clad in a peach suit not unlike Olivia's in style, she looked good but not *as* good. Which was probably why she was so thrilled to see Olivia being told off for wearing hers.

'You want to wear something more mumsy, less threatening for the cookery slot,' Nancy added, as if cookery was something only watched by bewildered women in floral pinnies who took fright at the sight of anyone in a suit.

'Not mumsy, exactly,' interjected Linda in a placatory tone. 'More viewer friendly.'

Kevin, the production assistant, who now sported a fake ponytail to go with his platinum crop, grabbed Olivia by the arm before she could say anything.

'Of course Olivia's changing her outfit,' he said cheerily. 'We're just getting it ironed.' He herded her away from the group, out of the studio and into the corridor.

'I haven't brought anything else to wear,' she protested, 'and that Nancy is an evil cow. I thought I was going to hit her.'

'So did I!' he giggled. 'Why else do you think I dragged you out of there? You can't afford to antagonise the bitch too much or you'll be history,' he advised.

363

'But the producer wouldn't stand for that, surely?' Olivia asked, thinking of what Max had said about how Paul Reddin was the one person Nancy couldn't wrap around her plump, bejewelled little finger.

Kevin smirked. 'Listen honey, *he* might not, but Nancy has plenty of friends in high places who'd do anything for her.'

'You think so?'

'Let me put it in a more delicate way,' he said. 'If this place went on fire tomorrow and the only thing left of the head honchos on the top floor was a collection of their dicks, Nancy would be able to identify precisely who'd been killed by just those parts.'

'Oh.'

'*Oh* is right,' he said. 'She's had more of the men in this place than I have and the difference between us is that she goes for the type who have power. Sadly I go for the muscular but dumb type who can't further their own careers, never mind mine.' He sighed theatrically. 'Now sit in your dressing room and study your running order, sweetie, until I can find a replacement top that isn't too "harsh".'

Good as his word, Kevin returned after ten minutes with a lilac silk knit top which, worn with her pin-stripe trousers, would look pretty and flattering. 'There's a girl in the library owes me a favour,' he said. 'I ripped this off her back so it's probably still warm.'

A woman who loved second-hand clothes, Olivia wasn't about to complain about wearing something still warm from the body of its previous wearer. She pulled it on, dragged a brush through her blonde hair and was ready.

'What a trooper,' Kevin said admiringly.

Back on the set, the programme was about to start and last-minute discussions were frantically going on in every corner of the studio. The floor manager strode around, yelling into his radio mike with every third word an expletive. The normally unflappable Linda Byrne sprinted across the floor in the direction of the control room looking anxious, and even the camera men and women seemed jolted out of their usual laid-back state in anticipation of the opening credits.

Nancy and her co-presenter, a kind-faced forty-something man named Theo Jones, sat on one of the giant raspberry sofas, as far apart as they possibly could.

Nancy, resplendent in her peach trouser suit with the usual six inches of heaving bosom visible down her V-neck, was facing one direction, sipping coffee and reading the stapled pages of the running order.

Theo, wearing a yellow handknitted jumper decorated with lambs, and a pair of fawn cords, was facing the other way reading his running order. You didn't need a degree in either psychology or body language to tell that the famous on-screen chemistry between the two presenters was as fake as the cheekbones the make-up department had attempted to give Nancy by the judicious application of blusher.

Theo looked plain uncomfortable sitting beside Nancy. But then, Olivia thought, grinning to herself, wouldn't anybody?

Nancy caught her grinning and glared back haughtily. But with the memory of Kevin's tale about Nancy's ability to identify men by their extremities uppermost in her mind, Olivia met the glare with a giant smile.

'Thirty seconds,' yelled a voice.

Everyone held their breath and the first guest, a pretty girl singer with her second single in the Top Ten, quivered with nerves on the sidelines and fiddled with her elaborately messed-up hair do with its collection of flowery hair clips.

'Twenty seconds! Ten seconds!'

Then the theme tune was thumping into the studio and Nancy and Theo, who'd automatically moved closer together on the sofa, were smiling buoyantly at the cameras.

'Good morning,' they said cheerily as one.

'And have we got a packed show for you this morning,' Nancy added breathlessly.

'Sure have, Nancy.' Theo patted her knees cosily. 'We've got gorgeous Zelda here to sing her new hit single, "Dance With You".' The pretty girl in the sidelines quivered some more in her electric blue hotpants.

'An update on our story on animal cruelty,' Nancy added.

'Author Anna Stavros is here to talk about her latest blockbuster,' Theo said, turning to Nancy.

'And we've got some fabulous cookery hints from our new expert, Olivia de Vere, who'll be showing you how to do interesting things with shepherd's pie,' Nancy simpered into the camera.

It was Olivia's turn to quiver: with rage. She wasn't making shepherd's pie, it was 'Ten Clever Things To Do With Pizza'. Nancy knew that! Linda Byrne, who had appeared from nowhere, put a comforting hand on Olivia's arm. 'We'll sort that error out,' she whispered. 'Must have been a mistake on Nancy's running order.'

Mistake my ass! Olivia thought. Nancy had done it on purpose.

She was speaking again: 'In a few minutes, we'll be covering our saddest story, the tale of one abandoned family of rabbits discovered in a plastic bag on Henry Street.' Nancy gazed mistily at the camera as if the plight of every injured animal in the world was on her mind constantly. 'We want you to phone us with your own stories – sad tales of poor abandoned animals or,' Nancy's face switched miraculously into a tender expression it never adopted off camera, 'funny stories about your own beloved pets. The number is on your screen now.'

'She just loves animals, folks.' Theo put an arm around Nancy and gave her a brief hug. 'Most soft-hearted woman I know,' he added.

Olivia wondered if she'd imagined the ironic gleam behind Theo's benevolent expression. She couldn't see Nancy letting any furry friendly creature dirty her clothes with a wet, questing nose or dirty paws.

'Now,' he added, 'let's welcome Zelda, glamour queen of the pop scene, and certainly the most beautiful creature to emerge from Limerick in a long, long time.'

Nancy's face tightened. *She* was from Limerick, if Olivia remembered correctly. And she *hadn't* imagined it: Theo was sticking discreet little barbs in Nancy's peach-clad side every chance he got.

She didn't waste any time getting her own back.

'Zelda,' she cooed, welcoming the nervous young singer on set with a saccharine smile. 'Sit beside Theo. He's perfectly safe,' she tittered. 'Poor dear wouldn't know what to do with a pretty girl like you.'

Theo joined in her giggles. 'She's only jealous, Zelda,' he said confidingly, 'because I haven't chatted her up for years. Not since they stopped paying me to, anyway! Only kidding, Nance, my pet,' he added, blowing a kiss to his co-presenter, who sat there, a smile welded on to her stony face.

If Theo had it all his own way during the Zelda interview, flirting and excluding Nancy totally, she was determined to make him pay when she held court during the abandoned animal story.

'Isn't it terrible the way people treat animals?' she said at the end of a heart-rending piece of footage narrated by the cats' and dogs' home representative who sat nervously between Nancy and Theo on the sofa. 'Not that you'd understand this, Theo,' she said tearfully. 'He eats veal,' she said dramatically to the camera.

'I don't,' hissed Theo, rattled. Not adoring children, old people and animals was death to any television personality's career, he knew. Eating veal was like being found to enjoy slapping little old ladies or, even worse, like a newspaper splashing your fondness for leather, peep-hole undies all over the front page.

'You do,' Nancy said. Then, noticing the look of horror in the producer's eyes, relented a bit. 'Or is it somebody else I'm thinking of?'

'Must be somebody else,' Theo snapped. 'I love calves – I love all animals.'

'Except little fishies,' Nancy said with her famous winning smile. 'You do eat fish, I've seen you.' She faced the camera: 'Meat is murder, viewers, but fish is justifiable homicide!'

Giggling as if she'd just made the most hilarious joke, Nancy patted the animal expert on the knee. Aware of the knife-edge tension on set, he jumped.

'Don't mind our teasing,' she cooed. 'Darling Theo and I love teasing each other. I pretend to destroy his reputation and he does the same to me. It's so much fun.'

'It doesn't look much like fun in my opinion,' Olivia whispered to Kevin.

'The viewers think it's a howl,' Kevin said softly. 'They don't realise that pair would have each other's eyes out if they got the chance. It's hard to tell which one of them is capable of throwing the bigger queenie fit.'

Five minutes later, as she stood in her gleaming television kitchen, Olivia reflected that whatever Kevin's job description was, it didn't cover half the things he did. Not only had he prevented her from murdering Nancy, he'd found her something to wear *and* kept her so amused with tales of Theo's and Nancy's long-running feud that she hadn't had a moment to be nervous about her first live appearance.

'You'll knock'em dead,' he said, utterly blasé.

And she did. From the first moment Theo introduced her to the viewers – and Olivia had sent up a silent prayer of thanks to Linda Byrne for making sure it was Theo and not Nancy who introduced her – she'd felt as if she was freewheeling down a mountain on a superb bike, heart lifting joyously with the thrill of it all.

For that first appearance, Theo hung around to help her in case she got stage fright. But in the end, it was Olivia who took charge, smiling at his efforts to grate cheese without grating his thumbs into the bargain.

'I'm hopeless at this,' he admitted, sad face incongruous above his happy lamb jumper.

'No, you're not,' insisted Olivia kindly, the way she would to a shy second year who was nervous about cooking. 'I'll do that, it's tricky. Why don't you arrange the Spanish sausage on top of this pizza? You're the artistic one around here.'

All in all, she and Theo made a far better team than Theo and Nancy, Olivia decided. Her ten-minute cookery slot was relaxed and fun. She and Theo chatted with the easy amiability of people used to each other's company.

'It's delicious,' he mumbled at the end, as he bit into a succulent slice of pizza decorated with goat's cheese and red onions.

Nancy, who'd been off having her inch-thick make-up touched up during the slot, appeared beside them suddenly, like a malevolent cloud dressed in Escada, and proceeded to look at the assembled pizzas as if they were decorated with rats' entrails instead of chorizo, mushrooms and tuna fish.

'Goodness, what a lot of pizza,' she remarked disdain-fully, poking at the most cheese-laden version with a fork. 'All appallingly fattening, no doubt,' she added maliciously. 'Not the sort of thing our viewers want to be stuffing their faces with.'

Olivia saw her chance and went for it. 'I don't find them fattening, Nancy,' she said pointedly, and cut a piece from the cheesy one in question while patting her own tiny waist. 'I can eat what I like.'

Under her sunbed tan, Nancy's face whitened with rage.

Olivia: one, Nancy: nil.

Kevin was still giggling when Olivia joined him behind the cameras.

'She walked into that one,' he squealed delightedly.

'She'll never forgive me,' Olivia pointed out. 'Although Theo seemed to like it. He gave me a hug and said "well done" when we went to the advert break, and I don't think he was simply referring to the cookery slot.'

'Olivia, you were brilliant.' Paul Reddin arrived from the seclusion of the control room to give her a congratulatory hug. 'You have this incredible screen presence. Everybody's going to be watching you and talking about you soon, and wondering where we found our marvellous TV newcomer.'

As it happened, quite a lot of people were watching her already. In Wentworth Alarms, Evie and Lorraine had abandoned their room for the sales office where, perched on the same swivel chair, they watched the show on an elderly television set normally only dragged out of its hiding place for the Grand National when the entire company all pulled a horse's name out of an envelope in an office sweepstake.

Watching Olivia's lovely face become animated as she laughed and joked with Theo Jones, while expertly dicing and slicing at the same time, Evie felt a lump of pride in her throat. Olivia looked so beautiful, so competent, so utterly charming. She was wonderful, just wonderful.

'Don't cry,' Lorraine said, seeing Evie's little face tremble and water collect in her huge hazel eyes from the emotion of it all.

'I know it's silly,' she said tremulously, 'but I'm so proud of her. Olivia's always lacked confidence, even though it was unfounded, but to see her doing this . . . she deserves to do so well!'

'Bleedin' hell, is she your friend?' asked one awe-struck sales exec, rooted to the spot with lust at the sight of Olivia's exquisite face and elegant figure clad in a lilac top which was marginally too small for her and, therefore, sensationally clingy. 'She married?'

'Cedric! You'll never guess who's on the telly . . .'

By the end of Olivia's cookery slot, Sheilagh was mentally figuring out what she'd wear to go into Navan town and casually ask people had they seen her Stephen's wife on the television that morning? Her new red blazer and navy pleated skirt, she decided, and the cream court shoes. So suitable. Her mind already working overtime, she could imagine the conversations: 'I'm getting a few last-minute things for our trip. Cedric and I are going to Dublin for a few days for a party to celebrate Stephen's wife going on the television. Oh, didn't you know? Well, we don't like to blow our own trumpets. Yes, with Nancy Roberts and Theo Jones. I believe Nancy is wonderful, just loves Olivia. Merciful hour, would you look at the time! I must rush. They won't start the party without us, we can't be late!'

Cedric's roar interrupted her fond imagining. 'Did you hear that?' he demanded, puffing up like an outraged bullfrog. 'They said Olivia *de Vere* – bloody de Vere. Not MacKenzie! Is our name not good enough for her? I'm going to have words with Stephen! There'll be war, I'm telling you.'

'I think we should go to Dublin,' Sheilagh interrupted.

'Stephen's away,' snapped her husband.

'We'll phone him,' she said. Then, as it occurred to her that her beloved son had kept this whole television thing a secret from her, she added, 'I want to find out why he never told us Olivia was going to be on the television.'

A hundred miles away, unaware of all this, Olivia was treating herself to a manicure in the beautician's on the basis that her hands were always going to be on show on the programme and needed to look nice. And she'd decided to treat herself. This wasn't Stephen's money she was spending, she thought, luxuriating in that fact. It was hers.

She was meeting Evie for a late lunch in half an hour, and then she was going to take Sasha to the zoo as a special treat. Stephen was away so there was no need to think about what complicated dinner she'd have to cook for him later. She and Sasha could have a McDonald's in Stillorgan on the way home and spend a relaxing evening watching telly. Bliss.

'You were brilliant!' yelled Evie when they met in The Orchard car park. 'We all watched you and there's one sex-mad sales executive who wants to know if you're married, single or otherwise available!'

'Probably otherwise available when Stephen finds out,' giggled Olivia. 'Was it really all right? I was so nervous in the beginning and then it just gelled.'

As Evie only had half an hour to devour her sandwich, they hurried inside. After ages spent discussing the ins and outs of television, Olivia suddenly said she must remember to phone Max and tell him how she'd got on.

'He's a lovely guy,' she added.

'Is he?' Evie sounded brittle.

'He is. And he really likes you, Evie. At that lunch, he wanted to talk about you all the time,' Olivia protested.

'I'd rather not talk about *him*, if you don't mind,' her friend said shortly.

'OK.' Olivia decided that something obviously had gone on between Max and Evie, something very odd. She'd been sure there was a spark between them but perhaps she'd been wrong. In any case, Max must have made his feelings plain to Evie and she'd rejected him. It must all have happened badly, although Olivia could hardly imagine Max messing up something like that. He was so polished, so sure of himself. But you never knew. The most polished people sometimes made a complete disaster of things.

The little red message light on the answerphone was flickering frantically when Olivia let herself and Sasha into the apartment that evening. Tired after a thrilling after-noon looking at lions, chimps and a baby goat, finishing up with a Happy Meal and a fudge sundae at McDonald's, Sasha padded into her bedroom to show her beloved teddies the new fluffy elephant she'd picked in the zoo shop. Equally happy and equally tired, Olivia shrugged off her jacket and decided to boil the kettle for a reviving cup of tea before listening to her messages.

So she at least had something hot and sweet to cling to when Stephen's irate voice came on the line: 'What's happened, Olivia? I've just got some message that my father is looking for me urgently and there's a problem to do with you. What the hell is going on?' He'd rung at half-four. The second message, which he'd left at half-six, just moments before Olivia had opened the front door, was much more to the point: 'My father tells me you're a bloody television star! I can't believe this,' he hissed. 'Did he get it wrong? I never thought the stupid eejit would lose his mind totally but he must have. Ring me back and tell me. I mean, I'm here trying to sort things out and . . .'

Being cut off didn't stop Stephen. He'd rung back two minutes later to continue in the same vein.

Clutching her cup convulsively, Olivia shut him up by deleting the messages. He knew. Oh, Christ, he knew. And in the worst possible way, at that. He would kill her, absolutely kill her. Nobody hated humiliation more than Stephen and having his father find out about his wife's television appearance before he did would certainly rank as humiliating. Why hadn't she thought that anybody connected to Stephen would see the show? Why had she been so bloody stupid?

Because you were so delighted with yourself, that's why, sang an evil little voice in her head. 'Pride goes before a fall,' her mother had always said puritanically, although she only ever said it during those years when Olivia's beauty had blossomed and never applied the proverb to herself.

Olivia stared at the phone, waiting for it to ring loudly at any minute with Stephen breathing fire and brimstone down the line from Germany. He'd phone again, she knew he would.

The piercing ring of the doorbell made her jump and spill half her cup of tea on to the floor. She gasped in shock. It couldn't be Stephen. He couldn't have got home from Germany that quickly. Opening the door gingerly, as if she expected something black, cloven-hooved and

brandishing a giant pitchfork to be standing there malevo-
lently, Olivia peered out.

There, hidden behind a giant bouquet of early-summer
flowers, stood her next-door neighbour, Gloria. A red-
headed air stewardess who lived alone, Gloria had
incurred Stephen's wrath years before for having the odd
wild party where seventies disco music blared through
the thin walls and, therefore, never called round when he
was there.

'Is this a good time, Olivia?' she said in her breathy,
little-girl voice. Meaning: Is your husband there? Olivia
knew.

'Wonderful time,' she said, just as grateful as Gloria that
Stephen was thousands of miles away. 'Do come in.'

'These were delivered earlier and I took them in for
you,' Gloria said, handing over the giant, sweet-smelling
bouquet. 'They are beautiful. I do hope you haven't been a
naughty girl.' She giggled. 'That's *my* job.'

Never seen without the expertly applied cosmetics that
transformed her from an ordinary-looking girl into a *femme
fatale* in an Aer Lingus uniform, Gloria was a complete
chatterbox who'd talk all day if you let her.

Normally, Olivia was too busy drumming up three-
course meals to keep Stephen happy to have time to talk.
But today, jittery with shock and desperate to gabble to
somebody about what had happened, she dragged Gloria
into the sitting room, made them two giant drinks and
spilled her heart out.

'I never meant not to tell Stephen,' she said, shaking so
much that Gloria was afraid Olivia's Bailey's and ice was
going to hit the floor. 'I mean, we all have secrets and it's
just the way it turned out. But if I'd ever dreamed he'd
find out this way . . . And he'll go mad! I know nobody
believes it, he's a bit of a house devil, street angel, but . . .'

Gloria, very kind and used to dealing with nervous fliers on the Dublin to New York route, sat beside Olivia and put an arm around her. 'Don't panic, lovie,' she said. 'Have your drink.'

Like a child being told to drink up her milk, Olivia obediently sipped her Bailey's while Gloria kept up a flow of meaningless conversation intended to relax her.

'Men are gas, aren't they?' she went on. 'We all think they're the answer to our prayers and when we have them, they drive us mad. I know your Stephen is a bit,' she paused delicately, 'sensitive and tricky. But he'll come round. The thing is, you've got to stand up to him, lovie. Tell him you're his dear wife but you've got your own career. It'd be different if you were fighting over something else but with this television show, he should watch out. There'll be dozens of men dying to date the glam telly cook and your Stephen ought to cop on to himself or he'll be cooking dinner for one soon. Now, let's see who those flowers are from. I'll put them in water and you read your card.'

She handed Olivia the envelope that came with the flowers and went into the kitchen in search of a vase. Feeling so much better after a bit of sisterly support and a glass of Bailey's, Olivia ripped open the envelope and smiled fondly.

'*Congrats on a brilliant TV debut. Paul and the team reckon they've found a new star. So do I. Best wishes, Max Stewart,*' read the card. Dear Max, he was so kind and supportive.

In the kitchen, she found Sasha and Gloria happily arranging the flowers. Kissing the little girl on top of her blonde head, Olivia asked Gloria if she could stay a bit longer.

'We've had a McDonald's,' she confessed, 'but we could open a bottle of wine and have some cheese and biscuits.'

They were halfway down a bottle of Frascati when the doorbell rang blisteringly. Much more relaxed and no longer expecting Stephen to arrive in a demonic rage, Olivia walked to the door in her stockinged feet and opened it. Her jaw dropped when she saw Sheilagh and Cedric on the doorstep, bristling with emotion and carrying suitcases.

'Well, you're the quiet one,' said Sheilagh, shoving past her into the hall, leaving Cedric to hump two cases and a carrier bag of bullet-hard scones in behind her.

'I can't say we weren't surprised,' Sheilagh went on, dumping her fat cream leather handbag on the floor and squeezing her plump arms out of her red blazer. 'But it's an interesting job. You'll have to get Theo or Nancy to do a special appearance in Miriam's Boutique in Navan. I was in there today and said I was sure you'd be able to, seeing as how you know them. All these famous types love personal appearances. But this'd be free, of course.'

Striding into the sitting room, she stopped at the sight of Gloria tucking into spiced Adare cheese and water biscuits. Not sure that Gloria wasn't a famous celebrity she just didn't recognise, Sheilagh's face creased up into a smile.

'Hullo,' she said, immediately adopting her posh phone voice. 'We're Stephen's porents, deloighted to meet you. I'm Sheilagh and this is Cedric.'

Gloria, who recognised Stephen's parents after being shoved rudely to the back of the lift by Sheilagh and numerous carrier bags in a January sale frenzy on several occasions, drained her glass and got up.

'Must go,' she hissed at a still-silent Olivia.

'So pleased to meet you,' she trilled at Sheilagh, in *her* first-class-to-JFK-lounge voice. 'Have to fly. Love to dear sweet Nancy. Tell her I'll be in touch,' she added wickedly.

'Who was that?' asked Cedric with interest as Gloria let herself out with a final goodbye pout at her hostess.

Sheilagh gave him the evil eye and he began humping their cases down to the spare bedroom.

'Television people are so rackety,' Olivia said, suddenly regaining her composure. 'Dear Gloria works on the News,' she lied, 'but she's so unassuming you'd never think she was in television.'

Sheilagh wasn't interested in the News. Only lifestyles of the rich and famous gave her the thrill that Cedric no longer wanted to. 'What's Nancy Roberts like?' she demanded, sitting down and helping herself to a lump of cheese the size of a hamster. 'Is she lovely?'

About as lovely as you pair are, Olivia reflected.

Cedric and Sheilagh had gone through half a quiche, four massive baked potatoes and an entire Vienetta by the time Stephen phoned again.

'Won't be a minute,' Olivia said to her replete guests, closing the door to the sitting room and taking the phone into her bedroom.

Stephen was beside himself. 'What the hell is going on?' he hissed, obviously not even slightly mollified by the posh dinner Olivia knew he'd have had in the posh hotel he always stayed in.

'By the way, your parents are here,' she said mildly.

'I don't fucking care! What's this about you on the television?'

'Don't swear. I did a television audition for a morning programme. They wanted a cookery expert and I went for the job. I got it and today was my first day.'

'What!'

Olivia covered the receiver. Gloria, in the apartment next door, must have heard his roars.

'I didn't tell you because I wanted to see if I was any

good at it. I thought you'd slag me off for even attempting to appear on television. But it was very good, everyone thought so.'

'Jesus Christ, Olivia, are you fucking mad? You go off and do this thing without even telling me about it and then I hear from my father. How do you think that makes me feel?' Stephen roared.

The telephone receiver is a powerful instrument, Olivia realised, the thought striking her out of the blue. She dared to say things to the cream plastic receiver she'd have been scared to say to Stephen's face.

'Stephen, do you ever for one moment contemplate the fact that what *you* think and what *you* feel aren't the most important things in the universe?' she said, finally snapping. If she could cope with the malicious Cheryl Dennis and the vicious Nancy Roberts, then her own husband wasn't going to trash her. 'I didn't tell you because I knew you'd try and destroy my confidence over this the way you do with everything else. It's that simple,' she said, every syllable enunciated perfectly. 'And now that I'm doing it, getting paid for it and enjoying it, I don't give a fuck what you think.'

She could almost hear him recoil at her unexpected use of the expletive. Olivia never swore.

'If you want to discuss this, then come home. But don't dream of swearing or screaming at me or you'll find all the locks changed. I won't even let you in the spare room,' she warned. 'You can use your precious gold card to buy you a hotel room. You've bullied me for too long, Stephen. The worm is turning.' She slammed the phone down vehemently, feeling the thrill of triumph coursing through her veins.

In the sitting room, her in-laws were channel surfing aimlessly. There was nothing on the TV they liked watching. All the films on these days were 'rubbish' and the late-night chat shows were all populated by 'young pups'. Olivia knew what would come next: bored, they'd start interrogating her as to why Stephen hadn't known about her television debut. So far, they'd been too busy stuffing their faces to ask. But the inquisition was nigh, she just knew it.

They'd love to be up all night talking about the proud MacKenzie name, about how much Stephen loved her, and probably ask if they could get tickets to see their favourite shows. Olivia, who had to get up the next morning for a class, wasn't in the mood. Seeing as how she wasn't taking any abuse from Stephen, she wasn't planning on taking any from his horrible parents either.

It was half-nine, she realised, wondering where the evening had gone. She could watch the TV in her bedroom if she managed to escape from Cedric and Sheilagh. As long as they had access to the kitchen, they'd survive.

'Was that Stephen?' asked Cedric, fixing her with his beady eye as she came into the room.

'Yes, it was. Actually, Cedric and Sheilagh,' she announced, 'I'm quite exhausted and I've a hectic day tomorrow so I'm going to bed early. You'll have to excuse me.'

Sheilagh, who had changed into one of her trademark velour tracksuits – mustard yellow – once she'd realised there'd be no more glamorous television guests turning up, looked furious at Olivia's announcement.

'After we came all the way up from Navan to see you?' she said hotly. 'We need to talk.'

Olivia's patience, which had taken a severe battering from Sheilagh and Cedric over the twelve years of their marriage, was wearing dangerously thin.

'Sheilagh,' she said, less tolerantly, 'I didn't know you

were coming or I would have tried to rearrange my day tomorrow.'

Her mother-in-law went a dark red at the not so subtle dig.

'But because you arrived unexpectedly,' Olivia went on, 'I haven't had a chance to rearrange anything and as I've got to be up at seven, I'm going to bed now.'

'There's no need to get up on your high horse about it,' Sheilagh snapped. 'I'm sure we'd have phoned if we'd had the chance.'

'You had the time to phone Stephen in Germany *twice*,' Olivia pointed out crisply, 'so I think you could have managed a call here.'

'We were worried, that's all,' Cedric interrupted, eager to get his four ha'pence worth in.

'Worried about what?'

'About how you'd got on the television and why we were never told,' he said. 'And about why you were using your maiden name,' he added sententiously.

'As if ours isn't good enough,' shrieked Sheilagh. 'We know when we're not wanted . . .'

'I don't hold with this modern carry on of women not taking their husband's name,' Cedric continued. 'It's a disgrace, should be outlawed. In my day, women were proud to take a man's name. Of course it's different now . . .'

'. . . what with all that divorce,' put in Sheilagh, her hard little eyes gleaming with rage.

'Well,' Olivia said, finally losing her own temper, 'thanks to your meddling, perhaps Stephen and I *will* be getting a divorce, so then I'll be needing my own name after all.'

Cedric spluttered and Sheilagh went another shade darker, a colour that usually made casualty department doctors ring up the cardiac specialist.

'There's never been divorce in our family,' she hissed with all the venom of a rattlesnake.

Olivia stared back at her parents-in-law. She'd have loved to have said that if they hadn't brought Stephen up to be a domineering, anal-retentive control freak, then divorce wouldn't be in prospect. But he was and it was, she realised calmly. Anyway, she didn't want to reveal her inner misery to Cedric and Sheilagh.

'Let's hope there won't be one this time either,' she said, 'but your *involvement* hasn't helped. Goodnight.'

She left the room and went quietly to her bedroom. They'd stayed here many times before: they knew where everything was, including the front door. And if Stephen had a problem with Olivia finally standing up for herself when it came to his parents, then tough.

It was too much to expect that they'd be gone when she came home the following day just after lunch, after having picked Sasha up from the crèche. The hum of a hairdryer and the blaring television still on in the sitting room told her that Sheilagh was doing her hair and Cedric was glued to afternoon TV. They may have known when they weren't wanted but that didn't mean they'd actually leave.

Tired of the air of gloom hanging over the apartment, Olivia went into the kitchen and turned the radio on full blast. Offspring's latest hit pumped out violently, all heavy guitars and an ambient beat that sounded as if you'd want to be taking at least a few kilos of drugs to really get into. She grinned. Sheilagh would *hate* it.

'We had our lunch,' Cedric said, appearing at the door looking mildly shamefaced.

'You have?' Olivia was surprised. Usually their idea of lunch meant half an hour tidying up for her.

'We're going in a few minutes, I've booked a taxi.' He

came further into the kitchen. 'I'm sorry, Olivia,' he said, startling her as much as if he'd just announced he was a transvestite. 'We shouldn't have interfered. I just reacted badly, although Sheilagh doesn't agree with me, if you get my drift.'

Olivia got it all right. Sheilagh had no intention of ever apologising for anything: she didn't think she'd done anything wrong, and she'd crucify her husband if she knew *he* was apologising.

'I didn't think about you or the trouble I might cause by telling Stephen you weren't using our name – I'm sorry. I've been thinking about it all night.' Cedric looked downcast. 'He can be hard to live with, I know. But he does love you very much.'

'Love shouldn't be about control, though, should it?' she asked bitterly. What a conversation to be having with your father-in-law!

Cedric shook his head. 'I know. That's my fault too. I wanted him to be strong, you see, not a wimp. I'm sorry he's so furious with you.'

Olivia's head shot up. 'He rang while I was out, didn't he?' she asked.

Her father-in-law nodded. 'I tried to talk to him but it was no good. His mother got in there and started giving out yards . . .'

'I did what?' Sheilagh, hair styled into hard grey sausage curls clamped to her head, appeared behind her husband, looking as if she'd been in an overpowering rage for twelve hours with no sign of a let up. Her face was red and she was sweating under her sensible white blouse and red blazer.

'I was telling Olivia that Stephen's getting a flight home this afternoon,' Cedric said, back to his usual strident tones.

Jesus! Olivia wanted to collapse. Stephen was coming home from Germany early. He'd kill her.

'Much she cares,' snapped Sheilagh.

Olivia looked at the woman who'd caused her so much grief during her marriage, the woman who'd always resented Olivia's family background and who'd found every excuse to complain about her to Stephen. Sheilagh had whinged about the food, her bedroom and Olivia's manners whenever she came to stay. She'd remarked that working women couldn't expect to rear children properly; anything to cause division between *her* beloved son and *that woman* he'd married. Olivia felt the years of doing her best to please Sheilagh slip away. You *couldn't* please Sheilagh, so why bother?

'You know what?' Olivia said, giving her truthful streak full rein. 'You're a nasty, vindictive woman and I'm sick of you. I'm not letting Sasha near you ever again in case you taint her with your horrible opinions on people and your venomous tongue.'

Her mother-in-law glared at her. 'You . . . you can't do that! She's my grand-daughter. What would people think?'

Olivia's face was a mask of disgust. 'That's all you really care about, Sheilagh: what people think. You couldn't give a damn about real people or whether you've hurt them or not. All that matters to you is the surface, your public face, and making sure you're in your rightful place at the altar on Sunday, piously praying. When behind it all you're secretly figuring out whose character to assassinate next.'

'Steady on,' Cedric said.

'I don't do that, said Sheilagh shrilly.

'Oh, come on.' Olivia was beyond being polite. 'When did you ever come here and say anything nice to me? When did you come and help, instead of arriving unexpectedly and demanding I drive you around like a bloody taxi? Did you think I didn't know you complained behind my back to Stephen if I wasn't ultra-polite to you or if you felt you weren't being looked after properly because you wanted an extra pillow on your bed?'

'How dare you speak to me like that? You're nothing but a jumped up little tramp, no matter how you pretend to be better than us, coming from that big house.' Sheilagh's eyes were blazing now as she said all the things she'd been hinting at for years. 'Well, we all know your mother's nothing but a drunken lush and that's probably what you'll turn out like too. I've warned Stephen.' She was almost spitting with rage. 'I've told him you'll turn out just like her: drunk and sluttish. You with that long blonde hair, too. It's ridiculous at your age! Makes you look common. And all your going on about your posh family . . .'

She went on and on but Olivia had stopped paying attention. What had Stephen thrown at her during that big fight before Andrew Fraser's wedding: that she'd turn out just like her mother? Obviously he and Sheilagh had been singing from the same hymn sheet. What a pair. No wonder she and Stephen had been struggling along together, with his mother as the anti-marriage guidance counsellor from hell in the background, dispensing her poison.

The doorbell rang.

'Our taxi,' said Cedric, desperately relieved. He scurried out of the kitchen to answer the door.

Olivia stood as close as she could bear to Sheilagh and whispered: 'I will get Nancy Roberts and Theo Jones to come to Navan, and we'll have a marvellous time – except *you* won't be invited. Nancy will make that plain. She'll tell everyone that she won't have anything to do with you because you're such a cast-iron bitch to me and Sasha.

Wait till *that* gets spread around Navan. You'll be a laughing stock.'

As if by magic, Sheilagh's high colour drained away. 'You wouldn't?' she breathed.

'Wait and see,' was Olivia's reply.

'Sorry,' said Cedric helplessly as his wife flounced out of the front door, not bothering to take either of the suitcases with her.

Olivia shrugged. 'I've always known what she thinks of me, now I've just told her what I think of her.'

'But this is so bad for the family . . .'

Olivia's voice was hard: 'Your wife and my husband worked hard to create this problem, so let them pick up the pieces, Cedric.'

'Where's Daddy going?' Sasha asked, sitting on the bed and playing zoo with her new elephant and a couple of old bunnies as Olivia briskly and efficiently packed Stephen's clothes into the two largest suitcases they owned.

'He might be going on a long trip, darling,' she said absently. 'Or he may be staying in the spare room.'

'Why?'

'He keeps waking Mummy up in the middle of the night with his snoring,' she said, abandoning her task to cuddle her daughter.

'Will he be cross with us?' Sasha asked, her face anxious.

'No,' Olivia promised. 'He won't.'

She hugged Sasha closer, grimly thinking that this was something she should have done a long time ago.

'Goodie. Can Rosie live with us then, and Auntie Evie?' Sasha loved Rosie with childlike devotion.

'Not really, love, they'll be living with Uncle Simon.' Or, at least, Olivia thought they'd be living with Simon. The last time she and Evie had discussed the wedding, it had gone from being the biggest thrill of Evie's life to something she apparently didn't want to discuss. Which didn't bode well for the future.

When Stephen's key turned in the lock that evening, Olivia had two suitcases and four boxes of stuff ready for him in the hall; the boxes containing his books, office files, CDs, the CD player, and the contents of his drawers. At first, she'd only packed clothes for him as if he was going on a particularly long business trip but after a while had decided that they needed a complete break. The only way to get him out was to shock him and packing up all his possessions would certainly do that.

'What the fuck is going on?' he roared on seeing the boxes.

It was business as usual. Olivia steeled herself for the inevitable battle. Do not back down, she told herself again and again as she walked from the bedroom into the hall.

'What's going on? Why have you packed up my stuff?' Tall, dark and handsome in a grey suit and charcoal tie, Stephen would have turned any woman's eye if it hadn't been for the fury on his face. Almost speechless with temper, he gestured at the boxes and cases and asked: 'What is going on, Olivia?'

Determined not to betray how scared she was, she stared back. 'Until we sort out our differences, it makes sense that you move out.'

'Differences! What bloody differences?'

'The differences that mean you scream down the phone at me, effing and blinding simply because I did something with my life you didn't know about.'

'Oh, yes, your "job",' he sneered, draping his suit jacket over the hall chair.

'That, Stephen, is my point. I have a new job and it's none of your business. I want you to move out. I want a trial separation, it's not open to discussion. Don't try to bully me.'

'You can't throw me out of my own house,' he said, outraged. 'I bought it, it's mine.'

'Is it?' she said coolly. 'I seem to recall my parents giving us twenty percent of the purchase price as a wedding present. Doesn't that mean I have a bigger stake in it than you?'

He shook his head impatiently. 'Let's get back to the main issue here. You're just fooling around like this because you want this job and I don't approve.' He advanced and took her hand in his, a pleading expression on his face now. 'We can talk about it, if it means that much to you. I don't approve . . .'

'Stephen.' She wrenched her hand away from his. 'I don't *need* your approval. I'm an adult, and I'm sick to the teeth of you bossing me around as if I'm some sort of half-wit. I'm not. I'm not Mother Hen or Dopey Olivia. I'm a person and you are no longer controlling my life. You're domineering, aggressive, and it's got to stop.'

Stephen sat down on a chair as if his legs had lost their strength and he needed to sit before he fell. He seemed genuinely amazed, astonished that she could see his behaviour as anything other than justified.

'But I love you! I only want what's right for you,' he protested. 'I only tell you what to do so I can protect you, take care of you.'

'I married *you*, Stephen, I didn't want to marry a force of nature. That's what you're like: a tornado or a tidal wave. You engulf everything that gets in your way. "Protecting" me means babying me, treating me like a kid. You never ask me what I want to do, you totally ignore my needs.'

'Needs?' he said, stung. 'I know where you've been getting all of this. From those bloody women's magazines with their "relationship" sections. *How to whip your man into shape – tell him he's a force of nature and doesn't listen to your needs.* God, that crap makes me sick! It's all psycho-babble anyway.'

Olivia felt herself weakening. It was so difficult, standing up to Stephen after all these years. Just then, she heard a noise and whirled around in time to see Sasha's terrified face peering around her door. One plump hand clutched her new elephant to her face; her thumb was lodged firmly in her mouth. She looked like one of those children you saw in newspaper photos about domestic abuse: trauma-tised and scared.

Olivia felt the final vestiges of fear chip off like the last bits of bright varnish from a nail.

'The final reason I want you to go is that you scare our daughter. When I disagree with anything you say, or when I don't immediately do what you've ordered, you go berserk. You change, fly into a rage. That rage terrifies her and me. I grew up in a house where I was always afraid: afraid my parents would get pissed and go crazy after me; afraid there'd be no money for food or bills; afraid of what terrible things my mother would say to me when she was in a rage.' She could remember it all so vividly. The terror of sitting in the kitchen when Sybil was in full flight – you never knew who'd be blamed for what or why. Waiting for bombs to fall in wartime must have been similar. You could hear it coming: you just didn't know where it would land.

'I don't want Sasha to go through all that,' Olivia said.

'I don't drink,' protested Stephen, looking strangely vulnerable for the first time.

'That only makes it worse,' she said simply. 'You have no excuse except your own total lack of control and the fact that anyone has dared to go against your wishes. We're all screwed up in some way, Stephen, we all have our demons and insecurities. But you can't see that about yourself. You think you're perfect. You're not and you need help.'

'Help?'

'Yes, help. To make you understand that you've got to take responsibility for your own temper. What happens when you hit Sasha or me?'

'I'd never do that.' The muscles in his jaw were corded with tension. 'You know that, Olivia.'

'How do I know that? I never know when you're going to change from Dr Jekyll into Mr Hyde so how do I know you'll never get violent? You have so much rage in you, Stephen. I don't want to put up with it anymore. You should leave. Perhaps when you face up to your problems, we might have a marriage.'

She wasn't being entirely truthful. She'd never been afraid he'd hit her. He'd never even touched her. But telling him she was afraid of it was the most shocking thing she could think of and it had certainly worked. Stephen looked shocked out of his mind.

'I'm sorry,' he said, 'I never meant to . . . Please, Olivia, don't let it end this way. I love you, and I love Sasha.'

'I love you too, but I don't know if I can live with you anymore. It would be better if you moved out, then we can decide if we do want to be together.'

He looked like a broken man. 'What about Sasha?'

'She's your daughter, I'm not stopping you seeing her. But I don't want her living with us when our relationship is so appalling. I don't want her to suffer that.'

'Maybe we could get counselling,' he said wildly.

'We can. But you've got to move out first, Stephen. If you won't, I will and I'll take Sasha with me. This is the only chance we've got to see if we can sort out our marriage. If you don't agree, I'll just file for divorce. End of story.'

In the end, he took only the suitcase he'd brought back from Germany. 'I'll come by tomorrow and pick up the rest,' he said hollowly.

'Fine.'

When he left, Olivia sat down on the chair in the hall and wept silently. Giant, heaving sobs wracked her body. She knew she had to do it but telling him to leave was the hardest thing she'd ever done. She loved Stephen, God help her, she still loved him.

CHAPTER TWELVE

Evie looked at the assembled bags and cases on the floor of her bedroom and realised that none of them was fit for a glamorous villa holiday in the south of Spain. None of them was fit for a wet weekend in a caravan park, for that matter, unless it was a seventies revival weekend where the older and grungier things looked, the better.

The delapidated old blue suitcase she and Tony had bought on their honeymoon had been stuck in a cobwebby corner of the attic for years and looked it. She used to store Rosie's old toys in the case and she'd had to jam a lot of headless dollies and threadbare teddies into an old laundry basket when she emptied it. But she couldn't throw them out, they were too precious for that. Every tattered but much-loved cuddly thing had a history behind it: the rabbit named Charlie that Rosie wouldn't get into her cot without; the little clown with the sad face she'd gone to sleep sucking until she was four. Evie dragged her attention back to the matter at hand – her lack of luggage.

The enormous barrel bag she and Rosie had taken to Ballymoreen for years wasn't in a much better condition than her honeymooning case. Only the black and red-edged weekender Olivia had given her one birthday in an attempt to get Evie to go away for a girls' weekend was fit to be seen. And that was so small it wouldn't have accommodated all the shoes she'd been considering taking.

The main problem, Evie knew, was all the advice she'd been given about the holiday destination.

Puerto Banus was stylish, the travel agent had said. Glamorous, one of Olivia's friends had pointed out, adding that everyone looked good with a tan.

'You'll feel like a bog woman beside those beautiful Spanish women,' said Lorraine's aunt mournfully.

Out of the three options, Evie was putting her money on Lorraine's aunt's forecast. She had nothing stylish and had never had anything close to the peanut butter tan Olivia's friend seemed to sport permanently. Which meant she'd almost definitely feel like Bog Woman on holiday.

'You can take the woman out of the bog but you can't take the bog out of the woman,' she muttered to herself forlornly.

Consequently, with all this contrasting advice, she had panicked over what to take and decided simply to take everything even vaguely summery. Plenty of non-summery things were also going on the basis that Ireland's climate meant Evie didn't have a vast summer wardrobe and just wore her winter clothes without the jumpers and opaque tights.

It was a glorious Wednesday evening, three – well, two and a half – days before she and Rosie were leaving for Spain: three days in which to transform herself from an ordinary office worker into a glamorous jet-setter who'd look at home sipping cocktails poolside and asking for *cafe con leche, por favor*.

Evie stood in her bedroom, arranging and rearranging the piles of clothes on the speckled duvet, valiantly trying to make each pile smaller by rejecting things that were too similar.

She'd never known she had so many pale pink T-shirts.

There were nine of them in varying degrees of washed-outness. Somebody must have told her once that pale pink suited her.

Holding one up to her face and looking critically in the mirror, she decided they'd been wrong. Pale pink made her look like a Beatrix Potter piglet. All she needed was a frilled mob cap and she'd have looked at home beside Mrs Tiggywinkle, which wasn't exactly the look she was going for.

'Shit!' cursed Evie with unaccustomed venom. She rarely swore but today just couldn't help herself.

The mellow July sun flooded in through the half-open windows and the scent of next door's freshly mown lawn mingled with the perfume of her aromatherapy burner which was overloaded with lavender in the hope of relaxing Evie. Some hope. Only serious tranquillisers could do that, she decided grimly. The holiday was a mistake, that was the problem. It wasn't simply her lack of clothes or lack of suitcases: it was her complete lack of self-control. She should never have agreed to go to Spain with her father, Vida and Max. What had she been thinking of? It was bad enough avoiding Max at home – how could she avoid him when they were staying in the same house?

OK, so he was only going to be there for two days as he was arriving at the villa on Thursday and she was leaving the following Saturday. But she'd still have to see him, to talk to him, to spend time with him.

How could she do that without making it terribly obvious that she was crazy about him? That she longed to talk to him; to sit with one hand on his thigh as they watched the sunset? Even though he was a terrible rake who went through women faster than a rock 'n' roll band did groupies.

Evie examined the denim mini skirt she'd found at the back of her wardrobe and had tried it on in desperation. It looked awful: so did she.

Her dark hair was lank and badly in need of a haircut, her skin was pale from too many hours spent in the office and she had the beginnings of a PMT spot the size of Texas on her forehead. It would be hard enough having to see Max without having to look terrible into the bargain.

But she couldn't suppress the excitement she felt at the thought of seeing him again. Banishing him from her life had been her only ammunition against him. She'd avoided Vida's birthday party with a fake case of 'flu because Max was going to be there, yet her sudden food poisoning had cleared up miraculously in time for dinner in their new house when she realised he wouldn't be present.

It was better not to see him, she'd told herself endlessly. That theory rang hollow on those hot, sweaty nights when she spent more time staring at the alarm clock than asleep. In her imagination, there was no escaping those flashing deep blue eyes. Night was when she thought about Max, giving him full rein in the hope that he'd remain one of her midnight fantasy heroes and would stop tormenting her by day as well. At night, she could remember every word he'd ever said to her and in a half-slumber, imagine his arms were around her, holding her, hugging her, making slow, passionate love to her.

In the daytime, she was ruthless with herself. Max was a rogue and she couldn't give up all the things she'd fought so long for simply because he'd waltzed into her life, nonchalantly assuming she'd dump her fiancé for a fling with him. And a fling was all it would be, she thought fiercely. After all she'd been through, Evie couldn't take that risk. Wouldn't take it.

'Does this top go with this skirt?' Rosie appeared at the

bedroom door, long bare legs clad in a pink pelmet of a skirt with her top half just about covered by a flimsy tie-dyed T-shirt that revealed her entire midriff. 'Of course, I've got to fake tan my legs,' she added, looking down at her slim brown limbs critically.

Thanks to a post-exam gift of three hundred pounds from her grandfather, Rosie had purchased an entire new wardrobe for her week in Spain. A cheap wardrobe of wondrously short and skimpy clothes that were youthfully sexy. Her mother shuddered at the thought of what the teenage male population of Puerto Banus would do when they saw Rosie wearing them. Or not wearing them, as the case may be. They were all so skimpy. One pair of shorts in particular looked like nothing more than a tiny pair of knickers and the thong bikini Rosie was so thrilled with would undoubtedly give anyone with a heart complaint severe palpitations.

'It's lovely,' Evie said truthfully, forcing herself to be honest about the skirt and not to say it was a pity they ran out of material when they were making it. 'But it's a bit short . . .' she couldn't help herself from saying.

'Oh, Mum, come off it.' Rosie threw herself on the bed, bouncing all of her mother's carefully folded piles of clothes as she did so. Lounging on one elbow with her legs swinging in time to the George Michael CD playing loudly in her bedroom, Rosie began to extract things from the piles and rearranged them in different combinations.

'Jeez, Mum, we're only going for a week. You're bringing tons. And this,' she said, holding up a white baggy T-shirt as if it was contaminated by Lassa fever, 'is terrible. You can't wear it. I don't know why you haven't turned it into a duster.'

Evie snatched it back. 'It's only three years old,' she retorted.

'A hundred and three,' Rosie replied. 'It doesn't matter how old it is, it's bloody awful on you.'

'Don't say bloody,' Evie corrected automatically as she pulled off her cardigan and dragged the white T-shirt over her head. Rosie was right: it was terrible. Baggy and shapeless. With her denim mini skirt on as well, she looked a complete slapper. All she needed was a pair of white stilettos, a tattoo and an ankle bracelet.

'See? It's terrible.' Rosie sat up purposefully and went through the rest of the clothes like a Medici poisoner searching for hemlock. 'You need some new things, Mum.'

For a laugh, Evie slid into a purple paisley midi-dress that hadn't even been that fashionable the first time round, smeared red lipstick on her lips and posed for her daughter. 'Surely not,' she simpered. 'This is all I need. A beach cover up by day and an evening gown by night!'

'Ugh!' Rosie was suitably disgusted. 'I've never seen that before.'

'It was in the attic. I thought I might find something that had come back into fashion,' Evie said. 'Hotpants did and flares. You never know what's going to be fashionable again.'

Rosie gave the dress a withering teenage stare. 'That thing is hideous and if it came back into fashion, I'd become a nun.'

'Sister Rosie, make us a cup of tea,' Evie joked, cheered by the presence of her daughter. When she was with Rosie, she didn't fret madly about Simon, Max and the future of her world.

'Not until I've gone through this junk,' Rosie pronounced. 'You can't take a quarter of this stuff. It's ancient! I've only spent some of Grandpops' money. How about if I give it to you to buy something nice? You deserve it.'

Eyes filled with tears, Evie kissed the top of Rosie's head softly. 'You are a wonderful daughter, you know that?'

'But you still want me to trudge downstairs and make you tea, huh?' she laughed, unfurling her long legs and dancing to the door as George Michael hit the high spots with 'Too Funky'.

'Choccie biscuits?' she asked.

'No,' Evie yelled after her, although she longed for one. She didn't want to look fat by the pool. Well, any fatter. Her bum and thighs were enormous: they got bigger every time she looked at them. She'd have to borrow a couple of sarongs from Olivia, who kept saying Evie was mad and that she wasn't in the slightest bit fat. Typical Olivia. Being kind as usual. Evie ripped off the purple dress and cricked her neck trying to gaze at her bottom in the mirror.

'Horrible,' she muttered to herself. So much for the anti-cellulite diet. She went on to the landing and leaned over the banisters.

'Rosie, I've changed my mind. Bring up some choccie biscuits, will you?'

Saturday morning dawned ominously dark. Clouds swollen with rain loomed like giant blackberries over Dublin airport as Evie drove up and parked the car in the long-term car park.

'We're miles away. Nearer Belfast airport than Dublin. Couldn't you have parked nearer?' grumbled Cara, lugging her sister's giant suitcase out of the boot and looking at the unfinished surface of the car park over which it would be hell to drag the cases.

'No,' snapped Evie, feeling nervy and irritated for some reason. 'The short-term car park is much more expensive, Stephen says. I'm not made of money, you know.'

Rosie, having listened to the two of them snapping like baby alligators during the drive across the city, was fed up.

'Stop bitching,' she said with rare sharpness. 'We're going on holiday, the first proper holiday of my adult life, I might add,' she added dramatically, 'and I want to enjoy it, not listen to you squabbling. *I'm* supposed to be the teenager, not you two.'

Head held high, she swept off, dragging her fit-to-burst bag as if it weighed nothing, long legs undulating in her faded denims, worn red espadrilles flopping off her heels with each step.

Chastened, Cara and Evie stared at each other for a moment before breaking into peals of laughter.

Evie dropped her smaller bag back into the boot and put her arms around Cara. 'I'm sorry. She's right. We're like a couple of old biddies fighting over the remote control.'

Cara giggled. 'Can't you just see us in fifty years, sharing a house with seventeen cats and nothing but the memory of our lost loves between us?'

'Do we have to wait fifty years?' asked Evie blank-faced, suddenly thinking how nice it would be to live with Cara and Rosie: safely, happily, with no horrible decisions about weddings and men or anything to torture her day and night.

'Why?' Cara was startled out of her Patsy and Edwina from *Ab Fab* reverie. 'What about Simon and the wedding? You don't fancy living with me now? You always say I'd drive you round the bend.'

'Lord, no,' her sister said briskly, recovering. 'Only kidding. We'd murder each other. You'd be better off with Ewan, wouldn't you?'

It was Cara's turn to look guarded. 'Yeah,' she said morosely.

Now wasn't the time to tell her sister it was all off between her and Ewan. Maybe later, over some Sangria by the pool. They could talk then. She brightened up at the thought of letting the sun warm her limbs and burn the memory of Ewan out of her skull. Although it would have to be very powerful to do that.

Two weeks of going out on the booze with Zoë hadn't accomplished it, so why did she think seven days in Spain would achieve what so many pints of beer had failed to do? Miserable again, but hiding it, she hauled her luggage into the airport.

The departures hall was like Henry Street on the first day of the January sales. There were people everywhere, manically rushing around with suitcases, trollies and push-chairs. All brightly dressed in anticipation of arriving in some scorching far-flung destination: all looking ludi-crously out of place in Dublin where the rain had finally decided to pelt down like some Biblical curse.

'It's certainly wet enough to be tropical,' Cara remarked, shaking rain off her black curls like a soaked dog just out of the bath. 'Pity it's so cold we've all got goose bumps. I can't wait to feel real Spanish heat.'

'I'm going to start queuing for check-in,' Evie said. 'It takes hours for charter flights. Will you wait here and keep an eye out for Rosie? Although, on second thoughts, she's probably gone off to Knickerbox to buy another bikini. Dad gave her money for clothes and she's bought four already.'

Cara prodded Evie's enormous borrowed suitcase. 'And you've just brought a couple of things yourself then,' she teased.

Her sister grinned. 'I couldn't make my mind up so my entire wardrobe is in there. If the airline loses it, I'll be naked for the rest of my life!'

'Simon will be a happy man on honeymoon, if that's the case,' Cara remarked drily, privately thinking that her future brother-in-law was such a wet, his eyes would probably stay glued to the cricket on the TV even if Evie stood in front of him starkers for hours on end and writhed around like a stripper.

'Now,' began Evie, starting to worry about her daughter's whereabouts in this massive, holiday-crazed crowd, 'if you can't find her, meet me in ten minutes in the queue and we'll have her paged . . .'

'Don't worry,' Cara said gently, not wanting to start a row and knowing that worrying was second nature to her sister. 'I'll find her. There's one advantage to being tall – you can see over crowds.'

They parted, Evie heading into the throng of travellers with her laden-down trolley and Cara striding determinedly in the direction of the shops, staring around looking for her niece.

Evie's trolley had a mind of its own, lurching in every direction but the one she was pushing it in.

'Sorry, sorry,' she gasped, barely avoiding colliding with a gang of golfers blindly steering club-laden trollies in the direction of check-in.

'If that's the way you drive, I'm not getting in the hire car with you,' said a deep voice, rich with amusement.

Evie, turning her head to see where the voice was coming from, cannoned into a barrier.

'I'll drive,' said Max, appearing beside her.

She furiously wrenched the trolley around like Ralf Schumacher on the chicane at Monza. 'It's my trolley,' she shrieked, utterly unnerved by the sight of Max, cool and holiday-ish in jeans and a comfortable denim shirt, looking for all the world as if he'd just stepped out of a Ralph Lauren advert.

'What are you doing here?' she demanded. Then, realising he didn't have any luggage with him, she assumed he'd come to see his mother off. Which was nice

402

but odd, particularly as he'd be seeing them all in Spain in five days.

'I drove out here and had a sudden longing to hop on a plane,' he deadpanned.

Evie blinked in disbelief.

'I'm flying to Malaga with you,' he continued.

'You said you were only coming for the weekend,' she accused, suddenly wishing she'd bothered with make-up. She'd been planning to plaster herself in Olivia's Lancôme eyeshadow palette on the plane before they landed.

Max shrugged. 'I changed my mind.'

'You promised you were only going for a few days, not the whole week,' she added.

'Did I?'

He could look irritatingly remote when he wanted to, Evie thought. He was doing it now: looking distant and blank. But he was, she realised, very pleased with himself.

'You did,' she hissed.

Gazing at her flushed little face, dark hair tied back in a tight pony-tail, the purple shadows under her eyes and not a scrap of make-up on her face except for hastily applied coral lipstick that gleamed on that full lower lip, Max appeared to change his mind.

'I need a holiday too,' he said casually. 'I didn't think you'd object that much, Evie. After all, I won't be able to get away again until after Christmas with the shooting schedule. We've been asked to come in on another production which will mean either myself or my business partner have to go abroad to sort it out . . . sorry, I'm boring you.' He flashed her a glittering smile.

You could never bore me, she found herself thinking.

'I just thought a week by the pool now would be perfect,' he added. 'If you wait here, I'll find my mother and Andrew. They were going to the bureau de change.'

403

'OK,' she muttered as he left abruptly. Evie couldn't think what else to say. The flurry of emotions she'd felt at the sight of him retreated before this reasonable explanation. Yet, paradoxically, she felt upset that he hadn't changed his plans to see her, that he hadn't turned up at the airport because he was desperate to go on holiday with her. That was the stuff of her sweaty night-time dreams: Max insane to spend time with her; Max rubbing sun cream into her golden-brown skin as she lay by the pool, soaking up sweltering heat from both the sun and him.

'I'll just undo your bikini top so I can do your back properly,' he murmured, as Evie lay face down on the lounger on a soft blue towel. His strong warm hands had been caressing her for at least five minutes, rubbing the coconut-scented cream into her toned, peanut butter-coloured body in languorously slow strokes.

She moved under his expert hands, like a great cat allowing itself to be touched by human hands for the very first time, letting the pleasurable sensations shimmer deliciously through her body. Apart from his caressing voice, the only sound breaking the tranquil peace of siesta-time was the distant hissing noise of the water sprinklers showering the lush lawn to the left of them with cool water. The villa was silent – everyone else was asleep, leaving Max and Evie alone by the white-tiled Moroccan-style pool. Alone for the first time.

'You don't mind?' he said, already untying the knot of her tiny white bikini at the nape of her neck before his fingers did the same with the knot halfway down her back. 'But you want an all-over colour, don't you?'

'Yes,' she breathed as his hands massaged Factor 10 into her flesh, fingers splaying as they travelled down her rib cage, exquisitely close to the curve of her breasts.

'You're so beautiful,' he said huskily. 'I never dreamed you

*had such a beautiful body beneath those baggy clothes you
wear. Why do you hide yourself?'*

*She knew she had to do it now. Evie moved sinuously,
sitting upright and facing him, hands holding the minuscule
white triangles over her breasts. His eyes were as hot with
wanting as hers were; he needed her just as much as she
needed him. Knowing this, she let her hands and the bikini
drop finally, feeling a flush of passion in her belly as his
eyes roamed over her naked flesh, staring with growing
hunger at her full breasts with their erect nipples aching for
his touch.*

One large, tanned hand reached out towards her . . .

'Aaagh!' Evie's shriek made all the people within twenty
yards of her stop what they were doing immediately and
stare open-mouthed in her direction.

'Evie!' cried Cara, shocked, jerking back the hand that
had just touched her sister's shoulder. 'Are you OK? You
looked like you were in dreamland.'

'I'm fine,' Evie gasped. She could hardly say she'd been
having the most deliciously erotic fantasy imaginable and
that Cara had jerked her back to reality. 'I'm just tired,' she
fibbed. 'I almost dozed off.'

'You'll never guess who's here,' Cara said excitedly.
'Max! He's coming for the whole week after all.'

Talk of the devil, Evie thought, as the hero of her fantasy
appeared behind her sister, towering over Cara. He was
devilish, a demon who always knew when to turn up to do
the most damage to her vulnerable heart.

Evie briefly wondered if Max could tell what she'd been
thinking. It had been so intense, she felt as if her face must
betray her excitement somehow.

He smiled at her, a lazy, confident smile, as if he *knew*.

He couldn't. It's just that he is so sure of himself, Evie
thought crossly, so bloody sure.

405

'Here,' she said, thrusting the trolley at Cara but staring up at Max defiantly. 'You take care of this for a moment. I'm going to phone Simon.'

With a toss of her pony-tail, she whizzed around on her new cork wedged-heel sandals and stormed off in the direction of the phones.

Simon was gratifyingly pleased to hear from her.

'Evie,' he said, delighted at the sound of her voice. 'I was sure you wouldn't ring me until tonight at the villa. Have you checked in yet? There are terrible queues for those charters.'

'We're checking in soon,' she reassured him. 'Cara's minding the luggage and, yes, the queue is a mile long.'

'I bet you didn't leave until after nine this morning,' he said fussily. 'I said you should leave earlier than nine o'clock if you wanted to get decent seats.'

Don't be such an old woman, she wanted to say. Instead, she replied mildly that the flight wasn't until half-twelve and they had loads of time to spare.

'I miss you already,' he said gloomily. 'I should have gone with you but I'd never get the time off. We're so busy right now at work.'

'I miss you too,' Evie said automatically and not altogether truthfully. Then she felt guilty. How could she not miss her fiancé? He'd generously told her to go off on a week's holiday without him, without once implying she should be saving her days off for when they were married so they could *both* jet off for a break. Simon was so good to her, so kind.

'I do love you,' she said impulsively. 'When I get home, it'll only be five weeks to the wedding. Isn't it exciting?'

'Yes, darling. Now don't have too wild a hen night in Spain,' he warned jokily. 'I don't want you running off with some handsome Spanish waiter!'

Evie joined in his laughter somewhat half-heartedly. Spanish waiters weren't the problem, she thought wryly. The danger was much closer to home. Poor, dear Simon would never for a nanosecond even dream that she'd fancy another man, which was why he'd made that crack about a handsome Spaniard.

Hanging up, after blowing lots of kisses down the phone, Evie went into the Ladies' and rinsed her hot face with cool water. Instinctively reaching into her handbag for her make-up to doll herself up, she stopped dead.

What are you doing? Plastering yourself in make-up to impress Max Stewart? she asked herself. A pale face with two bright spots of colour in the centre of her cheeks gazed wearily back at her from the mirror. A traitorous, trollopy face, she told herself fiercely.

Poor Simon didn't deserve a fiancée like her. He deserved a virtuous loving woman and that's what he was going to get. Redoing her pony-tail so that not one tendril of hair escaped to soften the almost nun-like effect, Evie swept out of the loo making more resolutions than a reformed alcoholic after a binge. I won't talk to Max, I won't flirt with Max. I'll be cool and distant. And phone Simon every day.

Her resolve strengthened, she marched towards the Malaga check-in desks. 'Watch out, Mr Stewart,' she murmured under her breath.

Evie was behaving very oddly indeed, Cara decided, flopping down on to a green chair beside Gate 26 and scrabbling around in her rucksack for the issue of *Company* she'd bought earlier. Evie had started being strange around the time Max had appeared on the scene, practically ignoring him in a manner that was verging on the rude.

Neither had she seemed very pleased to see Vida and their father when they arrived, out of breath and laughing after a scramble to get to the airport on time because they'd overslept.

'That's the last time I leave you in charge of the alarm clock,' Vida had teased Andrew affectionately.

'And whose fault is it that we were up so late?' he demanded archly.

They exchanged a private, utterly intimate glance and then started laughing again. Their closeness and obvious enjoyment of each other warmed Cara's heart. It was wonderful to see her father so in love and so happy.

Perhaps that was why Evie was snappier than a teething puppy. But she hadn't seemed *that* upset by the older couple's behaviour, Cara reflected. Apart from a tight-lipped comment that Vida could have told her Max was coming 'for the *whole holiday*', Evie hadn't appeared to notice her father and his new bride behaving like a couple of teenagers, always touching each other and exchanging long looks. It was clearly Max who irritated her, although Cara couldn't imagine why. He was so nice and had told Cara he wanted to sit beside her on the plane.

'Evie has the seat beside mine but maybe you two should swop so we can chat,' he'd said.

Cara didn't enlighten him with the news that Evie had already swopped, muttering that she wanted to read her book and didn't want to have to make conversation on the flight.

He and Rosie came into view; Max had obviously said something funny because Rosie was giggling hysterically.

'God, you'll have to get Max to tell you this story,' she giggled, sliding into the seat beside Cara. 'It's all about this actress and the things she wanted on location. Imagine – she wanted two kilos of handmade chocolates, a crate of bourbon, smoked salmon for her poodles, and Max found her on her hands and knees measuring the length of her trailer with a ruler to see if it was bigger than everybody else's!' She broke into peals of laughter.

'I can't tell you top-secret stories if you blab them immediately afterwards, you brat,' he said in pretend annoyance, sitting down on the other side of Cara and stretching out his long legs. He grinned at Rosie and Cara, white teeth lighting up his tanned, clever face.

God, he was gorgeous, Cara realised, suddenly struck by the thought that Max was friendly, kind and available. Gloriously available. And he liked her. *He* didn't think she was uptight, strange, and more neurotic than a roomful of therapy junkies. *He* hadn't told her she should have been a celibate. Correction, 'bloody celibate'.

The memory of that final, fierce row with Ewan flickered in her head like a video she couldn't stop playing.

'I don't know why you bothered going out with me in the first place,' he had said, forced out of his habitual cool. 'It's a game to you, Cara, a bloody game! I liked being with you, I still like being with you and I don't have a problem with letting people know that. But you don't want anyone to know we're going out. Nobody. I feel like you're ashamed of me or there's some weird thing going on in that weird head of yours and I can tell you, I've had enough of it. So goodbye.'

Goodbye, huh? After four months, a curt goodbye, was it? Well, she'd show him. Cara fought back the lump that swelled in her throat, threatening to make her gasp with misery. She'd show that damned Ewan Walshe she was no celibate.

Unbuttoning the top two buttons of her blue shirt so that a faint glimpse of creamy collarbone was visible above her white T-shirt, she leaned closer so that her shoulder was touching Max's.

'Sorry,' she said, not even vaguely meaning it. It was going to be a good holiday, she was sure of it.

★ ★ ★

The crowd around the baggage carousel in Malaga airport had practically disappeared, apart from a couple of elderly lady travellers who were sorting out their cases slowly and carefully, clutching tapestry vanity cases as if they contained the Hope diamond and a couple of Romanov tiaras. Cara sat on her barrel bag and took occasional slurps from her bottle of Coke. Rosie leaned against a pillar, eyeing up and being eyed up by a young mahogany-tanned airport security man. Vida and Andrew stood apart from the family, talking quietly to each other, seemingly unconcerned that the carousel had been rattling around for half an hour and there was no sign of either their or Evie's bags.

Tapping her foot in irritation, Evie watched as the carousel trundled on and an unclaimed, burst-open suitcase sailed past them for about the fiftieth time, the same pair of orange knickers sticking out at exactly the same angle.

'Maybe you should grab it, Mum,' Rosie called from her eyeing up position. 'Hopefully not everything in there is orange.'

Cara chuckled and Evie wondered which one of them she'd kill first: her daughter or her sister. Nobody seemed to care a damn that her luggage hadn't arrived.

Vida and Andrew were too insulated by love to care that they hadn't an item of clothing between them. Rosie was in exuberant form because this was her first grown-up holiday abroad and Cara was sleepily happy after four hours sitting beside Max, slurping back red wine and flirting with him over some lukewarm pasta and tunafish.

Across the aisle, Evie had pretended to be engrossed in her Jilly Cooper novel but she'd barely managed to read a couple of chapters what with listening to what the other pair were saying. There had been far too much whispering and laughing for her liking.

To her chagrin, Max had totally ignored her, apart from silently letting her go past him when they disembarked, a polite smile on his face. And now, to add insult to injury, her luggage was lost in the airport twilight zone and nobody gave a fiddler's. Evie didn't know whether to kick something with rage or burst into tears.

'The good news is that they've found your suitcases,' announced Max calmly, returning from his visit to the lost luggage department. 'The bad news is that they won't be here until the next flight arrives at nine o'clock tomorrow morning.'

'What?' squawked Evie.

'Relax,' he said calmly, 'they'll deliver everything to the villa.'

'Wonderful!' shrieked Evie, knowing she sounded like a fishwife and not caring.

'It'll be all right,' Max repeated in the same placating tone.

How could he be so calm? she raged inwardly. Because it wasn't his entire case full of swimwear, shorts and T-shirts that had gone AWOL. He wasn't the one wearing casual cream trousers that had got newsprint on them or a T-shirt that smelled as if it had been worn by a rugby international during a grudge match. How the hell was she going to go out to dinner tonight without fresh clothes? What about her toothbrush, knickers, moisturiser? She was about to explain all this heatedly when Vida sashayed up, looking remarkably unconcerned.

'Well, honey, what's the story?' she asked her son in her soft, American-accented voice. 'Breakfast in Dublin, lunch in Malaga, bags in Hong Kong?'

Mother and son laughed merrily. Evie ground her teeth.

'That's about the size of it,' joked Max. 'Seriously, Mother, they'll be here on the nine a.m. flight and they'll be delivered to the villa.'

411

Vida shrugged while Evie shook in outrage. How could anyone joke at a time like this? Vida was so bloody laid-back about the whole thing – didn't she realise what had happened?

'Lucky I've got this,' she said confidingly to Evie, indicating the small tote bag she carried. 'I've got so used to travelling and getting my luggage lost that I always bring a small bag with a few things in it. You know, pants and a change of clothes, toothbrush, that sort of thing. Your dad's got one too, so we can manage. I hate schlepping it around, but hey, it's useful. You can borrow from Cara, can't you, Evie?'

This time, she really thought she would cry with frustration. Yes, she *could* borrow Cara's stuff but it wasn't the same. She wanted *her own* things, her own T-shirt, her own moisturiser, her own toothbrush, her own grapefruit shower gel she'd treated herself to. She almost sobbed as she remembered the lovely fruity smell of it and how pleased she'd felt when she packed it. Now it was all ruined and nobody understood . . .

When Max slid his arm around her, she didn't experience that usual frisson of electricity: instead, his arm felt comforting, loving, somehow right. As if its rightful place wasn't clinging to some mini-skirted, perma-tanned blonde but wrapped around her, Evie.

'I'm sorry, we're just kidding around. I know there's nothing worse than losing your luggage,' he said gently, his breath fanning her ear as he leaned close. 'Mother hates it normally, she's just laid-back this time because she's so happy. The plane could have crashed and she'd be swimming with the sharks in the Atlantic, saying, "So what? I've got my overnight bag!" '

Evie laughed, a hiccuping sort of laugh, and let herself relax against Max's comforting body. She loved the feel of him. Big and solid, like a bear, yet graceful with it. As if sensing that she'd let her defences down and was relaxing, his arm wrapped itself around her, fingers tight on her waist.

OmiGod! Her spare tyre! Evie sucked her stomach in anxiously, wishing she could make her waist shrink. Why hadn't she stuck to the diet? And she must be hot and sweaty. Could he smell her? She sniffed the air near herself in horror, afraid she'd get a waft of BO. Why hadn't she brought any perfume with her – at least a quadruple blast of Anais Anais would overpower him so that he couldn't smell armpits that hadn't seen deodorant for hours.

'Come on, let's pick up the cars,' Max said, oblivious to her frantic sniffing and sucking in tactics. 'There's a guy waiting around the front with them. We'll stop off on the way so you can buy some clothes and toiletries. I hate borrowing other people's stuff and I'm sure you do too.'

Evie nodded.

'Lord, you smell great,' he said, breathing in the scent of her hair. 'A sort of fresh, fruity smell.'

Evie flushed with pleasure and relief. 'Apple shampoo,' she volunteered.

'Lovely,' he sighed, kissing the top of her head. 'I must stink like a long-distance runner. Sorry. How about we all have an hour in our rooms to beautify ourselves and then meet up for dinner, my treat?' He was walking her towards the airport doors as he spoke, still with one arm around Evie and the other steering his trolley as effortlessly as if he was steering a bowl of egg whites.

'That sounds lovely,' she said sincerely, and gazed up at him. 'Thank you, I was on the verge of screaming in there. I don't know why,' she added.

'Travelling makes people very, very strange,' Max pronounced. 'Look at that pair, for example.'

He raised his eyebrows in amusement as Vida and Andrew ambled out of the airport behind them, arms locked, oblivious to the world around them. Max grinned at the sight. 'What are the odds that the sun has a passionate effect on them and we don't set eyes on either of them until the end of the holiday?'

Evie giggled and realised she didn't mind if her father and Vida broke the wardrobe and the bed in their room jumping passionately from one to the other.

'That's not a bet I'd win, so I won't put any money on it,' she said primly.

'Not a gambling woman, then?' Max asked.

'No, never could afford it,' Evie admitted simply.

'I'll take you to the casino one night, you'll love it. It's fun,' Max promised. 'And you can get dressed up to the nines.'

'If I have any clothes,' she said mournfully, thinking of her lost luggage.

'If you don't,' he said, a wicked sparkle in his deep blue eyes, 'I'll buy you something devastatingly sexy to wear.'

That was when Evie felt the electric shock vibrate through her entire body. *Something devastatingly sexy to wear* . . . And take off, she thought longingly. Now there was a thought.

An hour later, she sat on the bed in her room, taking in the details of its high ceiling, cool white walls, terracotta-tiled floor and creamy muslin curtains rippling in the evening breeze. Richly carved Spanish wooden furniture gave the room an opulent feel, while the cerulean blue embroidered silken bedspread and soft cushions lent an air of sheer luxury.

The blue and white tiled bathroom was bigger than her kitchen at home and you could fit *two* people in the bath, if you felt inclined to. That wasn't even mentioning the balcony, which looked over an incredible vista, including a series of the prettiest white stucco villas set amid groves of orange trees, before your eyes reached the gleaming waters of the Mediterranean.

The balcony contained a sun lounger and a small white-painted iron table with two chairs which meant she could practically live in her bedroom, drinking in the sun that obviously bathed the balcony most of the day. It was a glorious room, in keeping with the glorious white villa, the most elegantly luxurious place Evie had ever stayed in her life. From the moment she'd stepped out of the car and breathed in the scent of the luscious crimson flowers that covered the entire walled courtyard at the front, Evie had felt as if she was living in a fairy tale.

She still felt slightly dazed by the whole trip, as if the sparkling, vivacious woman who'd sat in the front of the white Seat Toledo with Max had been a stranger. She hadn't been anything like the normal Evie Fraser, that was for certain. She'd been relaxed, happy and confident. It was like a drug running through her veins making her into a different person. Or maybe Max was the drug. Then, to arrive at this beautiful house set in the hills behind the Puerto Banus bull ring. Enclosed behind a high wall and with wooden gates, the villa looked like something from the Hollywood Homes of the Famous tour she'd seen on documentaries about Los Angeles.

Inside the gates, it was just as incredible: a verandah that stretched around the whole building, loungers and tall urns overflowing with succulent plants dotted at intervals around it; a pool and blossom-filled garden not a million miles away from the ones in Evie's fantasies; and a giant airy open-plan room that took up the entire lower storey of the villa containing a raised dining area, a marble miracle of a kitchen and a sunken seating area with huge floral sofas, wooden coffee tables and a giant stone fireplace should you feel cold.

'As if!' Rosie had said with delight when she'd seen it. 'Imagine being cold in Spain!' she enthused.

Oil paintings hung on the walls, pottery and silver treasures decorated each occasional table and the entire place reeked of being loved and lived in. Remembering the cramped one-bedroomed apartment she, Rosie and Cara had shared many years ago, with its consignment of cockroaches and a kitchen equipped for only the most basic cooking, Evie stared around the Villa Lucia in awe. This place must have cost Max a fortune. How could she repay him?

She'd thought they were going to some squashed little cottage where she, Rosie and probably Cara would have to share a twin room with somebody sleeping on a camp bed. This place was a bloody palace!

She stripped off her travel-stained clothes and stood under the shower until she'd washed away what felt like a ton of grime. In fact, the opalescent pink soap she'd picked up in the local supermarket had a subtle musky smell that she almost preferred to her grapefruit gel. And even though she didn't have her favourite apple shampoo, the almond-scented one she'd bought was just as good.

Wrapped in a giant creamy towel, Evie sat on her balcony and let the dying rays of the sun envelop her. She loved the sensation of the sun on her face and sat, eyes closed, face turned up skywards, for ages before suddenly realising she only had fifteen minutes to get ready. As if on cue, Cara marched into the room clutching several items of clothing that all seriously needed ironing.

'This is the best I can do,' she said apologetically, sinking on to the bed with her crumpled offerings.

Rejecting the peasant blouse in crimson because it was

far too bright, Evie held a sea green silk shirt up to her face and grimaced.

'Makes me look hungover,' she groaned.

Cara laughed. 'Then I'd better not wear it tomorrow when I plan to be *really* hungover. I'd look as if I was on the critical list.'

Cara's taste in tops was almost puritanical – lots of high-necked things that didn't cling. Her trousers were the same, baggy and unrevealing in the extreme. As Evie was so much shorter and of a totally different build, there was no way most of Cara's clothes would fit her. She'd look like a child after an hour in an adult's wardrobe because the sleeves and hems were all way too long.

The only garment that wouldn't make her look like a precocious child was Cara's new dress: a remarkably revealing mid-length sleeveless brown shift in crinkly viscose, the sort of thing that wasn't supposed to wrinkle, which was fortunate given Cara's packing technique of cramming everything in higgledy-piggledy and to hell with the creases.

'This new?' asked Evie, thinking it was years since she'd seen her sister wear anything with such a low-cut neck. She'd bet it looked stunning on Cara.

'Yeah,' Cara replied, 'I got it for the holiday, thought I'd break out and wear something a bit different. I'm not sure now. You'd be able to see my tonsils down the front.'

'Don't be daft. It'd be gorgeous on you, Cara. You should flaunt yourself a bit more. I'm glad to see Ewan is having a positive effect on you. I hate those bloody combats.'

Cara did not want to be drawn into a conversation about Ewan. 'Try it on,' she urged. 'It's a weird length on me so it's probably perfect for you.'

The dress wasn't the most flattering colour Evie had ever worn, as the combination of brown hair and brown dress was a bit overpoweringly chocolatey, unless you *wanted* to look like an éclair. But it fitted and certainly clung in all the right places, undulating around her small waist and flaring out over her hips to end in a swirl around her ankles.

'Sorted,' Cara said. 'I can't lend you shoes, I'm afraid.' She held up one bare size eight foot ruefully.

Fifteen minutes later, Evie was tottering along in a pair of what Cara had described as 'Rosie's fuck me sandals' when she'd seen them.

'She's only kidding, Mum,' a white-faced Rosie had hastened to point out, before shooting her aunt a killer look. 'They're fashionable, everyone's wearing them.'

Everyone must have bunions then, Evie decided, after a mere five minutes strapped into the shoes. It was like wearing shoe boxes attached to your feet with chicken wire. Still, they looked dressy and were about ten times more suitable than the cream loafers she'd worn on the plane. With lots of Olivia's precious Lancôme eyeshadow in place and her hair shining after a quick blast from Rosie's hairdryer, Evie felt ready for anything.

However, any confidence she'd been injected with on the trip from Malaga to Puerto Banus disappeared as if by magic when she stepped into Ristorante Regina. The style, glamour and effortless chic of the other female diners hit her like a Force Nine hurricane. Tanned, beautifully made up and looking as if they'd all just climbed out of Versace's window with a detour via Bulgari for jewellery, they made her feel instantly out of place.

The men were just as bad, all elegant and exquisitely dressed. Max blended in perfectly, handsome in grey trousers and a cream polo shirt that showed off his golden skin. Rosie looked glorious in a crimson mini dress, Cara was bolshie as usual in black combats and the striking sea

green shirt with her hair rippling down her back like a
Pre-Raphaelite maiden, and Evie – well, Evie felt as drab as
a mallard's wife in her dowdy brown dress. It had looked
OK in her bedroom; not marvellous, but not hideous
either.

Now, she wanted to rush into the nearest boutique,
throw her Visa card at the assistant and screech: 'Find me
something suitable to wear! I don't care about the cost!'
And dump Cara's dress in the nearest bin.

To make matters worse, their table wasn't in some
gloomy corner where Evie could hide behind a potted
plant or at least blend into the background. No. Their party
was escorted to a table in the middle of the restaurant,
where all the other glamorous diners could watch them.

Feeling as if she had headlice and everyone could tell,
Evie slid into her seat and immediately pulled the peach
linen napkin on to her lap. She wished she could pull it
over her head so nobody could see her.

Max immediately sat beside her, smiling broadly. 'You'll
love this place,' he said. 'The food is exquisite and the
people who run it are so friendly.'

If she hadn't been feeling so underdressed and out of
place, Evie knew she *would* have loved it. The restaurant
was so pretty, the walls a mélange of peach and
terracotta, with flowers, flourishing plants, beautiful
glassware and sepia-toned movie-star photographs adding
to the effect. As it was, she hid behind her huge menu
and studied it intently. She barely lowered it when a
beautiful blonde woman wearing what looked like a
Gucci jumpsuit entertained the whole table by telling
them the restaurant's specials for the night, switching
from English to perfectly accented Italian when she
named Italian dishes, and to Spanish when she named
Spanish dishes.

'There are more specials than dishes on the menu,' chuckled Max, as he went back to his. 'You pick something then they tell you about fifteen other gorgeous things you immediately decide to have instead.'

Despite all the exotic-sounding courses on the menu, Evie didn't feel in the slightest bit hungry any more. Peering around her, she spotted one elegant brunette in a grape-coloured silk sheath reaching for her pre-dinner drink: something in a pretty triangular glass with a couple of olives in it.

That was it – she'd have a Martini. They were classy and elegant, Evie sniffed. Nobody would think she was a bog woman when she was sipping a Martini.

'Vodka or gin?' inquired the waiter politely when she asked for it.

'Vodka,' Evie said recklessly, knowing that a moment's hesitation would let everyone know she'd assumed Martini came straight out of the Martini bottle. Did they put vodka in as well? Of course, they must, she realised, thinking that James Bond always wanted a vodka one.

'Olives or a twist?' inquired the waiter.

'Olives,' she smiled, since she wasn't sure what a twist was. When the drinks came Vida was regaling everyone with stories of her first time abroad with her first husband and how she'd drunk the tap water in her tiny Greek hotel room and been sick for three days. Acting nonchalantly, Evie took one confident sip of her elegant Martini and nearly choked. Christ! It tasted like neat vodka.

'I never had you down as a Vodka Martini woman,' Max murmured under his breath.

'Just love them,' said Evie gaily, taking another throat-burning gulp. The fiery liquid was doing its work: hitting her stomach like molten fire and spreading its heady warmth throughout her entire body. Halfway down the glass already, Evie, who practically never drank more than a couple of weak G & Ts, decided she'd have another.

If Max was surprised, he didn't say anything. Cara wasn't so reticent. 'Evie, you never drink Martinis,' she pointed out.

'Yes, I do,' she replied loftily. 'Maybe I'll borrow your hangover shirt tomorrow!' Going off into a fit of giggles, she finished her first drink, swallowed her olives and started on the next one.

Not even the delicious risotto she had for a starter could compete with the neat vodka swilling around inside her and Evie was soon well on the way to being plastered. No longer caring that she looked drab and uninteresting, she winked at her Martini waiter and waggled her empty glass at him.

'You sure you want another?' asked Max gently. He put an arm around her shoulders and she practically purred at his touch. 'Maybe you should have a glass of wine instead.'

Evie raised her eyebrows haughtily. 'I can decide for myself, you know. No man tells me what to do. I fancy a drink, that's all.'

Max grabbed the finger she'd been pointing at him. 'Fair enough, Ms Fraser, I don't want you to batter me. I simply don't want you to have a hangover in the morning.'

Smiling delightedly, Evie screwed up her eyes at him. 'Why?' she demanded coquettishly. 'Have you exciting plans for me?'

For a moment, Max dropped his guard and the laughing expression left his face. 'Yes,' he said simply. 'If you let me.'

The waiter set her third Martini in front of Evie. Feeling suddenly sobered up, nervous and excited all at the same time, she took a sip, anything to gain a moment's respite from the intense expression on Max's face.

This was dangerous, so dangerous. She'd said she wasn't

a gambling person and yet here she was gambling with her heart, her future and with the affections of two men as if she was a high roller in Monte Carlo.

'Not having another, Evie?' called Andrew across the table, shattering the intimate moment.

'Oh, Dad,' groaned Evie, 'not you too. Anyone would swear I was a teenager with her first shandy to listen to you lot!'

'Tell me about it,' muttered Rosie, who'd had terrible trouble persuading her grandfather to let her have one glass of wine.

'I thought we could drive to Ronda tomorrow,' Vida said, changing the subject because she sensed arguments looming. 'We can flop out by the pool in the afternoon but it'd be lovely to do some sightseeing in the cool of the morning.'

'Sounds brill,' said Cara, who got bored lying by the pool and was never too bothered about getting a tan. 'Doesn't it?' she said to Rosie.

'Yeah,' said Rosie, who longed to be mahogany immediately and had planned to stay glued to a sun lounger with her head in a book for hours each day.

Vida and Andrew began discussing what they'd read from their guide book about the region.

'Ronda is in a beautiful, mountainous position, and involves a nerve-racking road trip,' Max said, not looking at Evie. 'Not the sort of drive to take when you're hungover.'

She raised her glass defiantly and sank her third Martini, by now used to the fiery taste. 'Really?' she said cheerfully.

Bright lights hit Evie's head like the headlamps of an oncoming truck. They burned into her closed eyes, making her aware of the red hot needles being jammed into her skull.

'Go 'way,' she croaked, vainly trying to get hold of the sheet and cover her head with it to block out the agonisingly painful light.

'Mum, you have to get up,' Rosie shouted. At least, it sounded as if she was shouting.

'Don't yell,' Evie said weakly.

'I'm not,' yelled Rosie, opening the other curtain to let daylight pierce the gloom of the bedroom.

She sat on the bed beside her mother's inert form and looked at the grey face on the pillow. 'I've got some orange juice for you. I'm sure you're dead thirsty.'

Quite how her seventeen-year-old daughter knew that a hangover made you thirsty Evie didn't know, but she stored the information at the back of her head and decided she'd deal with that later. Right now, she had to cope with what was obviously either a brain haemorrhage or the worst hangover she'd ever had in her life. Lying prone, she felt as if the whole bed was vibrating, her body was bathed in a cold sweat and her skull was being Kango-hammered from the inside.

'We're going to Ronda in about half an hour, if you're up to it,' Rosie said. 'It's half-nine now. Vida and Grandpops got the most amazing little rolls and honey for breakfast and we had it on the verandah. I'd love to sunbathe,' she added, 'but Grandpops and Vida have their heart set on a sightseeing trip. Will you come?'

Evie moved a fraction in the bed and the Kango-hammer went into overdrive. 'God, no,' she moaned. 'I'm dying, Rosie. I can't go anywhere.'

'That's what Cara said,' her daughter replied prosaically. 'I've never seen you drunk before, Mum. You were very funny.'

Funny? Evie feebly tried to remember the night before. She could remember the Martinis and something funny about shrimps . . . oh, yes, feeding Max garlicky shrimps as if he was a seal, *insisting* he eat them as she dangled them over his mouth. And did she bang into the door on her way out? Or was it a person . . .

'It's just as well Max was here, otherwise we'd have never got you up the stairs,' Rosie explained, blithely unaware of how devastating her words were to her mortally embarrassed mother. 'Cara said she could probably manage to give you a fireman's lift but Max just picked you up as easily as if you were Sasha.' In her tangled sheets, Evie burned with shame. Max picking her up when she had passed out, after she'd been force feeding him shrimps and bashing drunkenly into people and doors on the way out. What must he think of her? He'd taken them all to that beautiful restaurant to celebrate their holiday and she'd got plastered and made a holy show of herself. Evie burrowed deeper into the bed with the disgrace of it all. She felt humiliated, demeaned and utterly mortified. She'd just remembered passing out once they got back to the villa.

'Are you dying?' asked Cara, loudly and irritatingly good-humouredly, plonking herself on the bed and jarring Evie's painful head.

'Yes,' she moaned. She lifted her head an inch from the pillow, opened her glued-up eyes again and asked: 'Was I dreadful? What did I do?'

'You were fine,' Cara said, 'apart from when you got up on top of the coffee table downstairs when you tried to pull up your dress to show us your appendectomy scar . . .'

'Oh, no,' Evie wailed before she realised she didn't have an appendectomy scar.

'Only kidding!' chuckled Cara. 'Listen, Evie, you got drunk, you passed out, you were fine. Big deal. We all do it.'

'I don't,' she said tearfully.

'Well, you obviously needed to or you wouldn't have,' Cara said with irrefutable logic.

'You were fine, Mum,' Rosie piped up. 'You had a big conversation with Vida about how you were sorry you were such a bitch to her before and that you didn't mind if, er . . .' Rosie hesitated, '. . . you didn't mind what she and Grandpops did.'

Not caring if her head fell off or not, Evie sat up shakily in bed and stared at her daughter. An appalling feeling that some part of this conversation was familiar crept over her.

'What were you going to add, Rosie?' she asked. 'What did I *really* say? Tell me.' Her voice was shrill with horror.

Rosie looked away cagily.

'Please,' begged Evie. It mightn't be as bad as she thought . . .

'What you actually said,' began Cara, 'was that you didn't give a fiddler's toss if they broke the bed and the wardrobe bouncing from one to the other having sex, so long as they were happy together.'

Evie's feverish hangover faded into an icy sweat and she lay down in the bed in shock. Being drunk obviously meant you parrotted things you'd thought earlier but would never have said aloud in a million years. If she'd said *that* to Vida, who knew what she'd said to Max under the truth drug effect of half a litre of vodka? Probably that she wanted him to take her to bed and make mad passionate love to her.

The fact that it was true was immaterial. That made it worse. *In vino veritas*, people always said. Now Max would know she was crazily in love with him, Vida would know she'd hated her for ages and the inhabitants of Puerto Banus would know she was Ireland's Bog Woman of the Year, incapable of going anywhere even vaguely sophisticated without carrying on like some dopey heifer who'd never been out of Bally-go-backwards before. That was it: she wanted to die. Now, as soon as possible, before she had to face Vida, her father or most especially Max, ever again.

'Is Evie coming with us?' called Andrew from the bottom of the stairs.

'No,' Cara yelled back. She got off the bed and kissed her sister on the forehead. 'We'll see you later, sis.'

Evie wished everyone would stop yelling. Didn't they know she had a hangover?

'Are you sure you're all right on your own?' asked Rosie anxiously, perching beside her. 'I'll stay with you, Mum. You look as if you need cheering up.'

Evie managed a weak smile. She'd feel a complete failure as a mother if her drunken behaviour meant Rosie had to miss a sightseeing trip on the first day of her holiday. 'I'm fine, darling, really. I just need some sleep and I'll be right as rain when you get back, I promise.'

Rosie left reluctantly, after making sure Evie had a big glass of orange juice beside her and some fruit by the bed in case she got hungry. Some hope, Evie thought, eyeing the basket of grapes, apricots and peaches. Just looking at a peach could make her projectile vomit like the kid from *The Exorcist*.

When she heard the front door slam, Evie sank back into her pillows with relief. She needed to be on her own to cope with the embarrassment and her hangover.

She drank her orange juice thirstily, barely tasting the just-squeezed juice as it rushed down her throat, slaking the hangover thirst. No sooner had she finished the last drop than she became aware that orange juice wasn't the right thing to drink with an acidic stomach.

Feeling the bile rise in her throat, she dragged herself out of the bed, staggered into the bathroom and was sick over and over again. Her stomach hurt and her throat was raw from puking. She was so tired, she sat clutching the toilet bowl for support, wondering if she'd ever get the energy to stand up.

'How's the patient?' said a voice.

Max! He hadn't gone with the others after all. Had he heard her puking?

'Go away,' croaked Evie, so weakly and feebly that he barely heard. She wanted him to leave her to her misery. But instead of going away, he marched into the room, saw her on the bathroom floor through the wide open door and hurried in to comfort her.

'You poor baby,' he crooned, hugging her, regardless of the fact that she smelt hot, sweaty and sick.

Another spasm grabbed Evie and she had no option but to retch again, this time with Max's strong arms supporting her.

'That's right, Evie, get it all out of your system. You'll feel OK when it's all gone.' She sank back on to the floor, too sick to feel embarrassed. At least whoever had dragged her clothes off the night before had put a T-shirt on her, so she wasn't naked. But with her hair plastered to her head and her face green, she might as well have been. She certainly felt vulnerable and bare enough.

'Sit there and I'll clean you up,' Max said, his voice as gentle as if he was talking to a small child or a frightened animal. He soaked a face cloth in cool water and gently washed Evie's face, neck and hands with it until she felt marginally better.

'Your T-shirt's a bit manky,' he said. 'I'll get you a clean one of mine.'

He returned quickly with a soft marl grey T-shirt, a small tablet and a glass of water with some grainy powder dissolving inside.

'Maxolon, perfect for your stomach, and this is some-thing to replace the lost salts in your body,' he explained, gesturing to the glass. 'I'll look away while you pull off your T-shirt and put on mine.'

She was so weak she'd almost have let him change her clothes, but she didn't. As she pulled his T-shirt over her head, a faint hint of the cologne she always associated with him filled her nostrils. A fresh, clean smell, like seawater on a warm summer's day. She breathed it in, her heart tender with longing. It felt wonderfully comforting to be wearing his clothes.

If this was the closest she was going to get to him, it was still wonderful.

Max made her drink the water and take the tablet before he picked her up and carried her back to bed. She felt too weak to reflect on the fact that he must have carried her like this the night before when she was roaring with drink and had passed out. Tucking her in like she used to Rosie, he kissed her on the forehead tenderly. 'Sleep for a couple of hours, my darling, and you'll feel much better. Then, I'm getting you up and making you something to eat.'

'I'll never eat again,' she said weakly.

'Yes, you will, after a few hours and those tablets, you'll feel fine and be ravenous.'

He shut the curtains, blocking out the sun to Evie's relief.

'Thank you,' she said, even in her weakened state unbelievably touched by how kind he was being to her.

Max didn't reply. He merely blew a kiss to her and left the room quietly. Snuggled up in his T-shirt, Evie let Max's face fill her thoughts. He was so kind, so sensitive. Imagine him holding her as she had her head down the loo. Not many people would do that for someone other than their own child.

She certainly couldn't imagine Simon doing it. He was the queasiest person imaginable: hated the smell of hospitals and nearly got sick at the sight of blood.

But then, Simon wasn't Max, was he?

The next time she woke up it was midday and she felt a hundred times better. Her head still hurt but the Kangohammer was gone. So was the nausea and the sense that the entire bed was quivering like a jelly.

Tentatively, Evie stretched one leg to the floor and levered herself into a sitting position. She felt weak but her skull didn't threaten to explode and her stomach felt almost normal.

Grateful that the worst was over, she padded into the bathroom and ran a bath. The restorative powers of the warm water soothed her aching body and by the time she was wrapping herself in one of the big towels, she felt quite good.

A soft tap on the door made her jump nervously.

'It's me,' said Max, 'with breakfast or lunch, whatever you want to call it.'

He laid the tray on the small iron table on the sun-filled balcony and Evie was amazed to find she was hungry. The scent of the coffee and the aroma of the mound of succulent scrambled eggs made her stomach contract. Silently, Max laid places for two people before sitting down with his back to the sun facing Evie. Strangely enough, she didn't feel in the least uncomfortable even though she was only wearing a huge bathtowel wrapped around her body, with her still damp hair hanging limply on her shoulders.

Max had seen her at her worst – plastered drunk and puking desperately into a toilet bowl. Washed and clad in a towel was an improvement, surely? She grinned to herself at the thought of what Lorraine and all the girls at

Wentworth Alarms would do if they saw her now, sitting undressed with the most gorgeous dark hunk imaginable.

'You lucky cow!' Lorraine would certainly screech delightedly. Evie found she couldn't keep the laughter to herself and it bubbled out of her.

Max raised one eyebrow. 'Have you been slurping back the vodka again?' he joked.

This made Evie laugh even harder. 'No,' she gasped, pulling the edges of her towel together as it threatened to come undone. 'I'm just thinking how this looks.' She went off into howls of laughter again.

'You, me in a towel, having late breakfast.'

'For it to look really bad, you should let your towel drop and I should eat my scrambled eggs off you,' pointed out Max, pouring coffee. 'Then you could shriek a bit in passion and we'd see the neighbours peering out of their windows to find out what was going on. The non-resident neighbours,' he added. 'The Spanish ones are so laid-back, they'd just shrug and smile to think that the beautiful Irish *señorita* was having fun.'

Evie grinned broadly. She *was* having fun, although a couple of hours ago she wouldn't have believed she'd ever have fun again.

'Was I terrible last night?' she asked, picking up her fork.

'Forget last night and eat up,' chided Max.

'I know I was,' Evie said, through a mouthful of eggs. 'God, these are delicious. I want to say I'm sorry, Max. I never drink Martinis, I don't know what came over me.' She grimaced. 'Ever heard the old joke about how some people have to be taken to certain places twice – once to go and once to apologise?'

'Forget it,' he repeated. 'You needed to let your hair down. Eat up because we're going out.'

'But I've no clothes,' she protested.

'Your suitcase arrived first thing this morning and I brought it upstairs. Cara dragged it into your room earlier.'

'I never even noticed it,' Evie groaned, 'I must have been in a bad way. Where do you want to go and what about the others?' she asked. 'They'll be back soon and they'll expect us to be here and . . .'

Max touched her face tenderly with one hand, tracing the curve of her cheek with infinite gentleness. 'You've had to spend too much of your life looking after other people,' he said, his voice as soft as his hand. 'This is your holiday too. I want you to enjoy yourself, just have fun. We'll leave a note saying we'll be back later. Rosie will hardly come to any harm with your dad and my mother, will she? The white slave trade doesn't get going until at least midnight!'

Evie wondered if the pretty backstreets of Marbella would have looked as lovely if she had seen them with someone else, someone other than Max? Wandering slowly through winding streets, past orange-tree-filled courtyards and little shops selling gorgeous blue and white pottery, the afternoon slipped by in a blur.

She wasn't sure how it had happened – perhaps it was when the kids on bikes had sped dangerously fast down one narrow lane, so that Max had to pull her safely out of their way – but he was holding her hand. Not loosely, the way Simon did when he briefly forgot his motto of never demonstrating affection in public and held on to her tensely. Max's strong fingers curled around Evie's small hand in a way that felt very different from when Simon did it.

They walked like that for ages, looking in shop windows, admiring the architecture and talking. They talked about everything imaginable, with just one exception: what was happening to them. Evie didn't want to break the magic

431

spell by discussing how she felt or mentioning Simon's name. Not that he was at the forefront of her mind, exactly. But she couldn't help but think about him when they passed a jewellery shop crammed with ginormous engagement rings. She was getting married in a few weeks' time, Evie realised dully, and here she was having the most wonderful time of her life with a man who wasn't her fiancé. A man she was crazy about.

She couldn't think about that now; she'd blank it out and deal with it later. Just enjoy the moment, she told herself, desperately wanting to break the habit of a lifetime and stop worrying. And, incredibly, she managed it. Simply being with Max made her block out all the anxious, tense feelings. She let them go and let herself drift off into the pleasure of the here and now.

After they'd strolled along the beachfront and had a cup of coffee in a tiny bar listening to the sea lapping gently against the sand, they walked back up to where they'd parked the car.

On an impulse, Evie turned to Max. 'Why don't we go to dinner ourselves here, have something early instead of waiting to go back to the villa? The others won't mind. We'll phone and say what we're doing.'

The gleam in Max's eyes was her answer.

Andrew answered the phone, saying he was exhausted after practically an entire day spent sightseeing instead of the planned couple of hours. 'Vida was navigating and we took a wrong turn, nearly ended up heading for Madrid. We're all shattered and are thinking of just nipping out for a pizza in that place near the Andalucia Plaza. When will you be back? Will we bring home a takeaway for you?'

'No, Dad, that's kind of you but don't bother. Max and I have been shopping in Marbella and we're hungry, so maybe we'll grab something to eat here,' Evie said, trying to sound blasé.

'OK. I'm glad to see you two are getting on after all,' her father confided in a low voice. 'It means a lot to me that you've accepted Max. He's Vida's only family, you know. I've got you three girls. Anyway,' his voice returned to normal, 'I'll see you later.'

Evie hung up, feeling like a teenager who'd just got away with lying about being at her friend's house doing home-work so she could see her boyfriend.

Giddy with the delight of spending more time with Max, she chattered away nineteen to the dozen as they walked, hair swinging on her shoulders and her eyes shining.

She looked beautiful, Max thought, watching her animated face as she chattered eagerly, huge hazel eyes alight with energy. Flicking back strands of hair as she talked, Evie was like a little whirlwind, lively and fascinating. How much more relaxed she looked when the weight of the world was off those narrow shoulders, Max realised. How he wanted to take away all her worries and make her look like this all the time: happy, carefree and able to enjoy life. He felt there were so many things he didn't know about Evie, things nobody knew. She was too proud.

Max could tell that she'd suffered in her life, that she still hid the scars of past sadnesses under that usually uptight façade. If only he could let her see that he loved her so she would let him past the façade, they could be so blissfully happy together. If only. Yet she was like a deep lake, full of uncharted depths she'd never revealed to anyone, and if he dived in the wrong place at the wrong time, she might never forgive him. Evie would have to reveal her secrets when she wanted to and not before.

'You aren't listening to a word I'm saying,' she teased, swatting him lightly. 'It's like having a conversation with Rosie when she's glued to *Friends*.'

'Excuse me, missus, I always listen to you, except when you're muttering on about how the other women in the place looked gorgeous and you haven't a thing to wear.'

'Pig!' squealed Evie, slapping him this time. 'Did I say that?' she asked with a grimace.

Max let go of her hand and wrapped his arm comfortably around her shoulders before replying. 'Yes, and I don't know why. You're fifty times more beautiful than any one of those painted women.'

Ecstatic with pleasure, she slid her arm around his waist, marvelling at his words. He preferred her to the other glammed-up women in their designer clothes and designer hair-dos, he really did. And she believed him. She didn't bother sucking in her stomach so her waist would feel skinnier. She didn't need any of that pretence with Max.

As they arrived in picturesque Orange Square, the sun was filtering through the fruit trees, gilding some of the tables under the trees with sunlight, leaving others in blissful shade. Max and Evie sat in the shade with glasses of cool white wine and gorged themselves on mussels with soft bread to soak up the juices.

'I feel a bit guilty for leaving Rosie on her own,' Evie confessed. 'I probably should be with her today. This holiday is so special for her.'

'Your first grown-up holiday is always special,' Max remarked, 'and it's obvious how close you two are. But she'd probably kill for the opportunity to swank around on her own, without anyone apart from Cara, I imagine. Cara looks enough like her sister for the pair of them to be a couple of Club 18-30 girls, completely devoid of parental guidance, on the lookout for talent. I daresay that would be Rosie's dream.'

Evie thought about what he'd said. He was right, she admitted grudgingly. Rosie would love to be able to socialise without her mother and grandfather. It was just difficult to let her daughter go.

'It's not easy,' she explained. 'I want her to be independent, to be her own woman. That's what I taught her. But . . .'

'. . . letting go isn't easy,' Max said softly. 'I guess there's a happy medium. We should let Cara take her out one evening, just to see how it goes. And I'll take you.'

'They'll talk about us,' Evie warned.

'No, they won't.' Max stroked her cheek lovingly. 'I'll tell Mother and Andrew to go for a romantic evening by themselves and then we'll slope off on our own for *our* romantic evening.'

'It's a deal!'

They were both silent as they drove along the road from Marbella to Puerto Banus. To keep her mind off the truly important matter, Evie was thinking that she hadn't actually bought anything, despite telling her father they'd been shopping. Hopefully, nobody would notice. Nobody appeared to. In the villa, everyone was slumped around the television watching an old Chevy Chase video.

'Cara insisted on getting it out of the video shop,' said Rosie by way of explanation as her mother sat down beside her.

'Shush!' hissed Cara.

'You must be feeling better,' Rosie whispered to Evie. 'You look great. I thought you'd still be in bed when we got back.'

'I slept a bit and then Max offered to take me for a drive this afternoon when you lot weren't back,' Evie said. 'I was a bit bored without you.'

'*You* were bored!' giggled Rosie. 'Try spending four hours in the car with Grandpops and Vida alternating between squabbling over the map, and then kissing and making up. If Grandpops said "you should never let the sun set on your anger" one more time, I'd have got out of the car and hitchhiked. I thought we'd never get home!'

'It is one of his favourite expressions,' her mother answered. 'Although I think his all-time favourite is "Oh, Evie, you do fuss over me"!' They both got a fit of the giggles this time.

A fierce glare from Cara, who'd had a huge crush on Chevy Chase in her teens, silenced them.

While everyone else enjoyed the movie, Evie sat quietly, eyes on the screen but her mind a million miles away. Max rarely spoke to her the rest of the evening, he was as coolly formal as he'd been the day before. Polite but distant.

Well, she thought, he understood that she didn't want anybody else to know about their new relationship. But his distant demeanour after their wonderful day made her feel subdued, as if she'd imagined it.

It was only when she was going to bed that he got a chance to speak to her privately. She'd gone into the kitchen to get some water when Max pulled her gently on to the verandah where they couldn't be seen.

'I've wanted to do this all evening,' he said, his eyes warm. 'I've been going mad pretending nothing's going on when I want to sit beside you and hold your hand like some besotted lover.'

Relief washed over her.

'You were barely looking at me,' she said, insecurity making her painfully honest. 'I wasn't sure what to think.'

'Evie,' he said, taking her face in his hands and gazing adoringly at her, 'I'm doing that for you. I'm free, I'm here for you, but you're engaged to be married and it's up to you to decide what to tell your family and when to tell them. I don't have the right to do that and,' he grinned, 'I

436

daresay you'd murder me if I did.'

She nodded ruefully. 'You're right, it's just that I thought I'd imagined it all, that you hadn't really spent this wonderful day with me . . .' She stared gloomily at her feet, pink-painted toes peeking out of the cork sandals.

'This,' he whispered, lifting her face up, 'is what I've wanted to do all day.'

His mouth came down on hers, softly at first, lips gently brushing against hers. Then his kiss deepened, his mouth crushed hers and they clung together, tongues entwining joyfully, clutching each other's bodies as if their lives depended on it.

For the first time, Evie felt herself melt into a kiss; she gave herself completely up to Max and felt him give himself to her. Perfect, sexy, delicious. Her legs felt weak at the strength of the body crushed against hers.

His mouth and hers melted together and she knew she wanted more from him; she wanted to feel his body naked against hers, spend hours getting to know every rib, every silken inch of skin, every sinew . . .

'Mom, are you out here?'

Jumping apart as if they'd been scalded, Evie threw herself on to a lounger and Max rushed over to the verandah wall. He was sitting, idly staring out at the pool, when Rosie poked her head round the door.

'Oh, hi. I thought you'd gone to bed,' she said.

'Really?' Evie replied calmly. 'I just thought I'd cool off before going upstairs. Max had the same idea.'

'No, I doubt if these flowers would grow in Ireland,' he said, as if he'd been interrupted discussing the Andalucian flora at great length, instead of having his tongue down Evie's throat and his hands roaming seductively under her T-shirt. 'What sort of soil do you have in your garden, Evie?'

She stifled an urge to snigger and replied: 'Acidic. Great for rhododendrons.'

'Honestly!' Sighing with exasperation, Rosie hauled herself on to the verandah wall, stretching out her long, fake-tanned legs and admiring the leather mules she'd bought in the mountains that afternoon after some thoroughly satisfying bargaining. 'Here we are in the most romantic spot in the world and we're all drearily stuck at home instead of being out in some great club sampling the real Spanish nightlife, with you lot talking about flowers!' She snorted with frustration. 'I hope we're not going to be doing this every night. I want to have some fun!'

Evie didn't dare look at Max or she'd have broken into hysterical laughter.

'You and Cara should go out together some night,' she said. 'On your own.'

'Really?' The surprise on Rosie's sun-kissed face was palpable. Bouncing over to her mother, Rosie hugged her fervently. 'You won't regret it, Mum. I'll be ever so well behaved. I just need to get out, you know what I mean.'

'I know,' Evie said gravely. 'Just be careful, that's all.'

CHAPTER THIRTEEN

It was three o'clock, when all native Iberians were resting and the sun was very hot. Evie knew she'd have to get into the pool soon to cool down or risk turning lobster red, in spite of all the sun protection cream she'd been assiduously rubbing into herself.

'Evie, is there any left in that bottle?' asked Cara lazily from her position on the lounger on the other side of Rosie's.

Without upsetting either her perfectly positioned sun hat or the book balanced on her knees, Evie delicately lobbed the blue plastic bottle of factor twelve over to her sister. The bottle fell short and landed between them on Rosie's flat stomach, which was turning a coffee colour after five days of intensive tanning.

'Ouch!' she yelped, waking up. 'What do you want this much protection for?' she demanded, squinting at the bottle. 'I'm using factor four,' she added with the pride of the young and unwrinkled.

This time Evie did dislodge her hat and book as she sat up in shock. '*Factor four!*' she gasped. 'You'll get skin cancer, you stupid girl. Put something stronger on immediately.'

'Oh, Mom,' groaned Rosie, lying down again. 'Stop panicking. I'm darker skinned than you. Like Max. He just has to sit out for five minutes and he's black.'

Evie was momentarily distracted by the thought of Max. The only time she'd seen him sunbathe had been for an hour the day before, his oiled body disturbing in its half-naked glory. Compared to Simon, whose body was angular and a little thin, Max was like an athlete: strong, wide shoulders tapering down to a lean waist, and long, muscular legs.

'Where'd you get that scar?' Rosie had asked, spotting a jagged raised weal that ran from his left thigh down to just above his ankle. Evie had wanted to ask but didn't dare.

'Mountaineering,' he said, rubbing the scar idly. 'It's too dangerous for me these days, I wrecked my knee and can't put that sort of pressure on it anymore. I'm supposed to rest it a lot, although I still can't cope with the idea of lounging around all day resting, even in the sun,' he joked.

He liked to sit on the verandah reading scripts and drinking strong Spanish coffee, letting the sun tan him naturally instead of baking himself beside a tan-obsessed Rosie. Max preferred driving Evie around the coast to lying in the sun.

Two days ago, they'd driven into the mountains to Ronda, where the others had been the first day. They hadn't dared stay out for dinner this time and had come home by four, to find everyone else splayed out by the pool soaking up the sun. Yesterday, they'd left separately for a walk and had met at the bottom of the hill near the bull ring, spending several hours meandering along the port and having coffee, talking as if they'd only just discovered how to and were desperate to practise.

'Your legs must be worn out,' Andrew had commented when Evie arrived back at the villa, purposely alone, with Max killing time until he could waltz in.

'I love to walk,' she'd said breezily. 'Did I tell you I'm going in for the mini-marathon?' she lied.

Today, Max had left the villa early to meet a friend who lived locally and still hadn't come back. Vida and Andrew were having a siesta, or 'bonk-esta' as Rosie giggled when the pair of them had sloped off to their room at half-two.

There was just Cara, Rosie and Evie by the pool, luxuriating in the silence and the sun. And Rosie had no intention of moving just when she'd got herself into the most comfortable position possible, not even to fling the sun lotion over to her aunt. 'Come and get it,' she said sleepily.

'You lazy thing,' Cara muttered. She clambered off her lounger and walked delicately on the hot terracotta tiles towards Rosie.

'She's not actually burning,' Cara reported back to Evie, standing over her niece's brown body which was just about decently covered in a tiny pink gingham bikini.

'See, Mum, I'm fine,' muttered Rosie, eyes closed as she lay in sybaritic bliss, adoring the sensation of the heat on her flesh.

'Maybe I'll cool her down a little bit, though,' added Cara wickedly. Scooping up water from the pool, she sprinkled it all over Rosie's belly.

'Ouch, you bitch!' shrieked Rosie, leaping to her feet. 'I'll get you . . .' The pair of them danced around in their bare feet, flicking icy water from the pool at each other, laughing and squealing as the drops hit their heated skin.

Evie grinned and retreated back to her book. She felt utterly, gloriously happy. Lounging by this azure pool, the people she loved most in the world with her and clear blue skies over her head, she couldn't ask for anything more. Well . . . she could but you couldn't have everything in life, could you? She wanted Max. He'd never be hers, but for these few wonderful days she could imagine he was.

When they got too hot, the three girls pulled on clothes over their bikinis, slipped on espadrilles, and wandered down the road to the supermarket where they bought mineral water and some of the juicy watermelon Rosie loved gouging the middle out of.

'God, it's hot,' said Cara, as they walked in happy silence up the hill to the villa.

A white sports car flew past them, raising dust into the air, and the driver honked his horn at the trio. They laughed delightedly and Rosie made faces. In bikinis and sarongs, Rosie wearing only the briefest of denim cut-offs over her bikini, they must have looked like typical tourists, Evie thought, wondering where the uptight woman of five days ago had disappeared to.

'All we do is laugh,' Rosie said, happily tired from the effort.

'Yeah,' Cara agreed, looping one arm around her sister's and the other around Rosie's. 'Isn't it great?'

It was, Evie thought to herself. She felt very relaxed and confident enough to be walking up a hill in broad daylight, wearing nothing but a white shirt knotted around her waist and one of Olivia's dusky pink sarongs covering her aquamarine bikini.

Her hair was in a tousled pony-tail, her feet were dusty from the road and her make-up consisted of a smear of pinky white lip salve to protect her from the sun. Yet she felt positively gorgeous and if Max roared up beside her and asked her to hop in and go *anywhere*, she'd go. She wouldn't need to fuss about her hair, her mascara or whether she looked like a mess in a hastily tied scrap of flowing chiffon. Was this the effect a holiday was supposed to have? Or was this the effect Max had on her? Evie smiled to herself as they ambled along, happy in her dream world.

'Evie, let's go out to dinner tonight. You're tired after a day at work. I want to take you somewhere romantic,' Max smiled at her.

How did he know, she wondered lovingly, that she was exhausted and couldn't cope with the idea of cooking? He just did. That was Max. He seemed to know her every thought, her every feeling.

Who else would run a bubble-filled bath on that evening when she had agonising period pains? Who else would pull her on to the couch beside him and stroke her knotted up belly, telling her he'd ordered in pizza, which he then fed to her as if she was an invalid.

Who else would whisk the dry cleaning off when he left for work in the morning, knowing she wanted to spend her lunch hour at her desk instead of hurtling to the cleaner's in the traffic? Who else would surprise her with breakfast in bed and a perfect pink rose in a new vase on the anniversary of the day they first met?

'I'd love to go out to dinner,' Evie replied, hugging her husband, wondering at her good fortune in having found this incredible man. 'After the day I've had, I didn't think I could bear to cook anything other than beans on toast.'

Max buried his face in her hair, breathing in the scent of her and making that little growling noise of pleasure she loved to hear. 'I know, love, and if I could cook, I would, but you know how dreadful I am in the kitchen so it's easier to go out. Can't have my pet slaving over a hot cooker all night. Unless you want spaghetti again . . .'

It was strange, Evie thought as Cara let them in the huge gates at Villa Lucia, her dreams were different now: less fantasy, more real. Real but with Max in them. Max, Max and more Max. The swarthy pirates and Germanic princes who whisked her away to their yachts had been replaced by a laughing face with probing, knowing blue eyes, and a smile that could light your heart up. All her heroes had turned into Max Stewart and the yachts and luxury hotels had been replaced by her cosy little home where she, Max and Rosie lived in utter bliss. She didn't need to dream of fairy-tale waltzes in glamorous evening gowns when she could be dreaming of watching TV on her old couch, snuggled up beside Max, his arms around her.

Vida was busy unloading the dishwasher and singing Ella Fitzgerald in a husky voice when they wandered into the kitchen with their purchases. Rosie began pouring them all glasses of mineral water, adding ice and lemon the way they never bothered to at home.

'Girls,' Vida cried, her face suffused with love, 'I had totally forgotten. Evie, you'll murder me.'

She sank on to a kitchen chair and fanned herself with a table mat picturing a crimson-clad flamenco dancer. They were so pretty; she'd planned to buy some before she went home. Vida had spotted ones like them in a little shop in the port. 'What will I never forgive you for?' she asked.

'Your hen night, of course,' Vida replied. 'I'm so sorry but it just slipped my mind. Tonight's the night, girls.' She beamed at all three of them.

'Yahoo, a girls' night on the tiles!' Rosie said joyfully.

'Cool,' Cara agreed. 'I could go for that. We'll have to leave Max and Dad here. They can go to that Milady's Palace and eye up the cocktail waitresses.'

'Tonight then?' Vida continued.

'Gosh, yes,' Evie answered in a small voice. 'My last night of freedom. I think I should buy something new for it.'

'Shopping!' said Rosie with glee. 'Even better. I'll get dressed.'

Rifling through the rails of lavish clothes in a tiny boutique in the port, Evie realised that she and Vida had totally different methods of shopping. While Evie looked at the price of everything before picking it out to admire in greater detail, Vida scrutinised it, tried it on, saw if she liked it or not and *then* glanced at the price.

Evie had already recoiled at the exorbitant cost of a glittery little T-shirt and was now merely fingering the clothes for something to do, on the grounds that she wouldn't be able to afford to buy so much as a keyring in this particular establishment. Cara and Rosie were mooching around the bikini shop next door. The only people in the boutique were Evie and Vida, who had the obvious bloom of wealth about her. The sales assistant was hovering hopefully, having spotted a potential gold card customer straight away.

'Evie, just look,' breathed Vida, extracting a coppery cocktail dress from the rack. With a low-cut back and a cross-over front with built-in bra, it was that rare combination of daringly sex and classy all at the same time. 'You've got to try it on.'

Evie caught sight of the price tag swinging from a silken cord and gasped.

'Are you mad?' she said. 'That's about a month's mortgage, Vida. I haven't got the Sultan of Brunei's cheque book with me, you know.'

'Oh, tish,' Vida said, thrusting the dress into Evie's hands. 'Try it on. I want to buy you a hen night present. This could be it. Go on.' She shooed Evie into the changing room and went back to rifling through the rails.

Evie was still standing in the room staring aghast at the beautiful copper dress when the tiny door opened and Vida thrust another couple of hangers in. 'Try these too.'

They were just as prohibitively expensive as the first

CATHY KELLY

dress. Evie shrugged. Vida was off her rocker, for sure.
There was no way she could afford the dresses herself and
equally no way she would let anyone else buy them for
her. But she pulled off her cream canvas trousers and her
vest top anyway. It wouldn't hurt to try them on, they
were so beautiful.

Once she'd slipped on the copper dress and saw how
beautifully it became her, she was lost. Gazing at her
transformed reflection in the mirror, Evie imagined how
Max would see her, how his eyes would widen at the sight
of her body so voluptuous outlined in the luxurious fabric,
how her breasts were enticingly exposed in the underwired
bodice. Visions of him gasping at her, holding her close,
kissing her neck and unzipping the dress filled her mind.
He couldn't but fall in love with her in this. The desire to
possess the dress fought hard with the knowledge that she
couldn't possibly afford it in a month of Sundays.

'Have you got it on?' Vida's voice inquired.

Evie stepped out of the changing room and slowly
walked in front of her.

'Oh.'

Vida's intake of breath told her all she needed to know.
She *did* look beautiful in the dress. Max would love it.

'That colour is stunning, I just adore it,' Vida said, lost in
admiration. 'Why don't you ever wear things like that, Evie
honey? You look just great.'

'I don't know,' she said dazedly, admiring herself from
different angles in a big mirror. 'I never think of wearing
colours like this and I can't afford clothes that cost this
much.'

'Nonsense,' Vida said briskly. 'I'll buy it. You've *got* to
have it.'

The assistant, scenting a sale, materialised beside them
with high shoes and a costume jewellery pendant that

hung tantalisingly in Evie's creamy cleavage like an arrow pointing the way for interested parties.

'No jewellery,' Vida said, arms folded as she eyed the combination critically. 'It's better to keep it simple. Now,' she added, 'try the others.'

The cream linen dress, so icily chic on the hanger, looked like an old flour sack on Evie and she didn't even bother stepping out of the changing room to show Vida. But the off-the-shoulder violet knit two-piece that clung to her in silken folds and turned her hazel eyes a hypnotic green was stunning.

'It's lovely,' she said, almost weeping at the thought of how much she'd love to buy it. 'But I can't let you buy them both, Vida, it wouldn't be right.'

In the end, Vida insisted so much and went on and on about how Evie was the daughter she'd never had, that she allowed her stepmother to pay for the two outfits. Cara and Rosie were waiting outside, eating ice creams and watching the world go by when Vida emerged, flushed with pleasure at having finally managed to spoil Evie. She, on the other hand, was flushed with guilt at the thought of how much Vida had spent.

'My second husband,' Vida had whispered as the assistant reverently wrapped the copper and violet garments in tissue paper, 'did not turn out to be a very nice man. Not like Max's dear father, Carlos,' she said sadly. 'But Dan Andersen was rich. *Very* rich,' she emphasised. 'It's nice to have a daughter to spend it on . . . well, a stepdaughter,' she added quickly.

'What did you buy?' Rosie asked, poking around the glossy carrier bag like a dog snuffling for food in the grocery shopping.

'Lovely things,' Vida replied, tucking her arm through Rosie's. 'Now what can we get for you, my girl?'

★ ★ ★

Dinner and drinks in a lively club in the port: that was Vida's plan for Evie's hen night.

'I've told the boys they'll have to do without us for the evening,' she said, arriving in Evie's room at half-seven that evening to find Evie dressed in her copper dress.

'Is Max back?' she asked anxiously, slipping her feet into high black sandals. She wanted to see him, tell him that the hen night hadn't been her idea, that she didn't even want to *think* for one moment about her wedding.

'He got back twenty minutes ago but he and your father have gone out on their boys' night. Lord knows where they'll end up. Some bordello!' Vida smiled affectionately, knowing full well that her beloved and besotted husband was as likely to end up in a bordello as she was.

I missed him, thought Evie, deflated. She'd never had the chance to explain and now he hadn't even seen her in her lovely new dress. She threw her mascara back into the top drawer. What was the point of bothering now?

Dinner was a lively, wine-sodden affair that she'd have loved if the circumstances were different. Cara, Rosie and Vida were all in fantastic form, determined that Evie should enjoy herself. Making a huge effort, she laughed at everyone's jokes and pretended she was having the time of her life. Inside, her heart was breaking.

Watching the others' faces recede in a blur around her, she thought that this was the end of her idyll. Tonight was the final proof that in just five weeks she was getting married. To Simon. Dear sweet Simon who'd once felt like the answer to all her prayers and now felt like a millstone around her neck, dragging her down to the bottom of the pond with him when she wanted to be swimming lazily on the surface with Max.

She twisted the engagement ring on her hand idly. It was looser now because she'd lost weight, despite the meals out every evening. Her appetite was non-existent. On her plate, some roasted peppers congealed in their spicy olive oil dressing, barely touched. Normally, she'd have wolfed them down. She loved roasted peppers.

'Tell me about the honeymoon,' Vida said cosily, delighted to be so close to Evie after all this time.

She smiled bravely. The last thing she wanted to talk about was her honeymoon, two solid weeks of being with Max in Greece . . . She breathed in sharply. *Max*. She'd automatically thought of him instead of Simon. Talk about a Freudian slip! She didn't want to be stuck with Simon so her mind had instantly and unconsciously replaced him with Max. This was ridiculous.

'Greece,' she sighed, trying and failing to put some animation into her voice. 'I've always wanted to go there.' But not now, she thought silently.

'Greece is so beautiful,' Vida said mistily. 'I remember walking miles to see the Oracle at Delphi after this party. We were all suffering from far too many cocktails and our car had broken down, so we walked, in evening dress, to the temple. We were insane to do it.'

Vida had many wonderful qualities, Evie reflected, and thank God one of them was the ability to talk in a stream of fascinating reminiscences about her life. Utterly entertaining, she could keep a crowd amused for hours on end. Cara and Rosie, engaged in a secret plan to give Rosie a lot more wine than her mother would normally allow, leaned forward over the remains of their dinner and listened.

Grateful that the spotlight was off her, Evie sat back and ran her finger around the rim of her wine glass. Her eyes roamed the room listlessly, as if she hoped Max would appear and take her away from all this talk of weddings and honeymoons.

A tanned blond man, sitting alone at the bar eating olives and knocking back red wine from a glass the size of a goldfish bowl, was staring at her admiringly. When she noticed him, he gave her a frankly appreciative look and, picking up his glass, raised it in her direction.

It was amazing the effect the right clothes could have, Evie thought ironically, giving him a polite smile back. She felt like a duchess in this dress and yet the man she most wanted to admire it, hadn't seen it and probably never would.

By dessert, Vida and a now tipsy Rosie were discussing men as if they were two seventeen year olds instead of one, and Cara, much tipsier, was telling Evie just what a lovely man Max Stewart was.

'He's so kind to me,' she confided, big dark eyes shining with a mixture of booze and affection. 'Asked me all about my childhood and about how you looked after me. He wanted to know about the whole family, really . . . It's so nice to meet a man who's interested in you as a person and not just as a pair of tits,' she said, a certain gloom entering her voice. Ewan hadn't thought she was just a babe with big boobs, Cara knew that. He'd loved her for the sort of person she was, but he hadn't been able to understand exactly what sort of person that was. All mixed up, she realised sadly. Totally screwed up, incapable of having a relationship thanks to that bastard Owen Theal who'd shattered her confidence.

And Ewan had ended up giving her back that confidence but she'd been too blind to realise . . .

No, she wasn't thinking about him. She was over Ewan. Finished, finito, ended. She needed another man to take her mind off things. A man like Max would do it.

'Do you think Max likes me?' Cara asked her sister earnestly. 'I think he does but maybe I'm wrong. He's so hunky, isn't he? Gorgeous body.'

'Yes, he's gorgeous,' Evie replied woodenly. What had she been thinking of? Max would be so good for her sister, he'd give her love, affection and the stability Cara needed so desperately. Evie had a fiancé, a man she was going to marry. Cara needed somebody. Just then, a picture of lanky, tousle-headed Ewan sprang to her mind.

'What about Ewan?' she asked suddenly.

Cara's eyes filled with tears.

'It's over,' she sniffed, fumbling around in her pocket for a tissue.

Evie put a comforting arm around her sister. 'You poor thing. Why didn't you tell me?'

'Nothing to tell,' Cara gulped. 'He's a pig, dumped me, ended it. Well, I can tell you,' her voice became flinty, 'I'm over him and I'm going to have one hell of a good time now that I'm here. Vida,' she said, interrupting a whispered conversation between her step-mother and Rosie, 'where are we going next? I want to party!'

The El Dorado nightclub was like a giant, purple velvet-lined cavern with smaller alcoves hollowed out from the walls like intimate rooms surrounding the dance floor area. A tail-coated waiter, bribed by Vida, led them to a quiet nook at the back of the club where voluminous banquettes were curved like fleshy Dali sculptures around glass tables and they could watch the dance floor without being deafened by the music. The dance floor was almost empty, apart from a few youthful blondes shimmying in white clothes that gleamed luminously in the disco lights.

As befitted a club where you had to pay a fortune just to get in, the clientele was of every age imaginable, from the very young to the very old. All of them appeared to be very rich. The ice buckets on the tables contained bottles of champagne and the handbags that lay close to their owners on the plump banquettes were all Fendi and Prada.

'This is some place,' Rosie whispered in awe, looking around.

'I'm sure it's far too sedate for you, girls,' Vida replied, waving a braceleted hand at a waiter, 'but I'm too old for most of the other nightclubs and this one was recommended as being suitable for old dears like me.'

'You're not an old dear,' said Rosie, horrified.

'Look at the price of the drink!' cried Evie, just as horrified as she browsed through the leather-covered wine list.

'Double tish,' said Vida, immediately ordering two bottles of champagne. 'It's not every day my stepdaughter gets married.'

Even Evie needed a drink after that.

Vida proved to be keen on dancing, especially when the DJ played a rock n' roll medley which saw half the club abandon their cigars to get up and dance. Rosie and Cara bopped energetically, but Evie, despite the appreciative glances her copper dress drew, soon sank back down into their corner and sipped her champagne meditatively.

She didn't feel like dancing or celebrating. She felt as if she was at a wake, where an old woman with white hair would start keening any minute. She didn't notice the man approaching her until he was in front of her, asking in heavily accented English if he could sit down.

Evie shrugged in a 'do what you like' way. She didn't care who sat where. She didn't care about anything anymore.

'You don't dance with your friends?' he asked.

Evie realised it was the blond man from the restaurant,

the one who'd raised his glass to her. He was forty-something, handsome from a distance. But up close his face was a road-map of red veins from too much alcohol or too much fresh air or both.

'You want more champagne?' he asked, eyes roaming over her body lasciviously.

Aware that any positive response might be interpreted as a come-on, Evie shook her head and slid back in her seat away from him, hoping Vida or the girls would come back and rescue her.

She didn't want to be rude but she wanted to get rid of this guy. Mr Red Vein moved along the seat after her, like a giant spider after a fly.

'You are too beautiful to be alone,' he crooned.

Evie smiled nervously, then stopped smiling because that would definitely be a come-on.

He stretched out a tanned hand and put it on her knee.

OmiGod, Evie thought with fear, this could not be happening to her. Things like this didn't happen to her. Encounters with strange men in nightclubs happened to glamorous women with exotic lives, not to boring little mice like herself. Why had she ever wanted interesting things to happen to her? She'd never wish for that again. She'd never wear this bloody dress again either. The crossover bit at the front was just asking for trouble.

'I saw you alone and thought you must be lonely,' he said, fingers caressing.

'Well, I'm not,' Evie said hotly, wrenching her knee away from him.

He laughed and gave her a scorching look that said, I like women playing hard to get.

'You British women are so sexy, so cool,' he murmured, eyeing her up as if trying to figure out how to unzip her dress. 'I bet you're not so cool in bed, huh?'

Evie felt repulsed. How dare he speak to her like that? He was disgusting, she didn't want him anywhere near her. His hand reached out again but she was too quick for him.

She slapped his face as hard as she could and shrieked: 'I'm Irish, I'm not at all cool and I'm not interested. No, no no! What part of "no" don't you understand!' She leaped to her feet, banging her shin painfully on the edge of the glass table in the process.

Whirling around, she walked straight into a giant of a man who'd suddenly appeared at the entrance to their nook, blocking off the light from the dance floor. Strong, comforting arms closed around her and the cologne that rose from the chest she was pressed against definitely belonged to Max.

'Evie, are you OK?' he asked anxiously, holding her by the shoulders and staring into her flushed, upset face.

'I am now,' she said, weak with relief.

She could feel Max's hands tighten convulsively on her shoulders as he stared furiously over her head at Mr Red Vein.

'So sorry,' muttered the other man, taking one look at Max's athletic frame and getting the hell out of there.

Evie leaned against Max's chest and laughed, relief flooding through her body. 'I thought he was going to pounce on me.'

'So did I,' Max said grimly. 'I'll kill Mother for leaving you on your own. She should have known you're fair game for every gigolo this side of Sotogrande.'

'I am not!' Evie said in outrage, pulling away and looking up at him crossly.

'Sorry.' He pulled her back into the circle of his arms and kissed the top of her head. 'I'm not rational where you're concerned, Evie. I want to protect you from everything and I should kill that bastard . . .'

'Shush,' she said softly, putting a finger against his mouth to silence him. 'Dance with me instead. I'd prefer a dance than spending the night trying to bail you out from the Puerto Banus jail.'

His eyes dark with longing as he looked at her, Max kissed her finger sensuously. Evie felt her belly quiver with desire, while her heart beat a fierce tattoo in her chest.

His head came down and he kissed her: a kiss so sweet and tender she wanted to drown in it forever. His mouth tasted of peppermints and his lips were soft as they moved against hers. Then he broke away and led her by the hand on to the dance floor, to a quiet corner where there were only a few other couples.

The music was still fast and Evie could see Cara's head over the crowd, swinging rapidly to the beat, long black curls flying. The people beside them were sweaty from their exertions but Max had no intention of jiving. They both knew they could dance beautifully together: they'd stunned the crowd at Vida and Andrew's wedding with their Fred and Ginger expertise. But Max wanted to hold her close this time, not trip the light fantastic for the benefit of the clubbers in El Dorado.

Smiling, Evie put her arms around his neck. He wrapped his around her waist, pulling her in deliberately close so that they were moulded together.

She could feel her body crushed against his, feel the heat of him as they swayed slowly, creating their own tempo instead of jerking to the frantic beat.

As if he'd seen them and knew they wanted to slow dance, the DJ let the frantic rock 'n' roll music fade, while gently turning up something slow and melodic. Al Green's 'Let's Stay Together' rippled around the nightclub and before long everybody else was dancing at their speed. Evie let the music flow over her, exquisitely happy in Max's arms. He'd have a permanent crick in his neck if they were married, she thought fondly, giving in to the impulse to stroke the sleek, dark head that was bent low next to hers.

'You look beautiful in that dress,' he murmured into the soft, dark cloud of her hair.

'I wore it for you,' she said simply. 'I could have cried when I heard you'd gone out this evening without my talking to you. I wanted you to see me looking like this just once.'

'You always look beautiful to me,' he said, 'even when you've just got up and are mooching around the kitchen in your dressing gown, rubbing sleep from your eyes.'

Evie laughed. 'That was yesterday, I bet. I was so thirsty I had to go downstairs before my shower. I didn't think anyone saw me.'

'You can't hide from me,' he said, fingers kneading the small of her back. 'I watch out for you, I always want to be seeing you.' His voice grew huskier. 'I want to see you in the morning after a night spent with me, so I can rub the sleep from your eyes and wake you up slowly.' They'd stopped dancing now and were standing very still, holding each other. Evie was also holding her breath, afraid to move in case she broke the spell.

'I want you, Evie,' Max said suddenly. 'I want to take you home with me now and never let you go. You've no idea how much I want to do that.'

His eyes were liquid with desire, matching Evie's. She lost herself in those eyes, knowing that she wanted him just as much as he wanted her. There was no pretence between them.

'I want you too, Max,' she breathed softly.

'Let's go,' he said roughly.

Rosie was delighted to see Max and threw her arms around him when he and Evie returned to the table.

'When did you get here?' she asked, slim hips swaying to the music.

'We've been dancing,' Vida added, fanning herself with her hand. 'Did you bring Andrew?'

Max shook his head. 'He's taking advantage of your night out to go to bed early. So I thought I'd drop in to say hello and it's just as well I did. Evie feels ill. Something she ate.'

Obediently, Evie tried to look sick, squinting as if she was in pain. Her stomach was certainly reacting wildly but that was butterflies fluttering around at the thought of what was actually happening.

'Poor thing,' Cara said with a hiccup.

Rosie hugged her mother sympathetically.

'I'll go with you,' Vida offered.

'No,' Max said quickly. 'You should stay with Rosie and Cara. Look after them,' he added, thrusting a handful of notes into his mother's hand. 'This is their night out too. Evie specifically wants them to enjoy themselves,' he whispered.

She did her best to walk away as if she was feeling terribly sick, but as soon as she and Max were outside the club, she grabbed his hand in delight. They ran to the car, like a couple of kids who'd escaped from some bossy relative, laughing and giggling at having outwitted everyone.

Max drove back to the villa with one hand on the wheel and one hand on Evie's thigh, as if he couldn't bear to let her go even for one moment. Beside him, she shivered with excitement, watching everything go by in a kind of blur.

As silently as they could, they crept in the front door, hoping Andrew would be asleep. The villa was in silence, only the light snores coming from her father's and Vida's room testimony that there was anyone at home.

'Your room,' Evie whispered, knowing that everyone would poke their head round her door later to see if she was asleep. 'I'll make my bed look slept in.'

Trying not to wonder where she'd suddenly developed this newfound skill at subterfuge, she crumpled her bed and arranged two pillows under the covers into a long shape so that anyone sticking their head in later would think she was in it. Then, she ran into the bathroom and cleaned her teeth before tiptoeing out on to the landing.

Outside Max's room, she paused, shocked for a moment at what she was about to do. She was going to bed with Max, she was betraying Simon. Was she some sort of slut? If somebody had told her she was capable of behaving like this, she wouldn't have believed them. This was not common or garden Evie Fraser behaviour, not in a million years. Talk about being caught on the horns of a dilemma.

She was still deliberating in desperation when the door opened silently and Max stood there, looking at her as if he knew what was running through her mind. He'd taken off his jacket and was wearing that white cotton shirt that made his skin look wonderfully bronzed by comparison. His face was in shadow but his eyes blazed out of the darkness, burning intensely with passion. Passion for her. His dark hair was unruly and he ran one hand through it impatiently, sleeking it back.

With a shiver of excitement, Evie knew that she longed to feel those hands touching her, wanted those lips burning against hers. She wanted Max. There was nothing else in the universe except her and him.

Nothing she could do to stop herself. It was as inevitable as the tide that lapped against the beach every day. Max and Evie. Evie and Max. She stepped into the room and gently shut the door behind her.

Max took her face in his hands and stared at her as if he was drinking in every hollow and bone of her face. He started kissing her forehead, moving to the arch of her eyebrows then her eyelids, her cheeks, her snub nose and her chin, before claiming her mouth, his lips at first gentle on hers, then hard against Evie's plump lusciousness.

She clung to him, standing on her tiptoes, letting her hands roam over him joyously. When she thought she'd die from the pleasure of kissing, Max pulled her to the bed, sat down on it and stood her in front of him, admiring her beautiful dress.

'It's wonderful,' he growled, 'but it's got to come off.'

His big hands traced the curve of her breasts through the dress, cupping them, then he slid his fingers under the crossover fabric to touch bare skin. Evie gasped as he caressed her. He ran his hands over her waist, marvelling at her hourglass shape, then roamed down to fondle the curve of her buttocks through the thin copper material.

Her face was flushed, her hair tumbled in curls around her shoulders, her mouth open as she gasped with pleasure. Evie thought she'd never felt such delicious sensations in her life before.

She reached back and her fingers found the zip. Slowly, she unzipped the dress and tantalisingly slid it down, exposing first the line of her sun-kissed shoulders, then the full curve of her breasts.

'You're beautiful, Evie,' Max said slowly. He didn't make a move to touch her, just sat like some Eastern potentate watching, drinking her in because he knew he'd be able to touch her everywhere when he chose. His watching excited her hopelessly. Breathing heavily, Evie continued her erotic striptease, sliding the dress over her hips to reveal tiny white bikini pants and nothing else. She was glad she'd shaved her legs that evening. Still, Max just stared at her, his pupils black with desire.

It was only when the dress fell to the ground like shed skin that he reached out and pulled her to him, arms and mouth exploring her body hungrily.

Evie heard moaning as Max's mouth fastened exquisitely on her nipple and then realised the person moaning was herself. She couldn't help it. The feelings his darting tongue unleashed in her couldn't be suppressed. She forgot all about keeping quiet in case they woke her father up.

'My darling,' Max said thickly, kissing her hungrily, 'I've wanted you for so long. You're so beautiful.'

Then her hands were on him, unbuttoning the soft cotton shirt, eager fingers exploring the hard, muscled body beneath it. As his hands roamed over her back, stroking and caressing, her hands touched his chest lovingly, slipping down to open the button on his chinos.

He groaned as they lay back on the bed, Evie quivering with desire as Max's probing hands slid her white cotton panties off her body. She arched against him as he touched her, trying not to make too much noise but helpless with excitement. When he was naked too, Evie didn't feel any of the prudery which overcame her with Simon. With Max, she wanted to have every light in the place burning brightly so she could experience every thrilling second of their lovemaking in full, well-lit colour. She shuddered when he pushed himself inside her, gentle yet insistent.

'Evie,' he said, his breath ragged. 'Are you all right, my darling?' In response her mouth caught his, kissing him deeply to let him know that she was as excited as he. She clung to him, sweat mingling as they moved as one. Every muscle in her body quivered beneath Max, every nerve ending burned with pleasure.

She wanted to be naked and wrapped around him for the rest of her life, skin on satiny skin, hip bones locked together . . . and then she felt the sweetness wash over her as she came, her orgasm flooding through her body like a great tidal wave of icy water: hitting her with an explosive force, then ebbing gently as it rippled through her body.

Fiercely excited by Evie's little cry of pleasure, Max came with her, groaning out her name in ecstasy.

'Evie!'

She didn't know which was more exhilarating: her own orgasm or the sheer pleasure of seeing how much she excited Max, seeing the effect she had on this incredible man.

She could feel his body spasm in bliss, every muscle hard against her as he came triumphantly, wildly.

They held each other tightly as they came back to earth, sated and shaking, bodies slick with moisture, breathing fast.

'My darling, that was incredible,' murmured Max, nuzzling Evie's ear.

She purred back at him, feeling like a giant cat lying in the tropical sun after months of Arctic winter. They shifted in the bed, Max curling his body around Evie's spoon-fashion, as if he couldn't bear even an inch to separate them.

Supporting his head with his left hand, he caressed her with his right, no longer exploring every inch of her flesh, merely stroking her lovingly. She wriggled until she was lying on her back, legs tangled up with his and looking up at his face. Max's fingers gently fondled every rib, splaying out to touch the full curve of her breast, touching her almost in wonder.

His face was tender as he watched her but the blue eyes were unreadable in the dark.

Suddenly, Evie wanted to ask the question all men were supposed to hate: What are you thinking? Rosie had gleaned this nugget of information from a magazine and had proceeded to read it out to her mother and Cara only the day before as they sat by the pool. It was women's favourite question and men's most hated one. But gazing up at Max, abruptly wrenched from feelings of joy to the sheer horror of making such a mistake, she desperately wanted to ask it.

What if their lovemaking hadn't been the most glorious, earth-shattering experience for him? What if she'd been nothing more than a quick lay, an available woman, and he was wondering how the hell to get her out of his bed so he could roll over and go back to sleep? Was that what he was thinking and if it was . . .

Max's fingers curled around hers and he brought her hand to his mouth, kissing it softly.

'You're wearing your worried face,' he said. 'Are you sorry now? Are you figuring out how to escape out of here as painlessly as possible? I certainly hope not.'

Laughter bubbled out of Evie as relief flooded through her. 'I was afraid that's what *you* were thinking,' she admitted. 'You weren't, were you?'

'You're a terrible woman for doubting me, aren't you?' he chuckled. 'How am I ever going to convince you I'm crazy about you? That I love you?'

His eyes weren't unreadable now; he was earnest, eager, hoping for a response. Evie gave it to him.

'I love you too, Max,' she said simply.

She reached up to kiss him, letting her tongue slip into his mouth, letting him see the force of her passion. God, he loved her! And she loved him, so very much. It was like a dream or a miracle. She wanted to sing from the rooftops with joy.

His hands were roaming over her body again, questing and passionate. Evie felt herself quiver as she responded to the erotic thrust of his tongue.

She could barely imagine that their kiss could be deeper, sweeter than before, but it was. As if those words of love had flicked a magic switch inside both of them, there was no holding back now.

'I love you, I love you, I love you,' she whispered joyously. Then, pushing him down and wriggling on top of him, she playfully pinned his arms to the bed and lowered her mouth to his. 'It's my turn to show you how much.'

They were satiated, entwined in each other's arms, when they heard the giggling, whispering and banging into furniture that heralded the return of the nightclubbers.

'It's half-three,' said Evie, scandalised at the lateness of the hour.

Max tickled her earlobe with his tongue. 'Oh, yeah? You're one to talk about staying up late, Miss Sexpot.'

'You're the one who's been up,' she retorted, her body exhausted after two frantic couplings in which she'd been stunned by how turned on he was. Simon had never been able for more than one session at a time. Max tickled her and she slapped his hands away, trying to muffle her giggles.

'Shush, they'll hear us.'

The footsteps stopped at the top of the stairs, outside Evie's room.

The pair of them lay silently and listened.

'She's asleep,' they heard Cara say.

After a flurry of goodnight kisses, doors shut noisily and the house was silent.

Evie curled herself back into the curve of Max's body, not wanting to leave and yet wondering if she should.

His strong arm stilled her. 'You're not going anywhere,' he said. 'I'm not letting you out of my sight.'

Feeling more comfortable in her nakedness than she ever had in her entire life, Evie wriggled up against his warm body and let herself drift off into sleep.

As if she wanted to remind herself where she really was, she found she woke up every hour to touch Max, just to make sure he was there and that she wasn't dreaming. Each time she woke up, he seemed to wake with her, stroking her softly and murmuring: 'Go back to sleep.'

Finally, she slipped into a deep slumber and woke to the sound of next door's lawnmower.

'Jesus!' She sat up abruptly, realised she was stark naked and, for one terrified moment, wondered where she was. Then she felt Max's arm lazily moving over her thigh and she remembered. Evie's face curved into a giant smile until she glanced at her watch.

Half-eight! Vida would be up soon. She always woke early and would undoubtedly peek into Evie's room to see how she was. A couple of pillows squashed under the covers might pass muster at half-three in the morning when everyone had a bottle of wine inside them, but it wouldn't fool the sharp-eyed Vida in the cool light of morning.

'Max!' hissed Evie, trying to be quiet but feeling nervous.

His response was to drag her down into the bed, pull her under him and kiss her in such an indolently sensual way that she forgot all about Vida, the pillows and why she was nervous about anyone discovering she'd just spent the night with Max.

By nine, the nerves were back.

Max was lying in such post-coital stillness that she thought he'd dropped off. She wanted to sneak back into her own room but couldn't bear just to leave him, not without talking to him anyway.

Evie stared up at the ceiling and fretted. What could she say to everyone? She was bursting with the news that she and Max were in love but she could hardly tell Vida, her father and the girls that she wasn't going to marry Simon.

Not without telling him first. That would be unfair and cowardly. But she didn't know how she was going to tell Simon. How did you start a conversation like that?

'What are you going to say to them?' asked Max.

Evie, who'd been convinced he was dozing, jumped in shock. 'I'm sorry,' she said guiltily. 'We shouldn't have to tell anyone anything – except the truth. It's just Simon, I have to tell him first . . .'

She paused. After all, Max hadn't actually said he wanted her not to marry Simon. But he must mean that, surely?

'I love you, Evie, I told you that and I meant it,' he said, interrupting her nightmarish thoughts. 'But I know you have to do what you have to do. Just don't take forever, please. I want you with me and I don't want to hide it.' He grinned, stroking the delicate skin of her collarbone. 'I'd never make a spy, I'm no good at lying.'

She smiled at him. 'Neither am I.'

Something banged against the door and Evie gasped, shooting out of the bed and into the bathroom like a rocket. Inside, she stuffed a bit of towel into her mouth to stop herself from giggling with a combination of nerves and lust.

She quivered when the door was wrenched open a moment later by a grinning Max.

'My mother tripped over the laundry basket going downstairs in the search for mineral water,' he said. 'She's dying of a hangover and even if you hung a sign over your bed saying "pillows – not a person. Owner bonking else-where", I doubt if she'd notice.'

They clutched each other, laughing as quietly as they could. Finally, Max kissed Evie's bare shoulder reluctantly. 'Get out of here,' he said, 'before I have to ravish you again.'

CATHY KELLY

'I don't know if I could manage another time,' she said ruefully, her body aching in the cold light of day.

'You and me both.' He smiled. 'I'm afraid I'm no toyboy, Ms Fraser.'

'No?' She pouted. 'Why else do you think I came in here?'

With her copper dress wrapped in one towel and herself enveloped in another, so she could say she'd been having a shower if anyone spotted her, Evie slipped across the landing to her own bedroom.

She shut the door and raced into the bathroom to see if she looked different. Surely her eyes were shining and her skin glowing with love? The sight that greeted her made Evie grimace ruefully. Her hair looked like a bird's nest, her eyes were ringed with smudged mascara like a ring-tailed lemur's and her face was deathly pale from no sleep. But she hugged herself gleefully. Max loved her.

Vida and Cara, both sporting the lemur look around the eyes, were sitting at the kitchen table looking like death microwaved up when Evie ventured downstairs.

'How are you?' she asked brightly, then remembering she was supposed to have been sick the night before, added: 'I'm feeling much better now.'

'Good for you,' groaned Cara, resting her head on her hands. 'We're dying. Hand us out the orange juice.'

'There's none left.'

'I had the last of it,' confessed Vida, who looked no better than Cara. 'I'm never going on a hen night again.'

'Look at the state of the pair of you,' Andrew said, arriving at the front door with Rosie, who looked the picture of health and was carrying a container of orange juice. He plonked the groceries on the table. 'You're a right couple of boozers. If you're not careful, I'm sending you

466

pair into a clinic to dry out when we get home.'

'Morning,' said Rosie cheerily.

Cara and Vida both winced at the loudness of her voice.

'Have mercy on the afflicted,' Vida said, 'or I'll make you suffer next time you have a pain in your head. And there's nothing wrong with the odd night out, Andrew.'

'Do you think you could both manage another night out?' Max said, coming down the stairs.

'I'll be fine when I've had my first coffee,' Vida remarked, ruffling her husband's hair before going over to the coffee maker.

Max hugged his mother. 'Good, because I met some pals in the port yesterday and they're having a party tonight. We're all invited.'

Evie glared at him from narrowed eyes. Why hadn't he mentioned this to her? They'd had at least eight solid hours of constant companionship and at no point had he alluded to a party given by friends of his. Was she suitable for bonking his brains out but not for hearing intimate little details of his life?

'Really?' she said crossly. 'Where's the party and who are the friends?'

Max took over spooning coffee into the filter as Vida looked too worn out to do it. 'Franz Lieber, a German director I worked with on a mini-series about Strauss. He and his wife have just bought a ranch down the road from here and it seems a lorryload of actors and crew decamped from his latest production the other day for the grand opening.'

'Anyone famous?' asked Rosie excitedly.

'Not really,' Max said, still fiddling with the coffee machine. 'Franz mainly pals around with the technical people on a production, although he says Ted Livingstone and Mia Koen are there.'

'Oh,' said Rosie, not interested in Ted, an American character actor, and not knowing who Mia Koen was.

The name 'Mia' flickered like a lightbulb above Evie's head, however. 'Who's she?' she asked, recognising the name but not remembering from where.

Max turned around but didn't meet her eyes. 'An actress,' he said casually. Too casually.

'Isn't that the girl who was crazy about you?' Vida inquired with a mischievous grin on her lovely face. 'The one from Atlanta, Queen of the Mini-Series?'

Evie felt a dart of sheer jealousy rip through her viciously. Mia . . . she knew she'd heard the name before. When she and Max had been surprised having lunch and she'd dreamed up a phantom, hugely pregnant wife for him, he'd automatically named her Mia. Not the sort of thing you would do on the spur of the moment unless the name meant something to you.

'We're *all* invited, are we?' she asked in an arch voice. 'Are you sure they don't want you on your own?'

Max shook his head and looked at her, amazement on his face at her caustic tone.

'We can't go,' Rosie said, patting Cara on the shoulder. 'It's our night to go out on our own. We've found just the right place to go, haven't we, Cara?'

She nodded. 'And I'm drinking water all night, I promise.'

'I hope you are too, Rosie,' said Evie, more sharply than she'd intended.

She spent the morning longing to get a quiet word alone with Max, determined to ask him about Mia. But every time it seemed as if she had him to herself, someone wandered in from the pool looking for mineral water or meandered down the stairs with the sun cream they'd gone up to find. Open-plan houses were a pain in the rear end, Evie thought angrily. To add to her temper, it seemed as if

Max didn't want a moment alone with her. He didn't look at all perturbed by all the interruptions.

Finally, bristling with indignation, Evie grabbed her book, her sun cream and her bikini, and flung herself into the lounger beside Rosie, who was determined to spend their last full day in Spain working on her tan.

When Vida called out from the verandah that they were driving down to the port for lunch, Evie padded barefoot into the villa, sleepy from the heat and sorry for being such a cow to Max. But he'd gone.

'Off to see his director friend,' Vida explained.

And Mia. Evie's heart hardened.

'Tell me about this Mia person,' she inquired idly. 'Do you think there's a chance she and Max might get back together?' Evie did her best to hide the fact that even *saying* it was like having heart surgery without an anaesthetic.

'I never met her but her reputation precedes her,' Vida answered. 'Evidently, she's beautiful and very demanding, a real drama queen from Georgia. She's never made it in the movies but she's huge in the sort of shows Max's company makes. He loves working with her because her name can make a show profitable. I'm not sure but I think they had a thing going together on location once.'

Evie gulped.

'She was married at the time to this Country and Western singer, which is why Max never told me what exactly happened. I think he was afraid I'd be horrified.' Vida shrugged. 'They tell me that happens all the time in showbusiness. DCOL they say – Doesn't Count On Location. I think I read that Mia's divorced now so maybe she's back for a re-match with Max.'

Evie was shocked to her fillings. Max had had an on-location fling with this woman who was married to someone else at the time! So, he had a history of running off with other men's girlfriends and not even staying around long enough to see what happened. How dare he try it on with her? How stupid she was for letting it happen.

Had stupid Mia believed Max's litany of lies and thought he'd stay with her if she dumped her husband? Like I believed him, Evie thought bitterly. Like she always believed men. She'd believed Tony and look where that got her.

Feigning exhaustion, she said she'd skip lunch and lay down on her bed while everyone else hopped eagerly into the car for a trip down the port to a cute seafood restaurant Andrew had discovered.

Tears rolled down her cheeks as she lay on the bed, staring blindly at the pretty little balcony outside, where she and Max had shared breakfast what felt like a thousand years ago.

At least Simon would never give her reason to doubt him. Dependable from his sandy hair down to his sensible lace-up shoes, he was the sort of man you could rely on never to give you a sleepless night. He didn't light fires within her either, but he loved her and she could trust him. How could she have betrayed him for a rake of a man who went around collecting women like Apache Indians collected scalps in old black and white movies?

And why did she always fall for the sort of man who didn't know how to be faithful, who thought monogamy was a great idea but not for him?

Evie's tear-filled eyes didn't see the cloudless blue sky through the open windows. Instead, she saw herself with baby Rosie in her arms, staring into her husband's grave and wondering why the tears wouldn't come. Of all the people standing there beside her, only Olivia knew the whole story. As Tony's mother wailed and screamed for her dead son, clutching her rosary beads in genuine anguish, Evie felt nothing but rage that he had left her with a six-month-old baby to bring up on her own. Rage at Tony, and rage at herself for having been conned by a man she'd thought she knew. No wonder she'd steered clear of the male of the species for so many years, preferring life as a single parent to the two-faced world of dating. Simon had been the first man she'd let close to her. Max had been the second.

Well, one out of two wasn't bad.

She swung her legs out of bed and sat down on the balcony, her face bleak as she stared out at the sea and the yachts dotting the shimmering blue horizon.

More than anything else in the world, she wanted Max Stewart. She loved him with all her heart but he wasn't what he pretended to be. She wasn't sure if he'd lied to her or not, but he hadn't told her the truth, that was for sure. And the truth was so important to her. A wave of guilt hit her as she remembered that she hadn't told Simon the truth.

Well, she would. From now on, she'd be the most faithful, truthful wife ever and he'd never regret marrying her. She'd make his life wonderful, be the perfect spouse, go into Wife of the Year contests, *anything* to make things the way they had been before.

The wedding was back on, she thought defiantly. And Max Stewart could go hang! But not, she decided grimly, before she saw what sort of women he *really* wanted to spend the rest of his life with. She pulled the violet outfit out of the wardrobe, broodingly aware that the infamous Mia would be studying the opposition if she went to the party. Well, Evie decided firmly, Ms Mia Koen wouldn't find her wanting.

'How could you?' Evie hissed, face proud and jewels glittering in the firelight as she faced the dastardly Max. 'How could you have another woman when you had my love?'

His swarthy face cruel and uncaring, Max advanced on her, mouth set in a grim line. His eyes raked over her figure, elegant in the amethyst ball gown, the corsets holding her tiny waist in to a slender eighteen inches. 'Because I wanted you, I couldn't help it. I admit it, she is to be my wife, but you and I can still be lovers. You want it, you know you do. You are the most exciting woman I have ever known. But I must marry her to save my family's fortune.'

'For your insolence, you deserve to die!' hissed Evie, producing a tiny pearl-handled pistol from the folds of her silken shawl. His cowardly face paled to the colour of his ruffled shirt.

'No!' Mia ran in, heavily bleached hair piled up in a ridiculous pompadour, wearing a vulgar, low-cut dress that was a riot of gaudy colours, with paste jewels clustered heavily around her thick neck. 'Don't shoot!'

'I must, he has dishonoured me,' Evie said grimly, thinking of the shame he could bring on her noble family.

'No, Madame Evie,' said a cool voice. 'I must shoot him for dishonouring you.' The Duke, elegance itself in his beautifully cut breeches, strode manfully into the room, his handsome face making Max look overblown and coarse . . .

'Mum,' said Rosie, sticking her head round the door. 'You missed a yummy lunch. I'm going to turn into a crab if I eat any more of it. Are you coming down to the pool for a last bit of sunbathing?'

Stretched out on her lounger, Evie turned the pages of her book listlessly and laughed as Cara and Rosie held races in the pool with Andrew doing the Olympic commentator coverage:

'And Cara Fraser has proved herself to be a champion

swimmer today even though she stuffed her face with *gambas pil pil* at lunch,' droned Andrew, in intense radio-presenter style, 'while Rosie Mitchell has just switched styles into the . . . er, butterfly flop and is drowning everybody else around the pool.

'Now, in a surprise move, ex-Olympic medallist Mrs Vida Fraser is getting into the pool to show these youngsters how it's really done. Mrs Fraser, better known as Esther Williams's sidekick, has great hip movement . . .' Andrew stopped when Vida and Cara managed to hit him with the inflatable plastic whale Rosie had bought to lounge on.

Despite all the high-jinks going on around her, Evie's misery never lifted. She kept her nose buried in her book but didn't manage to read a word all afternoon. Max was out until six, when he walked down to the pool and threw himself on to the lounger between Cara and Evie.

Instantly, Evie got up and collected up her things. 'Well, I'm going to get ready to go out. We're leaving at . . . eight, is it? I'll meet you all at the car then.' She ran upstairs and locked her bedroom door, just in case he tried to follow her.

By ten to eight she was dressed in the violet ensemble, which was, she realised glumly, the most beautiful outfit she'd ever owned in her life. Her bare legs were golden thanks to some of Rosie's fake tan, so that when the skirt's thigh-high side split parted revealingly, at least she wasn't displaying acres of white flesh. The off-the-shoulder cut to the clingy little top meant you couldn't really wear a bra unless it was strapless and, lacking one, Evie decided to go braless.

Tough titty, indeed, Mr Stewart, she thought mirthlessly, dusting her shoulders with bronzing powder and noticing that the outline of her nipples was ever so slightly visible when the top was pulled close down around her body. Once she'd pulled Vida's heated rollers from her head, her hair sat in perfect glossy curls.

It was as if she'd been given a make-over from Heaven, only tonight the man she'd wanted to look beautiful for wouldn't give a damn. He'd have eyes only for his bloody actress girlfriend.

Grabbing her handbag, she stomped downstairs and joined Andrew and Vida on the verandah, completely ignoring Max and the look of admiration on his face when he clocked her in the clinging violet.

If Max thought it was strange that the woman who'd writhed under him in ecstasy the night before was barely giving him the time of day now, he never got a moment to say so.

Evie sat in the back of the car with Vida after waving goodbye to Rosie and Cara, who were planning their own girls' night out, a night that involved Rosie borrowing half a ton of Olivia's eyeshadow and a lot of Evie's Pôeme perfume.

Andrew, Vida and Max chatted idly as Max drove out the coast road.

'Wait till you see this place,' Max said. 'Franz is obsessed with Westerns and says he fell in love with the ranch because it's half Spanish villa and half like something from *The High Chapparal*. When he took me there the other day, I almost expected him to strap on a couple of six guns and a stetson when we got home so we could round up some steers. He's a decent bloke, very sweet most of the time, but on set he's incredibly demanding.'

The car swung off the main road and headed into craggy mountains, rose pink in the setting sun. 'When we were making the Strauss biopic, we finished shooting *early*, which never happens.'

How thrilling, Evie fumed silently. Was that before or after your affair with nympho Mia?

They drove through the mountains for another half hour before taking a side road off into a dusty landscape. They passed a small village and then, to the right, perched perilously on a hill, saw a sprawling villa, gleaming white in the evening with lots of stables and outhouses extending behind it and tubs of blossoming flowers to the front.

Various cars were parked haphazardly on the drive, one a stretch limo so long Evie imagined you could play tennis in it. Mia's car, she figured, feeling her stomach knot with tension. Half-expecting a group of showbusiness harpies who all bitched relentlessly and looked like extras from a rock video, Evie was surprised when the huge wooden door opened and Franz appeared. Their host was a short bald man with an enormous belly and a friendly, welcoming smile. After kissing Vida and Evie as if they were old friends, he ushered everyone into a house decorated in typical Spanish style and yelled, over a background of opera, for Luisa, his wife.

'The others are here and there,' he explained, shouting over the noise, 'but they wake up when the champagne corks go bang!'

Luisa was grey-haired, motherly, and wearing an apron over a very sedate flower print dress. 'I'm cooking *paella* and everybody keeps stealing nibbles,' she groaned, waving a giant spoon. 'Come on, come on.'

The party was in full swing in a large room with a balcony off it, although Evie reckoned by the state of some of the guests that they were still partying from the lunchtime session. They all looked very ordinary, no rock-star types or movie moguls waving cigars and Rolexes around: just happy people red-faced from the sun, some still in T-shirts and shorts, others more formally dressed in summer dresses or polo shirts and casual trousers. Evie felt as overdressed as a strippergram in an eskimo suit.

Max was immediately swallowed up by the crowd, delighted to see him and shouting 'Max, over here!' in a variety of languages. Nobody was glamorous or desperately exciting. Instead, they all looked like Evie had after her first few days in Spain: tired but utterly thrilled to be away from work and in a place where the sun shone every day.

She soon found herself chatting to Franz's favourite cameraman, Lippo, who was supposed to be going home the next day but had decided that he and his make-up artist wife weren't going back for another couple of days because they were too worn out after a four-month production on location in the Black Forest. 'He works non-stop,' shrugged Lippo's wife, Hélène, before getting off the couch to phone home and tell their teenage twin sons the news that they'd return on Wednesday.

'They're nineteen and I'm afraid the house will be wrecked by their partying when we get back home,' Lippo confessed mournfully.

'I know the feeling,' Evie said. 'My daughter's seventeen but she's with us on holiday. She's out for the evening.' Evie accepted a glass of water from Franz, despite his attempts to get her to take alcohol. After her Martini débâcle, she was determined to remain as sober as a judge. 'I worry myself sick about her but I think she'll be all right tonight. She's with my sister who's nine years older than her and should be in charge, though when they're together, it's like having *two* teenagers.'

'The twins don't sound too upset,' remarked Hélène arriving back with a bowl of olives. 'The vacuum is broken apparently, and I ask how they *know* because they never use it!'

Marvellous *paella* smells coming from the balcony proclaimed that Luisa's dinner was finally ready.

'We're eating outside because the dining-room table disappear when we move,' Franz announced, leading everyone out to the enormous balcony where places were laid on two vast wrought-iron tables. Sitting with Lippo and Hélène, chatting and laughing and eating enormous black olives, Evie began to relax and stopped worrying about whether she was overdressed or not.

Max was chatting to Franz about work the whole time and kept shooting her almost pleading glances, as if to say, What have I done wrong?

Evie was on the verge of smiling back to say, Nothing, I was just fretting about something that happened a long time ago, when something caught Max's eye. Or someone.

The chattering and laughing continued unabated as Evie followed Max's gaze and saw a woman slip quietly into the room from the balcony and pick up a packet of Marlboros from a coffee table. Her lustrous chestnut hair was tied up in a casual knot and her heart-shaped face dominated by the most perfect mouth Evie had ever seen outside a lipstick commercial. Slanting, cat-like dark eyes were ringed with thick dark lashes and practically no other make-up. Lighting up, she put the cigarette between her perfect lips and inhaled deeply, with the finesse of a young Bardot.

Mia wasn't movie-star tall, the way Evie had imagined her to be. In fact, she was petite and so delicately slim as to make every other woman in the room look like a 2,000-passenger cruise liner beside a sleek racing yacht built for two. A minuscule white T-shirt stretched across her tiny frame had 'I'm Purr-fect' written on it and she'd tied a white sarong around her bronzed waist as if she'd only just got out of bed and had flung on the first thing to hand in order to cover herself. But Evie reckoned Mia would have no problem sashaying around clad just in a bikini no matter what time of the day or night it was. She looked stunning and, from the way she gazed around the room in predatory silence, she knew it. Evie loathed her on sight.

She glanced quickly towards Max, watched his Adam's apple contract as he gulped at the sight of Mia, and felt as if she'd been punched in the stomach. Nobody could remain unmoved by somebody as beautiful as that. And Max almost certainly *was* moved. His gaze flickered back towards Evie but, before he could catch her eye, she immediately turned to Hélène and muttered something inane about the weather.

Everyone was too busy to notice Mia and Max move into the hallway, Mia's tanned and slender arm wrapping itself possessively around his. But Evie noticed.

The meal continued, with applause for Luisa's cooking and even more applause when Franz brought out a bottle of Sambucca and a box of matches to go with the enormous fruit salad everyone was having for dessert.

Evie was on autopilot, wondering how long she'd be able to cope with this. It had been a huge mistake to come here. She couldn't bear the sadness inside her at the thought that Max was involved with Mia after all the things he'd said to her.

When Max and Mia arrived on the balcony half an hour later, Evie stiffened. Mia's face was happy, her mouth curved into a wonderful smile. She slid into Max's vacant seat beside Franz, leaving Max to search for a spare chair. He dragged it to the table and looked up as if to figure out where he'd position it, when Mia pulled his sleeve and made him sit beside her. She leaned forward, murmured something into his ear and then brushed her mouth against his cheek. He smiled. Evie watched, jealousy rattling inside her.

Hélène laid a soft hand on Evie's arm. 'Mia flirts,' she said simply. 'It is her way.'

'It's nothing to do with me what Mia does,' Evie said, with a false laugh.

Hélène shrugged. 'I think Max would want you to understand Mia. She and he were . . . involved,' Hélène said with a Gallic raising of eyebrows to imply that the involvement was more than just meetings to discuss production values. 'It is over but now Mia wants it back. She is bored and is used to having her own way.'

'I can see that,' Evie said drily, as Max obediently held a lighter up to Mia's cigarette. 'If she wants him, she can have him.'

Hélène leaned closer. 'I know him a long time,' she whispered. 'He doesn't want her but he is kind. He lets her down easily, as you say. It is you his eyes follow all the time.'

Stirring sugar into her cooling coffee, Evie spoke bitterly: 'Max is a man, Hélène. His eyes follow anything female with a pulse, and as it happens I'm getting married next month. So I really don't care whether he and Mia rekindle their fling or not.'

She pushed back her chair and rushed inside, desperate to find the loo before she started to blub again. The third door she opened led her into a small cloakroom decorated with French lithographs of semi-nude Edwardian girls advertising beauty soap. She stayed there, sitting on the toilet lid until Luisa knocked gently on the door and asked if she was unwell.

'Yes,' Evie said truthfully, opening the door. She was sick with despair, after all. 'Could you ring a taxi for me, Luisa?' she begged. 'I want to go home but I don't want to break up the party. I just want to slip away. Will you get Vida to bring me my handbag so I can tell her? But don't tell anyone else.'

Luisa's kind, understanding face nearly made her cry. 'I will do it,' she said.

Vida wanted to drive her home but Evie was firm. 'It's just a migraine,' she said. 'Please don't come, it's too early to break up the party on the last night of the holiday. I'll be fine. Don't say anything to anyone, please,' she implored.

The taxi cost practically all the money she had with her, but she was so grateful to the driver for getting her away from the party that she'd have paid him double. At the villa she roamed around downstairs for ages, tidying up the kitchen, wiping down surfaces with a cloth and sweeping the marble floors. When she heard the wooden gates being opened, she ran upstairs, left her bedroom light off as she pulled off her clothes and threw herself into bed. Her breathing had only just got back to normal after her dash upstairs, when she heard the bedroom door open.

'Evie,' said Max in a low voice.

Clutching the bedclothes tightly, she kept her eyes glued shut and didn't move.

'Evie,' he said again.

When he still received no reply, the door shut again quietly. She cried herself to sleep.

Cara flopped down on the bar stool Rosie had been holding for her, exhausted after boogying for half an hour with a tall, slim Greek boy named Tim. Lean and hungry-looking, he was one of the best dancers she'd ever met, with a pelvis that swivelled like Elvis's in *Viva Las Vegas*. He was proving to be one of the best kissers too. The way he'd French kissed her on the dance floor made her realise how much she missed the constant love making with Ewan.

When they'd been together, there'd never been a minute when they weren't touching, holding hands or giving each other small, affectionate kisses. It was that affection she missed, she thought, a shaft of misery piercing her. Why was it that marvellous moments made her sad? Even when she and Evie had been relaxing by the pool, in blissful sunshine, she'd felt maudlin. Being happy was so bloody bitter-sweet.

But despite thinking about times past, Cara was enjoying herself. Feeling Tim's mouth superglued to hers, his tongue plunging excitingly down her throat, had made her feel sexy for the first time since she and Ewan had split up. Maybe he was the one, the all-important post-relationship bonk. He was very charming and obviously fancied the knickers off her. Cara grinned, glad she'd worn her clinging sharkskin trousers, even though she was afraid she'd roast in them.

'Talk about tonsil hockey,' grinned Rosie, when she turned around on her bar stool to talk to her aunt. 'I was afraid I'd have to send a search party down your throat with a rope and crampons to haul him up.'

Cara erupted into laughter. 'I was a bit worried myself,' she said. 'But he's cute, isn't he?'

'Very cute,' Rosie agreed, 'and, boy, is he eager.' She leaned forward and whispered into Cara's ear. 'His friend was just as eager but I told him I don't rate a quick screw outside a Spanish nightclub as the ideal way to lose my virginity. That soon shut him up.'

Cara howled with laughter. 'If your mother ever heard you talk like that . . .' she said.

'She'd be pleased I wouldn't dream of bonking some complete stranger,' Rosie pointed out. 'I'm not throwing myself away on someone who won't remember my name in the morning. My generation has a different attitude to sex from yours,' she added reprovingly. 'Quick casual flings aren't true to the message of strong women. I have too much respect for myself to do that.'

'Yeah,' said Cara, feeling chastened that her seventeen-year-old niece had her head screwed on more firmly than she did when it came to sex. Lord knew what Rosie would say if she knew Cara had bonked her company's motorbike courier thanks to nothing more than about a zillion Tequila Slammers and a total lack of inhibition. Respect didn't even come into it.

'It's not a conservative morality thing,' continued Rosie, the stalwart of the debating society getting into full swing. 'It's about being strong and valuing yourself and your body. We have discussions about this all the time. You know, if Brad Pitt appeared and asked you to have sex, you'd go mad for him, wouldn't you? But,' Rosie sipped her beer thoughtfully, 'you wouldn't be doing yourself any favours. You'd just be some old slag to him and you'd never forgive yourself.'

'No, you wouldn't,' Cara murmured, thinking that if Brad Pitt landed in her flat looking for sex, she, Phoebe and Zoë would probably flatten each other in their attempts to get to him first. If it was a generational thing, then Rosie's generation were *so* different from hers.

Cara's peers thought it was a sign of equality to treat men on their own terms, to be a lad, to have sex with the thoughtlessness of men. Whereas Rosie's generation obviously thought that treating men with detachment until it suited them to get close was the way forward. Reflecting on the complete disaster she'd made of her own personal life, Cara decided that her niece had it all worked out.

'Wanna dance, Rosie babes?' said a voice. It was Gwynnie, a blonde Australian girl, who, with her two pals, had befriended Rosie while Cara had been off with Tim. 'See ya got rid of the geek!'

'Yeah, he obviously thought he was a customs officer,'

Rosie joked, 'hands all over the place. I told him to shove off. Let's dance.'

Cara watched the younger girls head for the cramped dance floor where they danced with abandon, hair and arms flying rhythmically, definitely not requiring any guys to make their evening go with a bang.

'You kept me a seat,' said Tim, appearing miraculously with a bottle of beer.

'Oh, er, yeah,' said Cara, not sure what to do with him after Rosie's sobering denunciation of casual sex. Perhaps that post-relationship bonk was a bad idea after all. But Tim, high on strong Spanish beer and turned on by dancing with this Amazonian beauty of a girl, was in the mood for lurve.

He sat close to Cara, nuzzling her neck and whispering sweet nothings in her ear in Greek. At least she *hoped* they were sweet nothings – he could have been reciting her extracts from the chemical engineering textbooks he was studying in college for all she knew.

It had sounded lovely earlier, when they'd been lulled by sexy music throbbing out an erotic beat. Now, with Rosie's condemnation of laddishness ringing in her ears, Tim's murmurings were decidedly less erotic.

It was after twelve, the club was growing hotter and it was jammed. There were people crowded around them, crushing Tim closer to Cara as they tried to get to the bar. Sweat glistened on his forehead and Cara could feel the back of her thighs growing damper by the minute in her sharkskin trousers. She took a cooling sip of mineral water but that only helped for a moment. It was so hot and sticky. What she really wanted was to get outside and feel a refreshing breeze on her face.

'I need some air,' she gasped to Tim. 'I'll be back in a minute.'

Smirking, he followed her through the throng and past the loos until they reached a small dark courtyard at the back of the club where heaving bodies swayed in the moonlight. The music was muffled out here but it was wonderfully cool after the volcanic temperature inside.

Cara flapped her crimson shirt around her body to cool herself and found herself jammed up against the wall by an eager Tim. The whitewashed plaster was uneven and ground into her back as Tim ground himself into her front, tongue on overdrive and hands body-searching madly. Like Rosie's would-be customs officer, Cara thought in shock. Frozen in surprise, she said and did nothing. She could hardly complain, could she? They had been glued to each other all evening and he'd evidently assumed her desire for a little night air was a coded message of desire for him. The Greek sweet nothings had dried up as Tim buried his head in her chest, moving downwards.

Cara felt suddenly weary. She didn't want this, she wanted to go home and climb into bed between cool, clean sheets to read her book. But it was all her own fault. She'd led him on and now he wanted to collect. It was always her own fault: a couple of drinks and she felt happy, confident and capable of flirting. The only problem was, flirting was only permissible when you were able to head the flirter off at the pass.

The way she handled it, they took her lack of resistance to mean all systems go and railroaded their way on through. Tim was groaning, frantically trying to open the button to her trousers. The waistband was tight after six days of glorious Spanish food and opening the button almost impossible, even when you wanted to. Cara didn't. What the hell was she letting this drunken kid unbutton her trousers for? What the hell was she doing out here? She didn't want to be here and she was going inside, now!

'Tim!' she barked, shoving him and his burrowing hands away from her with all her considerable strength. 'Whaddya think you're doing?'

'What we both want,' he said, smirking.

'I came out here because I wanted air, not you!' she said fiercely.

Stunned, his face like a spoiled child told he's not getting the latest Sony PlayStation for his birthday, he gazed at her. 'But you came outside . . .' he stammered.

'For air, Tim,' she yelled. 'I said I wanted air and that's what I meant. I told you I'd come back.'

Eyes flashing, he shrugged. 'Women never say what they mean,' he said dismissively.

Cara drew herself up to her full height, gave him a pitying look, and drawled: 'Well, I do, sunshine. And as we say in Ireland, you can rev up and fuck off. Goodbye.'

Feeling ten feet tall, she turned on her heel and strode majestically into the club, shoving her shirt back into her trousers and flicking back her hair in triumph. Talk about girl power and respect! Yes!

Why hadn't she done that years ago? Bloody Owen Theal would have benefited from some of that treatment – and perhaps a good left hook to the jaw into the bargain, she thought with satisfaction. Suddenly she was filled with longing for Ewan, for his arms around her and his mouth crushed against hers. What had she been playing at with Tim? What had she been playing at with Ewan, come to that? She'd completely screwed up their relationship thanks to her neuroses. It was about time she got to grips with her problems and started living.

Cara felt her head filling with plans and ideas. She'd phone Ewan the moment they got home, tell him she was crazy about him and announce to the entire office they were in love. And she'd find a counsellor in the phone book, someone to open all the locked doors in her mind, doors behind which demons lurked; ones that looked like Owen Theal.

She moved to the pulsating Euro disco beat and joined Rosie and Gwynnie on the swarming dance floor. 'Hey, girls, where are we going next?'

Evie dragged her suitcase downstairs and left it by the door. As if by magic, Max appeared.

'Evie, why didn't you tell me you wanted to leave early last night? I'd have driven you home.'

'There was no need,' she said evenly. After spending much of the night rehearsing exactly what she'd say to Max, she couldn't let herself down by screaming that she was as jealous as sin and he was a dirty double crosser to have her and Mia going at the same time. 'I was tired and needed a rest.'

Max looked as if he needed a rest himself. His face was drained and, despite his healthy bronze colour, there were shadows under the normally blazing cobalt blue eyes that today looked dimmed somehow.

'We need to talk,' he said urgently, 'about last night.'

'Why?' she asked briskly. 'I'm not your keeper.'

'I don't want you to get the wrong idea, Evie,' he said, raking a hand through his shining black hair.

She smiled coldly at him. 'I don't have any wrong ideas, Max. I merely needed to get away from everyone to come to my senses and consider what I nearly threw away.'

She meant the words to cut him to the bone and they did, she was sure of that. He recoiled slightly.

'What,' he said, eyes narrowed, 'does that mean precisely?'

'Just that,' she replied. 'Simon's a good man. I can't believe I nearly threw my whole future away for a hen night fling.'

The words nearly stuck in her throat. Her night had been nothing like a hen night fling. It had been wondrous, passionate, the most incredible night of her life. But she couldn't let him know that. No way.

'So that's all it was to you?' he said. 'A hen night fling?'

Evie could see hurt and bewilderment in his eyes but she ploughed on.

'Come on, Max,' she replied, words dripping cynicism, 'don't tell me it was any different for you?' "I love you" is very easy to say in the heat of passion, isn't it?'

'No,' he said flatly. 'It's not. Not for me.'

'Poor you then.'

She walked past him into the garden, wanting to put as much distance as possible between them. It would be so easy to crack, to cling to him and say she didn't care if he had ten women on the go at one time, so long as she could be one of them.

Swallowing deeply to control the lump in her throat, Evie walked across the lawn, still damp from the morning sprinklers. All she had to do was get through the journey home and then she'd never have to see Max Stewart again.

CHAPTER FOURTEEN

The washing machine repair man ate three Penguins and had two mugs of tea before he left.

'I'll give you a bell when I've got the part. Should be Thursday,' he said cheerily as Evie stood on the doorstep seeing him out. 'I still think it's better to get a new machine,' he added, shaking his head at the notions of women. 'That'll only give you another few months at best, but it's up to you.'

'No, it's not,' she muttered to herself, slamming the door. 'It's up to the bank manager.' Buying a new washing machine was undoubtedly the most sensible option since the motor in her seven-year-old one had conked out faced with acres of holiday washing.

But replacing the motor would give her at least another year out of the machine and, as she couldn't afford a new one, it was the *only* option. Irritatingly, not getting it fixed until Thursday meant she'd have to lug everything down the road to the launderette. Just as well she'd taken Monday off to sort herself out after the holiday. Some holiday! She may have looked happily tanned, but on the inside Evie felt as blue as Picasso's famous monochrome period. She sneezed abruptly and her eyes watered. A cold; she was also getting a cold. All she bloody needed.

The phone rang and she answered it listlessly, trying to reach the tissue she'd jammed up her cardigan sleeve to stem her sniffles. It was Simon, phoning for the second time that day to assure her he was on track for their lunchtime reunion. He'd been at his favourite aunt's hospital bedside over the weekend and so hadn't seen Evie since she and Rosie had arrived home from Spain.

Which was merciful, she thought, feeling the usual pangs of guilt whenever she thought about him. At least with a couple of days' grace, she'd be able to arrange her face into some sort of post-holiday smile and pretend she'd had a good time. Otherwise, he'd see the bleak, hollow eyes that stared back at Evie every time she looked in the mirror and even Simon, not the most sensitive person in the cosmos, would realise that something was wrong.

'Hugh gave me a wedding present this morning,' he was saying proudly, obviously thrilled that the senior partner in the firm had deigned to remember Simon and Evie's forthcoming nuptials.

'Oh, what is it?'

'A Lladro dancing couple,' Simon said excitedly. 'Apparently, it's very expensive stuff.'

'Lovely,' Evie replied. She hated Lladro.

'I've booked a table for one o'clock in Kite's in Ballsbridge as a special treat, is that all right?'

'I have a wedding dress fitting,' Evie reminded him, 'so I might be late. You know what the traffic is like.'

'I'll order for you if you're late,' Simon said cosily. 'Sesame prawn toast and chicken in black bean sauce.'

Evie suppressed an urge to shriek that she didn't want anyone deciding what she'd eat, she'd bloody well pick her own lunch, thank you very much.

'Great,' she said. 'Must go, love. 'Bye.'

She was running so late that she had to abandon the car on a double yellow line in Ranelagh to run into Bridal Daydreams where four women were oohing and aahing over a short blonde who looked miserable at being jammed into yards of unflattering satin in a design that looked like a meringue waiting for the cream and kiwi fruit to be ladled on.

'I prefer the shift dress,' the poor girl was saying, although nobody was listening.

At least I don't have a committee orchestrating *my* wedding dress, Evie thought gratefully, slipping into the alterations room. Sweating from her sprint, she ripped off her clothes and then had to fan herself with a *Brides* magazine for five minutes so she wouldn't destroy the dress with perspiration.

'Lord, haven't you lost weight?' squealed Delphine, the dressmaker, as delightedly as she could with several pins jammed into the side of her mouth. 'All my brides lose a few pounds but you've lost at least half a stone.'

'Really?' commented Evie, totally unmoved by information that, two months ago, would have thrilled her to her bones. What a way to lose a few pounds! The Max Stewart Disaster Diet – spend a few nights with our hero and you'll never fancy a mayonnaise-and-full-fat-cheese-sandwich ever again.

"You don't want to lose too much,' warned Delphine, on her knees and pinning expertly. 'Or it'll be hanging on you. This style needs some bosom.'

The dress was a Jane Austen classic: Empire-line oyster satin with an embroidered bodice and lace-covered sleeves. The sort of dress Evie had purred over on the cover of her favourite Regency novels. Now, it didn't give her the same frisson of excitement when she thought she was actually going to glide down the aisle wearing it.

491

Delphine was going on about being thin again and how she'd gone back to Weight Watchers in the hope of getting rid of that impossible-to-shift three stone.

Evie looked at her own reflection in the wall-sized mirror gloomily. Despite having lost a few pounds, she was never going to be thin. Not Mia Koen thin anyway. You were either born with that thoroughbred bone structure or you weren't. No amount of dieting would give *her* spindly legs perfect for wearing floaty knee-length dresses and strappy sandals in sorbet-coloured suede. Or even casually thrown on sarongs and minuscule T-shirts, for that matter.

They were now on to the knotty subject of low-calorie biscuits. Delphine, mouth still full of pins, was an aficionado of every calorie-controlled item in the supermarket. Evie let her chatter away and mentally drifted off to a warm Spanish night where the cicadas made sweet music and Max's body had worshipped hers. What was he doing now? she wondered. Was he tucked away in some remote cosy hotel with Mia, kissing and making love, hating themselves for having wasted so much time when they could have been together? Did Max cuddle Mia after they'd made love, spooning his big body around her fragile one, stroking her with a sense of affectionate wonder? Evie must have looked so desolate suddenly that Delphine stopped talking and stared at her little face, pale under the tan.

'Cheer up, love.' Delphine squeezed her arm encouragingly. 'All girls get last-minute nerves – so do the lads, come to think of it. But it'll be fine. He'd want to be out of his mind to leave a lovely thing like yourself standing at the altar. Anyway, as the bishop says, there's always divorce if things go wrong!' Delphine screamed with laughter at her own humour.

'Yes,' Evie replied politely, thinking that things had already gone wrong and they hadn't even got as far as the altar.

Simon was sipping mineral water with a very pleased expression on his face when Evie rushed into Kite's, twenty minutes late, having guiltily abandoned the car on yet another double yellow line.

'Had to park on Pembroke Road,' she gasped. 'I hope I won't be clamped.'

'Oh, Evie,' he said disapprovingly. 'You should have parked in the Herbert Park Hotel like I did.'

'You're not supposed to unless you're going there,' she protested, tired from all her rushing about and twice as tired of Simon's small-mindedness. He could bore for Ireland in the Olympics about car parking in Dublin city.

'Have you ordered?' she asked. Anything to stem the inevitable 'I know a little car park on Shelbourne Road that nobody else knows about' conversation.

'Yes. I hope you're in the mood for sesame prawn toast?' he added, looking unsure of himself. 'If you're not, you can have my spare ribs.'

Touched, she got up from her seat, leaned over the table and kissed him on the cheek. For once, Simon didn't shy away from the public demonstration of affection.

'I missed you,' he said in a whisper, and grabbed her hand under the tablecloth when she sat down again.

Evie smiled back, desolate at the thought that, after a separation of a week, Max would have grabbed her in full view of the entire restaurant and kissed her so hard she'd have needed mouth-to-mouth resuscitation and a moment in an oxygen tent afterwards.

After a quick squeeze, Simon withdrew his hand and began to describe the Lladro wedding present in great detail. He only stopped when their starters arrived and then, after a brief nibble of his spare ribs, went on to discuss the implications of receiving such a large and expensive present from the boss.

'It's a good sign,' he said earnestly, pushing his horn-rimmed glasses on to the bridge of his bony nose, one hand wielding a spare rib recklessly. 'Hugh wouldn't do that for just anybody, you know. It's fast track all the way to partnership, I tell you, Evie.'

Evie, thinking of the whiskey-drinking, bimbo-loving Hugh of the Christmas party and his sad wife, Hilda, reckoned it was far more likely that she had remembered Evie's kindness to her that night and wanted to reward it in some way with a decent wedding present. Hugh looked like the sort of man who only remembered golf handicaps and how much money he was worth. Simon's wedding wouldn't register in his mind. But she said nothing.

She picked at her sesame prawn toast, sorry that she was wasting such a nice meal by feeling ill and not even slightly hungry. Her throat was getting sore and she felt fluey. She wondered if Kite's could magic up a hot whiskey for her? That'd nip her impending 'flu in the bud.

'Now that's something else I wanted to talk to you about,' Simon was saying, having eaten all his ribs. 'Phillip Knight and I were having a discussion this morning in the boardroom . . .'

Evie didn't hear anything else. She dropped her dainty piece of toast in horror. Phillip Knight? The partner she and Max had bumped into when they'd shared that illicit lunch together. Had he told Simon that he'd disturbed a cosy *tête-à-tête* between his future wife and her handsome stepbrother? Of course he had. What else could such an intimate meeting mean? Simon had a bit of spare rib stuck between his teeth. She stared at it, mesmerised and silent, waiting for the knife to fall.

'The wedding list, Evie. We simply have to have one. I know you're dead set against it but come on, in this day and age, you need one.'

Evie hated wedding lists. Too often she'd felt ashamed at only being able to afford some tiny china cake knife on the list because she was broke and couldn't dream of coughing up for six exquisite John Rocha wine glasses. Today, she was passionately grateful for wedding lists.

'Simon,' she said, thrilled at the reprieve, 'you're right. We do need one. Would you like to organise it?'

Shocked, he blinked at her, grey eyes wide behind his glasses. 'I can't do it on my own,' he said. 'We've got to do it together, Evie. You are slagging me, aren't you?' he asked suspiciously.

She grinned. 'Yes, and you've got some spare ribs stuck in your teeth.'

Simon went pink and dashed off to the loo to remove it. Evie took advantage of his absence to order a glass of red wine for herself. Simon disapproved of drinking at lunchtime but she felt that something alcoholic would cheer her up.

'Are you sure you'll be able to drive home after that?' he said reprovingly when he came back.

The next topic of conversation was wedding acceptances. As it was her second wedding, Evie felt there was no point going on with all the palaver about her father inviting everyone to this joyous occasion, etc, etc, so the invitations had asked people to reply to her address.

The replies had started to trickle in. People were thrilled to attend the wedding of Evie Fraser and Simon Todd. A few wondered where to send the presents and inquired about a wedding list.

'Mummy wants to buy us something special,' Simon said.

She could start with a washing machine, Evie thought.

'Actually, she's getting miserable, thinking about next Christmas and all that,' he added.

Evie felt sorry for him. His mother, a sweet but clingy woman, treated Simon like an angel sent down from Heaven to make her life liveable. It was a huge burden on him, particularly as he was her only child. He'd spent every Christmas since he was born with his mother. Evidently, the thought that Simon would no longer be able to spend endless hours with her had made her even more clingy than usual.

'I had an idea,' he continued slowly. 'If we sold both houses and got one with a granny flat . . . What do you think? I know it's a lot to ask you but . . .' He trailed off, waiting for her reaction.

Evie was silent. She felt the door clang shut ominously. Like Sleeping Beauty trapped in her tower, she was trapped by Empire-line dresses, cream-embossed wedding invitations, wedding lists – and Simon's mother, Mary. She had a sudden vision of the three of them, all playing bridge in a noiseless house stuffed with anti-macassars, dusty dried flowers and old Todd family pictures in tarnished silver frames. All old before their time, days unbroken by anything except the drudgery of work and the occasional glass of sherry when the equally aged neighbours came round for tea and Mary Todd's famed shortbread. It was a vision which horrified her.

'It's a lot to ask. Too much, isn't it?' Simon said quietly.

Unbidden, another vision fought its way into Evie's head: a vision of herself in twenty years' time, lonely because she'd screwed up any chance of happiness, desperately hoping Rosie would take her in so she wouldn't have to live alone with the memories of Max and how he'd destroyed her future with Simon. That couldn't happen! She wouldn't let it. She didn't want to turn into Simon's mother.

'It's not too much to ask,' she said firmly, unable to look at him. 'I know how much your mother relies on you. You'd do the same for me.'

The key turned slowly in the lock, imprisoning her forever. Eyes shining, Simon beamed at Evie across his sizzling beef.

She forced herself to smile back, a false grimace that Max would have seen through in a moment. Why did it always come back to him?

'You're so good to me, Evie.' Simon couldn't contain his delight.

If only you knew, she thought bitterly.

Rosie arrived home at the same time as Evie, flushed with happiness and looking striking in a strappy little rust top and denim skirt, both of which looked suspiciously new to her mother.

'Hiya, Mum,' she carolled, practically dancing into the sitting room, long dark hair bouncing, sloe-black eyes glittering.

'You're in a good mood,' Evie said when she'd recovered from a sudden burst of sneezing.

Rosie grinned at her, white teeth gleaming in her sun-tanned face. 'You'll never guess . . .'

Evie threw herself on to the couch, lay down flat and began to massage her aching temples. 'I can't guess today, love. I can't think for that matter. I've been coughing and sneezing all day. I think I'm getting something.'

'Poor Mum.' Rosie perched on the edge of the coffee table, obviously dying to impart her good news whether Evie was dying or not. 'I've got a job for the summer!'

'Great.' Evie raised her weary head and blew a proud kiss in Rosie's direction. 'I told you I'd probably be able to sort something out for you but you'd hate Wentworth Alarms, so I'm glad you've got something else. What is it?'

'A runner in Max's production company,' Rosie answered joyously, not noticing the look of horror on her mother's face. 'I told him I'd love to do something fun like that for the summer and he said he'd set it up. I went to see the production manager today and I start on Wednesday. It's being a gopher really, but I don't care.'

'That's wonderful, darling,' Evie said, the band of pain around her temples tightening.

'They're starting filming scenes in Wicklow next week,' gabbled Rosie. 'I can't wait.' She rattled on energetically, talking about what a lovely office DWS Productions had and how she hadn't seen Max but had met his personal assistant, who was 'like that Indian Miss World, utterly, depressingly gorgeous'.

She would be, Evie muttered to herself. Probably couldn't type to save her life but she'd have other *skills*, none of them the sort of thing you could list on a CV – unless you wanted a job in a Soho lap-dancing club.

Trying to be happy for Rosie's sake, Evie made all the right noises and agreed that, yes, Max was wonderful to have set this up because lots of people probably wanted to work in a production company as it was so glamorous.

'I know I haven't got paid yet,' Rosie revealed, 'but they're paying me loads more than I got last year in the wool shop, so I went shopping and bought this.' She patted her new denim skirt and top happily.

When Rosie went off to phone her friends and tell them the wonderful news that she had a job and new clothes into the bargain, Evie made herself a hot lemon drink, added some honey so it wouldn't taste as vile, and took it off to bed.

★ ★ ★

Wentworth Alarms looked exactly the same as usual: squat, redbrick and undoubtedly full of irate customers all waiting for Evie to come back so they could be dealt with. She parked her car in her usual space at ten to nine on Tuesday morning and climbed out wearily. A blast of cool July wind shot past, making her sneeze madly. Everything felt so cold after the blissful heat of Spain. She'd been shivering since she'd got up, despite all the lemon drinks and the anti-'flu tablets.

'Evie!' yelled a familiar voice. 'Welcome back. Did you have a lovely time? You look great, *so* brown.'

Lorraine was much browner, in fact, a wonderful bronze straight out of a Clarins bottle. All in pale linen like something from *White Mischief*, she looked as if *she* was the one who'd just come back from a week in the sun.

'Keep away or you'll get this,' snuffled Evie, pleased to see Lorraine but not pleased at the thought of facing the office after her week off.

'I never get anything,' said Lorraine, giving Evie a hug anyway. 'Craig says I'm as strong as an ox. You've missed so much, you can't imagine!'

'What?' asked Evie, startled for a brief moment out of her Max and 'flu misery.

'Davis is resigning. Well, he *has* resigned. His health means he can't work anymore. What do you think of that?'

Evie shrugged. 'I'm not surprised,' she said wearily. 'He's been like a bear with a sore head for the past six months since he was diagnosed with M.E. I knew it was only a matter of time.'

'Aren't you gutted?' Lorraine asked, astonished. 'You worked for him for so long and he was always so nice to you. Never to me, I might add. But he loved you.'

They'd reached the front door. Inside, the receptionist

was waving and smiling at Evie, who had no choice but to smile inanely back.

She tried to bolster herself up. She couldn't go into work this gloomy. You had to separate work from personal life, or so she'd told various junior members of staff who'd sobbed from nine to five because their boyfriends had dumped them or because the dreaded blue line had appeared on their pregnancy testers. 'You have to rise above it and be professional in the office, no matter what's happening on the inside,' Evie would lecture, while dispensing hot tea and fig rolls. How irritating she must have sounded.

'Lorraine, all bosses move on and we've got to go with the flow,' she said finally. 'Davis was nearing retirement age, anyway, so he had to go sometime.'

'I suppose,' Lorraine said. She made no move to open the door, obviously loath to discuss this inside the building. 'His nephew is taking over,' she said quietly.

Evie did groan this time. 'That eejit!' she said. 'We may as well all look for new jobs then, because he'll have us in liquidation in three months.'

'Not *that* nephew,' Lorraine put in. 'God, he couldn't arrange a piss up in a brewery! Another one. Davis's brother's son from Belfast. Wait till you see him, Evie. He's blond, tall, an absolute screw. And his accent is beautiful . . . so sexy. If you and I weren't so in love with Simon and Craig, we'd be murdering each other to get near him!

'C'mere,' she continued, pushing the door open. 'I love the way you've left your hair down. It's much softer than in your usual plait. And where did you get that copper-coloured shirt? I don't know why you don't get glammed up more often, it suits you.'

Rosie was in love with the world of TV films and couldn't stop talking about the *hours* it took to shoot just five minutes of film.

'It's fascinating,' she told her mother, lying on her back on the grass eating an apple while Evie determinedly weeded her tiny back garden. Weeds put prospective house purchasers off, or so Simon had written in the painstakingly typed memo he'd given her on the art of selling. Weeds, peeling paint, and plants that looked as if they'd been holidaying in the Sahara were all no-nos, apparently.

So were untidy kitchens, lots of junk, personal knick-knacks and too much furniture cluttering the place up and making it hard for the buyers to imagine *their* bookcase where yours was.

Evie had spent all Saturday morning de-junking the sitting room until it was practically a Zen retreat, with no magazines, no books, no family photos and no trinkets. She'd removed the small table beside the window where she kept her collection of china animals until she realised that the table was always kept there to hide a bit of carpet where a thirteen-year-old Rosie had spilled neat Ribena. Evie stuck the table back and put a white geranium on it instead, gathering up her little pigs, seals, rabbits and elephants and putting them safely in a box with tissue paper.

Now she was grimly tugging dandelions out of the right-hand border to the accompanying barks of next door's bored Jack Russell, who could bounce up and down and appear startlingly over the fence when he was in an energetic mood.

'Boris, shut up!' howled Rosie, throwing her apple core over the fence. 'We're trying to have a conversation here.'

Boris took no notice.

Eventually, Rosie got up, leaned over the fence, picked up the squirming little dog and put him down in their garden, where he ran around delightedly, peeing all over the weeds Evie was about to pull up. Peeing finished, he ran back to Rosie and licked her face with adoration for having released him.

'Are you hungry, little baby?' she crooned, tickling his velvety toffee-coloured ears. 'Want a biccie?'

'Don't feed him biscuits,' Evie warned. 'Sophie has warned us not to. The vet has him on a diet.'

As if he knew he was being talked about, Boris immediately ran over to her and wriggled up against her adoringly, demanding attention, hopeful she'd relent on the biscuit front. She pulled off her gardening gloves and petted him. He squirmed happily under her touch and rolled obligingly on to his back, showing off his soft beige belly.

'Boris,' said Evie affectionately, tickling his belly and wishing she could have a dog, 'how am I going to get any work done with you here?'

After five minutes of unadulterated love from Evie, Boris scrabbled to his feet and trotted off to make an inventory of plants that required his own particular brand of watering. Evie went back to weeding and Rosie went back to describing just how incredible film-making was.

'It's got to be *so* boring for the actors,' she said. '*We're* always doing something – the crew, I mean,' she added proudly. 'But *they* have to hang around in their trailers the whole time. One of them knits. Maisie . . . she plays the housekeeper to this family it's about . . . she's making a lovely jumper for her daughter. And some of the guys play poker in Nicky Reilly's trailer.'

'Isn't he the guy who was in that detective series, *Rozzers*?' Evie asked, resorting to her trowel for one weed that seemed to have millions of roots going off in every direction.

'That's him. He plays the son of the Butler family, the

one who was at Oxford and comes back just before the First World War with a new bride, who's played by the horrible Mia.'

Evie stopped digging. 'You mean Mia Koen's in it?' she asked in an unnaturally high voice.

Rosie made a gagging noise. 'She's an absolute cow. Everybody hates her.'

Evie smiled.

'Well,' Rosie said grudgingly, 'not everybody. The director thinks the sun shines out of her every orifice but none of the crew can stand her. She whines about *everything*. The catering van doesn't do the right salad dressing, her caravan's too small, the heating doesn't work and the weather's too cold. I mean, you don't come to Ireland for the weather, do you?'

No, you come for the men, Evie thought, glowering.

'She's only been there two days and already we hate her,' Rosie continued. 'Max'll soon sort her out when he gets back from London,' she added gleefully. 'Remember how he said he dealt with that mad woman who wanted crates of bourbon and smoked salmon for her dog! He won't stand for Miss Bossy Boots.'

I wouldn't bank on it, Evie thought wearily as she started on another bed. He'd probably run to Mia's caravan and solve her heating problem immediately, mainly by jumping into her arms and . . . She couldn't bear to think of the '. . . and'.

'The Butlers go ballistic to find that their son and heir has married this Frenchwoman – Mia,' Rosie continued with her plot revelations, 'and they say they won't accept her. But she's got such a hold over the son that he'll do anything for her.'

That figured. Evie wrenched a petunia out of the hard soil by mistake.

'He goes off to war and gets killed and she has an illegitimate son with his brother, but everyone thinks it's her dead husband's. Then they find out and throw her out of the house.'

Evie was beginning to like the sound of the Butler family.

'And she goes to America where her son becomes a politician, so she starts an American political dynasty.'

'Is this based on anything real?'

'No. It's a book by this American writer. It's a DWS/American production. The rest of it is set in Boston in the twenties. I'd love to go on location with them there,' Rosie said wistfully.

'I know.' Evie pulled off her gloves again. 'But you'll be at college by then, won't you?'

'Yeah.' Rosie plucked at the lawn resentfully.

Evie held out her hand to her daughter. 'Come on, I'm going to get cleaned up and then let's go off shopping. We haven't done that in ages. Now that you're a working woman, you need new clothes.'

'Ace!' said Rosie, leaping up. 'I saw this amazing shirt in French Connection. Could we go into town?'

Unlike her elder sister, Cara practically ran into work, she was so keen to get there. Ewan hadn't answered his phone when she'd rung the night before, so she was eager to see him in the flesh and tell him about her Damascene conversion. Not that she could explain that playing tonsil hockey with some sexy Greek bloke had been the reason she'd suddenly, blindingly, realised she loved him and that she was as mad as a bicycle not to have realised it properly before.

She wanted to tell him so much it almost hurt. She'd been practising all night and all morning, beaming happily even though she got up too late for breakfast, the bus was delayed for ages by roadworks on Portobello Bridge and she didn't even have time to grab a takeaway cappucino on her way to Yoshi Advertising.

Darling, darling Ewan – I'm sorry! It's my fault, you're right. I shouldn't have hidden our relationship, it wasn't fair to you. I've been a bit mixed up for a long time but I'm going to sort myself out and please, please can we go out again. Dinner, my treat?

So when she raced upstairs into the elegantly grey copywriting department and found his chair empty and his desk suspiciously clear, she got a shock. He couldn't have left the company? she thought, stunned. He'd talked about it but would he have gone without discussing it with her? Of course he would. You don't discuss career decisions with your ex-girlfriend, do you? Deflated, she leaned against his desk miserably.

'Looking for Ewan?' his boss, Ken asked, poking his head out of his office.

'Oh, er . . .' Cara stuttered. How did he know she was looking for Ewan? She never came into copywriting.

'Didn't he tell you? He took a few days off.' Ken came out of his office, Dunhills and lighter in hand to slope outside for a quick cigarette. 'I thought he meant he was going away with you, actually, but you know Ewan. If ever there was a man for heading off when the mood takes him, it's Ewan.'

Cara was speechless. Not because Ewan was known as an impulsive creature: she knew that. But because Ken was so convinced she and Ewan were an item. How did he know? She'd never told anyone except Zoë. And Ewan wasn't given to discussing his personal life in great detail.

'Well, er . . . thanks, Ken,' she muttered, heading for the door. As she took the stairs up to her office two at a time,

Cara thought about something Ewan had said at the end of their relationship, something cynical about how the gimlet-eyed staff in Yoshi could almost tell when he was wearing boxer shorts instead of underpants. 'They notice *everything*,' he'd emphasised, 'so don't kid yourself that there's anything private in your life. They know but they just aren't talking.'

He must have been right. Perhaps everybody already knew she and Ewan were dating but hadn't said anything. And in attempting to keep it quiet, she'd managed doubly to insult him. The whole office knew, but could see that Cara Fraser refused openly to acknowledge the relationship, which meant she was ashamed of going out with Ewan Walshe.

She winced. Nothing could be further from the truth, but her behaviour had made everybody think so.

'Good morning, Cara,' squeaked Penny, Zoë's replacement, in her high Cork-accented voice.

'What's good about it?' growled Cara, and immediately regretted sounding so brusque. It wasn't Penny's fault that Ewan was away and she couldn't make it all up to him. 'Sorry,' she added. 'Post-holiday blues.'

Penny's broad, plain face curved back into a smile. Nobody could be further from the air-headed bimbo Cara had expected to have to train thanks to Bernard's fondness for nepotism. Penny was eager, clever, and if Cara didn't already know she was the daughter of one of Bernard's best friends, she'd never have discovered the fact from Penny, who was determined to learn everything the hard way.

And, as her computer literacy was non-existent, it really was the hard way. A marvellous artist, she fell apart when faced with a blank screen, a wacom tablet and the Adobe illustrator package.

This morning, she seemed thrilled to have Cara back.

'It's been difficult dealing with Bernard,' she said diplomatically. 'He's been in twice already this morning looking for you about a project he said he wanted done before you went on holiday.'

'It's only five past nine,' said Cara in exasperation.

'I know,' Penny said uncomfortably. 'I told him it wasn't due until this Friday but he insisted you'd got the date wrong . . .'

Cara, already deeply pissed off with the way the day was progressing, felt her hackles rise another inch. So Bernard wanted to play silly buggers, did he? Well, he could think again. Cara Fraser had spent too much of her life kowtowing to manipulative bastards who used her own neuroses to control her. She was starting again from scratch and Bernard Redmond was going to get the full blast of her rage.

The phone rang. Cara snatched it up. 'Yes?' she hissed, sounding as laid-back as a prison warden during a cell-block riot.

'Cara, welcome back.' Bernard's voice was oily with charm. 'I believe there's a misunderstanding between us about when an assignment was to have been finished. Penny says it's my mistake, so it must be. All the same, even though it's my error, I'd be so grateful if you could have it for me by, let's say, Wednesday evening.'

The wind taken out of her sails by his admission of guilt, Cara could only gape at the phone. 'Er . . . yes, sure,' she said eventually. Then she stopped. Because of his mistake, she'd have to work late all week.

'Actually, Bernard, it's not OK,' she announced suddenly. She rooted around on her desk as she spoke for the hastily scrawled memo he had given her about the job. The date he wanted it by was the forthcoming Friday.

'I've got the original memo in my hand,' she said, voice steady. 'It was to be ready by this Friday, not the previous one. And it doesn't say much for our relationship if you chose to believe my assistant and not me.'

Bernard, for once, was almost speechless.

'I can't imagine I'd have made such a mistake . . .' he began.

'You did,' she interrupted. 'Luckily for you, Bernard, I can manage to get it done for you on time, but we're really going to have to discuss my future with this company if you persist in treating me like some sort of idiot savant. Penny is doing great work but I don't imagine she'd be able to cope with this entire department if I left and, quite frankly, I'm thinking of it.'

Bernard began to bluster. 'There's no need for that sort of talk, Cara. You're a great addition to this firm . . .'

'Maybe you could start treating me like one, then,' she said pleasantly. 'I'll be down later in the week for a discussion on my package. 'Bye.'

She put the phone down slowly and looked at Penny.

'We're going to have to rush to get it done after all, Pens,' she said. 'Bernard admitted it was his mistake but we're going to have to work late.'

Delighted that Cara's outburst was over, Penny nodded enthusiastically. 'I bought Danishes for us,' she added. 'In case you needed a sugar boost.'

Cara relaxed. 'You're a mind reader, Pens. What if I nip down to the kitchen and get us coffee and you get breakfast ready?'

Ricky had just sneaked a large measure of Cara's litre of previously unopened Spanish gin when she burst into the kitchen that night at half-eight, exhausted after overtime on bloody Bernard's project and desperate for something to eat.

Ricky attempted to stand in front of the bottle so she wouldn't see it but it was no use.

'You bastard!' she roared. 'That's my bloody gin and you know it. It wasn't even opened.'

Ricky fluttered his long, girlish eyelashes bashfully. 'It is now,' he said, on the charm offensive. 'Can I pour you one? You look like it's been a bad day at the office.'

'No, you bloody well can't,' she shrieked back at him. 'You are a fucking . . . fucking . . .' She couldn't think of the word. Then she remembered. 'Parasite! You eat all our food, drink all our drink, borrow our CDs and never give them back. My Baz Luhrmann CD has the cover broken since you got your paws on it, and it's a waste of time buying biscuits round here because you snaffle them all, you big savage. I'm sick of you!'

Swiping her bottle of gin away from him, she stormed off in search of Phoebe to complain that, this time, Ricky had Gone Too Far.

'Phoebe,' she roared dangerously. Her friend wasn't in her bedroom so Cara, enraged, tried the bathroom where she found her flatmate sitting on the floor looking greener than the avocado bathroom suite. Phoebe's pretty moon face was desolate and her eyes were red-rimmed, all the eyeshadow rubbed away.

'Phoebe, what's wrong?' Cara asked, automatically forgetting her temper at the sight of her friend in distress. It was as though Phoebe had been holding in the tears until she heard a comforting voice, when she knew she could let go. As if Cara had turned on a switch, Phoebe's tears flowed like Niagara.

'Oh, Cara,' she sobbed, 'you'll never believe it . . . you'll never believe it.'

Cara, squatting down on the floor, found herself leaning on a pregnancy tester box, and could believe it all right.

'You're pregnant,' she said, matter-of-factly.

'How could you tell?' wailed Phoebe. 'Is it that obvious?'

'No.' Cara held up the box to enlighten her.

'My family will kill me.' Phoebe was sobbing heavily now.

Cara hugged her, wishing she could pass on some of her own strength. 'They won't. And even if they do, *I'm* here, *I'll* help you.'

'Thank you,' Phoebe cried.

'Does Ricky know?'

The sobbing grew louder.

'Does he?'

'I can't tell him,' Phoebe said, between giant, heaving sobs. 'He's stopped working to go back to college – he can't afford a baby.'

'He's given up his job?' asked Cara, aghast.

'He's given in his notice. He's going to take a month off to travel at the end of the summer and then go to college.'

Briefly, Cara closed her eyes, thinking of what she'd like to do with Ricky. Travel would certainly come into it: travel out the window after his rear end had connected with her Doc Marten boot.

'He doesn't know why you're in here?' she asked Phoebe gently.

Phoebe shook her head.

'You don't want to tell him right now?' Cara continued.

Phoebe shook her head frenziedly. 'Never.'

'I'll get rid of him then and we'll talk.

'Phoebe's sick,' she announced blandly to Ricky. 'She's gone to bed. I think it's one of those vicious twenty-four-hour bugs that give you the runs the whole time,' she added, interested to see if the thought of hours glued to the loo would put Ricky off saying goodnight to his beloved.

510

He took a step backwards. 'Jesus, I hate that! I'm off. Tell her I'll see her tomorrow.'

He was gone in a flash, leaving behind the crumbs of a packet of fig rolls and several dirty dishes in the sink. Cara made a mental note to demand fig roll money off him the next time he turned up.

She took the gin, which she'd brought back from the bathroom on the grounds that gin mightn't be good for someone in Phoebe's condition, poured herself a huge one, added tonic and took a giant, refreshing slug. Ricky had been right: it *had* been a tough day at the office, but nothing was tougher than what she and Phoebs were going to have to deal with now. And Ricky hadn't a bloody clue. At that moment, Cara hated Phoebe's feckless boyfriend more than anyone else in the world for what he was doing to her dear, kind friend. Phoebe was such an innocent, she hadn't an enemy in the world and wouldn't squash a spider if she could get some braver soul to pick it up and put it outside the door. She didn't deserve insensitive, brainless Ricky. Nobody did.

Cara boiled the kettle, quickly made a cup of weak, sugarless tea, the way Phoebe liked it, and took it and her mega-gin back to the bathroom. It was going to be a long night, she just knew it.

Olivia sat in her dressing room opening fan mail. She still got an enormous thrill at the sight of the kind, encouraging letters she got from fans of her slot on the programme, and despite the length of time it took to reply to each one personally, she did it.

Mind you, there were a few letter writers who weren't quite so kind or encouraging. They weren't sane either, she felt. 'Why would anyone want to send a letter like that?' she gasped to Kevin the first day she received one such letter, holding the offending sheet of paper between the tips of one finger and her thumb as if it was contagious.

'Ooh, give us a look.' Kevin read the letter, laughing merrily at the twisted viewer who said he thought Olivia had lovely breasts, and would she send him a pair of her knickers in the post? Worn, of course. 'They all want knickers, those pervie guys. I don't know why,' he said, wiping his eyes with mirth.

'Don't touch your face after holding that horrible letter!' Olivia shuddered, washing her hands feverishly in the tiny handbasin. 'You don't know what you'd get.' She shivered, shocked at the thought that there was anyone out there who'd watch her cookery slot, concentrating on her breasts instead of her cooking. It was horrible, horrible. Kevin stuck the letter and its envelope in a page of his A-4 notebook, obediently scrubbed his hands and patted Olivia's arm comfortingly.

'Olivia honey, all the personalities get the odd pervie letter. It's the price of fame, I'm afraid. I'll give this to the station's security office because this particular gobshite has included his address, so the security people will pass the details on to the police. But don't worry, most of these blokes are harmless.'

Olivia didn't look convinced.

'Probably forgot to take his tablets that morning, probably lives with his mother and the nearest thing he gets to a woman is watching you in the morning while Mummy irons his Y-fronts before he puts them on.'

'Ugh! That's worse.' She was sickened by the vivid picture Kevin had painted.

'I can get someone else to open your letters if you want,' he offered kindly.

Olivia shook her head. 'I should do them myself.'

'Nancy might volunteer to open yours,' Kevin added

innocently. He always knew how to make Olivia laugh. It was no great secret that Nancy Roberts was enraged that Olivia now got practically as much fan mail as she did. It'd kill Nancy to have to open Olivia's letters. It already killed her that Olivia's slot had been extended to four days a week because it was so popular with viewers. Nancy had been queen of the *Wake Up Morning Show* for years and it was entirely possible that she'd stab any person who took that popularity away from her.

Olivia slapped Kevin gently on the arm. 'Brat!' she said.

'Ooh, beat me, you sadist,' he squealed in a put-on falsetto. They both cracked up laughing.

'You're a head case, Kevin, do you know that?' Olivia said fondly.

'Not as bad as Nancy.' He smirked. 'She *loves* getting the pervie letters because she likes the idea that there are people out there who fantasise about her knickers. Mind you, there can't be many of them out there and you'd need an enormous envelope to send one of her used pairs in the post . . .'

Olivia grinned at the thought of how hilarious Kevin was on the subject of La Roberts. He loathed every over-bleached, cosseted hair on her head, and the feeling was entirely mutual. Unfortunately, since Kevin now worked so closely with Olivia, he was also on Nancy's hit list.

'I'd like to see the bitch try and get me fired,' he'd said bravely when he'd had too many post-show glasses of wine in hospitality. 'I'd rip her hair extensions out by the roots!'

But Olivia was suffering too.

In the four months she had been appearing on Nancy's show, the presenter's demeanour towards her had gone from chill-cabinet temperature to deep freeze. These days, Olivia was lucky to get a frosty 'hello' from Nancy at production meetings, and when Olivia had suggestions for

CATHY KELLY

the programme, there was always a dismissive snort from
Nancy's end of the meeting table. But she'd stopped being
outright nasty – mainly because Olivia had been winning
the battle of the ratings and consequently had Linda Byrne
firmly on her side, protecting the show's new star.

When Nancy's barbed comments began to earn her a
sharp 'Is that helpful, Nancy?' or 'If you're not interested,
would you like to skip the meeting?' from Linda, she soon
kept her bitchy little asides to herself. Except on the set
when there was nobody else around.

'Shimmery fabrics come up very tarty on screen,' Nancy
would hiss nastily just before the cameras rolled when the
two women were forced to stand side by side in the on-set
kitchen.

'Really?' Olivia would reply, smiling serenely for the
camera in her shimmery aquamarine blouse, before
launching into her spiel. Nancy didn't bother her. After
years of confidence-sapping carping from Stephen, who
could take the paint off a door with his remarks, childish
bitching from a blowsy television hostess just rolled off
Olivia like water off a duck's back. She could cope with
Nancy's jealousy. Just about. As she'd given up teaching for
a year to concentrate on her TV career, she had to!

Now Olivia ripped open another envelope with the
deadly-looking silver filigree letter opener Max had given
her: 'In case you're in danger of being stabbed in the back
and need to reciprocate,' he'd said wickedly in the letter
that accompanied his gift.

He knew what he was talking about when it came to the
world of television, Olivia thought with amusement, every
time she used his present.

She'd opened twenty letters and had begun writing short
notes on her Klimt-decorated notelets when Linda stuck
her head round the door.

'Great, you're here. I thought you might have gone home after the show.'

'My daughter's being taken to a birthday party today by her best friend's mum and because I did the last bouncy castle duty, I'm reprieved today,' Olivia explained.

Linda, mother of three and a woman who knew as much about childcare as any working woman, nodded knowingly. 'So you're free for lunch?'

'Sure.'

Lunch was in the canteen, a glass-fronted place where few of the staff felt inclined to linger too long after they'd finished eating. Olivia picked up a brown bap filled with tuna and decided she'd have some rosehip tea for a change. She was dunking her teabag by the string when Linda plonked her own tray down on the table. The heaped plate of chips and sausages smelled wonderful.

'I know,' she said, already looking guilty. 'I can't believe I'm having lunch with the cookery expert and I'm eating motorway cuisine. But I *like* chips and I adore sausages. And Nancy's driving me nuts so I need a carbohydrate fix!'

Olivia chose to ignore the reference to Nancy. 'Linda,' she remonstrated, 'one of my favourite treats is Cheddar cheese cooked in the microwave on top of cream crackers. I'm not Delia Smith, you know. I don't go home and spend three hours making my own *linguine*. Cookery on TV is half reality and half wishful thinking, you know that. In the real world, we all go home and have Marks & Sparks chicken tikka masala. And that's on the nights when we feel creative!'

Linda smiled. 'I always forget how normal you are, Olivia. I'm so used to dealing with these damn' prima donnas who let on they spend hours making their own bloody pesto sauce.'

'I'd love to do that,' Olivia confessed, 'but you need an

515

awful lot of basil and two apartment window boxes aren't nearly big enough to grow a bucket of the stuff!' She leaned over and grabbed a chip. 'I love chips too,' she added. 'I wish people realised that you can love cooking and still think beans on toast is a fabulous meal.'

Her tuna fish bap tasted unappetising after one of Linda's chips so she stole a few more.

'Please do,' said Linda, shoving the plate in Olivia's direction. 'I'm gaining weight at a fierce rate. It's Nancy, she's doing my head in. So I go home and even when Des is away on business, I open a bottle of wine for myself once the kids are in bed, cook an entire pizza and pig out. It can't be good.'

'Join the club.' Olivia took another chip.

'What are you talking about?' said Linda. 'You skinny cow.'

Olivia took a sausage this time. 'Usually I'm really thin when I'm stressed,' she explained, 'because I can't eat. But even though I'm stressed up to my eyeballs right now, I'm as heavy as I've ever been because I eat so much convenience food.'

Linda groaned. 'So says the woman who weighs about eight stone in her heaviest clothes. Anyway,' she continued, 'I didn't bring you here to slag you off for being sickeningly, naturally slim.' She put down her fork. 'You're seriously interested in a career in television, aren't you?'

This was a subject Olivia had given a lot of thought to, particularly when she'd had to decide whether or not to give up teaching in order to fulfil her four days at the station. She'd compromised by taking the rest of the year off from teaching with an agreement to take up where she'd left off if her television career didn't pan out. It had been a tough decision to make. The other teachers had been gratifyingly sorry to see her go, while the pupils

– apart from Cheryl Dennis – had moaned that the school's only TV star was leaving.

'Will you come back and talk to us when you're really famous?' they'd begged cheekily on her final day, when they'd produced Good Luck cards and a surprising number of autograph books for her to sign.

'You never liked me signing anything in the past,' Olivia joked, 'especially the section on your homework notebooks when I had to ask your parents how the dog managed to eat your homework five times in a row.' She missed the kids, Olivia realised. Teaching was very fulfilling – sometimes.

Linda was waiting for an answer. Olivia decided to give it to her. 'Yes,' she said, grasping the bull by the horns. She *was* serious about TV.

'Great, because we've got a marvellous idea for a show for you but I wanted to sound you out first before Paul Reddin brought you in for the serious talk.'

'A show for me?' asked Olivia, astonished.

'Don't look so shocked,' Linda said. 'You're fantastic on the screen, Olivia, you must know that. Everybody's talking about you. We want to hold on to our discovery, that's all.'

'Your discovery?' Olivia said, aware she was sounding spectacularly stupid but still feeling a little bewildered by the conversation. Was Linda asking her if she'd like a programme of her own or was she imagining it?

'If we don't sign you up, somebody else will. Ever since you got that terrific review in the *Sunday World*, people haven't stopped talking about you.'

Olivia grinned. It had been a wonderful piece written by an obviously besotted male reviewer: '*The only thing worth watching on the* Wake Up *Morning Show is the luminous Olivia de Vere, a natural TV performer who is singlehandedly responsible for making thousands of previously cookery-shy men take an interest in doing things with garlic and onions. Compared to the formulaic wittering of the ceramic-faced Nancy Roberts, Ms de Vere's performances are always fresh, funny and entertaining.'*

'I thought we were going to have to send Nancy into John of Gods to recover when she read that,' Linda said, referring to a private hospital where people went to be treated for nervous breakdowns. 'She went stone mad.'

Olivia bit her lip so she wouldn't laugh. 'I didn't know they did Advanced Jealousy Therapy in John of Gods,' she said finally, giving up on her attempts to stop laughing.

'Don't laugh,' said Linda, doing just that herself. 'Nancy rang me at home on the Sunday *insisting* we fire you.'

'Really?' Olivia stopped laughing.

'It's OK, I told her you were far too important to the show and that if she had a problem with that, *she* could talk to Paul Reddin about it.'

'Wow!' Impressed, Olivia drank some rosehip tea.

'You are important to us, too important to let Nancy's ego ruin things.'

'Was she the reason the last cookery expert left?' Olivia inquired slyly.

'What do you think?' whispered Linda, looking around in case anyone was listening. The walls weren't the only things with ears in the station canteen. 'She was a brunette version of Nancy but with a smaller waist and bigger boobs. Theo loved her and so did we, therefore Nancy was determined she'd get the boot.'

Olivia chuckled. 'Tell me,' she said, 'under the circumstances, how the hell did I keep my job?'

'Didn't you know?' The producer looked surprised. 'Max Stewart told Paul he knew you'd be wonderful and to keep Nancy on a long leash until you'd found your feet.'

'Max!'

'You didn't know? I sort of thought you and he were . . . you know.' Linda looked a bit embarrassed. 'Well, you said you were separated and Max was so interested in your career and all that.'

'Nothing like it!' Olivia said, astonished. 'Max is just a friend. He's actually crazy about my best friend, to be honest, although neither of them seems capable of doing anything about it. That's all! Wasn't it kind of him to speak to Paul, though?'

'Jeez, I'm so sorry, I didn't mean anything.' Linda's voice was down to a mortified whisper now. 'It's just that it was because you'd been having . . . er . . .'

'Difficulties?' supplied Olivia wryly.

'Sorry.' Linda looked very embarrassed. 'Sorry for thinking you and Max were an item.' She paused. 'I'm making an awful hash of this, but I feel that I have to explain, it's only fair. If you do decide to take on the new show, you'll have to be ready for some sort of intrusion into your private life. People will be interested in everything about you. Some journalists want to know everything about you, from what you eat for breakfast to whom you're sleeping with. They like "in-depth" interviews and it's real soul-baring stuff. They won't touch you if you don't agree to tell all.

'They're not all like that, of course. Plenty of papers are happy with a ten-minute interview and a couple of glamorous photos, but the point is, you've got to be ready for the worst.'

'You mean that some people will want to know if I'm married, and to whom, and why we're separated?'

'Exactly.'

Olivia thought about it. She and Stephen had actually been getting on quite well since the separation. He'd moved into a small apartment close by in Booterstown and seemed eager to go to the marriage guidance counsellor with her, despite storming out of the first session. Olivia had been horrified but the counsellor, Myra, had been utterly unfazed.

'Happens all the time, dear,' she'd said calmly, handing her tearful newest client the big box of tissues she kept on the desk. 'I've seen much worse.'

Olivia's mind had boggled. She couldn't imagine anything worse than a furious man practically breaking a chair and yelling he wasn't having some spinsterish old bag telling him how to behave with his wife. But Myra had taken the entire thing with equanimity and had welcomed a subdued Stephen back the next time with a serene smile on her face.

Since then, progress had been slow but they were getting there. Like peeling away layers of old wallpaper, uncovering the problems in their marriage was a painstaking process and Olivia didn't know how they'd have managed without Myra, who had apparently seen it all and then some. Thanks to her, they were learning new ways to talk to each other without yelling or accusing each other of terrible things. These frank, utterly honest conversations had been strange at first: like hearing Stephen talk about insecurities Olivia didn't know he possessed. Even stranger had been discussing things she'd bottled up for years. She didn't particularly want to discuss any of this with a journalist. But at least she wasn't having a secret fling with Max Stewart to muddy the publicity waters. She resolved to thank him for his kindness in keeping Nancy off her back.

'Would they be very interested in all that personal stuff?' she asked Linda, who was toying with her plastic cup and looking as if she wished she'd never brought the whole subject up.

'Maybe, maybe not,' she replied vaguely. 'You're not Pamela Anderson, but then you are a beautiful blonde woman and people will want to know who the significant other in your life is.'

'Maybe I should pretend I'm a lesbian,' Olivia said with a grin.

'Now *that*,' said Linda, 'would really sell papers. If you came out, maybe poor old Theo would have the courage to. Poor love keeps insisting that the public aren't able for his sexuality and always has a model on his arm for every posh party. People love him, nobody cares whether he's gay or not. Anyway,' she got back to the point, 'I'm just warning you now, so you can make an informed decision. We really want you to do this show – I can't breathe a word more about it until we know you're interested – but I think you need to know what it'll entail.'

'Would it mean keeping on the morning show too?' Olivia asked.

'Hell, yes. We couldn't let you go from that. You're a star.'

Everyone had advice for her.

Max Stewart's was: 'Get an agent.'

Evie advised Olivia to say she'd have to think about the offer and would get back to them in a week. 'Jumping right in would look too eager,' she said thoughtfully. 'Make them wait. You're a professional woman now, you don't make rash decisions. Think how delighted they'll be and how much money they'll offer you when you say "yes"!'

Sybil de Vere said a killer accountant and a hard-as-nails lawyer were vital. 'Those bastards will screw you out of every penny,' she screeched down the phone, obviously well stuck into the Scotch. 'If your father and I had had any sense and had accountants looking after our money instead of that lying little runt of a bank manager, we'd be rich today!'

Olivia knew it wouldn't be wise to point out that her parents' kindly bank manager had kept the wolf from the de Vere door on many occasions and that Leslie and Sybil's own profligacy was the only thing responsible for their financial state. Scotch and the bitter truth wasn't a combination her mother was fond of.

The only person who didn't have any advice for her was Stephen, the very one who once could have been relied upon to dole out shovelfuls of unasked-for opinions.

'It's your career, Olivia,' he said quietly when she told him as they drank coffee in McDonald's on a shared day out with Sasha.

Myra had suggested the trip: 'There's no point going to marriage counselling if you never spend time together to see if it's working,' she said brusquely, recommending time spent as a family as well as time spent as a couple.

'I don't want to force you to do what I think is right. I've done enough of that,' he added ruefully. 'Controlling behaviour is not what you need right now.'

'You sound like Myra,' Olivia said with amusement.

The guarded expression went from Stephen's face. 'Yeah, well, it's an effort sometimes to speak like a psychiatrist,' he said candidly. 'I know what I *should* say but I'm just about to launch into one of my "This is the correct way!" speeches when I remember I'm not Field Marshall MacKenzie anymore. It's a hard habit to break. When controlling behaviour works for you, you keep on doing it. It did work for me. I could control you, Sasha, people I worked with. I was in charge, I was the dominant person.' His eyes took on a faraway look. 'Stopping isn't easy. It's like learning to speak a different language.'

'So your counsellor helps?' Olivia asked. It was the first time she'd referred to the therapist Stephen was seeing on his own. She'd been astonished and thrilled when he'd obliquely told her about it. The fact that he'd taken her seriously gave her real hope for their future.

He nodded, watching Sasha playing with the toy from her Happy Meal. 'Sort of. I still think I'm one of those people, with some, I don't know . . .' he paused, searching for the right word '. . . darkness inside me. I don't know why and it wasn't fair to you. I only hope I can deal with it and that you come back to me. Sorry.' He looked at her, suddenly haggard. 'I wasn't supposed to say that.'

He'd looked so desperate that Olivia nearly let her defences down and said, Yes, come back and live with us. But she couldn't. It had all been too hard, too painful. She'd cried herself to sleep too many nights, wondering if she'd destroyed her marriage to give in to an impulse now.

Stephen couldn't come back until they were all healed, all ready, otherwise they'd be back at square one in a year.

'You shouldn't,' she said softly. 'But I understand why you did. We just need to give it a little longer . . .'

Their eyes met. He stretched across the table, over the tray littered with empty burger boxes, and took her hand in his. 'I can wait,' he said fiercely. 'You're so different now – so confident, so beautiful – that I get scared you'll meet someone else, someone who doesn't need fucking therapy so he doesn't scream at his own kid.'

Olivia glared at him. 'Language!' she hissed, swivelling her eyeballs to where Sasha sat talking quietly to herself and her new toy.

'Sorry. A father who needs therapy so he doesn't swear in front of his kid,' Stephen amended apologetically. He held her hand tightly, his voice almost a whisper. 'I don't care what you do so long as I've got you, Olivia, don't you understand? I love you. Please don't forget that or me.'

With her other hand, she softly stroked the corded veins in his hand.

'I'm not interested in anyone else, Stephen. I never was. It's always been you, but it has to be right. If what we have is worth having, then we've got to fight for it.'

He nodded. It was then she realised that his eyes were full of tears. Hard man Stephen MacKenzie was crying in McDonald's in full view of the general public. It was unbelievable, incredible. Promising.

Olivia beamed at her husband. They were both changing, thank God.

Lorraine flicked through *The Star* aimlessly, ignoring most of the news. She paused at a picture of a glamorous woman in a glittery dress and sighed.

'Wouldn't you love to be going to parties and premières every night of the week?' she said.

Evie, spending her lunch hour laboriously ticking off acceptances in her wedding notebook, murmured yes in response.

'I mean, look at this dress. It probably cost two grand and I bet she didn't have to pay for it. Designers give people like Mia Koen dresses whenever they want them just for the thrill of having her wear their outfit in the . . . news,' she added, as Evie whipped the paper from her, scanning the photo.

How could any normal woman compete with *that*? she thought furiously. Mia, clad in a bum-skimming sequinned number that dipped so low in the front that the décolleté nearly met the hemline coming the other way, was pictured on the arm of a famous singer leaving a private party at the Merrion Hotel. Her chestnut hair was in artless ripples around her slender shoulders and she was laughing, seemingly unaware she was being photographed. Cow! Evie bet that woman could sense a photographer at five hundred yards.

Staring at the photo as if she wanted to see every dot individually, Evie searched for Max. There were people behind Mia but none of them looked like a tall man with strong shoulders and a jaw that could chisel marble.

He had to be there. Rosie had said he was back in Dublin and although Evie would have loved to have asked a million questions about him, she daren't. It would kill her to learn that he and Mia were together, the glittering couple to beat all glittering couples: the successful producer and the woman he'd made into a star.

'She's beautiful all right,' sniffed Lorraine. 'But I don't like her. Po-faced, if you ask me.'

'Smug is the word I'd have used,' Evie said bitterly. Smug because she had everything in the world; everything Evie wanted.

The intercom on the phone buzzed. It was Nicky Wentworth, the dazzling blond new boss who sent Lorraine and most of the female staff into spasms of delight just by speaking in his husky Northern accent.

'Evie, I know it's your break but could you come into my office for a wee minute?'

Lorraine stuck out her tongue suggestively and pretended to pant like an over-heated dog. 'Lucky Evie,' she gasped. 'If he asked me into the office for a wee minute on my lunchbreak, I'd gallop in.'

'Slapper,' retorted Evie, sticking her tongue out in retaliation. 'I'm not interested in him.'

'Then you're the only one who isn't,' sighed Lorraine dreamily.

CHAPTER FIFTEEN

Scowling at her monitor, Cara repositioned Saturn until it was the third planet from the sun and rearranged a couple of stars as ordered. She didn't see why she had to mess with the solar system simply because the creative director wanted 'that planet with the rings' nearer the front of the ad. In a fit of wickedness, she put Earth closest to the sun and vowed that if any astronomer complained about this fatal and reckless rearrangement of the solar system for a washing machine advert, she wasn't taking the blame. The creative director, a man so obsessed with the world of advertising that he genuinely thought the Milky Way was a chocolate bar, could take the rap.

Intent on the job in hand, she heard the door to the office swing open but didn't turn around. 'I hope you've bought supplies, Penny,' she grumbled. 'I could murder some crisps.'

'No, but I could offer you dinner later if you're that ravenous,' said a familiar voice.

Cara dropped her electronic pen in shock and whirled around to see Ewan lounging against the door jamb, looking effortlessly cool and relaxed even in the humid atmosphere of her non-air-conditioned eyrie. His green eyes glowed like tourmalines in a face tanned caramel by the sun and his dark curly hair was longer than ever, brushing the collar of the white linen shirt he wore loose over khaki combats. Like a round-the-world traveller who'd just wandered back after trekking leisurely around Morocco, he looked so laid-back he was practically horizontal.

'Hi,' she said, flustered and wishing she'd had some warning he was back. Here he was looking wonderful after two weeks away and she was greasy-haired and hollow-eyed from yet another late night comforting Phoebe. And, she was wearing a desperate faded brown T-shirt over her jeans because she'd been too busy to do any of her holiday washing. It was too small, had a gaping hole under one armpit and looked like something Oxfam wouldn't allow in the shop.

'Have a nice holiday?' she asked.

'Great. I went to Tunisia.' He didn't move, just watched her with those intense eyes. 'And you?'

'Wonderful, marvellous. We had great weather in Spain and I actually ended up lying in the sun, even though you know I'm not the greatest sunbather in the world,' she rattled on, trying to fill up his meaningful silence with words. She knew she should say something but she didn't know how. Despite her nervous prattling, she was at a loss for words.

'Ken said you were looking for me at the beginning of the week?'

'Yeah, I wanted to say hello . . . No.' Cara went over to him. She had to say this and there was no point waiting until she was all dolled up like a dog's dinner with freshly washed hair to do it. 'It was more than that.' The words tumbled out: 'I wanted to tell you that I was crazy about you and that I was so sorry for the way I hurt you. Please let's try again?'

They were practically the same height and as she stood just feet away from Ewan, Cara searched his face for a sign that he understood, that he wanted her back.

For an agonising few moments he didn't say a word. Then, his hands were around her waist, his mouth was on hers and they were kissing, melting together frantically as if they couldn't believe this incredible thing was happening.

'Oh, Ewan, I've missed you so much, I've been so stupid!' cried Cara, her mouth buried in his hair while his blazed a white hot trail along her neck.

'Me too, Cara,' he said hoarsely.

'I wanted to tell you on Monday. I've thought about it all the time I was away, that it was all my fault with my stupid neuroses. I mean, who the hell does it matter to that we're going out with each other?'

'I know.' His lips were at her collarbone now, devouring her.

'There *was* a reason, you know,' Cara said, feeling the desire leaping in her belly like a salmon leaping upstream. 'A stupid reason but still a reason. I want to tell you about it. It happened when I was at college and I never let myself get over it.'

He stopped kissing her, his face anxious. 'What happened in college?'

His mouth was dark from being bruised against hers and his pupils were huge with hunger, mirroring her own eyes

Suddenly, Cara decided that she'd tell him later. They had all the time in the world.

'We'll talk about it tonight,' she said, bringing her mouth down on his, 'in bed.'

When Penny climbed the stairs to the graphic design department a few minutes later, carefully carrying two mugs of tea and a Kit-kat, she found her mentor wrapped in a heated clinch with someone who looked like that lovely Ewan Walshe from copywriting. Penny thought it was him but you couldn't be sure because most of his face was buried in Cara's T-shirt.

As quietly as she could, she shut the door, went back down to the halfway step and unwrapped the Kit-kat. She wished she looked exotic and dramatic like Cara. Those cheekbones, the huge, reddened mouth and the rippling black hair made her stand out. Men were always looking at her admiringly when they went out for lunch together. Penny longed for men to look at her like that: hungrily yet cautiously, as if Cara's fierce hazel eyes fascinated yet frightened them in equal measures.

Penny finished the Kit-kat. If reincarnation worked, she was putting her name down for a Cara Fraser body and face, definitely.

Mary Todd looked uneasy. Evie tried not to notice. Her future mother-in-law always looked uneasy.

'Do you think we'd be able to look after that big garden?' Mary asked fearfully, as if the property had several, sprawling acres at the back instead of a long, narrow wilderness even Evie's short legs could cross in fifteen large steps.

'Of course,' Evie said impatiently, determined that whoever did look after the garden, it wouldn't be her. Then, seeing Mary's pinched little face, felt sorry for sounding snappy and put an arm around the older woman. 'It'll be fun, Mary,' she said. 'Imagine it all tidied up with a bit of lawn there and some nice garden loungers where we could sit on sunny days. Herbs maybe, by the patio, so the smell would hit us and some plants in patio tubs.'

Mary didn't look convinced. A fragile seventy year old, she was in constant fear of crooked paving stones and wet leaves in case she fell and broke something. The patio in the property she and Evie were viewing had more uneven paving stones than even ones. It'd all have to be ripped up and relaid if Mary was ever to sit outside with any degree of confidence.

Evie thought of how Rosie carelessly left magazines, tennis rackets and school bags abandoned on the floor and on every step of the stairs at home and wondered how Mary would fare if they were all living in the same house.

This place was certainly big enough for the four of them: the ground-floor annexe had one bedroom, a small sitting room and shower room, while the rest of the house had four bedrooms, a sitting room-cum-dining room, two bathrooms and a big kitchen. Large and therefore expensive, it was only within their price bracket because Mary, Simon and Evie were all going to contribute money towards its purchase. It was also desperately rundown and needed huge amounts of renovation. Looking at the pre-war decoration, Evie gloomily predicted a lifetime of stripping wallpaper and sanding down wood.

'I don't know if it's right,' Mary said tremulously. 'I know Simon said I'd like it but I'm not sure . . .'

Evie cursed Simon and the inevitable meeting which meant she was the one using up her precious half-day off showing his mother around the latest house that was, 'Just perfect for us, Evie!'

'Mary, we've all got to love it,' she said wearily. 'Don't worry your head about it if you don't. Your opinion is just as valid as Simon's. He can just find another house.'

'But with the wedding only two weeks away, we'll have to get it sorted before you go away to Greece,' Mary said, twisting the handles of her beloved patent handbag with nerves.

'Not to worry if we don't,' Evie said with false cheeriness. 'We'll manage until later in the year. Houses will be cheaper in the autumn, anyway.'

She settled Mary in the passenger seat, closed the door and closed her eyes. She felt totally frazzled. And the day wasn't over yet. The hotel wanted to see her about some detail to do with the banqueting hall where she and Simon were holding the reception. The wedding co-ordinator had been strangely vague on the phone, muttering about 'wanting to make extra sure everything's perfect'. Which meant another two hours gone driving into the city centre and back.

With Mary installed in The Duchess of Ormond hotel's airy reception sipping coffee, Evie followed the wedding co-ordinator upstairs to the banqueting hall where bad news was waiting.

A fire had damaged the very room Evie and Simon had booked, the prettiest room with a terrace where the guests could gaze out over the Dublin skyline and sip drinks surrounded by Italian urns overflowing with white, star-shaped flowers. The only other option was the biggest banqueting room, twice the size, very grand, but sadly a lot too big for the small number of guests at the Fraser/Todd nuptials.

'We are so terribly, terribly sorry,' the wedding co-ordinator apologised for about the eighth time in a row. 'We know you had your heart set on the Leinster Suite but the Munster one is very nice and my superior says we'll only charge you half the corkage on the wine by way of making things up to you.'

Evie gazed around the enormous, icy blue Munster Suite and thought of how her guests would rattle around in it like the last few matches in a box. Very formal, it wasn't anywhere near as nice as the cosy yellow room with the elegant cornices picked out in gold and the marigold-coloured brocade curtains that fell in graceful swags to the polished wooden floor.

'There's nothing else we can do,' the wedding co-ordinator said desperately, seeing the bleak look on Evie's face. He could hardly know that she wasn't just thinking about the venue for her wedding. That she was, instead, thinking that this was just another terrible omen for a day that seemed doomed.

'It's fine,' Evie said, switching on to automatic pilot.

She decided not to tell Mary about the Munster Suite disaster. If she had, they'd have had to rent a hotel room so Mary could lie down for an hour and get over the shock. It was hard to believe that Simon's mother wasn't that much older than Vida. She was so vibrant and beautiful, loved life and embraced it with a passion. She wouldn't have dreamed of moving into a granny flat with Max and his new bride: if she was on her own at Mary's age, she'd probably book herself on a cruise, learn the Lambada, collect a whole range of men friends to take her out to dinner and decide to do a computer course.

'Problems?' asked Mary, hands fluttering nervously about her bosom when Evie came to collect her.

'Nothing,' she lied easily.

She couldn't lie to Simon. With his mother installed in his dining room, waiting for the first course of the meal Evie had flung together, she broke it to him. Simon, just home from work, took his glasses off and spent three minutes massaging the bridge of his nose tensely afterwards.

'This is too much to cope with,' he said, eyes blinking myopically without his glasses. 'Too much.'

His left hand began to flutter just like his mother's. Up and down, up and down. Just like Mary's. Evie stared at it in alarm. Had he done that before? Why had she never noticed it until now?

'Don't panic,' she said. 'It's only a room, Simon. It's not the end of the world.'

'I'm so stressed at the minute,' he said, voice rising.

His hand stopped fluttering and began to run through his sandy hair, fluffing it absently into mad little tufts. 'First my mother doesn't like the perfect house – and it *was* perfect. Now this. I don't think I can take any more.'

You and me both, Evie thought, a little hysterically.

'Simon,' she said, 'do you think we could have a bottle of wine with dinner? I could do with a drink.'

'Drink isn't the answer,' he answered in a shrill voice.

'I'll have a sherry then,' she said grimly.

When Simon went inside to – stupidly, in Evie's opinion – tell his mother about the crisis with the reception room, Evie drained her sherry and had another, this one filled to the brim instead of halfway up the Waterford crystal port glass.

This is terrible, she told herself, sticking a knife into the potatoes to see if they were boiled. She was turning into a lush. She was the one who usually gave out to Cara for drinking too much, and in the past month *she'd* been plastered once and consumed at least six glasses of wine on her hen night.

Like every other time she thought about that night, Evie felt her legs weaken at the memory of making love with Max. She couldn't help it: it was an automatic reaction, the same way she smiled when she saw a baby or gasped at the very thought of a rat. Max, Max, Max. He still ran through her head like Morse code, banging out the same word over and over again.

Simon came into the kitchen and leaned over the saucepan, steaming up his glasses immediately. Would he ever learn not to do that? Evie stifled the urge to thump him. He irritated the hell out of her much of the time. And she was going to marry him in two weeks and spend the rest of her life with him, being irritated. Her legs felt weak again and this time, it wasn't from thinking about Max.

'Here.' She handed Simon two plates filled with the tomato and feta cheese salad she'd made for the first course. She hadn't bothered washing the iceberg lettuce. No doubt Mary would discover half a slug in hers. 'Take these in, Simon, I'll be right behind you.'

Mary decided to stay at Simon's that night, which meant that Evie couldn't. It was a blessing in disguise, she knew, because she wasn't in the mood for a passionate encounter with her fiancé. Yet she was peeved that his mother's presence meant her staying over was out of the question.

'It's not as if we'd be having a one-night stand,' she said caustically. 'We're engaged to be married, Simon. We're not going to be at it like knives while she watches *Antiques Roadshow*.'

'I know, but my mother is very old-fashioned, very set in her ways.'

Like her son, Evie reflected.

For Olivia's dinner party on Saturday, Cara brought two bottles of red wine, strawberry cheesecake from the delicatessen – and Phoebe.

'I couldn't leave her at home,' she whispered to Olivia, briefly explaining the story as they stowed Cara's cheesecake in the fridge.

'You had to bring her, poor child,' Olivia said, determined to make Phoebe feel utterly at home.

'Now,' she said, arriving back in the sitting room with wine, mineral water and fruit juice, 'who wants what? I know you probably want wine, Cara,' she added teasingly. 'But I'm on the fruit juice tonight because I've a busy day tomorrow.'

'Me too,' said Phoebe, seizing the excuse to avoid alcohol.

'Wonderful,' said Olivia cosily, 'your bold best friend here often makes me feel like a boring old dear if I don't get pissed with her. I love fruit juice and I'm not much of a drinker.'

Phoebe smiled and accepted a glass of juice. When she wasn't looking, Cara shot Olivia a deeply grateful look.

Vida arrived with a fragrant bunch of Stargazer lillies, several bottles of Frascati and some Amaretti biscuits. 'I felt in an Italian mood,' she said gaily, kissing Olivia.

'Congratulations on your new show, darling,' she added. 'I want to hear all about it. Cara, hello. This must be your flatmate, Phoebe? Hello, dear. Cara's always telling me you're pretty and I can see she's telling the truth.'

This was exactly the right thing to say. Phoebe, who'd been looking out of sorts, beamed at Vida.

'Let's sit together and you can tell me all about my stepdaughter,' Vida said confidingly. 'I want the whole low down – men, money, and how many of those awful chocolate ice creams she eats a week!'

Phoebe giggled into her fruit juice. Olivia and Cara heaved sighs of relief. Vida always knew exactly the right thing to say.

Rosie and Evie rolled up twenty minutes later, clutching wine, mineral water and a huge container of Evie's homemade mushroom soup. The smell mingled with the heavenly scent of Olivia's famous seafood pasta bake which was emanating from the kitchen.

'I love that stuff,' Phoebe said hungrily, sniffing the soup container.

'Sorry we're late,' apologised Rosie, who looked like she was heading for a night on the tiles in a black Lycra catsuit and suede boots. 'My fault. I was late home from town. Shopping.' She did a twirl. '£39.99 in Miss Selfridge. Whaddya think?'

'If it'd fit me, I'd love to borrow it,' Cara said enviously.

'It'll never fit me now,' Phoebe added miserably, hand going to her non-existent bump.

'Nonsense! You have naturally good bone structure,'

Vida said briskly, patting Phoebe's hand. 'You'll never have a problem with your figure.'

The dinner party was great fun and the food and drink, though marvellous, were secondary to the conversation. Sasha, theoretically in bed but allowed to sit up and be petted by her adoring aunties, showed everyone the doll's house her daddy had bought her and then produced a painting that showed 'Mummy and Daddy living all in the same place.'

Olivia's eyes filled with tears as Sasha proudly showed her painting to everyone, but they weren't sad tears. When Sasha was back in bed with her cuddly toy menagerie, Cara soon had everyone in knots over how she and a half-undressed Ewan had hidden under the computer desks in her office when they'd heard Bernard Redmond pounding up the stairs.

'Penny must have been waiting outside the door while we were there. She kept insisting to Bernard that there was nobody else in the room and he kept insisting he hadn't seen me go out so I had to be there!' Cara recounted, laughing till it hurt. 'Ewan stuffed his shirt in my mouth to stop me from giggling out loud. I bit a hole in it! He didn't mind, but he said he'd only bought it new that day to impress me.'

Olivia told them all about her prospective new pro-gramme: an hour-long afternoon chat show where she'd interview people, with some pre-recorded stuff on local events from a roving reporter. Nancy Roberts had heard about it through the grapevine and had smashed the glass coffee table in her dressing room by dropping her wine cooler on to it in a fit of rage.

'It was priceless,' Olivia said, wiping away tears of laughter. 'Nita, her assistant, ran out for fear Nancy was going to stab her with a sliver of glass and nobody else would dare go in to clean it up because she was ranting and raving like a banshee, so Kevin locked her in until she calmed down.'

Rosie had lots of tales of similar tantrum-throwing at the Wicklow location where Mia Koen had taken to refusing to get into costume every day until after Max arrived.

'She's such a tart,' Rosie said scathingly. 'She's got this see-through white dressing gown and prances around in it with no underwear until he gets there and sees her. *Then* she goes into the costume van. You can't move for technicians on set every morning, hoping for a glimpse of her tits. Not that she's got any,' Rosie sniffed.

Vida noticed that the only person who didn't convulse with laughter at this was Evie. Remarkably quiet during the meal, she'd stiffened at the mention of Mia Koen and stopped eating, pushing pieces of succulent cod and fat, juicy mussels round her plate aimlessly. She'd lost weight too, Vida realised. She'd also lost the sparkle in her eyes that had been so blindingly obvious when they'd all been on holiday in Spain. The reason had to be Max.

Vida hated interfering but she suddenly decided that it was far too important not to let poor Evie throw herself away on that nice but drippy Simon if she was actually in love with Max. Some not-so-subtle prodding would do the trick.

'How are the wedding plans going, Evie?' she asked brightly.

'Thrilling,' Evie said tonelessly. 'Simon's mother Mary doesn't like any of the houses he keeps picking, and to be honest, neither do I. The wedding reception is going to be in a different room, a horrible room, because there was a fire in the one we'd booked. I daresay the wedding dress shop will be struck by lightning and the isle of Crete will sink mysteriously into the sea, just so the dress and the honeymoon will be ruined too, to balance things up.'

Nobody spoke for a moment.

'More wine, girls?' asked Olivia in desperation.

Vida waited until Evie went to the bathroom to say her piece. Following her, she pulled her stepdaughter into the blue-and-white-tiled room and shut the door.

'We've got to talk.'

Evie was silent. Talking was beyond her. She felt as if she'd run out of words. She slumped down on the edge of the bath and stared at the floor.

'Max said the oddest thing to me the other day,' Vida said slowly.

Evie looked up. Her every sense quivered, like an insect with antennae sensitive to the slightest nuance of the breeze.

'Really?'

Vida seemed to be considering whether she should say this or not.

'I should preface this by saying that I thought the two of you were getting close when we were in Spain. You spent enough time hanging around together.' She smiled at the memory. 'But I'm a great believer in letting life sort itself out. I keep my distance over affairs of the heart. Don't interfere, that's my motto. I also thought you were very happy with your fiancé and that you knew your own heart, that you'd go to whichever man was the right one for you.'

'How do you know who's right for you?' Evie said despondently.

'You just do,' Vida replied. 'I knew that Max's father, Carlos, was the right one, the same way I knew my second husband wasn't the right one. In my heart of hearts I knew it but I still married him and, honey, you wouldn't believe how unhappy Dan and I were. I don't know if I believe in hell but I'm pretty sure I went through it during those years.'

'Why did you marry him then?' asked Evie, eyes glued to Vida's.

She put one of Olivia's fluffy white towels down on the toilet lid and sat down gracefully on it, facing Evie.

'We'd been seeing each other for a long time and I was lonely. He'd been a friend of Carlos's and I thought he was being kind to me. He took me to Colorado skiing and to San Francisco for weekends. I was numb after Carlos died and Max was in Ireland studying . . . I guess I still don't really know how it happened but one day Dan asked me to marry him and I said yes. I'd never really seen him that way, as a husband, but he was a good man and I didn't want to end up alone. We got married and that was when the trouble started.'

'What sort of trouble?' asked Evie gently, her mind taken off her own troubles by this fascinating story of Vida's past.

'Dan was a complete control freak,' she said. 'God, I'd love a cigarette,' she added, looking around as if Olivia might have a packet and a lighter lying casually beside the basin. 'I used to smoke then and even talking about Dan makes me yearn for one of my Gauloises. He hated me smoking but it was the one thing I wouldn't give up for him. I did it for your father,' she grinned, the love apparent in every line of her face.

'Dan couldn't bear me to be out of the house unless he knew exactly where I was and who I was going to be out with. Charity work was fine because he was rich and expected me to be a rich man's wife and sit on endless committees with all the other rich men's wives. But, Evie,' Vida's eyes were suspiciously bright, 'I'd worked all my life in hospital administration, I couldn't stop to sit around all day or go shopping, with the odd committee meeting thrown in to keep me amused. And Dan hated that. He wanted me to be there when he got home in the evening, the perfect little wife.'

'He doesn't sound a million miles away from our own Stephen MacKenzie,' Evie commented.

'Got it in one, honey. I don't like that man, I can tell you, and I doubt he'll ever change.'

'Olivia says he's getting counselling,' protested Evie.

Vida looked surprised. 'That's great to hear. I'd be very happy for Olivia if he does change. She deserves a good man. Unfortunately for me, Dan would have needed more than a shrink to change the way he thought. He'd have needed a brain transplant.'

'What happened in the end?'

'After seven years of torture, he did us both a favour by totalling his speedboat off Martha's Vineyard. I wasn't with him at the time, thankfully, so nobody could blame me for driving it into the rocks and jumping to safety,' she said, her voice raw with irony. 'Although anyone who knew us as a couple wouldn't have been surprised if I *had* killed him.'

Evie couldn't help but smile as she thought of her initial and utterly insane impression of Vida: a glamorous black widow who married and killed. How terribly wrong she'd been. And how unfair.

'Do you think anyone in this apartment block smokes and we could ask them for a couple of emergency cigarettes?' Vida asked, emotionally worn out by her story. Normally unflappable, she looked rattled.

'I'm ashamed of what I was like to you in the beginning,' Evie said earnestly.

'Tish, we've gone over that before. It's forgotten.' Vida waved a hand dismissively. 'It was tough on you because you loved your mother and because you're so close to Andrew. But look how well it's all worked out now.'

'I didn't have anything in my life, you see,' Evie explained darkly, feeling the need to explain. 'I needed to make my father terribly important, I needed somewhere to go for weekends, someone to fuss over. You can't fuss over Rosie anymore: she's too old. Dad was my project. I could spend time with him and nobody would think I was strange because I didn't have a husband or a boyfriend. People at work used to ask what I was doing at the weekend and I could say, "Spending time with my father, he's lonely and he needs me".' She laughed bitterly. 'He wasn't lonely, I was.'

'Didn't that change when you met Simon?' Vida asked softly.

Evie shook her head. 'Not really, to be honest. He went to his mother's most of the time and I went to see Dad. Business as usual. Then you came along and I lost it. I couldn't cope. It was the shock of realising he wouldn't be there for me in the same way, that I couldn't drive to Ballymoreen on bank holidays when everybody else was with a partner and fuss around him.'

She stopped, remembering exactly when she'd got over her father's remarrying: on the very day of his marriage, the day she'd met Max Stewart. Meeting Max had crystallised everything in her head. She'd fallen crazily in love with him and all the pieces of her life thereafter had fallen into place. Andrew could stop being the focus of her worries because he now had somebody else to worry about him – and Evie now had somebody else to think endlessly about, someone to dream about at night, someone to think of as soon as she opened her eyes in the morning: Max. Only he didn't know how deeply she felt about him, and now, he never would.

'You know, I must be losing my marbles,' Vida said, getting up and splashing water on her face. 'Age is a terrible thing. I came in here to talk to you about my son and I've got weirdly sidetracked.' She carefully patted her skin dry with some tissue paper. 'I asked Max would he be around for your wedding because, as you know, your father and I are having a little party for you before you go on to your honeymoon, and he said he couldn't bear to. He'd rather be in hell than be here for that.'

Evie's heart leapt.

'He did?' she said, her voice barely a whisper.

Vida nodded. Evie didn't have to know she was lying through her teeth. Max had said nothing to his mother but she wouldn't be much of a parent if she didn't know he was crazy in love with Evie Fraser. As it was now plain to Vida that Evie returned the sentiment, a little fib was a small price to pay for getting them together.

'Yes, he did,' she said fervently. 'He didn't have to spell it out for me, Evie. He meant he couldn't handle being around while you got married when he wanted to be the guy in the suit at the altar with you.'

'You think so?' Evie could barely talk. Her throat was overcrowded with frogs.

Vida put her arms around her trembling stepdaughter and held her close. 'I know my own son, Evie. I want you to be happy and I'm not going to interfere any more than I've done now. But,' she held Evie away from her, determined to get one message across for certain, 'don't marry anyone unless you really, really want to. Rings, dresses and gifts can all go back. Hurt and humiliation go away eventually. It's much harder to mend a broken heart ten years down the road when it's all gone wrong and the marriage is over.'

Evie bit her lip. You didn't need to be a rocket scientist to figure out what Vida was telling her: she shouldn't marry Simon.

She knew that herself, of course. She was merely terrified she'd left it far too late to back out now. The ceremony was in eight days' time; the church was booked, the reception too, and the honeymoon. Sixty people had bought new outfits, borrowed hats, organised babysitters and arranged to meet other friends, planning who'd be on taxi duty that night when they were all plastered and incapable of driving after celebrating Evie and Simon's marvellous wedding.

How could you cancel all that? And how could she ever tell sweet, trusting, anxious Simon that she wasn't going to marry him after all?

Picking the venue was hell. People picked special places for special moments and this was definitely a special moment, unforgettable really, so she had to pick somewhere special. Somewhere he could cry if he wanted to; somewhere *she* could cry. Evie thought of the restaurant where Simon had taken her to propose. At the time, she'd wished he'd put a bit more thought into the choice of venue. They'd had the Early Bird menu, she remembered, and a child at a nearby table had driven them mad screaming for fish and chips. God, it all seemed like a million years ago. Had she really said she wanted to marry Simon then?

Evie sighed. What Vida had said last night was the truth: there was no other way. She had to call the wedding off.

'I don't think we've got the money to be buying paintings, Evie,' Simon said when she phoned and asked him would he like to take a stroll around Merrion Square and look at the marvellous street gallery that appeared there on Sundays. Come rain or shine, every Sunday the railings around the pretty garden square were hung with oils and watercolours, big, small and indifferent. The artists sat on deckchairs and talked among themselves while people meandered along, looking at oils of desolate Western land-scapes and bright pictures of Dublin's Georgian doors. Evie used to take Rosie there on Sundays when she was younger. It was fun and it was free, ideal for a broke single parent.

She'd never gone to Merrion Square with Simon. The place held no memories of them, which was why she chose it. Probably neither of them would ever want to go there again afterwards.

'I'll meet you there,' she said, trying to finish the phone conversation.

'What would you want to meet me there for?' he asked. 'I'll drive us.'

She panicked. They had to go there in separate cars so they could go home separately. There was no way she'd be able to cope with sitting in the car with Simon after she'd told him the wedding was off.

'No! I've got to go to Olivia's afterwards,' she said hurriedly.

'I don't know why you've got this fancy to go to Merrion Square all of a sudden,' he grumbled. 'There's a special on Sky One about the FBI and serial killers.'

You'll probably turn into a serial killer yourself with rage after I tell you the news, Evie thought sadly as she put down the phone. She wished she didn't have to do this, wished it with all her heart. But she had to.

She parked her car at the Mount Street end of Merrion Square as arranged and sat waiting for Simon to drive up. Her heart was thumping along with nerves and her palms were sweaty. Celine Dion was sweetly singing 'Think Twice' on the radio, begging her lover not to end it. Evie switched the radio off.

She should have had a drink or a tranquilliser or something, *anything*, to help her through this. Simon was a lovely, kind, decent man and he didn't deserve this. She was a bitch and a cow. She deserved to be sent to prison for hurting . . .

'Evie, are you staying there all day?' Simon yelled in through the wound-up window.

They joined the procession of people strolling around the square.

'I don't like these type of pictures,' he whispered to her as they passed some modern oils, vibrant slashes of colour painted thickly on huge canvases.

Evie barely saw the paintings. All she could see was a horrible vision of the church where they'd intended to get married, full of flowers and people, with Simon standing open-mouthed at the altar.

'If you want to buy some paintings for the house, I don't think we have the money,' he added apologetically. 'Budgets will be tight for quite a while. Of course, my mother wants to get us something special and if you saw one you really liked . . . I fancy something with boats. Do you think they have anything with boats in it? Dalkey harbour, maybe?'

'Simon, I don't want to buy any paintings,' Evie announced. 'I brought you here to talk to you. Let's go into the gardens.'

She led the way into the actual square, along the path to a bench that looked out over a manicured lawn. Purple and yellow pansies bowed their soft petals under the heat of the sun. Evie wished she was a pansy: flowers never had to break off engagements. She sat down and took a deep breath. This was it: she had to do it now.

Looking a little bewildered, Simon sat down beside her. He reached for her hand and stopped, his own hovering in mid-air over Evie's left hand which was bare apart from her watch.

'You're not wearing your ring,' he said in an accusing voice.

'No.' She had it in its little box, nestling in the velvety pink fabric. She hadn't wanted to take it off her finger and hand it back to him: this had seemed nicer. That way, he wouldn't fling it away with rage and then later regret it on the grounds that it had cost a fortune and he could always sell it and realise his investment.

'I can't marry you, Simon.' *There!* She'd said it. Blunt but truthful.

'What?' He shook his head, confusion and hurt written all over his pale face.

There was no going back. 'I'm sorry, Simon. I should have said this a long time ago but I don't want to get married to you. I wish there was a nicer, less hurtful way of doing this and I wish . . .'

He interrupted her, shocked. 'But it's less than a week away. It's on Saturday, next Saturday, Evie. You . . . you . . . you're joking, right?' he stammered.

She didn't want to face those hurt grey eyes but she had to. Evie stared steadily at her fiancé and said, 'I'm not joking, Simon. I can't marry you.'

'But I love you, Evie,' he pleaded. 'Say you're only upset, say it's just last-minute nerves . . . please?'

'I can't,' she said in anguish. 'I wish I could but I can't. I'm calling it off, Simon. I'm sorry, there's no other way.'

'What about all our plans? I mean, can't you think about it, can't you give me a few days and try?'

He didn't get it, she thought in desperation. Closing her eyes, she launched into the real reason why.

'I'm in love with Max Stewart, Simon. That's why we have to break it off. I'm not seeing him but I fell in love with him and that means it would be wrong to marry you.'

She opened her eyes gingerly.

Simon wasn't running his fingers through his hair or shoving his glasses anxiously on to the bridge of his nose. He was simply sitting there looking at her with an expression of such desolation Evie thought she couldn't bear it.

'You did say you didn't know if you believed in true love and that people just sort of got used to each other and learned to live with each other,' she said desperately. 'I needed something more than that, Simon. I needed love, true love, romantic love like in my novels. I'm sorry, so sorry.'

'I should have known that someone like Max would steal you away from me,' he said quietly. 'What hope did I have beside him? I can't change your mind, I know. Not when it's someone like him.'

His voice was resigned. There was no question of her staying with him, he seemed to be saying, when she'd fallen for a man like Max.

Evie was stunned by his reaction, his passive acceptance of the situation. How sad to accept that your own girlfriend could quite easily find someone else more interesting than you. Simon's opinion of himself was so low it seemed reasonable to him that Evie could fall for another man.

She put her hand on his. He didn't pull away or scream abuse at her. He let her hold his hand quietly.

'I don't deserve how good you're being to me,' she said truthfully. 'I never wanted to hurt you, Simon. You've been such a good friend to me. I just couldn't marry you knowing what I do. It would be wrong, it would destroy both of us.'

He nodded numbly.

They sat like that for half an hour. Evie spoke about cancelling all the arrangements as calmly as if she was a third party brought in to deal with the fall-out of someone else's shattered engagement. She said who she'd telephone and who Simon should telephone. She said he was to tell people whatever he felt was right: if he wanted to say he'd broken it off, then he should. She didn't mind. He deserved to save face.

Finally, she fished the ring box out of her handbag and handed it to him. There were no words for that sort of thing, no script for the handing back of an engagement ring. That was the way she left him: sitting with the little ring box in his hand, gazing at the flowers with unseeing eyes. Evie cried all the way home, barely able to see the traffic lights or the other cars because of her tears. She cried for poor Simon who'd loved her but who'd accepted that she loved someone else. Guilt and self-hatred mingled with sheer, blessed relief. She'd done it, it was over, finally over.

At the sight of her mother's tear-stained face, Rosie had hugged her and made them tea, before making something stronger with far too much gin and not half enough flat tonic. Her face swollen with tears, Evie had begged Rosie to tell no one until she told people herself. She didn't mention why she had ended the engagement, she didn't mention Max at all. Yet Rosie didn't seem surprised by the news.

'He wasn't right for you, Mum,' she said earnestly. 'I always knew it. He's a nice person but he was wrong for you. You need someone heroic, someone like Dad was.'

Evie cried even harder at that. More guilt. She should never have made Tony out to be this wonderful person. She couldn't tell Rosie what he'd really been like, that she'd gone back to using her maiden name when he died because she couldn't bear to use his. Evie had always said it was because the people in her office knew her as Fraser and she'd never changed it. Only Olivia knew that Evie would have killed herself rather than be called Evie Mitchell, the name of the man who'd been in love with a married woman when he married Evie. He'd married her because she was pregnant and within a month, had made it plain that he wanted a child but not a clinging wife. His affair would continue and Evie could like it or lump it. No wonder she'd never cried at his funeral.

Rosie should have known the truth but it was Evie's fault she didn't. She felt like a congenital liar who ran through life lying to everyone she cared about, telling huge untruths. She was a terrible, terrible person.

'If only Dad hadn't died, none of this would have happened,' Rosie said solemnly. 'What you need is somebody like him.'

She went off to work reluctantly on Monday morning. 'I should stay with you, Mum,' she protested. 'You're still in shock.'

'Please go, darling,' Evie said, grey in the face after a sleepless night where she'd thought of nothing but Simon. 'I'm not going into work today. I've got to start cancelling things, telling people. I'll be OK on my own.'

She cringed at the thought of telling friends and relatives that the great wedding was off, but the worst was over. Telling Simon had been like hitting some trusting wild animal you'd coaxed out of the woods to feed by hand.

Yet in the middle of her guilt-ridden misery, a spark of pure unadulterated joy burned brightly in her heart. Now that she was finally free, she could be with Max. It was the one thing that had kept her going during the endless hours of the night. Max . . . he'd told her he loved her, hadn't he? He'd told Vida he couldn't bear to be around for Evie's wedding, so he couldn't be with Mia Koen after all.

He was waiting for Evie, like the knight with a white charger, all saddled up and waiting for the damsel to call him. It seemed terrible to be happy in the midst of Simon's pain, but Evie was incredibly happy. She was free. She fantasised about Max's exultant cry when he discovered she was his. *'Evie, my darling, I can't believe it! I've dreamed of this moment for so long. I've driven past your house and wondered what you were doing so many times. I've rung your phone number a thousand times just to hear your voice but I never spoke. I knew you had to come to me. Now we'll never be apart, ever . . .'*

She found the number in her daughter's diary. The phone number Max had given Rosie in Spain so that she could ring him and arrange the job in his company.

Evie wrote it down, replaced the diary in Rosie's drawer, and went downstairs, feeling as nervous as a kitten. She dialled with shaking hands, wondering how she was going to start the conversation. *Hello, Max, I'm not getting married after all. Does that invitation to lunch still stand?*

After six rings, an answering machine kicked in: Max's voice filled her ears, his rich, gravelly tones telling her he wasn't in but to leave a message. Evie could have listened all day. She smiled as she thought of him getting her message. She waited for the beep, still smiling. Then the phone was picked up.

'Hello?' said a woman's voice. A soft Southern drawl that sounded like icy Mint Juleps, ripe peaches and long, sultry days in the Atlanta sun. Mia Koen's voice. 'Max, is that you, honey? I can't hear a thing. I bet your mobile phone's on the blink again. You're in a bad signal area, honey. Call me back in a minute.'

Evie put the phone down quietly. Thank God she hadn't left a message. Imagine Mia playing it and laughing to herself, laughing at the idea that the hick Irish woman was in love with her Max. Max who lived with her in some luxurious loft apartment with wooden floors and exposed beams. Imagine Max listening to it with her, both of them laughing hysterically at the very idea.

Evie went out into the garden, put on her gloves and began to weed the flower bed at the back of the garden. When the tears began to drop relentlessly on to the hard, baked earth, she didn't bother to wipe them away.

CHAPTER SIXTEEN

Phoebe looked at herself sideways in the hall mirror. At five months pregnant, her bump was visible but still small. She was lucky she could still get away with wearing bigger sizes of normal clothes instead of maternity things, which all seemed to be horrendously expensive when she and Cara trekked around the shops.

'Maybe I do want to know if it's going to be a boy or a girl,' she said thoughtfully, going back into the flat's sitting room which was crowded with shopping bags and Christmas wrapping paper.

Zoë groaned from her position on the chair with the dodgy spring, where she was eating crisps and reading her horoscope. 'Phoebs, every second day you want to know what sex it is, and every other day you don't want to know. Make up your mind.'

'It's important,' Phoebe protested. 'If it's a girl, perhaps I should be doing something different from what I should be doing if it's a boy.'

'If it's a boy, you'd be ravenous for beer and pizza all the time,' Zoë theorised, 'and if it's a girl, you'd be getting cravings for chocolate and re-runs of *Dynasty*.'

'It's definitely a girl, then,' Cara said, returning from an emergency trip to the grocery shop in Rathmines with another box of Mars Bar ice creams and a lot of assorted chocolate goodies. 'They think we're all mad in that shop,' she said. 'The woman behind the counter can't understand why we're buying ice cream in December.'

'Did you explain it was for a pregnant woman?' Phoebe grinned, ripping open the carton almost before Cara had taken it out of the plastic carrier bag.

'Phoebe, we were eating just as many last December when you weren't pregnant.'

'True.'

They were all quiet for a few minutes, eating happily and half watching *The Sound of Music* with the sound turned down. Phoebe loved old films but Zoë said she couldn't bear to hear 'Edelweiss' one more time and could they turn it down for a while?

Ice cream finished, Zoë went back to reading horoscopes. 'Listen to this,' she said. ' "Leos will find happiness away from home this Christmas but be sure to think before you speak." I'm glad I'm going to your dad's for Christmas, Cara. I couldn't bear another festive season with the boys and my father killing each other.'

'You're sure your father and Vida are happy we're coming?' Phoebe asked a bit anxiously.

'Vida says that's the whole point of the annexe, so guests can stay and do their own thing,' Cara pointed out patiently. 'There's only two bedrooms so you'll have to share because Ewan's going to be in with me. Poor Rosie is in bits because there's no room for her in the annexe. Evie can't understand it because Vida has a lovely bedroom with a half-tester bed in it for Rosie.'

'Rosie probably thinks we'll all be drinking and sitting up till very late being wild,' Zoë said, 'and she's wrong. Phoebe will be watching old films all day, I'll be going round like a mad woman at the relief of missing the testosterone-filled war zone at home, and you and Ewan will be breaking the new bed in your bedroom as you practise for the Sexual Olympics.'

'Ha bloody ha,' retorted Cara good-humouredly. She was feeling so very happy. She was spending Christmas with Ewan, her family *and* the girls. Vida's idea had been a marvellous one. The new house in Ballymoreen was finally finished, a masterpiece of Victorian architecture and a testament to Andrew's ability to sweet talk the builders into actually finishing it when they'd said they would.

The main house had five bedrooms, four reception rooms and a huge, stone-floored kitchen where the dogs, Gooch and Jessie, took great delight in sliding up and down on the tiles when they were excited. One of the stables had been converted into a self-contained apartment with two bedrooms, a bathroom and a large kitchen-cum-sitting room with a real fireplace.

When Cara had turned down the offer of a family Christmas at home and explained that she was going to stay in Dublin with Phoebe for the holidays because she was getting so much grief from her father about being pregnant and unmarried, Vida had immediately suggested the annexe.

'You can be in peace there and do your own thing but it'd be lovely to have you with us over the holiday,' she said hopefully. 'Phoebe could do with a change of scene, I'm sure, to help her get over being abandoned by that awful boyfriend of hers. Your father would be heartbroken if you didn't come to us.'

Zoë, hearing about the plan, had immediately given Cara a sad-eyed, Andrex-puppy look that plainly said, 'Please, please, can I come too?'

It was now two days before Christmas and they were leaving on the six o'clock bus that evening. The morning's shopping had yielded all sorts of Christmas gifts and plenty of edible goodies for the holiday. But nothing was wrapped, nobody had packed so much as a pair of knickers and Zoë had been saying she had to drop home and grab her stuff for at least the past hour.

'Why don't you wrap the presents and I'll start packing?' Cara suggested to Phoebe. 'And you go home, for God's sake,' she added to Zoë, who was now reading Cara's horoscope. 'It's nearly three and we have to leave here at half-four to get to the bus.'

' "Librans will be fulfilled this Yuletide," ' Zoë giggled. 'You can say that again! Ewan is very keen on fulfilling you. "They should be aware of overindulging in rich foods but this will be a time of rejoicing for them." '

'Go home,' Cara said, shooing her out into the hall. 'I will not be rejoicing if we miss the bus because of you, you big eejit.'

'Ah, sure, if we miss it, we can all drive down with Ewan tomorrow afternoon,' protested Zoë, who hated travelling on buses.

'Oh, yeah? Four suitcases, ten bags of presents, three boxes filled with chocolates, booze and cake, and four people are going to fit into one small sports car? Get out. We are not missing the bus and that's that.'

In the end, they made the bus at the very last minute which meant the luggage compartment was almost totally full with the other travellers' Christmas packages and the three of them would have to sit with boxes and bags on their laps for the entire journey.

'I'll kill you, Zoë,' muttered Cara, failing to get comfortable as the bus edged along in the horrendous Christmas traffic, moving a foot at a time. 'The journey is going to take three hours at this rate and I'll have no circulation left in my legs with this box on my lap.'

'Ah, shut up,' said Zoë from the seat in front, just as

uncomfortable with the wine box on *her* lap. 'We got here, didn't we?'

Battling hordes of crazed Christmas shoppers desperate to abandon cars in the already-jammed city centre car parks, the bus crawled out of Dublin at a snail's pace. The Christmas spirit was noticeably absent with much bickering about being squashed and grumbling that the heating didn't work.

'I'm buying a car next year,' Cara growled to Phoebe, who was beside her. But Phoebe was asleep, her round face content as she slept, hands clasped around her belly, protecting her precious cargo. Cara smiled. Her flatmate was being so strong about having this baby on her own. If she could deal with that *and* with being dumped by Ricky, then it was ludicrous Cara and Zoë bitching about being stuck on a crowded bus. So they'd be squashed for a while? Big deal.

The bus driver had had enough of his bad-tempered passengers. He slotted a tape of Christmas carols into the tape deck. As the sound of a children's choir singing 'Silent Night' drifted into the air, the entire bus seemed to take a collective breath and remember the whole point of the season. A hand holding a packet of toffees shot back from the seat in front. 'D'you want a sweet?' hissed Zoë, her red head appearing around the back.

'Love one,' said Cara. 'Sorry I was so cross with you. I'm a bad-tempered old cow sometimes.'

'That makes two of us,' Zoë agreed.

They chewed their toffees companionably for a while. 'I think I'll try and doze,' Cara said eventually, realising that the journey would feel like forever if she couldn't block some of it out.

She closed her eyes but couldn't sleep. There were so many things to think about that she just couldn't switch off.

Ewan, lovely Ewan, was in her head all the time. They'd discussed moving in together and the very thought of it gave Cara a warm glow in the pit of her stomach. Imagine waking up with him every morning, sharing the bathroom with him, curling up watching TV together, doing the grocery shopping together, spending hours in bed on Saturday mornings, reading, snoozing, making love . . .

The only problem was Phoebe. Cara didn't want to abandon her friend in her time of need. If only they could get two flats together so that they could be just down the hall if she needed anything. Then they could both help looking after the baby. Cara rather liked the idea of that. She could imagine herself and Ewan strolling along the canal, talking baby talk and pointing out the swans and ducks. Phoebe had already insisted that Cara should be godmother.

'You've got to be,' she said at least once a day. 'You're so good to me, coming with me to scans and stuff.'

'Your mother would go with you if you asked her,' Cara said delicately, hoping to heal the rift that Phoebe's desperately religious father had started within her family.

'She hasn't so far,' Phoebe replied gloomily.

The next thing Cara knew, Zoë was shaking her awake. 'We're here. Get up or the bus will drive off again and God knows where we'll end up.'

Like the three wise men burdened with gifts, the three of them staggered off the bus. Andrew stood waiting for them.

'Dad!' Cara practically collapsed against him from the weight she was carrying. 'I've never been so pleased to see anyone in my life.'

He hugged her back tightly. 'I'm so glad you're here, love,' he said. 'So glad. Christmas just wouldn't have been the same if you hadn't come.'

'Unfortunately,' said Zoë, 'you've got us pair into the bargain.'

Andrew gave her and Phoebe hugs as well. 'We're thrilled to have you all. Vida has lasagne, baked potatoes and mulled wine waiting for you, and the dogs are hysterical with the excitement. They know someone is coming and every time the doorbell rings, they go insane. Gooch has all his teddies lined up inside the back door, ready to give them to guests as presents. Just be warned, girls: Gooch's teddies are all covered in drool and dog food.'

Cara beamed as she started shoving bags and boxes into the boot of her father's car. It was wonderful to be home.

Olivia shut the front door, dropped her briefcase and bags on to the hall floor and levered her feet out of the spindly stilettos she'd worn to the office party. It had still been in full swing when she'd left, despite the fact that it had started at lunchtime and the time was now seven o'clock. The *Wake Up Morning Show* set in Studio One would never be the same again, what with all the booze spilt on Nancy's precious settees and the amount of abuse the fragile set had been given by giggling and sozzled staff falling over things as they danced to the seventies disco music some bright spark had put on.

'Don't go, Olivia,' Kevin had wailed when she'd said goodbye to everyone and put her plastic cup of mineral water down on the only inch of the make-shift bar that wasn't already covered with wine bottles and empty cups.

A silver paper hat sat sideways on top of Kevin's peroxide crop and there were multi-coloured streamers hanging around his neck. He was plastered.

He threw his arms around her. 'Don't go,' he pleaded, breathing booze fumes at her. 'We love you, don't we, everyone?'

Anyone who could still speak slurred, 'Yesh.'

'See?' Kevin was so proud. 'Nobody would say yesh for Nancy.'

Olivia kissed her friend and confidant on the cheek and untangled herself. 'I have to go home, it's a special night for Stephen and me.'

'Sorry. Forgot. Hope it all works out for you both. Kissy-kissy and I'll see you in January.'

Olivia put her winter coat in the hall cupboard and padded quietly to the kitchen door.

Something that smelled delicious was bubbling away in the oven. Stephen had his back to the door and was bent over the sink. Sasha was sitting up at the table, small face solemn as she inexpertly stuck cotton wool on to Santa's crayoned-in red hat. Scraps of paper, crayons, fluorescent pens and a tube of child-friendly glue lay scattered on the table.

'How are you getting on with Santa?' asked Stephen, moving away from the worktop where he was washing peppers for the salad to go with the *coq au vin* he'd been labouring over.

Neither of them had heard Olivia come into the apartment. She watched silently, her heart bursting with happiness at the scene in front of her.

Stephen bent over Sasha, nuzzling her hair as he admired her handiwork.

'That's very good. You're so clever,' he said proudly.

'It's for you and Mummy,' Sasha said, still concentrating on her cotton wool.

'Mummy loves it,' Olivia murmured, going over to the table. She kissed the top of Sasha's head then turned to Stephen. He wrapped his arms around her and kissed her full on the mouth. He tasted of garlic. He tasted wonderful.

She kissed him back, closing her eyes and giving in to the sensation.

'I didn't expect you back so soon.'

'I wanted to leave for ages, I wanted to get home to you two. But it was so difficult. Linda's about the only sober person left at the party,' Olivia explained. 'The studio is a disaster area and she kept wandering round, saying, "We'll never get this fixed!" '

'I'm delighted you're home early,' Stephen said, still holding on to her.

'Christmas starts here.' Olivia leaned her head tiredly on his shoulder.

'I don't know why we never did this before: have Christmas at home on our own,' Stephen sighed. 'It's so relaxed here, just the three of us.'

'And the guinea pig,' Sasha piped up.

Her parents burst out laughing. Santa had been asked for a guinea pig. Two were arriving the next day, complete with a palace of a hutch and all sorts of guinea pig goodies.

'Just the five of us for Christmas, then,' whispered Olivia into Stephen's ear before nibbling it tenderly.

He held her closer to him. 'If you keep doing that,' he said with a smirk, 'there'll be six of us next Christmas.'

She smiled contentedly. 'That sounds wonderful,' she said dreamily.

Evie unearthed her handbag from behind the driver's seat, pulled her coat on over her old sweatshirt and locked the door. She felt exhausted after the drive down to Ballymoreen. It had been all endless traffic and maddened drivers overtaking on dangerous corners. Thanks to the traffic, it was now half-nine at night and Evie wanted nothing more than to sink into her bed in her own home and not have to make polite conversation with anyone. There was no chance of that.

As soon as they'd pulled up outside Andrew and Vida's

new home, Rosie had bounced out of the car and run around to the back door. The security light had come on when she had passed it, lighting up the graceful redbrick building and casting malevolent shadows down the long garden. It was freezing and dark, but Evie couldn't face going into the house just yet. She knew it'd be warm and welcoming; the Aga roasting hot; something appetising on the table; Vida and her father thrilled to see her. Cara was probably already there with the girls, all laughing and chatting, happy in the joyous Christmas atmosphere. But Evie didn't feel Christmassy. She felt like the horrible spirit of Christmas past – gloomy and ancient. She didn't know if she'd ever feel happy again. All she felt these days was numb.

You couldn't remain numb forever, could you? Then again, maybe you could. She'd been numb for four months already.

She opened the boot and looked wearily at the suitcase and bags piled higgledy-piggledy inside. She'd probably forgotten loads of things. Imagine that! The once perfectly organised Evie Fraser not having her Christmas presents wrapped, labelled and indexed since November. She looked at the boot grimly. That Evie was gone forever, along with the naive, innocent woman who'd dreamed of true love and kept herself insulated from real life with a diet of romances.

The only thing she was sure she'd packed was her latest serial killer novel. Cannibalism and mutilation weren't the best subjects to read about before going to sleep but at least they kept the human ghosts out of her dreams. Nightmares about killers were easier to handle than desolate dreams of a man she'd loved and lost. She heard a crunch on the gravel. A figure was coming from around the back of house. Her father to help with the luggage.

Only it wasn't her father. It was the last person she'd expected to see: Max. Vida had said he'd be out of the country, had been for months. Knowing he wasn't going to be there was the only reason Evie had agreed to go to Ballymoreen for Christmas. She'd get back in the car and drive straight home, she decided hysterically. She couldn't wait. He'd be here with Mia and she couldn't cope with that.

Now he was advancing on her, still handsome even in an old jumper with dog hairs on it and worn jeans. His face was in shadow as his back was to the security light. The shadows couldn't hide the glittering of his eyes as he looked at her. He seemed thinner than she remembered, still a great big bear of a man but more big cat than grizzly. Evie took a step backwards nearer her car.

'What are you doing here?' she snapped, nerves making her sound harsh.

'Waiting for you.'

'Why?' she hissed, feeling like a trapped fox.

Max was beside her now, his face tender as he towered over her.

'To tell you we've wasted too much time and we're not wasting any more,' he said firmly.

Just the sound of his voice made Evie melt. She longed to touch him, to run her fingers through that thick black hair, to feel his mouth against hers. Then she blinked. What had he said?

'What did you say?' she asked.

He repeated it. 'I love you and I'm not letting you out of my sight until you agree to spend the rest of your life with me.'

Evie stared at him. 'Why?' she asked, knowing it sounded stupid.

'Because my mother phoned me up in South Africa three days ago and told me to stop being such a bloody

563

idiot and come home. That you weren't married and you were wasting away after me and why hadn't I done anything about it?'

'B-but why . . . how?' Evie couldn't get the words out. This was so bewildering. She'd dreamed of him so often, now he was here it felt very strange. This had to be some hallucination, some after effect of several hours' driving down country roads in the dark.

'How is a good one,' Max said, a grin lighting up his face. 'Trying to get a last-minute flight home in Christmas week is damn' near impossible. I've been flying on and off for the past thirty-six hours to get here.' His face darkened. 'Why is because I didn't know you weren't married. Why didn't you tell me, Evie?' She could hear the anguish in his words. 'If I'd known you'd called it off, I'd have thought there was some hope for me, some hope you might love me.'

'I did call,' she breathed. 'Mia answered the phone and so I knew she was living with you.'

'She was living in the company flat,' Max said, stunned. 'She's never lived with me. I gave you my phone number at the wedding, you never rang me. The company flat is a different number. I stayed there for a couple of days when we got back from Spain because the decorators were still in my place . . .'

'You gave that number to Rosie, didn't you?' Evie asked, an excitingly heady sensation coming over her. 'So she could phone you about a job with the company.'

'Yes.'

'And I used that number to phone you.'

Max grabbed her shoulders. 'Evie, what made you think I was with Mia? I told you I loved you, didn't you believe me?'

She closed her eyes at the pleasure of his touch and then shivered from a mixture of cold and excitement.

'You're freezing, my love,' he said, anxiously. 'I shouldn't be keeping you out in this.'

My love . . . he'd called her 'my love'. Evie reeled at the thought of it. All those months of torture and he did love her after all.

Taking one of her small, cold hands in his large, warm one, he led her round to the back door. In the hall, surrounded by wellington boots and walking sticks, Max Stewart pulled Evie Fraser into his arms and held her to him as if they'd die if they were parted.

She clung to him, feeling his heart beating as wildly as her own through his sweater. Then, he lowered his head to hers and their lips met.

It was the sweetest kiss in the world. Gently, as if he was kissing porcelain, Max's mouth touched hers. Evie let herself lean into him, feeling his taut body hard against hers, his chest crushed against her breasts. She'd never thought she'd experience this again, this wonderful, joyous love. Her whole body felt alive next to his and her heart was free as a kite soaring into a summer breeze. His mouth became more insistent. Suddenly they were grinding their lips together, as if to make up for all that wasted time when they could have been clinging to each other, making love and plans.

'Evie, Evie, why did it take us so long to sort things out?' he muttered into the soft cloud of her hair. 'Why didn't you believe me when I said I loved you? What made you think I cared about Mia?'

'It was so like what happened to me before, with my husband. I thought I couldn't trust you,' she said, tears suddenly appearing in her eyes as she stared at the cable stitch on his jumper. 'I couldn't trust Tony, you see. He was involved with another woman when he died. He'd only married me because I was pregnant but this woman had been with him for years. She was married to a friend of his. I never knew anything about it until Rosie was born. He told me then, told me he didn't want me to think anything was going to be different. He loved her and that was that.'

'Jesus,' Max said, eyes full of pity for what she'd gone through. 'You poor little love.'

Now that she was telling him the whole awful story, it was like a plug had been pulled and everything rushed out.

'I never cried when he was hit by the car. It was a relief after what he'd told me. Nobody knew but Olivia; Rosie hasn't a clue what he was like. That,' she said passionately, 'is why I never contacted you again. It was like history repeating itself. You and Mia . . . you'd been with her before me and you'd never give her up . . .' Her voice broke finally with the strain of saying all the terrible things she'd lived with for the past four months.

'I saw you talking to her in Spain that last night. She's so beautiful and I was sure you wanted her. How could I think differently?'

'That night in Spain, Mia was telling me she wanted us to get back together,' Max explained earnestly. 'She was bored with her life, thought I'd liven it up.' He stroked Evie's face tenderly as he spoke. 'I told her I wasn't interested, that I was in love. With you. The next morning you told me you were still marrying bloody Simon!' He spat the name out. 'So I left you alone and left the country before your wedding. I haven't been back since. I couldn't bear to ask my mother about you. It's been hell.'

Evie could imagine exactly what that was like: the same hell she'd gone through. Pain and suffering, living like a robot, doing everything automatically because of the ache in her very soul.

'I thought you were with Mia, that I'd been a one-night stand or something,' she whispered. 'I kept looking at her picture in the papers, expecting to see an announcement that you two were engaged or having triplets or something.'

'And I thought you were living in married bliss and that I'd meant nothing to you.' He laughed. 'What stupid morons we've been! If my mother hadn't rung me . . .'

'What have I done now?' inquired Vida, sticking her head round the hall door.

Max and Evie both jumped at the interruption. Then they relaxed against each other, arms instinctively wrapping around each other's waist.

'Given us one hell of a Christmas present,' Max said.

Vida beamed at them.

'Now, Mother, could you shut the door for another few minutes? We've got some catching up to do,' he asked politely.

'Charming,' said Vida, sounding thrilled. She shut the door softly.

'Catching up?' Evie asked, a twinkle in her eyes. 'What did you have in mind?'

Max's eyes glittered. 'We'll think of something,' he murmured.

Millie's Fling

Jill Mansell

When Millie Brady saves Orla Hart's life she doesn't realise how drastically it will change her own – not least because the boyfriend who is asking her to move in with him at the time promptly storms off in a huff.

Actually, Millie's relieved. She's quite happy to enjoy a restful man-free summer in Cornwall. But best-selling novelist Orla has other ideas. She's determined – for her own reasons – that Millie should meet the man of her dreams.

Dropped wallets, roller-skating gorillagrams, the world's most flirtatious boss and a helicopter in the back garden all conspire to produce a summer neither Millie – nor Orla – will ever forget.

Acclaim for Jill Mansell's novels:

'A jaunty summer read' *Daily Mail*

'An exciting read about love, friendship and sweet revenge – fabulously fun' *Home & Life*

'Slick, sexy, funny stories' *Daily Telegraph*

'Fast, furious and fabulous fun. To read it is to devour it' *Company*

'Riotous' *New Woman*

0 7472 6486 4

headline

For Better, For Worse

Carole Matthews

Josie Flynn is in New York for the wedding of Martha, her American cousin.

Having just been through a messy divorce, she's hardly in the mood to don a lilac bridesmaid's dress, especially when she thinks Martha is about to marry the wrong man. In fact, Josie is all for talking Martha out of what could be the biggest mistake of her life.

Which is all very noble, until Josie meets Matt Jarvis and appears to be about to fall for the wrong man herself. And when an ex-husband, an old flame, a dubious boy-band and a seriously determined duck enter the picture who can tell where it will all end.

'A story that'll make you laugh out loud, as well as shed a tear' *Woman's Realm*

'Warmly written' *Express*

0 7472 6327 2

headline

Now you can buy any of these other bestselling
Headline books from your bookshop or
direct from the publisher.

FREE P&P AND UK DELIVERY
(Overseas and Ireland £3.50 per book)

Olivia's Luck	Catherine Alliott	£5.99
Backpack	Emily Barr	£5.99
Girlfriend 44	Mark Barrowcliffe	£5.99
Seven-Week Itch	Victoria Corby	£5.99
Two Kinds of Wonderful	Isla Dewar	£6.99
Fly-Fishing	Sarah Harvey	£5.99
Bad Heir Day	Wendy Holden	£5.99
Good at Games	Jill Mansell	£5.99
Sisteria	Sue Margolis	£5.99
For Better, For Worse	Carole Matthews	£5.99
Something For the Weekend		
	Pauline McLynn	£5.99
Far From Over	Sheila O'Flanagan	£5.99

TO ORDER SIMPLY CALL THIS NUMBER

01235 400 414

or e-mail <u>orders@bookpoint.co.uk</u>

Prices and availability subject to change without notice.